She Who Waits

About the Author

Daniel Polansky was born in Baltimore, Maryland. He can be found in Brooklyn, when he isn't somewhere else. The *AV Club* called *The Straight Razor Cure*, Daniel's debut and the first novel in his Low Town series, 'an assured, roaring, and rollicking hybrid, a cross-genre free-for-all that relishes its tropes while spitting out their bones.' *She Who Waits* is Daniel's third novel.

You can follow Daniel on Twitter @DanielPolansky or Facebook at Facebook.com/DanielPolanskyAuthor, or visit his website to find out more: www.danielpolansky.com.

The Low Town Novels

The Straight Razor Cure
Tomorrow, the Killing
She Who Waits

She Who Waits

DANIEL POLANSKY

HODDER &
STOUGHTON

First published in Great Britain in 2013 by Hodder & Stoughton
An Hachette UK company

1

A CIP catalogue record for this book is
available from the British Library

Hardback ISBN 978 1 4447 2139 3
Trade Paperback ISBN 978 1 4447 2140 9

Typeset by Palimpsest Book Production Limited,
Falkirk, Stirlingshire

Printed and bound by CPI Group (UK) Ltd, Croydon, CR0 4YY

Hodder & Stoughton policy is to use papers that are natural,
renewable and recyclable products and made from wood grown in
sustainable forests. The logging and manufacturing processes are
expected to conform to the environmental regulations
of the country of origin.

Hodder & Stoughton Ltd
338 Euston Road
London NW1 3BH

www.hodder.co.uk

*To my family and friends; I am grateful there are enough of
you to make enumeration impractical.*

I

That autumn the bottom fell out.

You could tell it was coming if you were paying attention, though most weren't. A low background hum, the faint smell of brimstone. They'll deceive you, those stutter steps into the abyss. You get to thinking the descent goes on indefinitely.

Everything ends. Looking back, it's not surprising that things came apart – it's surprising how long they stayed together.

'Warden, you around?' asked a voice from behind me.

'No,' I said, my first lie of the day.

It was nearly noon, late for breakfast but awfully early to be boozing, though I suppose the handful of drunks sharing the bar with me disagreed. I've often suggested to Adolphus that we keep to stricter hours, keep out the clientele until after nightfall. At other times I've suggested maybe going one further and just not letting anyone in at all. I really didn't have any business owning a half-stake in the Staggering Earl, in so far as I find people unpleasant as individuals and altogether loathsome when amassed into a crowd.

The voice walked over to my table, revealed itself as belonging to Fat Karl Widdershins. Karl lived two doors down, though he spent the majority of his waking hours inside the confines of the Earl. A drunkard living off his pension, Karl's recreational activities centered around inebriated stumbling interspersed with the occasional bout of spousal abuse. Which is to say he was all but indistinguishable from the better half of our patrons. He didn't bother to sit down, just buzzed around my shoulder. 'There's something you ought to come take a look at,' he continued.

The only thing I felt like looking at right then was the plate of runny eggs and fried ham in front of me. After that I was thinking I might spend some time looking at a full glass of beer, and then at some point probably at an empty one. 'I'm busy.' It was my second lie of the day.

'The guards have Reinhardt cornered inside his house. They're getting ready to make a move on him.'

'That's unfortunate for Reinhardt.'

'Don't you want to know why?'

I didn't, in fact, though Karl was thrilled to his socks to tell me. I don't know what it is about the species that makes us enjoy passing along bad news – if Reinhardt had hit today's racket numbers, I didn't imagine Karl would have ran himself breathless coming to tell me. 'Why?'

'His kid came sprinting out of his building a half-hour back, screaming that Daddy had chopped up Mommy with a butcher knife.'

The ham and the eggs would wait. I slid off my chair and out the front door.

Reinhardt was a Valaan from the far north, one of those rocky islands so barren and brutal that it made the slums of the capital pleasant by comparison. He'd served his stint in the war, settled into Low Town, spawned children and taken a wife. Not quite in that order. He was a foreman down at the docks, made decent money, nothing to a noble or a banker but good enough for a man that labored for a living. We weren't friends, or anything close to it, but maybe I wasn't so far gone that I didn't keep an eye on those veterans that lived in the neighborhood and hadn't turned their skills over to a syndicate. He used to nibble away at my stock of breath, a vial or two on the weekend, a handful at Midwinter and High Summer. At some point he'd started to show up more often, and we'd had a long conversation at the back of the Earl, come to an arrangement. I'd spot him a vial a month for recreation, two on the holidays, and apart from that I wouldn't find him knocking at my back door, wouldn't need to think about him taking money away from his rapidly expanding brood. That had been a year back, maybe a year and a half. Since then I hadn't seen much of him, and was glad of that fact.

It was the kind of autumn afternoon where you can smell winter in the air, that scent that's part wood smoke and part the cold that makes the first necessary. Karl walked a few steps ahead of me, playing the guide, though there wasn't a corner of Low Town that I didn't know better than a toddler does his mother's teat. Reinhardt's apartment was down near the docks, one of a hundred crammed into a tenement that had been intended for a quarter of that. I didn't sprint down there, but that was only because I was still pretty hung over.

The war had done mad things to everyone, broken most of those it hadn't killed, turned stout men into drunks and quiet boys into murderers. But the war had been gone fifteen years, and while you never forgot it – while you might wake up in a sweat and breathing heavy, your wife or the whore you'd bought bug-eyed at your madness – at some point most of us had brokered an uneasy truce with memory. It was like anything, you put it behind you or you let it put you in the ground, and most of us had made our decision one way or the other long years back.

'This is as far as I go,' Karl said as we got in sight of our destination. 'I just thought I'd let you in on the gossip. The rest isn't any of my business.'

'You've an admirable sense of community,' I said, tossing over a copper coin. Karl bit it, then disappeared back the way we'd come.

There were a handful of guards standing outside of Reinhardt's building, looking useless and maybe a bit frightened. One of them, so innocent as to be unaware that I effectively paid his salary, made to brush me off. But his captain shut him down, even opened the door for me. They give good service, the hoax.

I didn't know exactly which hundred square-feet were Reinhardt's, but another coterie of law enforcement was waiting on the second stairwell, and I figured they weren't doing so for their health. The men upstairs were the very cream of Low Town's finest, hardened veterans of a thousand back-alley shakedowns, clean as a latrine and bent as a penny-nail.

I knew the lieutenant, as I knew all of the officers in the neighborhood and most of the patrolmen. He was about fifty, an aging Tarasaighn with muscle all but warped away to fat. You could see he was a drunkard by his nose, which was the color and rough shape of a radish, though several times the size. I couldn't remember his name right at that moment, but then it didn't really matter. 'By the Firstborn,' he said, 'I'm glad you're here.'

This statement shouldn't have bothered me, but the truth is at bottom there's some part of me that never quite got over the world being upside down. 'What's the situation?'

'Got word a half-hour back that Reinhardt's daughter was running through the streets, screaming about blood. Came up here to see what's what, but he's not answering and neither is his wife. We were getting ready to kick in the door.'

Getting ready, getting ready, getting ready but not doing it. The hoax were tough as all hell when jumping on a manacled prisoner, but going toe-to-toe against a veteran with death in his immediate history was enough to unglue them. 'Where's the kid?'

'Back at the station. She's pretty shaken up.'

'Wouldn't you be?' I muttered, then said, 'I know the man. We go back a ways.'

'Yeah?' the lieutenant said, eyes brightening, thrilled at this sudden opportunity not to do his job. 'Any chance you could talk him down?'

4

'We're about to find out.' I knocked three times, loud enough to get the attention of anyone inside but not so hard as to bust the door down. A narrow middle, as these tenement houses were about as flimsy as wet paper. 'Reinhardt, you in there? It's the Warden – I'm coming in, I'm by myself, and I'd as soon not have any surprises, dig?'

No response. It was moments like this – a lot of moments, if we're being honest – that I found myself aching for a hit of breath. Steady your mind, settle your hands, get you so the idea of seeing blood or making it doesn't seem any particular trouble. But I'd sworn that off a few years back, and the fact that I still missed it was a pretty good argument that I'd been wise in doing so.

The door was unlocked. I wasn't sure what to make of that. It swung open easy and I came in quick after it, like I'd done a thousand times back when I was an agent. And like every other time, the muscles in my neck tensed up, anticipating the shiv.

A fate delayed. She Who Waits Behind had left the building – though she'd been in residence not long before.

Reinhardt's daughter had not been lying, I could tell that before I saw the body, tell it from the smell of blood in the air, hanging like washing over a line. I could taste egg yolk in the back of my throat, managed to swallow it before it came out on the floor.

I'd only met Gertrude once or twice, and she hadn't occupied any particularly distinct spot in my memory. All the same I was pretty sure that when we'd seen each other last, she'd had both her arms attached to her body. I'd say she was cut up like a hog but that would be a lie, because you slaughter a hog for food, and you do it careful. It's not pretty and it's not clean but it wasn't anything like the specimen of madness on the floor in front of me. I'll spare the specifics, though sadly it isn't because I've forgotten them.

It was a small apartment, a back bedroom and a slightly bigger living area, and though Reinhardt was in the corner it took me a while to realize it. Not wise on my part, as I had firm and concrete evidence of his willingness to kill. But I was stymied, all the same. You never quite get numb to the things you see. At least, I never did.

He was sitting on a stool that was too small for him, big ass balanced carefully, awkward and incongruous with the rest of the scene. He was staring at the kitchen knife in his hands, the blade slick with red. I stepped a long ways around Gertrude, and got a little closer to her murderer but not so close that I wouldn't have a chance to flee if he jumped me.

'Hello, Reinhardt.' I had a small blade in my back waist band, and I kept my hand on my hip so that I could go for it if things moved in that direction. Reinhardt was more fat than big these days, but he was still plenty big, and anyway those excess pounds hadn't stopped him from going to work on the woman who'd born and nurtured his seed.

'Hey,' he said slowly, without looking at me. Reinhardt was an oddly shaped character, his shoulders too big and his arms too long and his legs too short. He had a face that seemed to have been assembled from a random selection of spare parts. His nose was big and angular and his lips were thin as an old woman's and he had a head like a melon topped by a pair of ears that seemed sized for a child and jutted out abnormally. In the past I'd found his ungainly visage made him oafish and easy to like. At that moment it was uncanny and rather horrifying.

'Maybe you could do me a favor, go ahead and toss that blade into the corner.'

If he heard me he didn't let on. There was no sound in the room but the buzzing of the flies, croaking a symphony over their feast. Flies come quicker than you'd think, quicker than the hoax, near as quick as remorse. Up close I was reminded of what a big fellow Reinhardt was, almost tall as me sitting, with thick biceps and a gut that bulged out like a battering ram. But the look on his face was of a man with nothing left, and even with him holding the knife I still couldn't quite bring myself to feel fear.

'Were you fighting, Reinhardt? She just kept talking and talking and talking, and then you snapped?'

He blinked twice, hands on his weapon, eyes on his hands. 'I don't know how it happened,' he said finally.

I'd heard a lot of men tell me that back when I was an agent, leading them away in chains or buried in a room beneath Black House. And I didn't always believe them but I believed them more often than you'd expect. Because most of us aren't as bad as the worst things that we do, though it's those things that define us all the same.

'The hoax are outside. They're nerving themselves into coming in, and I don't imagine they'll be too long. It'd be better for everyone if you came out with me. I'll make sure it doesn't go rougher for you than it has to.' Though you didn't need to be a scryer to see that Reinhardt's future ended with a short drop from a gibbet.

He nodded at what I was saying but it was clear he couldn't really hear it. 'I can remember doing it. I can remember every single second. But I don't know why it happened.'

'I get it.'

'She asked me if I wanted soup for lunch and I got up from the couch and I went over to the kitchen and got the knife that she was using to chop celery and I picked it up and then I—'

'It's done now,' I said, cutting him off. I didn't need any reminder of the meat rotting behind me, not what it had been before it was meat, and not who made it that.

'Sarah saw me do it,' Reinhardt said, as if he had just remembered that. 'By the Lost One, she saw me do it.'

'It's done now,' I repeated, though it wouldn't ever be done, not for him nor for his child, not while they were still up and breathing. 'You need to come with me. There's no sense in making a bad situation any worse.'

For the first time since I'd entered the room Reinhardt turned his attention off the weapon in his hands, looked up at me with eyes vast and empty and unblinking. 'I'd have done her too,' he said. 'If she hadn't run away. I'd have done her too.'

There's nothing so terrible that it can't get that little bit worse. I took a step back, and the revulsion I'd been trying to keep off my face since I'd walked inside flooded over me. I could feel my lips curl up like paper thrown onto a fire.

Maybe that look of horror was what sparked it, or maybe he'd just been waiting for the chance. Either way it happened quick – Reinhardt knew what he was doing, he'd learned to kill during the war, and he'd had recent practice since. I bet his wife had wished he'd done her as easy, one smooth shot straight into the jugular, a spurt of blood that nearly reached me from halfway across the room. His hand didn't tremble, not with the first plunge and not as he worked it across, and though that wasn't the most horrible part of the afternoon I'd as soon have not seen it.

The hoax rushed in, late as always, two through the door but the second one ducked out as soon as he saw Gertude's corpse, started retching in the hallway loud enough to wake the dead. Not literally – we had a pair within earshot and neither so much as quivered.

The lieutenant at least held it together, though I wouldn't have so much blamed him if he'd done like his partner. There are only two kinds of people in the world – the first would carry the memory of what was in that room with them to their graves. The second would get off on it. Happily the former outnumber the latter, though it's an open question to what extent.

'By the Firstborn,' he said finally. Haimlin was his name, for some reason I remembered it all of a sudden.

'Yeah,' I agreed. The appearance of the hoax did something to steady me. I was back on solid ground. It was a point to hold onto, amidst all the madness – the guard were hopeless and incompetent. If there was anything in the apartment to give indication as to why Reinhardt had decided to murder the mother of his children then play havoc with her remains, I'd be the one finding it.

Not that there was much to look through. Whatever impulse had driven Reinhardt to murder had left the rest of the room all but untouched: no broken furniture or shattered crockery, nothing to suggest the sort of scuffle which would have preceded his violence. I nosed around the shelves a bit, saw little of note. An old vase with a bouquet of flowers withering inside, some prayer medals, a tarnished candelabra. Keepsakes you'd have called them if they were yours, junk if they were anyone else's.

I opened the door to the bedroom, a windowless box the size of a small tomb. It was too dark to make anything out. I struck three matches trying to find a candle, struck a fourth lighting the one I'd found. Even with its assistance there wasn't much to see: a marital bed that wouldn't get any more use and a closet with a broken leg, leaning on a wooden crate. Inside this last was a winter coat too big to be anyone but Reinhardt's. Inside the front pocket of the winter coat was a small tin about the size of a playing card. Inside the small tin were a pair of red crimson disks, looking like nothing so much as hard candy. I closed it and slipped it into my pocket.

I'd spent about ten minutes inside the bedroom, though you couldn't have known it by Haimlin, who hadn't moved three steps in my absence. The crowd of hoax that had formed in the hallway outside seemed no more willing to enter with Reinhardt dead than they had been when he was up amongst the living. At some point they'd get around to tossing the joint, though they wouldn't have found anything even if I hadn't already taken the only thing worth finding.

'I've never seen anything like this,' Haimlin said finally.

'I have,' I said, then nodded goodbye and headed outside.

2

I walked east. There was work that needed doing, if you could call what I do work, and I was happy for anything to take my mind off what I'd just seen.

Strolling down Cove Street a pusher, new to the game or just dumb as all hell, tried to sell me a vial of hop, apparently ignorant that his boss's boss cops breath from me and thanks the Firstborn for the privilege. Hooking through Cross Market I spotted two urchins setting a tinker up for a smash and grab, one loud and flamboyant, while the other slinked in from the side. The tinker bought protection from me but my sympathies were with the children, and I kept silent. At a bordello past Pritt Street I dropped off an ochre of dreamvine to the madam. It was early, and the girls were lounging on the balcony, cackling the news of the day between fucks. We passed a moment trading gossip, and I got back to moving.

I was only in Kirentown for the length of time it took to follow Broad Street to the docks, but it wasn't near fast enough to outrun

Ling Chi's eyes. He owns Kirentown like I own the leather in my shoes, and a fly don't land on a fresh turd without him hearing about it. A pair of heavies picked me up after a block and a half, pastel tattoos swirling from collarbone to brow, machetes swinging freely at their waists. They offered polite greetings and made sure I kept an even pace out of their territory.

A caravel from the Free Cities had come into port, and there was work unloading for anyone who wanted it, rare those last six months since the Crown instituted a tariff on anything coming from Nestria. It would be a good night at the Earl, and at the whorehouses and the wyrm dens. Tomorrow morning I'd have a line of distributors slinking in to re-supply. I cut through the bustle and had a quick word with the ship's purser, a high-yellow Islander with a stutter that became more prominent whenever it was time to settle accounts. I gave him a piece of paper with a dishonest man's signature at the bottom and he gave me a purse heavy with coin. Back out again I dropped the smallest of these into the bowl of a fake cripple – I mean he was a real beggar, but his legs worked fine.

It went on that way for a while. Low Town is a lot of things – the Empire's dumping grounds, an open-air prison, the beating heart of the city. But it's also my business, a broken-down engine that needs constant tinkering. Palms to grease, backs to stab. It takes a lot of energy, running in place.

The daylight was growing thin before I was through with business, could turn my attention towards other affairs, and my feet towards the bay. To a banker from Kor's Heights, anything below the Old City was the deep slums, forbidden territory without an escort of guardsmen. But those of us in Low Town had a more sensitive palette, could distinguish between simple poverty and true barbarity – though even we connoisseurs generally avoided the small finger of land east of the docks jutting out into the bay. There were levels of hell that compared favorably to the Isthmus.

Despite what half the drunks in the Earl would have you believe, the Islanders are no worse than anybody else – which is to say they're treacherous, callow and cruel to the weak. The character of the Isthmus didn't have anything to do with the peculiarities of the Islander people. Too much flesh, too little of everything else – we're all a bare step up from animal. Just how small that step is becomes abundantly clear walking down narrow alleys in the late afternoon, and I moved along the unpaved roads at a speed more frantic than brisk. Best not to present myself as a target any longer than absolutely necessary, and between the fact that I had the money to clothe myself fully and my obvious foreignness, I was definitely a target. White folk don't come to the Isthmus, if they can help it – black folk don't generally come to the Isthmus if they can help it either.

I'd made the journey with enough frequency to have the route more or less memorized, but the natives had the unfortunate tendency to shift the grid, close up alleyways and build over by-lanes, like silting up an estuary. More than once I'd taken a cut down a well-remembered side street only to discover a family of ten had erected a shack in the few weeks since I'd last been there, toothless grandmothers bobbling a brood of half-wits. And the Isthmus isn't the sort of place you want to be doubling back on, running around in circles, reminding anyone who's watching that you aren't one of them. I was pleased when I finally made it to my destination.

Mazzie's hovel was nothing to brag about. In broad form it resembled every domicile on the block, a cramped one-room shack with a thick hide covering – a door was an unseen luxury in this part of town. With what I was paying her, no doubt only a sliver of what she made, she could have afforded to live elsewhere. But one of the few virtues of the Isthmus is that the Crown isn't in any greater hurry to swing by than everyone else, providing a cover for her activities not to be found in any other part of the city. For instance, if Mazzie had lived elsewhere in the metropolis, she might have found her neighbors taking umbrage at the bull's skulls and squiggles of cock's blood that decorated her facade.

Inside the room was dark, the only light coming from the

cooking fire Mazzie kept perpetually stoked in the corner. The gimcrack ornamentation to the contrary, Mazzie's was an austere existence. Her furniture consisted of little more than the boiler itself and a wooden table so ragged as to be only distantly recognized as such. A faded curtain stretched across a back corner, a bed behind it, though it wouldn't have shocked me comatose to discover Mazzie never slept. The matron herself took up one of the room's two chairs, and the alley rat I'd made my surrogate child took the other.

It was a stark contrast. Wren was at the last threshold of boyhood, seventeen or eighteen; I'd picked him up off the street years back, so we weren't altogether clear on his age. Likewise, I could only make a guess at his heritage, though he had the vague features and stern constitution of a mutt. Long threatened, his most recent growth spurt had stretched him a few inches over my own six feet, a humiliation only partly assuaged by the fact that his mustache was a scraggly brown line that I often considered shaving while he slept. Apart from that he had dark hair and the sort of blue eyes that women would do things for one day, if they hadn't already started.

Mazzie was opposite in every particular. Unmixed Islander to go by the jet black of her skin and the rich cocoa of her eyes. Standing she wouldn't have reached my collar, though her back would have been the envy of a stud-bull. A gentleman doesn't speculate on a lady's age, and I wasn't sure it mattered – Mazzie was too tough to give up a step to time, she'd walk into the grave with her back unbowed and her head raised level. She wore a calico dress, and an ivory hoop the size of my palm hooked through her left nostril.

In one regard only were they similar, though this last outweighed the rest – was indeed the cause of their association, the reason I'd tracked Mazzie down three years ago and cajoled her into taking Wren on as a student. In the long gestation prior to their birth, the daevas had reached down inside them and kindled a spark which remained dormant in the rest of us, which allowed them to will into existence things wondrous and horrifying.

14

Mazzie was playing with a deck of oversized cards, strange things, precious looking but well used. She reordered them with easy dexterity, using a type of shuffle with which I was unfamiliar – and I'm a deft hand when it comes to cheating at poker.

'What are you doing here?' Wren asked. Amongst my many failures as a guardian, I had yet to learn the boy the basics of etiquette.

'I was in the neighborhood. I thought I'd give you a walk home.'

'We've got a couple of minutes yet.'

'Finish your lesson,' I said, stepping inside and pulling shut the curtain. 'I paid enough for it.'

Wren turned back to Mazzie, who noted my presence in her brilliant, imperturbable eyes but gave no greeting. 'You ready?' she asked the boy.

'I'm waiting, ain't I?'

Mazzie cackled, but didn't stop what she was doing.

'The Zealot.'

Mazzie cut a card from the center of the deck, randomly so far as I could see, and flipped it over. On it was a robed figure kneeling beside a bound woman, holding a lit torch to a fagot of wood at her feet.

Wren smiled confidently. 'The Crumbling Throne.'

Mazzie dropped another card onto the table – a crowned man on a stone chair, the top inlaid with gemstones, the bottom decaying into nothingness.

'Why you looking at my hands?' Mazzie asked Wren. 'I got nothing to do with what's coming.'

'I gotta look somewhere.'

She shook her head adamantly. 'Your eyes just gonna lie to you – don't you listen to anything I say?'

Wren shrugged but didn't bother to answer. Mazzie had kept up her shuffling during the back and forth, and dropped another card in the boy's direction. 'The False Friend.'

An ugly man standing between two halves of a mob, hands raised in supplication, a sly smile on his face.

I was conscious of the heat – over-conscious, to judge by the fact that no one else seemed to feel it. My brow was moist with sweat, and my head was heavy, like I'd wrapped it with cloth. I blinked it away, but it didn't go.

'Bitter Enemies,' I heard Wren say.

Two figures locked in a death grip, a scarred man strangling his opponent into final submission.

'The Untrue Lover.'

A man and a woman intertwined, the first beatific, the second cold and even.

'Five for five,' Mazzie said. 'Let's see you finish it.'

To judge by Wren's smirk, certain and over-clever, this would be no problem. 'The Broken Cage.'

Mazzie drew the last card from the deck, looked at it and smiled for a moment. But only a moment – then the grin dripped off her face like wax from a candle, and what was left was bitter and contemptuous.

The card showed a galleon breaking against a reef. It was surprisingly intricate – I could make out a tiny figure leaping off the topmast, taking his chances with a furious sea. 'Dashed Hopes,' she said.

The smoke from Mazzie's kitchen fire had wrapped itself inside my throat. My ears were buzzing like I'd taken a full snort of breath. Each stroke of my pulse sounded in my ears. Wren was saying something, but it was a few seconds before I realized it was directed at me.

'What?' I broke out of my stupor.

'I said that was it for the day. I'm ready when you are.'

'Start without me, give the elderly a moment to themselves.'

'You said you were here to walk me home.'

'What I say is a long way from what I do – I'd have thought you'd have picked up on that after six years.'

'Get on out of here,' Mazzie agreed, waving her charge out the exit.

Wren grumbled himself to the door, and I stopped thinking about him. The boy didn't need to worry about the inhabitants of the Isthmus. Mazzie had spread clear word throughout the neighborhood that he was off limits, and even the most hardened thug felt their mouth dry up at the thought of crossing her. Besides, he could handle himself, much as it galled me to admit it.

I took the seat he'd vacated and started on a cigarette. My hands were stiff and numb, and it took me longer than it should have. I managed it finally, though it was far from my best work. 'How's he doing?'

'You ask after what you just saw?'

'Parlor tricks. And he missed the last one.'

'I didn't know you were such an expert on the Art.'

'I know everything about everything Mazzie – it's one of my many charms.'

She about half-laughed at that. The three years she'd been teaching Wren hadn't made us friends, but we'd at least acclimatized to the other's occasional presence. 'Took me more years than I'd admit to learn that parlor trick. Took the boy six months. He's coming along. Coming along fast. As it happens, I've been meaning to speak on him for a while now.'

'I'm within earshot.'

'When you first came to me, you said to make sure he didn't kill himself with the gift.'

'You've upheld your end of the bargain admirably.'

'Said to teach him a few basic charms, set his feet on the path.'

'That's what I said.'

'I done it – done it and more.'

'So what would you say – he's fifth rank? Fourth?' I tried to remember where apprentice ended and initiate began. It had been a long time since my days picking up second-hand bits of magical trivia from the Blue Crane.

Mazzie rolled back her eyes. 'You fucking Riguns – you put a number on something, think you own it, think you know what it is.'

'Yes, the acquisition of knowledge – an unfortunate hobby the Empire has bent itself towards.'

'Learning's fine. Better to remember that you don't ever know very much. Say you go ahead and do something a hundred times – if you ain't dumb as dog shit, you ought to make a fair guess as to what happens the hundred and first. That don't mean you understand why it happened, don't mean you can do anything but read a pattern once it's been burned into your head. I spent twenty years sitting at the feet of the greatest Practitioner in Miradin. I once saw him tame a storm that would have swamped half the capital by whispering kind words over a wooden bowl.' She spat on the ground. 'Should have let it drown the place, but that's not the point – he didn't need a number written onto his forehead to know he knew how to do something.'

'And that's all they do in the Academy? Lie to themselves about what they know, what they're teaching?'

She shook her head. 'All this nonsense about ranks and scales, the idea that you could master the Art like you would your times tables – that's a lie. The learning ain't no lie. But the learning takes different forms for everybody. My way isn't Wren's way – he's stronger, and his mind goes in different directions. I've taken him as far as I can.'

'He's learned everything you have to show him?'

'He's learned everything I'm going to.'

That sat just fine with me. There were things Mazzie of the Stained Bone knew of which I'd prefer Wren remain ignorant. 'So what are you suggesting? Get another teacher? You know as well as I do, no practitioner would be willing to take on an unlicensed student – and you know double I won't let the Crown hear of what he can do.'

'He's got talent – real talent, talent like I never had and never seen. And he's smart, and he wants it. He could be a master – there aren't half a hundred folk in the world you can say that about. But he won't be it here. Not with me, and not if you can't get him someone knows more of the Art than I do.'

'You're telling me to leave the city?'

Mazzie took a thumb-sized cheroot out from her seemingly

limitless supply. 'I told you what I'm telling you,' she said, and pared off the tip with a curved knife far too long for the job.

'Fair enough.' I added the concern to a not insignificant tally. 'But the boy isn't what I came to see you about.'

Mazzie leaned her muzzle over the candle and lit the stub in her mouth. 'Then what was?'

'Yancey.' The Rhymer was our single shared acquaintance, beyond the boy himself. Had, in fact, been the one to put me in touch with Mazzie, when I'd been looking for someone capable of training Wren that I could be sure wouldn't be whispering anything about it to the Crown. That also made him one of a half-dozen people in the world who knew what Wren was capable of. There weren't many men I'd have left alive knowing that secret, but I trusted Yancey as far as anybody could trust anybody.

Mazzie stretched back into her seat, puffing at her cigar till it had a decent draw. 'I'm listening.'

'He's sick.'

'I hear so.'

'I thought maybe you'd look in on him, see if there's something you can do. I'd make it worth your time.'

Reading Mazzie was like staring into an overcast sky at midnight – I'd have better luck playing Wren's side of that card game. Still, I thought I saw something resembling regret. 'He been sick for a while?'

'The last six months. Maybe longer, but you'd notice it the last six months.'

'Nothing to be done.'

'You can say that without seeing him?'

'Folk come to Mazzie, they say they sick. I tell them quit eating fried chicken livers for every meal, give them something so they can shit better. Sometimes they come to me in the winter with a child, getting that wet cough, that cough that's gonna get worse. They come to me early enough, sometimes I can help him, smooth it over, see to it the child sees spring. Some nights I hear loud noises outside of the door, and I know the rough boys got someone who took a blade, and are trying to get the courage to bother me 'bout it. They stop being fearful, they bring the man in, Mazzie look at him, tell his friends to come back in the morning. Sometimes the man come out at first light with his flesh reknit, owing Mazzie till the day he die for true. Sometimes that man don't walk out at all, if Mazzie decide it better he be going in the ground.'

She had a smile like the last thing you see before the end. I made sure I didn't look away, but it was a strain. After it had gone on long enough, Mazzie ashed her smoke and continued.

'But when a body decides it don't want to keep breathing, nothing to be done. Least nothing I ever learned.'

'You can't take a look?'

'What the point of that? Give the man hope for something ain't coming?' She shook her head. 'I tell you I can't do it. That's all there is to say.'

'I guess so,' I agreed. 'I'll see you next week with coin.'

If there had ever been a moment when Mazzie was expressing concern as to the Rhymer's future, it was gone completely. She grunted, my presence or lack thereof not worth an entire syllable. We had enough in common for understanding, but too much for friendship. I stubbed my cigarette and left without a final retort.

It had been a vain hope, barely that even, a passing fancy I'd decided to cling to. Forty years, you'd think a fellow would start to get used to disappointment. But it always burns the same. Wren hadn't bothered to wait, which suited me fine. I spent the walk home eyeballing passersby, hoping one of them would jump. But none of them did – they never do when you want them to.

3

I stopped off at a bar on the way back from Mazzie's, a little neighborhood joint a few blocks from the pier. I needed a drink, and I needed to be left alone, and back at the Earl I'd only get the first. It had been a nasty day. Two stiff glasses of liquor didn't improve it, but they at least blurred some of the details.

Folk started to trickle in around dinner time. A man asked if he could borrow the empty chair from my table, and I paid my bill and left without answering.

I followed the canal north, away from the docks and towards the big industrial districts that ring the west corner of the city. Hempden had been a nice place, once, but it wasn't anymore. I guess that holds true of a lot of things. The population was Vaalan, with a smattering of Islander, the men working at the huge pig-iron foundries they'd built after the war. A working-class neighborhood, where a man could come in from the provinces without anything but a strong back, find himself some labor he needn't be ashamed of doing, and that could pay for whatever family he managed to put together.

But the Nestrians stopped buying iron from us after we stopped buying wool from them, and the forges started to twinkle out, one after another. They weren't any great shakes, as many a bitter old drunk with a mangled hand or a limp could tell you, but they were better than nothing. Their absence left a chancre where a community had once been. When you got nothing to do all day but sit around and pretend to be mean, you find that's exactly what you end up doing. Then one day you find you aren't pretending.

The three men on the stoop weren't even up to that moderate task any longer, an object lesson in just how much a person could lose without dying. I had a sudden image of three toads on a log – blank eyes and mouths stretched horizontal. I smelled piss, but then I'd been smelling piss for a solid ten-block stretch, so I couldn't pin that on them for a certainty.

'The Professor around?' I asked one of them.

He didn't answer. None of them answered.

'You going to let me through?'

The one in the middle leaned very faintly to the left, as if blown by the wind, and I slipped up the stairs. Someone had busted the front door off its hinges – I had to pick it up and move it aside. The entryway was the sort of place that made you wish your boots were thicker than they were, that you were wearing gloves and a winter cloak and a few layers of long underwear.

I didn't linger. At the end of the hallway was a door, and I rapped at it.

'Who's there?'

'Queen Bess.'

A moment's pause. 'But your majesty, you weren't expected till tomorrow! We haven't even made up your chambers!'

I opened the door, but hesitated before going inside. I'd found my way through the foyer with the little bit of light coming in from the outside, but it wouldn't take me any further. The interior was black as the inside of a cenotaph.

'Just a moment,' said the voice. 'I'll light a candle.'

There was some scuttering about. In the pitch black it seemed very loud, and the odor was almost overpowering, mildew and flesh-reek and wyrm-smoke baked into the foundations.

Finally, there was the sound of a match being struck, and the dim light of a candle helped me with my bearings.

'You aren't the Queen.'

'No,' I admitted.

'Well,' the Professor said, shrugging. 'Come in anyway.'

The Valaan tend towards tall and broad, but the Professor wasn't one to walk with the crowd, and he'd bucked convention by being short, fat and round as a cannonball. His clothes had been expensive when he'd bought them, loud purple pants and a silken shirt, but these days you'd be hard pressed to pawn them off on a rag-picker. He extended his hand like he wanted me to kiss it. He had to settle for a handshake, though he didn't seem to mind.

Pleasantries completed, the Professor returned to the big green comfy chair that sat in the corner of the room, set his candle on top of a neighboring table. Apart from a wooden stool in the corner, they were the only furniture left in the room. I could remember a time when the walls had been lined with shelves and the shelves lined with books, but they'd disappeared long since, sold off volume by volume to pay off the Professor's cravings. I've heard people speak of themselves as addicted to reading, but I think those people never stole from their family so they could afford this month's serial, or sucked off a sailor for a new book of short stories.

'What do you want?' the Professor asked, feigning annoyance. Whatever else he had lost, he maintained a keen sense of the theatrical.

'Do I have to want something?'

'You only come by and see me when you want something.'

'You wound me.'

'So you're just here to chat?'

'No, you were right. I do want something.'

He laughed and gestured towards the stool. I dragged it over and perched myself across from him.

Seen from the outside, crime looks as anarchic as a jungle, every man against the other. But in fact it's as strictly hierarchical as a counting house or a caravel. Every member of the fraternity knows their place within it, from the biggest syndicate kingpin to the most decrepit Low Town streetwalker.

Nowhere is this more true than when it comes to picking pockets. You start off as a slip, ferrying away with the purse once it's been snatched, returning with the proceeds, getting your ass whipped red if you've been cutting into the group's take, or maybe even if you haven't. You pay your dues in that long enough and you move on up to stall, bumping into passerby, distracting the fish for those few critical seconds during which they lose a week's wages.

That's as high as most folk go. It doesn't take anything but a set of hands and feet to be a slip, not much more than that to work as a stall. You want to take a turn making the grab yourself, you'll need sly fingers and hungry eyes, and the sort of nerves that don't get rattled by making something that was someone else's yours. We call that working point, and it's not for the faint of heart.

Of course, if you get right down to it, picking pockets isn't so far from getting your pocket picked. It's not like people go to the corner grocer with their life savings – you're lucky to end your days with half an ochre, and you've still gotta split that a couple of ways. People who have a lot of coin on them tend to notice us that don't, and the guards in the Old City are less apt to look the other way at a felony, or at least demand enough in bribes to make the whole thing pointless.

Anyway, if you do decide to start cutting purses you can expect to spend about six months as a slip, maybe a solid year or two as a stall. I made point in nine months, and what I learned, I learned from the Professor.

'How you been?' I asked.

'Oh, I get by, I get by,' he said, in no great mood to discuss the present. 'What happened to that dagger you were carrying?'

'In one of your pockets, I suppose.'

He laughed, pulled out the blade and threw it over to me. He did this every time I saw him, though even knowing it was coming I never caught him doing it.

'That was your downfall, you know. Once you started carrying one of those it was all over,' he said, shaking his head sadly. 'You could have been one of the greats, if you'd kept at it. One of the all-time greats.'

This was untrue. I'd been a good pickpocket – still was, if it came down to it – but I'd never been anything close to elite. My hands weren't quite fast enough, and the few fractions of a second between what the Professor was capable of and what I could manage were enough to get you jailed. Besides, to be a really great pick, you had to be the kind of person that other people didn't mind letting get close. Needed to look friendly, or at least harmless. And I never really could pass for harmless, not even when I'd been a kid.

The Professor knew it was a lie, but it was a good segue into talking about the past. He started unraveling the yarn about how he'd once stolen a pocket watch from the Duke of Stockdale, then returned it because he'd been so moved by the inscription. It wasn't a true story, and I'd heard him tell it before. But I didn't interrupt. It was part of the tithe, letting him recall his glory days.

And I owed him something, a lot of people did. He was the Professor because at one point he'd all but run a school for wayward youth, turning ill-bred larcenous miscreants into – well, more successful ill-bred larcenous miscreants. Of the five best pickpockets in Rigus, three of them had come up under the Professor's tutelage. That was how he scraped by these days, former protege's coming by to drop off a few coins to the man that had gotten them started in the business. If they were smart, they'd take a look at how it ended, learn one last lesson from the greatest pickpocket in the history of Rigus about stepping off before you're forced. Most of them probably weren't that smart.

'. . . but you didn't come here to listen to an old man ramble,' the Professor ended.

'Always good to catch up. But like you said, I only visit when I want something.'

'And what would that be?'

Even when the Professor had been at his best, he'd been a sight too flashy, with his colored handkerchiefs and a touch of rouge on his cheeks. He had this trick he'd do, hand a mark some 'dropped' item while removing another of greater value, returning a wallet with one hand and lifting a golden bracelet with the other. Watching the vic stumble all over themselves offering their thanks, it was just about the funniest thing we'd ever seen.

Till one day it wasn't. He miffed a snatch on the wrong chump one evening, got beaten half to death for his trouble. Kind of thing that could have happened to anyone. Will, if you ply the trade long enough.

Anyway, that was pretty much the end of the Professor as a serious 'pocket. His body healed but his nerves were shot. He could still manage a smooth lift from a friend, but that thing that let him smile into a man's eyes while impoverishing him, that thing was gone. For a while he managed to fake it with the assistance of pixie's breath, a quick shot of courage before going into battle. But the thing about being a junkie is that it doesn't leave room for much else. For a while a person is a junkie and a bartender or a junkie and a father or a junkie and a thief, but after a while he's just a junkie.

Not that I'm one to judge. If it wasn't for the Professor and his cohort, I'd have to work an honest living. I'm a real swell character, in case you hadn't already gotten the drift.

I slipped the tin I'd taken from Reinhardt's out of my pocket, tossed it over. He caught it, rattled it up next to his ear, opened it, looked inside. Then he whistled a jaunty little tune. 'How did you get your mitts on this?'

'I found it in my sock drawer when I woke up this morning. House elves, is what I'm figuring.'

'See if you can't get them to come out my way.'

'They're sedentary sorts, house elves. Don't like to move much.'

I don't think I'm being unduly flattering in suggesting I have some passing familiarity with narcotics. But still, there's being an expert, and then there's being an expert. You want to know about bread, ask a baker. Want to know about iron, ask a smith. Want to know about greed, ask a banker, or a politician, or pretty much anyone else you see. But you want to know about drugs, you ask a fiend. They're not exactly a rare species, not in Low Town at least. Course, one that you can trust further than you can piss, that's a bit more difficult to find.

'What you know about it?' I asked.

'They're calling it the red fever.'

The red fever had killed half the city and most of Low Town when I'd been about five. Amongst the numberless dead had been my parents, sister and pretty much everyone else I'd ever known. It was still spoken of in hushed tones – your average citizen makes the sign of the Firstborn when speaking of it.

It was a pretty good name for a drug. I was surprised it had taken so long for someone to use it. 'Who's calling it that?'

'Everybody. It's the big talk. Expensive as hell, but they say it's the closest thing to heaven a sinner is likely to find. You try it?'

'No. You?'

'A bit out of my price range, as I said. A hit will set you back an argent.'

An argent was a lot of money for a real down and outer, maybe three or four pipes of choke, if I had my junkie math down. A person in the Professor's position would need to save up for it, and people in the Professor's position were not renowned for their thrift.

'Where's it coming from?'

'Part of the mystery. Just showed up on the streets about a month ago.'

'You must know where I can cop some.'

'I hear Truss has a stash, and maybe Gerald the Idle. But they're strictly bottom-feeders, unaffiliated with anyone. They're not making it, or bringing it in.'

27

'Then who is?'

The Professor shrugged. 'Can't say.'

I was old enough to remember when wyrm had started to be a big moneymaker, the Tarasaighn immigrants bringing it with them from the bogs of their home country, the rest of the population quick to catch on. But that had been the last panacea that had broken into the mainstream. The good people of Rigus can be quite parochial, when it comes right down to it.

'That seem strange to you?' I asked.

'Of course. You'd think whatever syndicate is sitting on this would want to make their mint while they still have a monopoly. Sooner or later the opposition will figure out the process, even up the field.'

'Unless it's not one of the syndicates. Could be some up and comer, doesn't want their new game shut down before it gets started.'

He shrugged. 'More your territory than mine.'

'Truss over on St Marc's street?'

'And Gerald the Idle. You thinking of paying them a visit?'

I got up off the stool, dug an argent from my pocket and set it next to the candle. The Professor shot me a look. I sighed and added another.

He smiled and rattled the tin. 'Can I keep this?'

'I'm afraid I've still got some use for them,' I said.

He held onto it for a moment longer than he should have. Then he handed it over to me.

I put it back into my satchel. 'In fact, it would be a good thing if you stayed away from this altogether, hear? It's not like breath, or even wyrm. The side effects are . . . severe.' Warning him was a waste of air, I knew it even as I said it. The Professor had made the decision to die in that chair a long time ago. There was no point in clinging to any standards of prudence, no point except in chasing whatever alchemical pleasure you could get, for as long as you could get it.

'Oh sure, sure,' he said. 'I'm too old to be acquiring new habits.'

Bad to end on a lie. At least it wasn't mine. 'I'll see you soon, teach,' I said, tipping my hand to my head.

'You forgetting something?'

I held out my hand, and the Professor tossed over my coin purse.

'Do I need to check it?'

He puckered his lips up in protest. 'I'm an honest thief.'

One day I would walk out of the Professor's and not ever walk back in. It's the rare wyrm-fiend that reaches their natural end. Then again, two-copper crime lords don't generally meet She Who Waits Behind All Things in bed, gray-haired and surrounded by their grandchildren. Just as likely the Professor would be coming to my funeral as I would be going to his.

For some reason, that thought warmed me during the cold walk home.

4

'Y ou've been moping for two hours,' Adolphus said.
'Longer than that, probably.'
'Longer than that certainly, but the last two hours you've been going at it something fierce.'

He wasn't wrong. I'd come back from the Professor's to find the Earl busy bordering on raucous, an inimical counterpart to my mood. I'd taken a corner seat at the counter and stitched my mouth into a shape which would not attract company. Then I'd started drinking.

'I wish you'd knock it off,' he continued. 'You're scaring away the customers.'

I glanced around at the small mob surrounding us. 'We seem to be doing all right.

'All right, sure,' Adolphus said, leaning fleshy arms onto the bar. 'But compared to what? Often I find myself thinking of the success I could have if you weren't weighing me down.'

Adolphus the Grand was a sight to bring despair to the mind

of any middle-aged man. In the height of youth he'd been as perfect a specimen of the human race as could be imagined, if you discounted aesthetics and just went on sheer physical ability. He was half again as tall as a tall man, and twice as big as a big one. His hair was black as midnight and he had a beard thick as razor wire. Course he was cur-ugly, but that wasn't no hindrance to killing a man.

Twenty years later he was still strong, and he was still ugly, but only the last had increased with age. To the pockmarked skin and crooked teeth his parents had given him, and the single eye the Dren had taken away, you could add a dense cobweb of wrinkles and a gut that would shame a prize pig. I wouldn't have bet against him in an arm-wrestling competition, and there was more than enough left to keep the drunks honest, but he was a far way from what he'd been. And if a superhuman like Adolphus couldn't last two falls with time, what chance did we mortals have?

'Can't be good for your back, carrying me so long,' I said.

'I'm serious. If it wasn't for you this would be the most happening joint in the city. I'd have a half dozen pretty girls serving drinks, and an ogre in a suit manning the door.'

From the drunk a few seats over came a loud belch, followed by the scent of onion and minced meat. 'This isn't exactly the velvet rope crowd,' I said.

'You feel like talking about it?' Adolphus asked.

'Do I seem like I feel like talking about it?'

'No – but you have a backwards way of doing things. A person could take this brooding as a sign you had something to get off your chest.'

'Or they might take it as a sign I genuinely want to be left alone.'

Our conversation was interrupted by a patron shouting from the other end of the bar. 'Hey, one-eye! You bringing my beer or not?'

Adolphus broke his attention off me for a moment, swung around to face our heckler. 'Denis Traub, you've owed me three argents since weekend-last, and you'll get your beer when I feel like fucking bringing it.'

The crowd laughed, Denis Traub included. People liked Adolphus. He was friendly and sympathetic, and he didn't mind letting a tab slide a ways, as Denis Traub could attest. I liked Adolphus too, though for different reasons.

'You give away a lot of booze,' I said.

'You want to be the bartender?'

'Very much no.'

'Then stick to your own end of things. I don't tell you how to hustle pixie's breath and bitch endlessly.'

'I don't need much help with either.'

Adolphus turned to the tap and filled a few glasses. He made like he was going to go over and serve them, but then he pulled up short and went back to talking to me.

'I guess that thing today wasn't lovely.'

'Wasn't lovely,' I agreed.

'Well, the world sometimes isn't. No point in holding onto it.' He gave me Denis Traub's ale. 'Have a drink.'

I had one. 'It's not nightmares that concern me.'

'Then what is it?'

'You knew Reinhardt, didn't you?'

'Here and there.'

'You think him the sort to do what he did today?'

'I did not. But it isn't my first time being wrong. Nor yours, though I know that's hard to hear.'

'No point being nasty.'

Adolphus shook his big head back and forth. 'I'm not used to this end of the argument. Normally you're the one pushing on the fallen nature of man.'

'I'm thinking maybe it wasn't him.'

'Word from the guard was that you came in on Reinhardt holding the murder weapon. That he turned it on himself out of remorse, or fear out of what was coming.'

'I mean it was him that chopped up his wife obviously – I'm just not sure that it was his fault.'

33

'You're about as clear as a coal fire.'

'You remember last week, that greengrocer near the warrens snapped, went after one of his patrons with a hatchet?'

'Yeah.'

'And the week before, when they found Old Tom Shepherd hung in his basement, the bodies of two whores keeping him company?'

'Vaguely.'

'Lot of people been killing people lately.'

He shrugged, nonplussed. 'This is Low Town.'

There was that.

'So you think there's something more to this than meets the eye?' Adolphus asked.

'I think there might be.'

'Any idea what that is?'

'Yes.'

Adolphus's face was big as a shovel head, and every feature marring it was similarly oversized. It was like having a conversation with someone while staring at them through a magnifying glass. 'If you want to talk, talk – if not, keep quiet. Saying nothing loudly is no good middle ground.'

'What's the worst thing you've ever done?'

Adolphus looked at me a long time without answering. Then he reached over and took hold of the half mug of beer I had left, set it beneath the counter. 'You're cut off.'

'I'm serious.'

'I'm serious too – you only get maudlin when you're full of liquor, and soon after you get maudlin you get violent. I've got enough to worry about without having to figure out where I'm gonna hide a corpse.'

'I guess you've got less to regret than I do.'

'You've no monopoly on remorse.'

But I continued on without hearing him, anxious to add further errors to my tally. 'What do you really have blackening your slate? A cruel word to Adeline, maybe a backhand to a drunk that didn't quite warrant it. I'm not talking about vice, Adolphus. I'm talking about sin.'

'You forget where we met each other?' he said, and I could feel the weight of his eyes pulling at mine. 'Five years I spent in the trenches, same as you. I wouldn't think you'd need a reminder of the things we done there.'

'But you couldn't very well say that was our fault, could you? I mean not like other things.'

Adolphus scratched a fingernail down the crooked grooves of his face. 'What are we talking about, exactly?'

'I've done things make the war look like a tea party,' I said. 'I've done things make the war look like a prayer service.'

Time passed. The room was loud and getting louder, inebriated half-wits talking to keep themselves from thinking. The wife couldn't keep her mouth shut for a thirty-second stretch, and the kids weren't any better, you unload cargo for ten hours and come home to a pack of spoiled little ingrates wailing like they'd been beaten. And you're lucky you have a job, what with those damn heretic Kiren willing to break their backs for a clipped copper, and they should ship them all back to where they came from, wherever that was, and let's have another beer, and whose turn is it to pay? Bipeds, all of us, but that was as much relation as I'd admit.

'No one gets to our age without doing things they wish they hadn't,' Adolphus said finally. 'You make good, or you forget about them.'

'Some things can't be made good.'

'That's a nice excuse not to try.' Adolphus reached beneath the counter and grabbed the glass he'd taken from me. 'Finish your drink and go to bed. I've got customers to serve.' He set a quick hand on mine as he passed me the drink. Then he was gone down the line, spreading solace to drunkards.

I watched him walk away, the best friend I ever had – which is underselling it really, because I never had very many, and most of those weren't any good. For a moment I thought maybe I ought to have told him what was on my mind, disregarded that notion near as quick as I thought it. Part because it wasn't clear in my head yet, part because telling him wouldn't have done any

35

good; if my worries held water there wasn't anyone could handle it but me.

But mainly because there are some things that you don't tell anybody, no matter who that person is, no matter how quick they are to believe in the brighter shades of your character. Adolphus had been my friend for twenty years. I'd served with him in the war, saved his life more than once, put up half the stake in the Earl, lived above him for more than a decade. And I knew if he ever had any really clear idea of who I was I'd be as dead to him as a rose bush in December, he'd turn his face from mine and never look back.

It wasn't late but it was late enough. Walking up the stairs to my room I could hear the clatter of the not-candy in the tin in my pocket – like a locust atop carrion, like a death rattle, like the end.

5

Around noon the next day I walked into a lunch place across the street from the house that Truss dealt from. I took a seat by the window and ordered a plate of eggs.

Following up on a re-supply is a pretty easy process. You stake out a place and wait for someone to walk inside who isn't obviously a junkie. Then you follow said non-junkie back to his headquarters. It was just a question of killing time till Truss's stash ran down, though there was no way of saying how long that would be. Work this dull I'd usually pass on to Wren, but for the moment I wanted to play things close to the vest.

Time dragged on. My server kept coming over to refill my coffee, though my bladder was about ready to burst as it was. I felt kind of bad about taking up a seat for so long, but he didn't seem to mind. He was that gregarious sort that only appears when you want to be left alone.

The sun had moved a fair way from its zenith before I saw the man I was looking for slip into Truss's. He was out again five minutes later, and I was waiting for him.

With my second look I was certain I hadn't seen him before, a tall, broad-shouldered character of indeterminate parentage. He wasn't dressed well enough to be working for the Rouenders, and his olive skin meant he wasn't part of Ling Chi's crew. He wasn't looking for a tail, and he wouldn't have noticed me even if he was. We made our way south down Broad Street, then cut west on Paul. I felt a brief flash of something when I realized where we were heading, but ground it down and kept walking.

It had been six years since the Blue Crane – the greatest sorcerer in the Empire, the city's noble protector, plague-banisher and the common man's friend – had put a straight razor to his wrists, and in the interim his estate had pretty much gone to shit. I'd heard the Crown had tried to sell it, but there weren't many interested in purchasing a palatial tower located in the heart of the slums, especially not one with such ominous affiliations. The locals had avoided it for a time, love or fear of its ex-tenant keeping the site intact. But people have short memories, in Low Town and everywhere else. These days the Aerie no longer enjoyed any special status, and the locals treated it with their usual sense of civic pride.

The maze that I had played in as a child was littered with cigarette butts, broken bottles and all sorts of refuse. The tower itself – a magnificent structure, azure-hued stone shooting straight up into the skyline – had become the preferred canvas of anyone with a can of paint and an adolescent's grasp of vulgarity. 'THE CRANE LIVES', read one epitaph, a sentiment which I appreciated but couldn't agree with. Next to it, in bigger letters and a cleaner hand someone had written 'FUCK THE CRANE'. There were a few more dealing with the former owner, but mostly it was just the usual nonsense, tags and doggerel verses of the more profane variety. Some enterprising young fellow had managed to scale the sheer face of the edifice and stolen the head off the gargoyle that once sat in watch above the doorway.

Vagrants had been using the area as a sleeping space, to judge by the worn palettes scattered about. A toilet as well, to judge by the odor.

I told myself I wasn't bothered, seeing the place like this, and there was no one around to contradict me.

We continued south for a little while longer, till we were just off the east docks. My man disappeared inside a small pub, shuttered windows and a 'closed' sign on the door. I gave him five minutes to settle, then walked in after him.

The bar was a bar – tables and chairs and whatnot. Sitting at one of these last, in the back, was the man I had come to see. I knew he was the man I had come to see because the only other person in there was the one I'd been trailing, and even in a small-time operation, the boss doesn't run product.

'We're closed,' the seated one said as the door shut behind me. He was picking at his fingernails, and didn't bother to look up.

The guy I'd been tailing recognized me, though. 'Sully,' he said.

'I said we're fucking closed,' Sully repeated, still working furiously at his talons.

'Sully!' his partner said again, rather more nervously.

Sully looked up, saw me, blinked twice, avoided pissing himself through a great act of will.

I walked over to the guy behind the bar, the one I'd followed from Low Town. Up close he was bigger than I realized, solid shoulders and a crew cut and a gut pushing past his waistband. He stared down at me from across the counter, trying not to show fear.

'You're pretty short,' I said.

He laughed awkwardly.

'I said, you're pretty fucking short.'

This time he didn't laugh. 'I heard you.'

'Shorter than me.'

'I guess.'

'Say it.'

'Say what?'

'Tell me you're shorter than me.'

'Are you fucking serious?'

'Yes.'

He shot a look over at Sully. I put my hand up to block the view, snapped my fingers. 'Your boss can't make you no taller.'

He weighed his manhood against his sense of self-preservation. 'I'm shorter than you,' he said, and he said it without a stutter.

I stared at him for another few seconds, then walked over and took a seat opposite his partner. 'You're Sully?' I asked.

'Yeah.'

Sully looked like someone who wasn't important enough to notice. I guess Sully's mother didn't think that, but I did. 'I guess I don't need to tell you my name.'

'No,' he said. 'I know who you are.'

'Are you sure?'

Sully didn't answer. 'Can I get you a drink?'

There was a full glass of beer already on the table. I reached over and raised it to my lips, chugging along till it was empty. Then I held it over the side of the table and let it fall from my hand. 'No,' I said.

For some reason the sound of glass shattering served to remind my new acquaintance of the fleshy appendage snuggled up to his spine. 'This isn't your territory,' he said. 'You got no business coming in here and playing the asshole.'

'I am an asshole, Sully. We haven't even scraped the surface yet. I'm a dramatically unpleasant individual, the kind of person you don't want hanging around. You take my word for it, the quicker I'm out of your hair, the happier you'd be.'

'And how do I make that happen?'

'You could kill me, if you've got a half dozen men tougher than you are waiting in the back.'

Sully didn't say anything.

'No, I thought not. In that case, the simplest expedient is to give me what I want.'

'What do you want?'

'Let's go through it together, shall we? Am I here because I want to drink some watered-down ale? Do I find your conversation profoundly stimulating? What might you have that's of interest to me?'

He shook his head fiercely. 'I'm not giving up the stash.'

'You can keep your drugs,' I said. 'I've got plenty.'

'Then what the hell is this about?'

'I want to know where you're getting them,' I said, raising my voice for the first time.

The atmosphere in the room, which I think might rightly have been described as frosty, chilled further.

'I can't tell you that.'

'That's bad news for one of us.'

'I know who you are.'

'You said that already.'

'And I've heard your reputation.'

'Word spreads.'

'But you've overplayed your hands, and your big talk ain't nothing but. What are you going to do? Beat it out of me? In my own bar, in broad daylight?'

'No,' I said, pointing a finger at his man at the bar, but keeping my eyes on Sully. 'I'm gonna beat it out of him. You I'm just gonna kill straight off, so he knows I'm serious.'

Sully's little spark of fortitude burned out as swiftly as it had ignited. 'Let's just stay calm here.'

'I'm not agitated,' I said. 'I'm just violent. What gets done to you will be the consequence of cautious premeditation.'

'My man wouldn't like his name being mentioned.'

I leaned back into my chair, folded my arms together and made like I was pondering. 'I understand. You're worried about the future.'

'Damn right.'

'Let me tell you something about the future – it isn't the present. And in the present I'm guaranteeing you that there's nothing that your supplier will do to you tomorrow that I won't do to you today, now, right this very moment. Might as well postpone getting dead. When you think about it, isn't that all we're ever doing?'

Sully turned his eyes to the man at the bar, then to the ceiling, then to the table we were sitting at.

'So,' I began again, after he'd stewed for an appropriate interval. 'Who's your supplier?'

Sully mumbled something that I couldn't quite make out.

'What?'

'Uriel Carabajal.'

I didn't say anything. Then I said, 'Fuck me.'

'Yeah,' Sully agreed.

'You got in bed with the Asher?'

'It was a sweetheart deal,' he said, though he was more lamenting than celebrating it. 'They wanted someone to distribute this new drug they've got cooked up. Someone unaffiliated – not one of their own. The money was good. And they're Unredeemed, it's not like they wear the outfit.'

'He tell you where he got his hands on this stuff?'

'What do you think?'

I wouldn't have told Sully the name of my barber. I didn't suppose Uriel felt any differently.

'They aren't so bad,' Sully said, mostly to himself. 'The Asher are just the same as anyone else.'

'No,' I said. 'They aren't at all.'

Sully put a hand up to his head.

'You ever hear that story about Uriel and his brother, about why they left the fold?' I asked.

'Yeah.'

'No way to prove it, of course – not like the Asher are going to go swearing out a complaint with the hoax.'

'No.'

'But having met him, I kind of think it's true. You think it's true?'

'I don't know.'

'Sort of person who would do that to his own people, folk he grown with, folk whose blood he shares – don't bear pondering, kind of thing he'd do to some stranger who betrayed his trust.'

'No.'

42

'I'm saying, things would go bad, he ever finds out we had this conversation. Not for me – nothing bad ever happens to me, I lead a charmed life. But for you, Sully. I imagine things would get very ugly for you indeed, if Uriel ever found out that you'd let a few harsh words pry his name out of your mouth.'

To judge by the look on Sully's face, forlorn and near to weeping, this thought had already occurred to him.

'Well,' I said, standing, 'I'll do my best keep you out of it.'

It took him a while to hear what I said. 'What?'

'I won't mention you to Uriel,' I said, 'when I go to see him tomorrow.'

'Why the hell would you be talking to Uriel?'

'What did you think this was all about? You roll on Uriel, he rolls on whomever he rolls on. It's the way of the world. But don't worry about it – I'm looking out for you. I'm gonna make sure you come out of this OK.'

I waited to see if he'd thank me, but he didn't. Poor breeding, that's all that was. Kids today, and so forth.

I buttoned up my coat. 'You'll remember, Sully, that I did you this favor? When I come back and see you, next week or in six months or in five years, you'll remember how I helped you out this time – and you'll be happy to make good on your debt.'

By that point, Sully would have sold away his firstborn if it meant getting me out of the bar. 'I won't forget.'

'That's good to hear,' I said. 'At the end of the day, all a man is is his word. Don't you think?'

I didn't wait around for an answer. But then, I was pretty sure where Sully stood on questions of personal loyalty.

6

The weather had turned from early to late autumn by the time I made it outside. The wind was blowing – a month earlier it would have been a breeze, but by now you'd have to go ahead and admit it was the wind. There had been some sunlight a few hours earlier but there wasn't any now, the sky was gray and so was the mood. I pulled up the collar of my coat and headed east.

Yancey had never moved out of his mother's house, and I guess now he never would. A solid thing, brick walls and a bright red door, the kind they didn't seem to build anymore. Everything these days is cookie-cutter mansions or slum tenements, shacks with tarpaulin for a roof. It was in a decent neighborhood too, there weren't many of those near Low Town. A good spot to grow up, as good as any to die. Better than most.

I knocked on the door. It was a long time before it opened.

Once upon a time, Mrs Dukes had a certain genial affection for me – misplaced but appreciated. Later this had turned into a rather exaggerated contempt, though I suppose from her perspective it was well earned. I wasn't sure what she felt for me at this point. Not a lot, I supposed. What was left of her was consumed by her son.

She'd been a handsome woman well into middle age, with an infectious smile and lively eyes. That had been burned out of her with Yancey's illness, and now she just looked tired. She wouldn't long outlast him – you didn't want to think it but you couldn't help yourself.

'Hello, Mrs Dukes.'

'He's upstairs,' she said, with no great excess of kindness. She started to warn me not to make trouble for him, but she didn't finish. Things could not, after all, get much worse.

He was lying in bed when I came up. He was always in bed these days.

I'd met the Rhymer some fifteen years back, long enough ago that it was a struggle to recall the specifics. When I used to enforce the law he'd let me in on the gossip, what everyone knew that Black House didn't. When I started breaking it for a living he'd been of even more help, dropping my name at the parties and nightspots he frequented, letting anyone looking for a pleasant escape know I was the man to act as tour guide. He'd been a musician and a poet, still was I suppose, though his body was no longer capable of focusing his inborn talent. For a while it had looked like he could do no wrong, that his ascent would be continuous and uninterrupted. At his peak, there wasn't a drawing room or garden of the empire's elite that wasn't graced with the presence of Yancey the Rhymer.

But nothing lasts forever – not success, not life. Four years back, Yancey had roughed up a noble after one of his sets. No doubt the blue blood had deserved it, but go ahead and try telling that to the hoax. He'd gotten off light, apart from being tuned up like a lute string. Six months inside, not so terrible in the scheme of things, but it had changed him. He'd fallen out of favor amongst his old patrons, had to stoop to playing dive bars and busking for coin. Then he'd started to get sick, real sick, for days and weeks on end. I'd see him out one night and then he'd be gone for half a month, holed up while his body ate away at itself. Whatever was killing him had been growing for years – but I think it was prison that let it take root, prison and the shame of falling from such heights.

Back when Yancey was Yancey he was constantly in motion, his body echoing the rhythm pulsing through his skull. He swiveled his shoulders when he walked, bounced his head when he talked and drummed his fingers when he laughed, which he did often. He was a small fellow but he took up twice the space of a normal man.

So it was the stillness that I noticed more than anything else, the long moment it took him to look up from the spot on the wall he'd been aimlessly staring at, the longer moment it took for him to react to my presence. I dropped in to see him whenever I could stomach it, which was less than I should have. You could read every minute I'd been gone in the loose folds of his face, and his jaundiced eyes.

Still, he did the best he could, offering a smile that still carried some flicker of the man he'd been. 'So you stopped by?'

'I was in the neighborhood.'

'You bring me a present?'

'You need to ask?' From inside my coat I took out a ball of dreamvine, wrapped in brown paper and tied tight with thread.

I tossed it on over and he brought it up to his nose, savoring the smell. 'Where'd you get this?'

'Dread Mackenzie himself.' It was widely believed that Mackenzie had the best vine in the city. A boutique business, far too expensive to warrant farming out through my dealers. What I bought from Dread I kept for my own personal use. It wasn't cheap, but it was worth it.

'Coming through strong for me?'

'I wouldn't drop by with anything less.'

The Rhymer took that as his due, then swung his legs off the bed. 'Help me up,' he said.

'Where we going?'

'The roof – Mom would kill me if I smoked in the house.'

This was not a good idea. The weather was bad, and Yancey was in no shape to be spending twenty minutes outside without a coat. But his eyes were firm, though bloodshot, and I knew there wasn't any point arguing. And I knew it wouldn't make any kind of difference anyway, not in the long run.

I helped him up, trying not to grimace at the wasted shell he'd become. In his prime, Yancey had been a solid block of muscle. After getting out of prison he'd started to swell up some, a curious precursor to the wasting process he was now undergoing, his body bloating unpleasantly before failing all together. He leaned on me as we walked out of his room and up the stairs, leaned on me and hated doing so. But his legs were spindly things that seemed barely able to support his torso, for all that he'd withered down to half what he'd once weighed.

Yancey's house was built over the Beggar's Ramparts, a deep ravine that cut down towards the docks. I'd passed many an afternoon looking out over it, listening to Yancey practicing new material or just burning through vine and time. There were two chairs left on the deck built over the top of his house, relics of a summer that seemed long distant. I settled him into one. On the other was a thick wool blanket. I covered his shoulders with it, then joined him in repose.

He undid the wrapping on the dreamvine, and got to rolling. After a moment he had a twist as wide as my middle finger and twice as long. 'Not so bad,' he said.

'Not at all.'

'I can still do that, at least.' He let his hand sink back to his lap. 'When a man can't roll his own joint – that's when a man knows it's time to put razor to wrist.'

I didn't say anything. Under the circumstances, Yancey was entitled to a little self-pity. Śakra knew I indulged deeper than he did, and for less cause. The breeze picked up. It would rain tonight.

He managed to light the thing against the wind. The first puff rumbled through him, he started coughing, had to hold on to the rest of his chair. If he died up here in the cold, his mother would throw me off the balcony, and I wouldn't do anything to stop her. But he straightened up, even managed a decent smile. 'Good shit,' he said. 'What's the news?'

The Rhymer had always been a font of gossip, the repository of all Low Town's secrets and sins. It was one of the many things his illness had taken from him, I think he craved information more than he did the drugs I brought. 'Things roll along. You remember Zaga, giant Islander, used to be part of the Bruised Fruit Mob, back when there was one?'

Yancey scowled. 'Sure.'

'He dead.'

'Yeah?' Yancey brightened up a bit.

'Found him bobbing in the bay yesterday morning. People who seen it say the corpse was . . . mistreated.'

'Who done him?'

'Let's just say there are a lot of dry eyes in Low Town. One of the Tarasaighn mobs, maybe; they've been going back and forth over the west docks.'

It couldn't have happened to a nicer fellow.'

Yancey passed the joint over and I took a puff. Dread's reputation wasn't no lie – this was as good as it got. You could tell from the sweet taste on your tongue, and you could tell from the color of the smoke, royal purple and star orange. And you could tell from the way it swelled up in your chest, made your head full of light and empty of trouble.

'What else?' Yancey asked.

I could feel Reinhardt's tin in my pocket, nor was my mind far from the events that had preceded me finding it. But there was no point in tracking that mess to the Rhymer, and anyway I'd come over here as an excuse to not think about it. 'The Sons of Śakra don't show any signs of disappearing. There's half an army of them handing out tracts down by the docks, trying to convince men been on a ship for six months they'd prefer a church pew to the arms of a whore.'

'Two of them woke me up banging on the door the other day, asked Mama if she had a few minutes to talk about the end of days.'

'What did she say?'

'She said the end of days would be coming for them sooner than they expected, if they visited a second time.'

It would have been funnier if I didn't know that Ma Dukes had it in her to murder a pair of men and hide their bodies. 'There are always folk that look around and decide what they see isn't enough. Start searching for something to believe in, aren't altogether partial on what it is.'

'Flies on a wound,' Yancey said. 'They won't be what kills you, but they're a sure sign of rot.'

The wind snapped at us, carried the particolored smoke out into the firmament near as soon as we breathed it.

'So that's Low Town,' Yancey said.

I nodded.

'And how are you?'

I shrugged. Things were not great, but then again I was not rapping on the last door. 'I'm old,' I said, feeling it.

'You've been saying that for years.'

'It's only gotten truer.'

'How's business?'

Business was a steady moneymaker in the degradation of fools, taking resources off men too stupid to use them properly, out of the hands of their womenfolk, the stomachs of their children. It hadn't bothered me as much, back when I was on the breath. Part of that had been because nothing particularly bothers you after a good whiff, but part of it had been that I could at least pretend I wasn't selling anything I wasn't already doing. That had been a lie, of course, but a tolerable one. You could claim prohibition as the chief ill, and it was – if the Crown had any sense they'd slap a tax on it and sell it in shops, stoke their coffers and choke the life out of the criminal organizations that flourish off its sale. But even if they did, it wouldn't make the trade smell any sweeter. At the end of the day I was helping people kill themselves, and there's no dignity in that.

'Booming,' I said, with sad accuracy.

'You feeling that way, maybe it's time you started looking for an out.'

We all of us only have the one out, and Yancey was well on his way to taking it. 'Thing about being a small-time criminal, there's not much in the way of retirement.'

'You ain't so small time.'

'I don't have an organization – there won't be anyone following behind me, kicking up a percentage.'

'How about the boy?'

'You know the answer to that.'

He hocked and spat some of what was killing him over the side. 'So step off.'

'To where?'

'Not here. Isn't that the point?'

'Just leave everything?'

'What you got keeping you here? A shithole bar, a network of pushers and lowlifes. The junkies will find another person to buy breath from, I can promise you.'

'The bar's not so bad.'

'I don't have the time to flatter anyone,' he said, and looking at him I was forced to agree. 'Stick around, you won't live to enjoy your dotage.'

'I've stumbled through so far.'

'You used to be hungrier.'

After that we didn't say anything for a while. Just sat there and let smoke blow away. It started to rain, light but getting harder, and I helped Yancey up out of his spot and into the house. By the time I'd gotten him back downstairs he was ready to pass out on my shoulder. I eased him into his bed, pulled the covers up around his neck, blew out the weak light coming from the lantern on his night table.

'You're all right,' he said to me as I was leaving. His eyes were little slits in his head, and his voice was weak. 'You're all right.'

There weren't but a handful of people who would say that to me and mean it. I didn't like the thought that there would soon be one less of them.

7

So back when I was a kid I spent a few months working as a spotter for a Valaan named Martinus the Bull. That wasn't really his name, but it was what he told you to call him, and Martinus was not the kind of guy with whom you argued nomenclature, making up for a limited wit with biceps the size of ripe melons. Anyway, we had this little scam where I'd hang around some of the more lucrative dice games, wait around for a player to walk off deep in the black, then shadow them back through the city and mark him out for Martinus and his boys to thump. It was a dangerous gig – the sort of person who pulls out of a dice game heavy in the purse is often the same sort of person capable of defending it, and as a general matter of policy the people running these little gambling dens dislike it when their best customers are robbed, and have concrete and unsavory ways of making manifest this displeasure. And all the money I made for Martinus, I didn't see much of it, and most of that I ended up gambling away, cause how long really can you watch a group of men throw the bones and not want to give them a toss yourself? I bowed out of the whole thing about six weeks before one of the less forgiving tycoons had some thugs find Martinus in an alleyway and cut a half-circle into his throat. If I could have held onto such a fine sense of timing, I'd have saved myself a lot of trouble over the years.

Anyway, I found myself thinking about old Martinus the next morning, while running a few vials over to a whorehouse in Brennock, when I turned around and caught a guy tailing me.

He wasn't the worst shadow I'd ever shaken, but he was far from the best either. He had the basics down – kept himself at a reasonable distance, made sure his eyes weren't near me when I turned around. But his costume wasn't quite right, he was too well dressed to be a laborer and too clean to be a criminal. He might have passed for an artisan or maybe a counter at one of the merchant houses, except for the long sword swinging at his side. This in itself was something of a giveaway, weapons of that length being uncommon in Low Town, outside the price range of most of the rabble, and rightly seen as an encumbrance in stealth and movement. Some of the Bravos carried them, quick-handed fools trying to make names as duelists, but no bully-boy in the city would be caught dead in such bland garb, or be awake before late afternoon.

I'd first noticed him back at Keogh Street, near Brennock, and if for some reason you'd felt like tossing away the benefit of the doubt you might have allowed him some reason to be there. But an hour later we were deep into the bowels of Low Town, passing through the sorts of areas only natives would have reason to be. So it wasn't really so much any failure of camouflage on his part – he didn't belong in Low Town, and when you'd been there as long as I had, that was easy to see.

We were just south of the river, on the edge of the spider-web spread of alleys and side streets known as the warrens. It was market day, and even in the slums the autumn markets were pretty good, rich with the smell of roasted chestnuts and burned coffee and blood from the butcher stands and smoke from everyone.

Set up in the middle of the thoroughfare a group of Islanders were playing a folk song, an upbeat thing with a nonsensical chorus of yelps and half-rhymes.

I stopped in front of a fruit stand, rich from the harvest, plump red apples and sour-looking cherries. It was being run by what I took to be the daughter of the owner, a doe-eyed girl with blond hair hanging past her shoulders. Wasn't an easy life these peddlers had, a little farm on the outskirts of the city two-thirds entailed to the bank, the grinding need of the land, the pittance it gave out in return.

But for the moment she looked bright as the foliage, and she gave her little set speech as if it was the first time. 'Good morning, sir. Apples are three a penny, cherries are two copper for a tenth-stone. All are fresh from our family farm, sir, barely eight miles away sir, in North Hempston.'

I gave her a smile and began inspecting the produce, though of course I hadn't much need for them. I'd only called a halt after noticing the lanky Kiren leaning against a cask of dry cider next to the stand, sipping at a cup of what I assumed to be the same, a floppy boater obscuring his face down past his nose, the brim of the hat and the brim of the mug meeting in the middle.

'Hey Warden.'

'Knocker.'

The first big surge of Kiren had showed up some fifteen years back, driven by an internecine conflict in the old country the nature of which we pale faces were too simple to understand. They'd followed the path tramped down for them by previous waves of immigrants, the weak-willed or honest being ground up for cheap labor, those unsuited to carrying water carving out territory at the expense of their countrymen new and old. It wasn't long before the Kiren had gained a reputation for exoticism and brutality that had once been firmly the property of the Tarasaighn. Their hitters were short men with dark eyes that spoke an incomprehensible tongue and seemed no more mindful of blood than a fish is water. With their numbers and desperation they'd quickly become a force to be reckoned with throughout the city, would have become top dog if they'd continued to grow at the same rate.

But of course, they didn't. You can't stay hungry forever. What the father earns the son squanders, and that's a universal reality, true regardless of skin color.

Knocker was of the first generation to be born on foreign shores, knew no other world than Low Town. I'd first noticed him a few years back, he'd been running confidence scams near the docks, once took a few ochres worth of breath off one of my less acute couriers. I'd kept an eye on him since then, an up and comer to make use of or run off.

I was surprised to see him awake this early. If he'd stuck to habit he'd have been up half the night, dicing and generally being a nuisance. For all his bluster there was a sort of sweetness to him, though perhaps it was more a lack of savagery than any particular sense of decency. Regardless, he still hadn't seen fit to slap a blade on his side and call himself a killer, and for a boy his age, in Low Town, that made him damn near a saint.

'Feel like doing me a favor?' I asked.

'No.'

'Feel like making an argent?'

'Depends on how.'

'There's a guy following me a few blocks back or so, got a too-big sword hanging from too-clean pants.'

Knocker spat some of the slime in his throat onto the slime in the street. 'Do I look blind to you, or just stupid?'

'You aren't using a cane.'

'What you want done to him?'

'I want you to get a friend or two together and shake him down, then let him follow you into the warrens.'

'How many ways you expect me to split an argent?'

'Fine, two then.'

'Where you want him led?'

'You know that dead end off Ash Lane? Across from what was Old Man Gee's wyrm den, before Old Man Gee torched himself inside it?'

'Yeah.'

'There.'

From behind his ear, obscured by the long black tangle of his hair, Knocker brought the last half-inch of a joint to his lips. He lit it with a match from his boot, sucked at it a while.

'Don't tell me you're too lazy to make a dishonest silver,' I prompted.

'Bad for my rep, getting caught slipping a purse.' He banged a bony fist against his stained white undershirt. 'I've got a name to live on – I'm the sharpest pickpocket south of the Andel. People can't be hearing I miffed a simple snatch.'

'No one would believe it.'

He puffed his sallow chest out, considered that for a moment. 'What happens once I get your man to the warrens?'

'You leave. But first I give you two silver.'

'Can I keep his purse?'

'No.'

'He isn't so tiny.'

'Are we just going to sit here all morning trading insights?'

'Point being, more certain if I had three friends, 'stead of two.'

'You seem a popular fellow – I'm sure you won't have any difficulty rustling up support.'

'Three men, three argents.'

'By the Lost One, you're exhausting. Fine, three argents, but that's the ceiling, and this has already gone on longer than it should have. You don't want to earn supper, you aren't the only man in Low Town up for trouble.'

I watched his spliff burn down to where the ember was near touching his lip, wondered if it was a parlor trick for my benefit or if he just couldn't bear to waist a single curl of vine. 'All right, I'm in – but I wouldn't do it for anyone else.'

'I'll remember you in my prayers.'

He nodded and went back to sitting very still. I bought three apples from the blonde girl, who was either too young to understand our conversation or old enough to know it was better not to. I gave her an extra copper and she smiled rather fetchingly. Then I stepped back into the crowd, let it carry me south.

The market ended after a few hundred yards, and the mass of people eased out and quieted. A little further down I pulled off the thoroughfare and took a backways look at the action. It was something of a risk – if my shadow was paying attention it might be enough to spook him. But if Knocker and his boys miffed their play and things went to blood I wanted to make sure I'd have the chance to intervene.

And indeed, I was halfway concerned when I turned around and spotted Knocker approaching the target all by his lonesome – three argents split best one way, apparently. 'You got a spare copper, mister? Spare copper for me to get something to eat for my mother?'

'Shove off heretic, I've got nothing for you,' the outsider growled, with more force than you needed to put on it.

'Just a copper, a copper's all I need? For my mom, see? Been a week since she's had a decent meal. You ain't gonna go ahead and tell me that you can't toss a copper for my mother to get a loaf of bread?' All the while Knocker doing his best impression of a wyrm-fiend, hands waving meaninglessly, slack-jawed, bug-eyed and blinking.

'Don't make me tell you off again,' the mark said, this time with a palm on the hilt of his blade.

Knocker put his hands up in front of him like he was about to beg forgiveness – a dead giveaway if you knew him – then he gave the man a solid push.

It's the most basic thing in the world for all it can be hard to remember – never let anyone get behind you. Knocker dazzled the mark with a show, while the one confederate he had chosen to assist him, a mixed-race boy no older than twelve, slid in from offstage and took up position on all fours behind him.

The muck he fell into was good for his back, but bad for his dignity. Also bad for his dignity was Knocker slipping his purse before he could react, then laughing and sprinting off down an alley.

Here was the one part where my plan might go sideways – because if our patsy had any sort of head on him at all, he'd give the purse up for lost, brush the mud off his pants and head back home. Chasing a native through alien streets is a sure way to find yourself not living. But something about this guy made me think he kept his brain near the hilt of his weapon, and my suspicion was gratified when I saw him sprint off in the direction of his attackers.

The warrens aren't so big, maybe a square quarter mile, maybe less. If you know what you're looking for you can pace through it in ten minutes easy, though of course, if you don't, you could wander around for half a day before finding an exit, in the unlikely event that the people living there decided to allow you free passage. Point being, it was easy to make up lost time, navigating swiftly through the labyrinth while Knocker led my pursuer around in circles for awhile.

I reached our destination and took a seat on a broken crate in the back end of the alley. From inside my satchel I took out a clasp knife and started to peel one of the apples I'd bought, separating out the red skin from the flesh beneath. The wreckage of Old Man Gee's den stared at me, ruined windows like vacant eyes, the bottom floor collapsing in on itself like a set of broken teeth. It was the sort of place to give you the heebie-jeebies, if you were the sort of person to get them. I wasn't, really, though I could see why the neighborhood kids maintained that strange lights could be seen coming from the place on moonless evenings, and a wailing heard above the wind. Never held much belief in that sort of thing myself – all the men I'd seen go into the ground, I never knew a one of them to come back for a visit. Still, it would be just like the daevas to curse Old Man Gee by sticking him in his old den. All that effort spent slipping the place, just to spend eternity staring at it.

My ruminations were cut short by the sudden arrival of Knocker, who sprinted in stage left with a face red from labor and a smile wide with sin. He dropped the purse at my feet, grabbed three argent from my hand and then dodged back across the street and out of view. I could hear his pursuer, formerly my pursuer, chugging towards me at a fair clip.

Knocker had led the man a merry chase – if he'd intended to lose him he wouldn't have had any trouble. The man was fit, and enthusiastic enough about catching his quarry, but his sword was too long to comfortably run with, he had to hold it back so it wouldn't trip him up. It was an awkward sort of locomotion, and it wasn't improved when he came around the corner and saw me waiting for him – near enough jumped out of his coat.

'Fancy running into you here,' I said.

It was the first chance I got to look at him up close. I wasn't impressed. His skull was prominent beneath his face, the hair above it cut to flat stubble. His limbs were long and fleshless – indeed from heel to brow you'd have been hard pressed to carve an ounce of fat from his frame. Give me a fat man any day, at least it means he enjoys something. In the scheme of things, gluttony is a pretty mild evil.

Wrath is a far more serious one, and he was moving quickly towards it before I cut him off. 'Don't do anything stupid – I didn't lead you here to offer a convenient spot to be stabbed. The man I've got waiting on the rooftop yonder with a crossbow is a paranoid sort, and if you were to make any move he were to interpret as threatening – pull your blade say, or maybe just come any closer to me – well, I couldn't vouch for your safety.'

Despite my warning, he went ahead and put his hand on his basket-hilt, though what good he imagined the sword would do against a bolt I can't imagine. 'You're bluffing,' he said, but he said it the way people say things they wish were true.

'You're welcome to die thinking that.'

His eyes stayed angry, but he eased his hand away from his weapon. 'What are you doing here, and why do you have my purse?'

'I'm here because I live here. Lived here my whole life, nearly. Might even say I belong here. On the other hand you, my friend, look about as out of place as a whore in church.'

He let out a quick hiss of breath, like I'd landed a punch.

'I don't have any idea what you're talking about. I've got business to attend to at the docks, I was just cutting through the market to save time.'

I smiled a little, ate another piece of my apple. 'I'm trying not to let myself get insulted, friend, but you're making it awful difficult. It's one thing to follow me around like a border collie, a person could have all sorts of reasons for doing that. But now you're standing there telling me that black is white and up is down and toenail tastes like taffy. It's rude – it suggests you think me an idiot. No one likes being called an idiot.'

I watched him consider and discard a series of lies. 'All right,' he confessed. 'I was following you. But I'm not here looking for trouble.'

'Then you picked the wrong neighborhood to go strolling in.'

'I was hoping the two of us might have a talk.'

'We're talking right now. And I have to admit, thus far it's been less than entertaining. And when I get bored I get grumpy, and when I get grumpy my man gets fretful. And when that happens people have a way of falling down and not getting back up.'

'I don't know who you think I am,' he began, drawing himself up to his full height, hand back on the hilt of his blade.

'I think you're very far from home,' I finished for him. 'And I think I'd knock off the bluster if I wanted to ever get back there.'

I put a little edge on that last one, and he seemed to feel it. He relaxed his grip on his weapon, and he even tried to force a smile, an awkward, fluttering thing that died stillborn on his narrow lips. 'This wasn't the way I'd intended our conversation to go. Perhaps I went about finding you the wrong way – but I assure you, my attentions are entirely peaceful. My name is Simeon Hume,' he said. 'And I'm here on behalf of—'

'The Sons of Śakra,' I finished. 'Yeah, I know.'

An unexpected shot of truth hits harder than a fist to the gut, if you can time it right. The unconvincing smile on Hume's face became an altogether honest look of shock.

'It's an amateur mistake, frankly,' I continued, cutting another slice of apple, then pointing the blade of my clasp knife down towards his feet. 'You clean up so nice and then you don't even bother to change your shoes.'

If you'd told me five years back that the Sons of Śakra – better known amongst those of us unaffiliated with the organization as the Stepsons, or just the Steps – would have risen to a position of social prominence, would include in its ranks nobles and members of parliament, I'd have laughed right in your face. A pack of zealots listing as a cardinal vice everything from hard liquor to sex on feast days – hardly the sort of creed to find fashion amongst the hedonistic citizens of Rigus. But that was before trade with the Free Cities dried up, and the mills started to shut down, and the last two harvests had all but withered on the vine. Since then their ascent had been impressively rapid, buoyed by the collapse in trade and industry and the general sense of misery that seemed to loom omnipresent over the city. Despair breeds conviction, when you can't afford a pleasure it gets damn easy to decide it's not one you'd lower yourself to enjoy.

Nowadays their church services were packed to the rafters with old women weeping and young men beating their breasts, and their brown-robed leaders made a ruckus in parliament about anything they could find to make a ruckus about. They ran orphanages and poor houses and occasionally led raids down into Kirentown, proving that theirs were loving gods with the aid of brick bats and cobblestones. Otherwise they could be found throughout the city, passing out tracts and preaching and generally being a nuisance to those of us whose labors focused on this world rather than the next.

In truth, I hadn't been paying much attention to them, seeing as the only thing I care less about than politics is religion. I'd spent enough time in the corridors of power to know that the people you think are running things aren't ever the people that are really running them. And I'd been alive long enough to know that if the Firstborn reigns above, he's not paying much attention to what we're doing down below.

'I hadn't thought them so recognizable,' Hume said, taking a moment to inspect his treads.

'I tend to notice jackboots when they're threatening to march over my face.'

He bristled. He seemed like the kind of person who bristled easily, though I was hoping our association would be too brief to confirm that one way or the other. 'There are many false rumors spread about the Sons of Śakra, spread by our enemies, jealous of the love we have amongst the common folk and our success in parliament. We seek nothing more than an active role within government, for the greater glory of King and country.'

'You can't imagine how little this conversation interests me,' I said, tossing away the core of my apple and pulling out a fresh one from my satchel. 'I assume you haven't been following me through Low Town to debate politics, and I can assure you that I didn't lead you here hoping for a lecture on your sect. Now how bout you tell why you *were* shadowing me, before I make good on these threats I keep offering.'

'My superior has a proposition for you. We wanted to know what sort of person we were dealing with, before we offered it.'

'I'm the sort of person who doesn't like being followed. I wonder whether that point would best be conveyed to your boss from you, or with your corpse?'

'I may not seem like much to you, but my people feel otherwise. They'd be unlikely to take my being harmed with much grace.'

'A lot of men have said that sort of thing to me before I made them dead. I wonder that it gave them much comfort.'

Credit where it's due, the credible – though in this case, fictitious – threat of his demise didn't rattle Brother Hume overly. One of the benefits of being certain about the afterlife, I suppose, is you aren't horrified at the thought of reaching it. 'I work for a man who is very much interested in meeting with you.'

'And who would that man be?'

He pursed his lips but didn't say anything. I waved my hand

63

as if batting away a fly. 'This is pointless – if you've got nothing to say, you can say nothing without me listening.'

'Egmont,' he said. 'Director of Security Cerial Egmont.'

I hadn't been paying much attention to the Steps, as I said, but still that was a name with which I was familiar. 'And what would this meeting be about?'

'That's not for me to say.'

'Cause you don't know?'

You would think ignorance being the common state of mankind, fewer people would have trouble copping to it. 'It's not for me to say,' Hume repeated. 'Come in and meet with Director Egmont, he'll make everything clear.'

'Everything? That's a tall order.' It was clear Hume didn't know anything more than what he'd said, and therefore pumping him any longer for information was pointless, if faintly enjoyable. 'This has been a swell little interruption from the day to day, but I'm afraid I'm not interested in helping you.'

'How can you say that, when you don't know what it is we want you to do?'

'Because it's you asking me to do it. Your side isn't mine. Rats don't give no help to cats, and the cats offer their prey the same courtesy.'

'They say politics make strange bedfellows.'

'I sell drugs for a living, Brother Hume – I don't lower myself to deal in politics.'

He was getting back to talking but I cut him off. 'There's no point in arguing with me anymore. My mind is set as a broken clock. So here's what's going to happen – I'm going to slip out of this alleyway, and you're going to wait three minutes and do the same. My man on the roof is still watching you, and if he gets the sense you're watching me, I'm afraid your superiors are going to have several things to be unhappy about. Dig?'

'I understand,' he said after a moment, though his eyes blazed rather furiously.

'Good. Now after three minutes, you take your first right, then a left two more down, then straight on ahead till you hit the canal

– I know, it's not the way you came. The way you came isn't the way you get back. That's a crooked truth, but it's one you run into more often than you'd think.'

He mulled that over for a while. 'Can I have my purse?'

I fished it up off the ground and tossed it to him, noticing as I did that it was lighter than it should have been. Fucking Knocker – that kid was too damn smart for his own good.

Dull knife that Hume was, he had the thing halfway to his waistband before he bothered to check it. 'I had eight argents in here,' he said.

'My fee for a consultation is a flat ochre – I assume you're good for the rest?'

He belted his purse back on rather furiously, as if by strangling the leather he was getting some payback on me. 'You might think about what it means to go against us.'

'I get a deal on bolts. And on men who fire them.'

You can only push a person so far before they buck a little. That's not true, some people you can push all day and they'll come back begging for more, but Hume wasn't one of these. He gave me the sneer he'd been waiting to offer since he'd seen me, the sneer of a man born on one side of the line for a man born on the other. 'You can put on airs, but I know your big talk is nonsense. You've got a dive bar and a mutt boy who runs poison for you. You might act like the King himself, but it's a bluff, and no good one at that.'

I hopped down from my spot on the crate, eased over towards him, turned my face nasty. 'I hope for your sake that the people who make your decisions aren't operating under that misimpression. Low Town is mine. Every broke-down whore shaking her ass on a midnight thoroughfare is keeping her eyes out for me, every lost youth leaps at the chance to do me a favor, every thug fingering his knife shivers when he hears my name, and makes sure to stay on the right side of it. The bricks in the street, the cracks in the walls, the smog and the smoke, the shit in the canal – I snap my fingers and an army rises up from the muck.' I dropped the apple core at his feet and leaned into him. 'There ain't nothing here worth having – but by the Firstborn and every one of his siblings, there isn't a man alive who'll take it from me.'

He wasn't quite quivering, but let's just say if you'd been looking at us then, you wouldn't have said he was the taller man. I went back to smiling, brushed a bit of dust off his shoulder. 'And since this is my fiefdom, I can assure you – it's your first right, then a left two more down, then a straight shot back to the river. You do that and you'll be back in the Old City in a half hour.'

I tipped a finger off the brow of my head and walked out from the alley. After a short ways I took quick shelter in one of the many abandoned buildings that girded the warrens, rolled a cigarette and waited to see what the Step would do.

Just shy of three minutes Hume walked briskly out of the mouth of the alley we'd been occupying, swiveled his head back and forth, as if trying to make up his mind about something. Then he cut back the way he'd come. With his unerring sense of direction, it would be three hours before he found his way back to a main road. I'd spend a fair portion of that trying to figure out what in the name of the Firstborn the Steps wanted, and why they'd detailed an incompetent to try and get it.

8

Low Town's borders are ill-defined, the squalor and waste stretching out further every year. But there's a change in the air after you cross Lisben's Square, spirited anarchy giving way to dull urbanity, blank neighborhoods of hard-working nobodies, eight hours a day for fifty years, earning them their six-square feet. I didn't know many people there. There weren't many worth knowing.

The pedestrians are pale-faced Tarasaighn, bony children and women that look older than they are. But after a slow mile you start to get pepper with your salt, olive-skinned and clad all in black, unfriendly eyes making an effort not to look at you. Another twenty minutes and it's all pepper, as if after passing Whey Street you'd been transported to a foreign country. Another twenty minutes and you come to the hive itself, stone walls twice the height of a man, a single wooden gate guarded by a scowling tough with a blade at his side.

Rigus is the capital and the largest city in the Empire, maybe the largest in the Thirteen Lands. I was born here, grew up here, made a life and will die here, and I've seen all of it – from the mansions up in Kor's Heights to the wyrm houses where the Kiren smoke away their souls.

But I've never been in the Enclave – no one has, not no one who wasn't born Asher. There's an Enclave in every metropolis in the Thirteen Lands, a walled-off ghetto behind which the Pure Folk are free to obey the dictates of their harsh, single god. They've got their own schools, hospitals and courts. They eat their own food and spit their own curses in their own foreign tongue. During the war they'd even had their own units, silent ranks of black-clad men with long, curved swords, clear eyed and looking to die. An entire world crammed into a few square blocks, the apotheosis of a culture sprung from the millennial exile of a damned people.

But all that shit's academic. Everything there is to know about the Asher can be summed up in four short syllables – don't fuck with them. The central tenet of their faith is that a violent death is the only means of squaring accounts with the almighty. No percentage in troubling a man that's looking to die and been trained long to do it.

It was a sentiment I'd have been happy to go on upholding, if events hadn't overtaken me. Not shockingly, the stark creed of the nameless Asher god fails to find favor with every one of his children. Each generation sees a slow trickle of apostates, forswearing the doctrine of their fathers and joining the rest of us in sin. The Unredeemed, they're called, these Asher who left the fold – and the faithful would cross a street to avoid them, cross it crawling over broken glass. Some of these outcasts take up a trade or go to sea, but most decide that they hadn't given up one set of commandments so they could strictly adhere to another. This last year had seen a steady expansion by these Unredeemed Asher, pushing out from the Enclave west towards Low Town and south against the docks.

The underworld is a delicate ecosystem, and the sudden rise of a new power had threatened to wreck that fragile equilibrium that keeps people from getting murdered in their beds. In particular, the growth of the Unredeemed threatened the interests of the Gitts family, a clan of backwoods savages claiming a swathe of territory running from the eastern docks out past the city walls and into the Glandon suburbs. Squatters' rights, sure enough, but it would be no simple thing to evict them. Throughout Low Town, an interested party could make book on when violence between the two groups would pop off. As of yet, no one had collected – but it wouldn't be very long.

Headquarters was a few blocks from the ghetto, two stories in gray slate, indistinguishable from every other building on the street. I might have missed it myself if it weren't for the heavies – squat men standing motionless, dour by the standards of a sullen race. I'd only been there once before but they must have remembered me because I got waved in without comment.

The interior had the look of a place that was meant to be left quickly, and thought of little thereafter. A wooden table took up most of the room, two men sitting on the far side of it.

Uriel was clean-looking and pretty, the sort of person to whom you'd extend credit. He wasn't tall but he had the broad stature common to his people, the kind that let you know there was more there than you could see. He wore a snow white suit and his smile wasn't half a shade darker. His hands were red, but you couldn't see it looking at him.

Qoheleth was taller and broader than his brother, though I didn't imagine fiercer. He had dull, flat eyes and a head like the business end of a bludgeon. The Unredeemed had a thing about garish clothing, presumably a reaction against spending their youths in sackcloth. Uriel was pulling it off, but his brother looked like a circus performer, each item of clothing at cross purposes with another, a polka-dot tie clashing with a checkered shirt, bright orange pants and a too-tight mauve hat. While not the person I'd choose to double-check my arithmetic, credit where due he was supposed to be very good at his job – which was sticking metal into wriggling things. Uriel was even better at his, which was telling Qoheleth what needed sticking.

'Warden, what a pleasure,' Uriel began. He made as if to get out of his seat, but then didn't.

Qoheleth grunted something I decided to take for a greeting. He had a strong dislike for me, as he had for that segment of the world to which he was not directly related.

'Can I offer you anything?' Uriel asked. 'Coffee? Liquor? Something stronger?'

Uriel didn't take anything but tea – but he liked to have it all on offer when you came in, liked it more if you took him up on it, a reminder of your moral weakness. Not that I needed one.

'I'm solid.'

'As a rock.'

'What kind?'

Uriel crinkled the brow above his nose. It was a pleasant affectation. I imagine he practiced it in the mirror before going to bed. 'I'm sorry?'

'Lots of different kinds of rocks. Shale, for instance, you can pull right apart.'

'I hadn't taken you for such an expert on the subject.'

'There are depths to me, my young friend, heretofore unhinted.'

'I don't doubt it.'

We smiled at each other for a while.

'How's business?' I asked.

'We scrape by.'

'Barely breaking even?'

'Something like that.'

Qoheleth snickered.

'I would think the fever must be adding something to your bottom line.'

Qoheleth looked for a moment like he might choke on his tongue. But Uriel didn't so much as blink. He gave me a fingertip clap that lasted a long few seconds. 'How'd you figure it out?'

'I have my sources. Where are you getting it?'

'I've mine as well.'

That was as much as I'd expected. Getting to Uriel had been easy. Getting past him would be less so.

'As impressed as I am with your acumen,' Uriel continued, 'I'm not clear where your interests lie in the matter. We've been . . . careful to make sure that our new enterprise doesn't infringe on your own prerogatives.'

'Frankly, I'm hurt that you didn't think of including me in this exciting opportunity. But that's not what I'm here for.'

'Do continue.'

'You've done a solid job of keeping things a secret as long as you have. But you can't stay under cover forever. Won't be long before people start wondering where this new drug is coming from, and who's making money off of it. I don't imagine they'll have much more trouble finding the answer than I did.'

'Our obfuscation is only a short-term strategy – testing the waters, as it were. Soon we'll be ready to give the thing an official roll-out. When that happens, we'll make sure the bigger boys get their cut.'

'You've been growing pretty quickly as it is. I don't imagine everyone will be happy to hear of your new-found success. The Gitts may well have feelings about this new narcotic – where you're peddling it, in particular.'

'The pie's big enough for all of us.'

'Depends how hungry you are.'

'I'm a man of . . . modest appetites,' Uriel said, grinning ravenously.

'Self-restraint is a virtue.'

'I've heard that.'

Having swelled up like a boil during this last exchange, Qoheleth took this moment to burst. 'Fuck the Gitts – they don't mean a damn thing to me. And while we're on the subject, fuck you – what business is it of yours where we peddle our merchandise? Glandon ain't your territory. Keep to Low Town, and leave the rest of Rigus to those of us man enough to take it.'

'Now, now,' Uriel clucked, but that was as far as he went. His feelings were more or less in line with his brother's, though it wasn't his style to air them. That was why Qoheleth sat in on these back and forths. It offered Uriel the opportunity to seem reasonable, while making clear where the hard line lay.

'It's no great shakes, getting old,' I said. 'Your knees creak and your hair goes gray. You need to piss all the time, and you can feel your muscle turn to fat. But one minor compensation is that you get to bore your juniors with unwanted advice.'

'Respect for one's elders is a central tenet of the Asher faith,' Uriel said.

Small comfort, given his apostasy. 'Then take a moment and hear one – the Gitts don't look like much to you, I suppose. A bunch of illiterate hill folk, pumping low-grade junk into neighborhoods no one cares about. You ain't wrong – but what they are, they've been for a long damn time. Every so often some sharp young fellow gets it into his mind that the Gitts need changing, gets it into his mind that he's the one to change them.'

'And?'

'We're having this conversation, aren't we? That would suggest that the Gitts disagree. Might even suggest that sharp young fellows, assuming they're the first and not just the second, ought to look for wiser places to expand.'

Uriel stroked the dimple in his chin. He had a talent for making it seem like he was listening to what you were saying. 'Let me set your mind at ease – we've got no interest in making trouble, only money. We're still working out distribution for our new product. It's possible some of our . . . intermediaries have been less than diligent in respecting the Gitts' territory. If that's the case, I'll make sure to put a stop to it. None of our people will be selling fever in Glandon – I imagine that should prove satisfactory, even with a party as . . . temperamental as the Gitts.'

'That's all I wanted to hear.'

'And now you've heard it.'

I recognized a dismissal when it came down to me. 'Before I split – I don't suppose I could get a taste of your new concoction?'

Uriel's perpetual smile widened slightly. He nodded, and Qoheleth disappeared rather grudgingly into the back room.

'Only be a minute,' Uriel said.

'I can't think of a more pleasant way to spend it.'

'What you make of this new guy they put in as High Chancellor?' Uriel asked, small talk one of the many aspects of human behavior he was capable of mimicking.

'Thrilled to my armpits. I figure he'll have the whole thing wrapped up in six months or so.'

'The whole thing?'

'Crime, poverty, disease – all in the past. We're staring into a golden age, Uriel. Soon all men will be brothers, and the sun won't never set.'

Qoheleth slipped back into the room and set a wooden box onto the table before dropping himself back into his chair. Uriel picked it up and held it out towards me. 'On the house. In appreciation for your coming over to talk with us, and in hopes that it's only the beginning of a lucrative relationship.'

'Very kind, but I like to pay for what I own. Gratitude sours quick as young love – mutual self-interest is the basis of all cooperation.'

'Mutual self-interest,' Uriel repeated. 'I like that. If you insist, five ochres is the going rate.'

I paid the man, shoved the box into my satchel and stood. 'Always a pleasure seeing you boys. This goes down well with my customers, we might have to talk about a more permanent arrangement.'

This time Uriel made the grand effort of joining me on his feet. Qoheleth, predictably, remained seated. 'It would be an honor to do business with such a venerable and accomplished man of business.'

I pretended that was a compliment, and not a threat.

A few blocks out I took a moment to open up the box I'd been given. Inside were a stack of tins siblings to the one I'd taken out of Reinhardt's house. I closed the box back up, returned it to the safety of my satchel. The sun had come out while I'd been inside. It was shaping up to a nice day – for some of us at least.

I whistled tunelessly and headed towards Low Town.

9

It was a good night at the Earl, the best we'd had in weeks. Customers stepped over each other to beg drinks, Adolphus kept the flow moving and the chatter pleasant. It's a skill, running a good bar, and Adolphus had it. Next to killing men, it was probably the thing he did best.

Course he had a pair of capable assistants. More than assistants really – tending bar is the glory gig, smiling and pouring drinks. The Staggering Earl ran on the back of Adeline, Adolphus's wife, who, apart from cooking, cleaning, keeping the books and maintaining our stock, was also the sole reason we hadn't gone out of business on the strength of Adolphus's generosity. Between her and Wren the work that needed to get done got done, which left Adolphus free to take the credit.

I'm more of a silent partner to the whole operation. When Adolphus and I had gone in on it together, I had made two conditions clear – first, I could drink all I wanted. And second,

I was never, ever, to be expected to do work of any kind. So far we'd managed OK.

It was late before things started to trail off, well after midnight. Wren had taken a seat with three of our less savory customers, and in a bar like the Earl there's a fair amount of competition for that position. One-Thumb Alain supposedly did work for the Skinned Rabbits, a mid-sized crew of Tarasaighn, though he didn't do it in Low Town. Dubois and Herrold were just run-of-the-mill freelancers, picking up jobs from whoever threw them their way, blowing their money on girls and liquor and holding on till the next one. Just the sort of company a growing boy needs.

One-Thumb fancied himself a gambler, and if you judged by frequency rather than success, he'd fair claim to it. He had a cup and a pair of dice out, and he was displaying his preferred method of throwing. Wren took the advice with good humor, though like any neighborhood boy he was no stranger to the bones, and his sleight of hand was damn near professional.

Midway through the evening I'd switched from ale to liquor, which meant I didn't have to make the trip to the tap every time I wanted a refill. It also made it easier to slide from buzzed into inebriated without being entirely cognizant of it. Standing, I was surprised to find my legs loose and my steps uncertain, which is to say that I more rolled over to the table than walked. Alain had one hand curled conspiratorially over his dice cup, and rattled the four fingers of the other in an even tempo on the table next to it.

'You holding clinic?'

Alain knew I didn't like him. I don't like most people, but with Alain there had never been a reason to pretend. On my end, I mean – he knew enough to smile when he saw me.

'The boy ought to learn how to roll the dice.'

'And you're the one to teach him?'

Alain took a long, slow sip from his drink. Dubois and Herrold shifted uncomfortably in their seats, trying to make clear through posture that their sitting at Alain's table ought in no way to indicate their being his friend, or having a stake in what came to him.

'I've sat in on my fair share of games,' Alain answered finally, trying to keep good humor.

'If you had any idea how to cheat, Alain, you'd still have ten fingers.'

Alain didn't laugh, and he knocked off with his tapping. The stare-down that followed was just riveting, let me tell you. He broke contact, as of course I had known he would. 'On your way, boy,' he said.

Wren was the only one sitting who seemed unfazed by the interaction, but then he was the only one who knew for dead certain he was going to walk away from it. 'Maybe you could show me tomorrow, Alain.'

But Alain didn't answer. I suspected I'd ended Wren's apprenticeship before it had gotten moving.

Wren waited till we were back at my table before calling me out. 'There's no reason to go aggravating customers.'

'They're my customers. I can aggravate them if I want.'

'They're Adolphus's customers.'

That was a fair point. 'You spend too much time with half-wits. It'll stunt your development.'

'One-Thumb's not a half-wit.'

'He's in a dive bar at two in the morning, drinking hard liquor – I wouldn't be too quick to follow in his footsteps.'

'You're in a dive bar at two in the morning, drinking hard liquor.'

'I wouldn't be too quick to follow in mine neither.'

This was pretty standard stuff, common any time I was in my cups, and Wren didn't pay it much attention.

'I ran into Knocker this evening.'

'Next time you run into him tell him next time I run into him he's going to give me eight argents or I'm going to put his head through a wall.'

'He says he helped you corner a Step down in the warrens.'

Little bastard must have had a set of ears planted somewhere in the scenery. 'Knocker ought to learn to keep his mouth shut about things he's not supposed to know.'

'What do the Sons of Śakra want with you?'

'I'm thinking of joining up. Get me one of those cute little hats they like so much.'

'I'd figured you and the Sons might have something of a shine for each other. Enemy of my enemy, and all that.'

'Enemies? What enemies? I'm universally loved.'

'Last time I checked, you weren't the biggest fan of Black House. And if this pamphlet I picked up is accurate, neither are the Sons.' He set a piece of paper onto the table, a standard one-page broadsheet, the kind the Steps had been flooding the city with this last year or so.

'Damn censors – standards have gone to shit. Back in my day a person couldn't buy a book with a purse full of ochres, now they just hand out reading material on the street.'

'I assumed you'd want to bone up on the specifics – they might make you take a test before they hand over the headgear.' Wren picked the notice up and made an exaggerated show of reading it. 'Enthralling stuff.' He puffed out his chest and affected a proper speaking voice. 'The King is beset on all sides by false friends and whisperers of lies. It's the duty of every true born patriot to martial all resources in defense of the Crown, and against the forces that seek to betray his ancient line.'

'And what prescriptions, dare I ask, do the Sons of Śakra suggest for our ailing Empire?'

'Increased vigilance against the Dren threat.'

'Saber-rattling – the remedy to all domestic misfortunes.'

'Renewing ties with our ancient allies in Nestria and Miradin.'

'Pig fuckers and zealots, and neither of them worth a damn in a fight.'

'A halt to the unjust privileges for those yet to accept the blessings of the Firstborn.'

'What unjust privileges do the Kiren hold exactly? The right not to be strung up to a lamppost by every drunken dockworker who takes the fancy?'

'And finally,' Wren continued over my objections. 'A return to the virtue and dignity of our forefathers.'

'I knew our forefathers – bunch of drunken, violent cretins, like their kids.' I was getting hot. I'd like to say it was the liquor, and that certainly didn't help, but primarily it was Wren. Most people I've learned the trick of not listening to, but he had a way of getting up under my skin. 'Lay off it, boy. Today's been long enough without you poking me.'

He folded up the notice and put it into his pocket. 'I'll admit it doesn't sound like much. But they've got the numbers – couple thousand in the city, growing every day.'

'Popularity is no guarantee of value – more often it's the opposite.'

'Not just the lower classes, either. You see a lot of young nobles walking through the Old City with those pretty brown bonnets you've so taken to. You know their leader's a Duke?'

'I did.'

'Charles Monck, the Honest Pater they call him. He's a member of parliament, one of the good ones, supposedly. He even stood with the Veterans' Association during their march.'

'How'd that end?'

Not so well, to judge by the fact that Wren decided to stare fixedly at the wall for a while.

'It doesn't exactly suggest much for his sagacity.'

I suppose the boy realized he'd overplayed his hand, because he didn't answer that either.

'I wouldn't be so quick to bet against the establishment. And even if there was to be a change of guard, it wouldn't make a damn bit of difference to me or you. There are people up top, and people at the bottom. Today it's King Albert and the Old Man. Tomorrow, could be the Steps. It's all the same – whatever you were on the climb is lost once you hit the summit. Call it altitude sickness.'

Wren had heard this line often enough not to pay too much attention to it. Wasn't like he was for the Sons of Śakra either, just for generally pissing me off as best he could. Still, he waited a solid moment before speaking again, to at least give the impression that my monologue held some weight. He was kind that way. 'What did you and Mazzie have to say to each other?'

'Words, mostly.'

'I hope you aren't mistaking that for wit.'

'It's awful late,' I explained. 'She says that it might not have been entirely a waste of her time training you these past three years.'

'Not entirely,' Wren agreed. 'What else did she say?'

'I guess if she'd wanted you to hear, she'd have told you herself.'

Wren nodded, slow and serious, as if this last touch was worth holding on to. My tobacco pouch was on the table, and he reached over and started to roll up a cigarette. His movements were sharp and neat. 'And what did Uriel say?'

I was halfway to answering before I stopped myself.

Wren winked, and handed over the smoke. 'You're not the only one keeping their eyes open.'

I lit it, smoked it, and coughed for a while. 'But I'm the only one who seems to stay quiet on what I see, which is half of everything.'

'Doesn't seem likely, the Unredeemed continuing to grow unchecked.'

'Stranger things have happened.'

'The Gitts never struck me as the amicable sort.'

'I see you've been giving some thought to this.'

'So what are we going to do about it?'

'I'm going to do nothing about it, and you're going to do less.'

'Glandon is pretty close to Low Town.'

'Isn't exactly Nestria.'

'Can't be good for business, dead men piling up on our borders.'

'I don't imagine it would make my life any easier.'

I went to take a sip of my drink, and discovered that Wren had his hand on my wrist. 'I'm not a child,' he said, suddenly very serious.

'That's the kind of thing children say.'

Wren rolled his eyes but didn't get hot, an admirable equanimity which suggested he might not be lying about his new-found maturity. He was also kind enough to release his grip, and allow me to get back to my liquor.

'What's your point?' I asked after I'd finished off most of my glass.

'I've carried my share of water.'

'You want a raise? I can double your current salary of zero.'

'I want you to give me something real to do – I want a stake in the enterprise.'

I waved at the assorted drunks. 'You're asking me to share all this?'

'It's time you let me in. I know Low Town as well as you do, I can handle a blade and I've got fast hands. Everyone likes me, even our competitors, which is more than anyone would ever say about you.'

'Now you're just being hurtful.'

'And I've got other talents.' It was about then I noticed his hand beneath the table, pulsing with a low blue light.

'Stop that,' I hissed.

His eyes bored into mine, and it was a long second before the glow faded. 'I'm just saying – I could be of more use than you're allowing.'

I finished my cigarette, ran some things over in my head.

'You know Kitterin Mayfair, slings breath east of the docks?' I asked.

'Yeah.'

'He know you?'

'No. Not really.'

'No, or not really?'

'No.'

I pulled the wooden box out from my satchel and handed it over. 'Run this out to him. Tell him it's a gift from a new friend, hoping to become an old one.'

'What is it?'

'It's a box you're going to run over to Kitterin Mayfair, who slings breath east of the docks.'

When I'd met the boy he'd run on savage pride – anything that smacked of insult was repaid twice over. It made having a conversation difficult, given my predilection for causing offense. But he'd run down a bit in the last six years, certain enough in himself to not need to be reminded every moment of the day. 'I'm worth more to you than as an errand boy,' he said. He kept his eyes on me for a tick, steady but not angry, then paced out into the night.

I went back to drinking. It was something I'd had good practice at. After a couple of minutes Alain shook off, his pair of drinking buddies joining him. Wren was right, I'd lost the Earl a customer – but then the Earl isn't really how I make my money anyway.

The evening passed, and I followed along with it. Closing time rolled around, and Adolphus slipped out from behind the bar and started brushing out those patrons so deeply inebriated or desperately miserable that the thought of a walk home required encouragement. I stayed where I was – between his good humor and the size of his shoulders, Adolphus never had much trouble walking anyone out the door. And the real troublemakers don't wait till the end of the night before causing violence.

It was a while before I noticed that Adeline had crept up next to me. I'd been drinking for a solid six hours, not fiercely, but consistently, and my powers of perception were far from their height. Besides, I'm all but deaf in my left ear, casualty of lying down too close to a black powder bomb. Not that I'm complaining – I had been the one to set it off, after all.

I assumed she hadn't been waiting too long, though with Adeline you couldn't be entirely sure.

'Hey there,' I said.

'Hey yourself.'

It had been more than fifteen years since Adolphus had brought her to meet me, blushing like he'd robbed a bank. I hadn't seen the appeal – a tiny little Valaan, already running to plump, and so silent I'd near taken her for a mute. But she made him happy, damn happy, and this was right after the war, when we were watching comrades who'd survived years in the trenches drink themselves to death in six months, or drag a combat knife along an artery. I figured anything that kept his mind off his eye couldn't do any harm.

It didn't take me long to realize my first impression was for shit. Adeline didn't miss a leaf falling in autumn, and she was done adding the sums in her head before you'd gotten around to breaking out scrap paper. Youth is dew on the vine, beauty lipstick on a whore. I wouldn't give a piss for either. Adeline was solid as a cornerstone, a sure port in a thunderstorm. And if she was quiet – well, time goes by you realize that's no kind of vice either.

'How was your day?' she asked.

'Twenty-four hours long.'

'We need to talk.' Adeline was not huge on pleasantries.

'I'm listening.'

'It's about Wren.'

'Who?'

The list of Adeline's virtues would scroll down to your feet, but you'd be hard pressed to find a sense of humor amongst them. She didn't mind it exactly, so much as she just didn't quite see the point. 'I'm worried about him.'

'I'm worried about all of us.'

'He can't go on like this, tending bar.'

'It's worked out fine for Adolphus.'

Adeline had this look she'd give you, not quite contemptuous, she was too kind for that – more like she was disappointed in your refusal to live up to your potential. 'You know as well as I do that Wren isn't Adolphus.'

'No,' I agreed. 'He isn't.'

'How long you think it'll be before Alain or one of the others realizes how valuable he'd be to them?'

'They know to stay away from him.'

'But he doesn't know to stay away from them.'

'It's not something I'm unaware of, all right? But there aren't so many options for a street child.'

'He's clever.'

'No one likes clever people, they make regular people feel stupid.' I sighed and went to pour another shot. Discovered the bottle was empty. Sighed again. 'He's too old to join a trade, and anyhow I can't quite see him cobbling shoes.'

'He's already got a trade.'

I took a casual look around, making sure we were unobserved. 'Not one he can practice.' Since the end of the Great War, the Crown had gradually tightened control over the Empire's practitioners. Anyone with the spark was required to register with the Crown, and actually working magic without a license was strictly forbidden and unpleasantly punished. I'd made Wren a criminal by keeping him off their rolls – a cruel decision, but the alternative was unacceptable.

'What does Mazzie say?'

'She says she's taken him as far as he can go. She says we ought to find him another teacher – a proper Artist.'

'What did you say?'

'That both the Artists I knew are long dead.' Though I could only claim one scalp between the pair. 'Mazzie says we ought to look outside of the city. Maybe outside of the Empire.'

'That might not be such a bad idea.' Adeline was sharp, sharp enough that she didn't feel compelled to show it off. But she saw what I did, had noticed the smell of smoke, had enough presence of mind to note the direction the city seemed to be running towards.

'It might not.'

One last smile, then she paced back to the kitchen. Another nice thing about Adeline – she didn't belabor a point.

'I might be able to get him something at a counting house,' I said to her back. 'There's a merchant or two who owes me something – the boy's a good haggler. It might do him good, get him out of Low Town.'

'He wouldn't take it. He wants to be you, you know.'

'Śakra, that's a depressing thought.'

I went to pour myself a tipple, and remembered I was out of

84

liquor. I thought about calling for Adeline but decided against it, opting instead to fill some paper with tobacco and leaven some dreamvine over the top of it – just enough to ease me into a nice stupor.

So the boy wanted to be me, did he? Maybe it was time for him to see what that really meant.

IO

The morning found me trudging through the east gate and out past the city limits. To the north and west the metropolis's suburbs have started to devour the neighboring villages, and you could walk a long ways without seeing tilled earth or a tree worth the shade. But out this direction the land was worthless, low-lying swamps that flood in the spring, miles and miles of ground you could buy with a few spare copper. It was autumn, however, and the road was dry, and the sun still warm.

For a different man it would have been a pleasant enough errand, a few hours constitutional in bucolic surroundings. Me, I go mad without the bustle. This was business, pure and simple. If my druthers meant anything, I'd have still been asleep. But then, they rarely mean much.

After a mile or so the road turned to track, vague and increasingly ill-defined. Then that began to split, peeling up into the hills or down towards the water. I know the city better than the lines on my face, but this wasn't the city, and I kept to the bit of turf that I was certain of. This wasn't a place to get lost – the natives here weren't any friendlier than in Low Town, and past the walls my name doesn't carry much weight. Further on and the land itself started to seem foul, gnarled oaks embracing each other, knee-high weeds overgrowing the route. The whole country had been like this, back in the day, before the city's founders had drained the swamp and erected the monument to greed and vanity known as Rigus. You got the sense it hadn't quite forgiven the insult, was still waiting for the chance to repay it. I took a fork in the road, following it as it ascended into a steep ravine.

The house was a misshapen thing that sprawled its way up the hill, additions like tumors grafted onto what had once been an oversized shack. A large hog pen extended off one side, crammed to overflow with humanity's closest relative, squealing loud enough to break the dawn. There were a lot of people living in the house, but none seemed to be going to any great effort to see their trash was disposed of properly. What the pigs couldn't eat lay strewn about at random, broken bottles and heaps of scrap metal, rotting cord wood and decayed stock. Amidst the squalor a man was chopping wood into kindling, and I stretched my legs to meet him.

Calum was big for a Tarasaighn. Big for a Valaan, big for any creature not mythic. He had a red mane that circled his skull like a vertical halo, and blue eyes large even by the standards of his frame. His ax was about two-thirds the length of my body, but he swung it without difficulty, each movement methodical but not plodding. He was bare chested against the season, and his matted red fur was thick with sweat.

He did for another sapling before passing over a greeting. 'Warden.'

'Calum.'

'Suppose you're here to jaw.'

'If you've got the time.'

He left his ax in the stump and passed over to a neighboring trough. I'd assumed it had been intended for the use of swine, but if so it didn't seem to bother him. He cupped his hands together and brought a solid pint of water to his lips, drinking some and spilling the remainder over his brow. 'Aunt and Uncle are inside,' he said. 'I'll join y'all directly.'

Calum wasn't one for small talk. I took his suggestion and slipped inside.

By all rights, the Gitts shouldn't still exist. They ought to be a casualty of the city's growth, like the copse of giant oak that used to grow in the hills above Kor's Heights. They were an anachronism, a throwback to a wilder age, before mankind had developed civilization as cover for vice. They bred like rabbits in their warrens of backwood swamp huts, and they died off nearly as fast. As far as the Gitts were concerned, labor was purely a mug's game, and only the lowliest of them, the weakest and least capable, ever put their back to a plow. Crime, petty and other-wise, was their *metier*. They knew the bayous like their mothers' tits, knew a dozen hamlets where a boat could stop off for a few hours without any chance of being caught by an outbound patrol, knew a hundred more where you could weigh down a body without it ever bubbling back up. Mostly they dealt wholesale, farmed the work out through a network of small-time dealers working east of the docks. It bumped up against my territory, but we'd never had any problems. The Gitts lacked the infra-structure or the drive to expand – indeed, staying still was sort of their reason for being.

On the one hand, you had to give it to them, living a few miles from the heart of human civilization without bending knee to its advance. On the other, ten minutes in their company you found yourself rooting for civilization.

The family den had started life as a one-room shanty, but it had seen unceasing decades of development since, expanding every time another Gitts popped into the world, which was all too frequently to my mind. They'd turned the front room into a communal space and filled it with furniture acquired at random from the refuse of other people. Passageways led off at all angles to further wings of the house, and an unceasing stream of Gitts stumbled out of them, pausing to yell abuse or belch or fart or scratch themselves unwholesomely before disappearing back into the warren.

Aunt Cari sat on one corner of a sofa that was dilapidated near to the point of uselessness, a stocky woman well past forty. Responsible for a gaggle of children and a posse of grandchildren, it was an open question whether she'd brought more life into the world than she'd taken out of it. Cari had been pretty once – she had the eyes and the laughing temperament of a woman men had wanted. But that was a long damn time ago, antediluvian, almost past remembering. Booze and smoke had done what the years hadn't, her face was well-used as a soiled kerchief. She wore a dress of homespun cotton, barely strong enough to hold her sagging dugs.

Cari was loud, dirty and clever. Boyd was just loud and dirty. His face and a good deal of his collar were taken up by a bushy white beard. If you cared to spend long enough staring you could watch lice leap out of it. He had thick arms and a thicker belly, and they say he'd been swift with a razor, back when he'd served in the lower ranks of the Gitts' empire. I imagined he could still cut a fellow up. I was certain he'd be willing to try.

Aunt and Uncle were the ones to speak to, but there were endless more of them, strung throughout the area and holed up in their shithole shack, coming in and out of the living room without thought or pause. I'd never bothered to learn any of their names. One wyrm-fiend is the same as another, and the Gitts tended to die or get jailed before you could form an attachment, even had I been the sentimental sort. Cari and Boyd held authority by virtue of having made it to early old age, a rare feat for a family that thought of the morrow as being as distant as the moon. It seemed to indicate they were tough, or smart, or just lucky. I tended to think it was mostly the latter.

As for Calum – well, Calum was something of a different story.

'Warden!' Boyd pulled himself up from his spot next to Cari, a broad smile revealing the rotting green teeth of an habitual wyrm user. 'What you doing sneaking in here, without so much as a by your leave! If we'd have known you was coming, we'd have arranged a proper greeting!'

For reasons which I was not entirely clear, Boyd had a strong shine for me, indeed thought of us as something closely resembling friends. I had to match his enthusiasm or risk causing insult, and even by my standards such deception sat uneasy.

But I was up for it. I took him by the forearm and pulled him close, forcing myself not to react to the stench. Then I slapped him on his back and returned him to his perch. He laughed uproariously. On a side table an ashtray sat overrun with half-smoked ends. Aunt Cari pulled out the most substantial of these, lit it, took a hit and pointed it towards me.

'A little early, but thanks just the same.' Generally speaking I wasn't one to turn down an offer of narcotics, but the Gitts weren't your run-of-the-mill smoke-heads. Dreamvine was a little light for them, they'd fallen into the habit of mixing it with whatever was on hand, ouroburos root or wyrm, maybe even a few drops of widow's milk if they were feeling feisty.

'You know what your problem is, Warden?' Boyd asked, taking the joint from his sister and putting it to his lips. A cold sore about the size of my thumb peaked through the white of his beard.

'Enlighten me.'

'You don't never let your hair down.'

'I'll work on being more corruptible.'

'How's the bar?' Cari asked.

'People always gonna need a place to drink.'

'And how's business?'

'People always gonna need something stronger than liquor.'

Boyd slapped his leg so hard I thought he might unloose his incisors.

'Speaking of which – this isn't a social call, strictly speaking. Ling Chi wants to up his order of stem.'

The best wyrm, that is to say the wyrm which would kill you the quickest, came straight from Tarasaighn, grown wild in the swamps, dried, cured, cut and shipped. I figured the Gitts had kin back in the homeland, distant cousins more inbred and primitive. A disturbing thought indeed.

'Damn the Firstborn, but there ain't enough choke in the Thirteen Lands to satisfy the heretics,' Boyd said.

'Money in the purse,' Cari responded happily.

As a whole, the Gitts were the sort of folk who thought it good sport to catch the occasional Kiren too far from home, roll him, strip him naked and leave him in the bay. They were strong proponents of the belief that the heretics were stealing jobs from honest citizens, not that any of them had ever had a job, or were honest. But, generally speaking, greed trumps racism, one of the few virtues of the vice. I'd made a pleasant couple of ochres playing intermediary between the two organizations.

Calum had slipped in through the door while we'd been talking, but didn't interrupt. In one corner a wooden rocking chair sat motionless, the only piece of furniture that wasn't broken, breaking or defaced. Calum took a seat on it, pulled out a brick of chewing tobacco and cut a lump off with his boot knife.

I'd known Calum before I'd ever met his family, curiously. We'd served together in the war, different companies but the same regiment. Afterward, he'd spent a while working steady at the docks, honest labor for low pay. At the time he wouldn't have nothing to do with his kinfolk, put a cousin through a wall when he'd come to try and beg money. An admirable independence, but one that couldn't last. He'd returned some ten years prior, after his grandfather, at that point the head of the enterprise, got his throat slit playing loose with one of the Rouender syndicates they'd contracted with. We are what we are, in the end – you can only fight it but so long.

'He says he wants twice what you've been moving,' I continued.

Boyd looked at Cari. Cari looked at Calum. Calum looked at me.

Boyd scratched at his armpit, tufts of off-white hair sticking out from beneath his undershirt. 'That's a lot of stem.'

'Don't like dealing with the heretics. They ain't quite human, you know, not like us.' This from one of the youths I hadn't been paying attention to, a pale, skinny kid missing a chin. His nose was oddly upturned, stared at you dead on – a feat his eyes, vague and tweaked, couldn't quite manage.

'Their silver spends like anybody else's,' Cari responded, still thinking things over. Calum leaned towards an overflowing spittoon and added a short dash from between his teeth. He nodded slightly at his aunt and went back to rocking.

Cari stroked at the ash-blonde hairs that stubbed her chin, unsure if I'd seen Calum's signal and anxious to give the impression that it was still her decision that mattered. 'You tell that slant-eyed old bastard, he brings double the money to the next meet, he'll leave with double the product.'

'If it's all the same, I'll paraphrase it.'

Boyd laughed and stubbed out the end of the joint.

'What the hell did you go and do that for?' Cari asked angrily, all thought of our business forgotten.

'Weren't nothing left but the nub,' Boyd answered.

'A nub will get you high, won't it?' Cari pulled said butt out from the dirty ashtray and spent a few moments trying to relight it. Boyd had been right, there wasn't much left. A lesser addict would have given up, but Cari managed the feat at the cost of a few wasted matches and a burned lip. 'When does the heretic want his next batch?'

'He'll let you know, I imagine.'

'And what's your cut gonna be out of this, Warden?' the unnamed youth asked. He'd been eyeballing me the last few minutes, though I wasn't sure if he was offering insult or just cross-eyed.

'You're here to listen, Artair,' Calum rumbled. It was his first words since he'd entered, and for a moment the room came to a halt. 'You ain't here to speak.'

Artair mumbled something disagreeable, but had the good sense not to buck outright.

'Ain't no ill in a man seeing to his end,' Cari said, half-soothingly. 'You could learn something from him, a respectable type like that.'

93

Only in comparison to the Gitts could I possibly be considered respectable. Deciding the joint was well and truly done, Cari dropped it onto the floor and ground it beneath an unshod foot. 'I was about to roast up some bacon,' she said, turning back to me. 'You got time for a plate?'

'We aren't done with business yet, Auntie,' Calum said quietly. He always spoke quietly, and everyone always listened.

Cari cocked her head. 'No? That true, Warden?'

I smiled. 'It is indeed – I had ulterior motives in dropping by.'

'Did you now?' Cari asked, the vocabulary beyond her. 'You had ulterior motives?'

'I'm hearing stories in Low Town.'

'Is it the one about King Albert's cock ring?' Boyd snickered.

Calum blinked his eyes slowly, swallowing his temper. If he lost it every time his uncle made an ass of himself, there would be very little left of the house.

'That one's funny,' I said. 'The ones I've been hearing ain't.'

Calum nodded and waited for me to continue. I was talking straight to him now, dispensing with pretense.

'They concern you and the Asher.'

The mention of the Unredeemed unsettled everyone in the room below six-four. Uncle's eyes, blood-rimmed and vacant, fluttered unbecomingly. The youth snarled and dribbled tobacco juice into the spittoon. Auntie started to roll another joint.

Only Calum stayed steady. 'And what do these stories say?'

'That you'll be killing each other in a few weeks' time.'

Calum had this slow way of starting a sentence, like he was building towards something critical. He took a shallow breath, then a deeper one, his chest swelling. 'Your concern is appreciated.'

'I'm not here pretending we're brothers to the bone. You've got your people and I've got mine – but neither of them are served by bloodshed.'

'Then you ought to go and tell them black robes to keep the hell on their side of the line.' Cari had lost most of her teeth, but she'd kept her bite.

'I did tell them. I told them yesterday.'

'We should head over there and tell them ourselves,' Artair said.

'I don't want to hear you talk anymore,' Calum told his cousin, though without bothering to look at him. 'If Uriel's so interested in keeping the peace, why is he selling red fever in our territory?'

It doesn't do to underestimate anyone. I thought I had a fair idea of Calum's abilities, but it was clear I was wrong. 'You figured that out, did you?'

Calum shrugged. 'You aren't the only one with a pair of eyes in their head.'

'Regardless, I spoke to the man about that in particular. Conveyed that you lot would be less than pleased about the development.'

'And?'

'A mistake, he says. One Uriel will make sure isn't repeated. No fever will get sold in your territory. I have his word.'

'You trust him?'

'I don't trust anyone. But then I don't quite not trust him either. At the very least, it'd be worth waiting a while before doing anything rash.'

'Do I strike you as a rash person?'

'No,' I said honestly. 'You don't.'

'If I do something, it'll be because it ought to be done,' Calum said. 'But until then – so long as the Asher stay out of Glandon, we'll keep the peace.'

'All I ask,' I said, rising and reaching out my hand. It disappeared inside of Calum's, though to his credit he didn't squeeze.

'Don't be so long in dropping by, you hear?' Boyd said. 'Why don't you come over Sunday, we're gonna roast up a hog. Plenty of fine-looking women around here, even for two old farts like us!'

Stretch-marked slatterns to whom you're directly related, but that was no objection so far as Boyd was concerned. 'I'll have to take you up on that soon,' I said, nodding and seeing myself out.

On the stoop sat two children playing with a broken whiskey

bottle. The boy was towheaded, and seemingly well fed. The girl ran more to the Gitts' norm, bony and blank-eyed. Her dress was a re-purposed cotton sack. It also looked like a hand-me-down. My arrival upended their game, though they took a moment to stare at me before speaking.

'Say, mister?' the boy asked.

'Yeah?'

'You got a spare copper?'

'No.'

They looked at each other for a moment, then the boy turned back up to me. 'Well, fuck you then!'

'Yeah.'

The girl giggled as I walked off.

II

That night was another busy one. A lot of busy nights lately, it seemed. The ale flowed quickly, and the talk was loud and meaningless. The more obvious it is things are collapsing, the more desperate folk get to ignore it. I guess there's no point in pinching copper when the world's about to catch fire.

The man who came over to sit next to me was near faceless, successfully cultivating anonymity. If he'd punched me and run off, I couldn't have given a description beyond his sex, and even that I wouldn't have been a hundred percent on. I was fairly certain who he was working for, but I figured I'd wait for him to prove me right.

It didn't take long. 'I've got something to show you,' he began.

'You aren't gonna flash me, are you? Cause I know what a dick looks like.'

He held his hand open below the table, and I took a peek. Nestled in his palm was a sky blue jewel in sterling silver. A beautiful thing, the setting alone worth more than an honest tradesman would see in a year. Of course, you couldn't have found a pawnbroker to take it, not the most crooked back-alley fence, not for two coppers on the ochre.

Because what the man was holding was only a piece of jewelry in form – in function it was the power of the Throne made manifest, and only those deputized by it have the right to hold one. The Crown's Eye, they call it, the foremost possession of every Black House Agent. They aren't easy to make – there's a handful of Artists who have a permanent commission, laboring for six months or a year on each piece. Using it isn't easy either, but that's another story.

They'd broken mine when I'd been cast out of Black House, smashed it with a hammer, held me down and made me watch. At first there was a flash of pain like I couldn't imagine, and I've been stabbed before. Then there was nothing – not nothing, the absence of something, a void I could feel around the edges for months after. I still thought about it, sometimes.

I shook the past away and faced the present. 'Yeah?'

'The boss wants to see you,' the agent said before slipping the eye back into his pocket.

'I don't want to see him.'

He looked tired, shopworn. This was a waste of both of our time, but I figured I had more of that to spend than he did. 'What you want don't really enter into it. He would prefer this was done quiet, but he's insistent it be done. I can walk back to Black House, gather a couple of savages, bust up your bar and jail anyone in here with a warrant – which is everyone, I suspect. And you'll end up talking to him just the same.'

I knew all of that. The Old Man got whatever he wanted – but you have to give the ice a certain level of pushback or they start to think they can muscle you just for fun, and that's a slippery slope to being a straight snitch. I finished what I was drinking, put on my coat and followed him out.

We walked in silence for a couple of blocks. As a child I'd loved the fall, the smell of rotting leaves, the colors. Lately autumn seemed to get squeezed tighter and tighter between the moist unpleasantness of summer and winter's bitter chill. 'This isn't the way to Black House,' I said, after that fact became clear.

'We're not going to Black House.'

'Why not?'

'You'll know if he wants you to know,' said the agent. He was a good time-server, a happy, or at least willing, fixture in the machine – just like the Old Man liked them.

We stopped at a two-story building in one of the duller neighborhoods near Brennock. It was the architectural equivalent of the man who'd guided me there, utterly without distinguishing features. The agent tapped twice on the door, paused, then tapped once more. It opened in response.

Two agents stood in the doorway, heavy men with dull eyes, eyes that weren't impressed with your reputation or how hard you thought you were. They patted me down with a thoroughness that came close to violating basic rules of hygiene.

The corridor was dark, the only light coming from a small sconce. In its distant glare I could make out the curve of a staircase. 'He's upstairs,' the faceless one said.

I had something pithy on the tip of my tongue, but I swallowed it. I'd need everything I had for the fellow at the top of the steps.

The room was almost identical to his office in Black House, which was to say, dismal near barren. A worn table, two chairs, a bookshelf largely empty. All furniture of the institutional sort, to be found across the breadth of the Empire wherever an owner doesn't much care what fills his space. The walls were a soulless sort of gray, more the absence of color than a color in and of itself. No, you couldn't say there was anything particularly noteworthy about the setting. It was the man that gave it character, and that character was unpleasant to the point of terrifying.

The first time I'd met the Old Man I'd decided I was going to become him. He'd never forgiven me for changing my mind. There was no one else in the room, which was unexpected. We'd only spoken a handful of times since I'd been cast out of Black House, but in the past he'd preferred to have someone standing near by, implicitly offering violence. Or, often, explicitly. I wasn't sure what to make of this development, or the change of venue.

'My boy,' he began. 'What a fond pleasure it is to see you again. Please,' he said, pointing at a chair opposite him, 'take a seat.'

I'd known the Old Man for most of my adult life, since I'd come back from the war and joined Black House. The line you heard about him as a rookie – that he was the chief architect of the Empire, that he molded souls like clay, that he knew your next step before you got around to standing – did not seem to hold when you met him. He looked like someone's grandpa, as if at any moment he'd reach out to tussle your hair. He had bright blue eyes, eyes that smiled whatever the rest of his face did. He had salt and pepper hair in a neat but not severe cut. He had strong hands with long fingers. He had a vacant spot somewhere down inside him, where a person was supposed to be.

It was one of the Old Man's many strengths that he did not appear to be what he was. And what he was was evil, pure and undiluted. I've broken cultists on the rack, tracked serial killers to their workspace and sat down with every syndicate heavy worth his carving knife, and never have I met anyone to come within pissing distance of the Old Man. He was one of a kind, and you can thank the daevas for not making any more.

I was used to all that, of course. I'd known what he was even when I'd worked for him, and it had been a long time since I'd had a reason to pretend he was anything else. But there was something new, and it took me a moment to put my finger on it. The Old Man looked old – he'd always looked old, but old like an oak, ancient when you were born but sure to outlive you. Now he just looked regular old, not quite feeble but far from whole. Like a man past his date, over the final hill.

I guess nobody's immortal – though I wouldn't give odds to anyone trying to prove it on the Old Man.

And indeed, when he spoke it was with the same easy lilt he'd always had, like the issue at hand was barely a passing concern.

'I appreciate you seeing me on such short notice. No doubt you were in the middle of some sort of pressing business, for which I do apologize.'

'Why aren't we in Black House?'

'I wanted a change of scenery.'

'A man gets called in by the chief himself, he expects a certain amount of formality.'

'We own everything, my boy,' he said, taking a moment to inspect his nails. They were very clean. 'This house, your inn, the Old City, the Palace. The mountains, the ocean and the sky. There is no spot of ground in the Empire which is any less mine than is Black House.'

'That's not an explanation.'

'It doesn't have to be. I don't have to explain the things I do.'

He did not. I took out my makings and started rolling a cigarette.

'I'd prefer if you didn't smoke.'

'But I'm going to anyway.'

'That's rather petty.'

'I take what pleasures are available.'

He thought about this for a moment. 'I suppose we all have to.'

I punctuated his observation by lighting a match on the table, then puffed along in silence. He'd get to what he wanted at his own pace, there was no point trying to hurry him.

'Why do you think you're here today?'

'An agent came into my bar and threatened to discontinue my existence if I didn't.'

'But why do you think I sent him?'

'You're in the mood to pick up an ochre of vine?'

'You caught a man following you yesterday, a man sent by the Sons of Śakra.'

'Did I? I have trouble remembering back that far.'

'He's going to return in the next few days.'

'You read palms too? Cause I'd love to find out if I'm ever gonna get married.'

'He's going to ask you to take a meeting with his superior.'

I shook my head, almost bemused. 'By the Firstborn, did you

call me in here to tell me to stay out of politics? You really think I'm stupid enough to get in the middle of whatever you've got going with the Sons of Śakra?'

'I think you're incredibly stupid,' he said flatly. 'And if you interrupt me again, I'm going to have the boys downstairs come upstairs and cut off one of your ears.'

The Old Man did not make empty threats – it was part of his gag, like his smiling eyes and easy manner. I determined discretion to be valor's better half, and went back to smoking my cigarette very, very quietly.

'As I was saying – I didn't call you down here to tell you to stay away from the Sons of Śakra. Quite the opposite. Sometime in the next few days, their Brother Hume is going to approach you a second time. He'll ask that you take a meeting with his boss. You'll agree to do so. During that meeting his boss will ask that you take on an assignment.'

'And?'

'You'll agree.'

'To what?'

'Whatever he asks you to do.'

I stamped out my cigarette, then started to roll another, slowly, trying to work out the Old Man's deviousness – though I could have twisted up a year's supply and not have run my way through all his angles. 'What if they ask me to kill the King?'

'They won't ask you to kill the King.'

'But what if they do ask me to kill the King?'

'Whatever task they assign you, I'm sure you won't be able to complete it without the sage counsel of your friends. I would imagine Agent Guiscard, in particular, would be a useful asset to you in these troubled times of confusion and despair.'

I lit my second smoke. The Old Man frowned unpleasantly. He was quite the prude, though that wasn't much vice stacked against the fact that he was also an amoral lunatic. 'I'm not so sure I'll get a second bite at the apple. I somewhat . . . forcefully declined it the first time.'

'You underestimate the persistence of Mr Hume and his ilk.'

'What use could I possibly be to the Sons?'

'I'm sure we'll discover the answer to that, as the situation progresses.'

'But whatever it is, I'll have your backing?'

'We wouldn't want to make it too easy for you. Guiscard will offer what advice he can, and he'll involve me as he sees fit. But I'm afraid you'll need to be operating without Black House support for the time being. We couldn't very well sell you as a credible aid to the Steps if you carried a squad of agents in your hip pocket.'

'You trust Guiscard to do his job?'

'Implicitly,' he said, wounded on behalf of his subordinate. Though of course he trusted no one – hadn't trusted me, even when he'd been willing to turn the shop over.

I puffed little ringlets of smoke in his direction. He twitched his nose but gave no other sign that he'd noticed. 'So you're asking me to get in tight with the Steps, then wait for the opportunity to fuck them?'

'You've a vulgar way of putting things, as always. But in essence, yes.'

'Then I suppose I've only one question.'

'I wait patiently to hear it.'

'Why would I do anything to help you?'

The Old Man leaned back in his chair and laced his fingers together. 'I can think of several reasons. First, you're not doing anything for me – you're doing something for the Crown, the Empire, and the nation. The Sons are fanatics, a few steps from howling at the moon. They're also well funded, highly organized and competently run. Sad though it is to say, they are popular amongst the rabble, and amongst the wealthy that are like rabble. If they aren't stopped, the ramifications could be . . . quite unfortunate.'

I looked at him blankly for a moment. 'Did you really just make an appeal to my sense of patriotism?'

'Second,' he continued without answering, 'I'm not yet starved of resources. Your cooperation in this matter would be directly beneficial to you, in the most pecuniary fashion.'

'I'll let you in on a little secret – people love drugs. Really, it's not that much work getting rid of them. Which is to say, I got money.'

'You never did take to the carrot, did you?' Said in a way that almost made me feel bad about it. 'Here's the stick. If you don't do what I'm asking, I'll be forced to take – how shall I put this without sounding melodramatic – rather vigorous steps against you and yours.'

'Yeah, yeah, burn down the bar, massacre my people, lay their corpses at my feet. This isn't the first time I've heard this song. It's starting to lose its novelty. And dead I'm no help to you.'

The Old Man fell silent, though it was clear from the simple fact that he hadn't yet gotten what he wanted that our conversation still had a way to go. He turned and stared out the tiny window at the alley below, though it was too dark to see anything. At least, it was too dark for me to see anything. Who the hell knew what the Old Man was capable of?

'There is, of course, a final reason,' he said, after the silence had started to drag.

'That's good, cause the first few weren't doing much for me.'

'Albertine Arden is back in Rigus. She's working for the Sons.'

'I'm in.'

The Old Man nodded happily. 'I thought you might be.'

12

Alistair Reginald Harribuld the Third did not like me.

Didn't like the set of my jaw, the tan of my skin or the color of my eyes. Didn't like that these last stared back at him unwavering, without the dip customary to men of his stature. Hadn't liked it when I'd knocked at the entrance of his Kor's Heights estate, three solid raps on the main door. Didn't like my ice blue uniform, didn't like that my wearing it meant I couldn't be sent away by the butler.

No, Alistair Reginald Harribuld the Third did not like me – which was all to the good, because I fucking hated him.

'I'm afraid what you're asking is absolutely impossible,' he said in his slow, patrician drawl, as if the concept of haste to him was as foreign as the earth is the sea.

'Squaring a circle is impossible,' I answered smiling. I smiled a lot in those days, an affectation I'd stolen from the Old Man.

It was easy to smile with the full weight of the Crown at your back. 'What I'm asking is well within your capacity.'

'My capacity, certainly. But contrary to my disposition.' We were sitting in his drawing room, one of several public spaces within his mansion – the one he kept for entertaining riff-raff, baronets and foreign princelings. On the walls were a series of paintings depicting the Duke in various elaborate situations. The Duke on a battlefield, the Duke at hunt, the Duke overlooking his lands, the Duke on the shitter. I made up that last one. The furniture was fantastically uncomfortable, the antique chair I sat in could have been ensconced in a torture chamber. But they were old and fabulously expensive, and for a man like Harribuld, that was all that really mattered.

'Motivation is the issue?'

'In a sense.' Harribuld was nearing forty and doing everything he could to convince the world otherwise. His shoulders were still broad, and he was admirably fit for a man who did nothing for a living – but the buttons on his shirt were taut from holding in his gut, and his hair was too dark to be anything but a dye job, midnight blue-black. The fashion at court that year had tended towards the intricate, and he was well in keeping with it. His mustache drooped down almost to his shoulders, and his goatee had been waxed to a rapier point. I didn't care to guess how long it took him to dress every day, but certainly it would have been impossible without the best efforts of the small army of stewards, butlers and pages that kept supplied his every conceivable need.

'My understanding was that relations between you and Lord Aekensheer were less than cordial.'

'It's not a question of how I feel about him,' Harribuld said. He had this way of enunciating his words like he thought Rigun was your second language. 'It's a simple matter of honor – there are certain things a gentleman simply does not do, and informing on a fellow gentleman is one of them.' He took a delicate pinch of snuff out of a silver box on the table and brought it to his nose. A good deal of it was caught by the wire-mesh barrier of his facial hair, but I thought it impolite to point that out. 'I wouldn't imagine you'd understand.'

'Loyalty towards your peers is admirable,' I said. 'But trumped by fealty to the Crown. I tell you in strictest confidence, the avenues we've been investigating would shock, I say shock, the conscience of even the most jaded villain.' This was not true, as I remember. Lord Aekensheer was involved in some vaguely shady financial dealings, and we were going to use those to swing him in the direction we wanted on an entirely different issue. It was pretty standard stuff, really.

'I'd do anything for the Crown,' Harribuld said, affronted, though of course he'd never done anything for anyone. Had he served in the war, I wondered? Probably he had spent his tour attached to some elderly general with four stars on his lapel, never came close enough to the front to smell the shit and blood. Probably had himself a chest of medals somewhere, commemorating his noble service. I made a mental note to look it up in his file when I got back to Black House. We had files on everyone – getting to sift through the dirty laundry of strangers was one of the perks of being an agent. There were a lot of perks, truth to tell.

'Then it won't be any trouble for you to answer a few questions.'

'But then you see, there's the Crown,' he continued on as if he hadn't heard me. 'And then there's the Crown.' It was clear which end I sat on.

'A neat distinction – we make a similar one, at Black House. There are loyal subjects, and there are disloyal subjects. Amongst the latter would include anyone unwilling to participate in an ongoing investigation.'

Arrogance gives the upper crust a dash which can occasionally be mistaken for courage, though of course it stems from a different root entirely. It's not a disregard for danger, rather the belief that their position keeps them immune from harm. He twisted his mustache till I thought it might detach from his face, then snapped his hands to his sides and stood up. 'I've heard all about the policies of your superior. You can go back and tell him that there are still men in the Empire unaccustomed to cringing like dogs before their lessers. You can tell him that my father's father led the King's armies into battle, and I'll be damned before I bend knee to some trumped up tradesman.'

I let his words hang in the firmament for longer than necessary. I always enjoyed watching them right at the crest, so certain of themselves, so unprepared for what was about to come. 'Is there anything else you'd like relayed?'

He didn't bother to answer that.

'Here's what's going to happen, Harribuld. I'm going to walk up out of here, because the stench of unearned wealth is getting too much for me to stomach. I'm going to roll, light and enjoy a cigarette. Then I'm going to go back to Black House and find whatever it is you don't want found.' His mustache quivered, prelude to an objection but I continued without pause. 'There's no point in arguing – everyone's got something, you bluebloods more than most. Gambling losses, taxes, girls, boys – it doesn't matter. It's there, and I'll get it. Then I'll come back over here and bend you over it until you break right in two. We'll cart you off to a cell in the tower, and a dozen men in jackboots will trail mud onto your carpets and get their fingerprints on your heirlooms. Your house will get sold at auction, your prized possessions find their way to sidewalk antique dealers.' I laughed loud enough to scandalize the butler. 'You fucking nobles, you crack me up. You traded power for wealth and comfort, and while you were sodomizing the help and perfuming yourself, fresher men, men like me, we came and picked up what you cast aside. And now, right now, this very second, you're looking at me and realizing it. Because your name, and your line, and that fake mole affixed to your cheek, they don't mean shit. I'm the new breed, Harribuld, get a strong whiff. What I don't own now I'll own soon. Acclimatize yourself and your retirement can be comfortable. Fuck with me and I'll snap you like a toothpick.'

I stood up. 'But first, there's that cigarette.' He was near spitting in fury at this point, shaking with it, but that would pass in a moment. The aristocracy had their spine bred out of them long ago. 'If I was you, and I thank the Firstborn I'm not – I'd spend a moment considering how seriously you take class loyalty. Your father's father led the King's armies into battle – what do you want your son to do?'

It had been pissing rain all day, and even in Kor's Heights they hadn't gotten around to laying down cobblestone. Back then there weren't two paved miles of track in the whole city, just a few streets by the Palace maybe. My boots were thick with mud after a few steps, and the rain beat against my coat, but even so it was a distinct improvement over the atmosphere inside.

I took up a spot across the street from the Duke's main gate. I wanted his butler to have to tramp through the grime when he came to get me. It took a while to light my cigarette, what with the weather, but when I managed it, it tasted fucking incredible. I was savoring the thing, about halfway through it, when one of our official carriages rolled up next to me. The door swung open, and a man in ice gray slipped out.

Maggins was not prone to overreaction – he wasn't particularly bright, and he had something of a temper, but I accepted both because he stayed calm when others didn't. It was what had earned him a position as something of my second-in-command, and it was why I was very concerned that he seemed distinctly out of sorts. 'Chief needs to speak with you.'

'Tell him I'll swing by after I wrap this up. Shouldn't be long.'

Maggins shook his head, and now I noticed that he was in a very dark humor indeed. 'Not later. Now. It's about your woman.'

Harribuld's butler was sprinting over to meet us, petticoats raised above the mud. 'Agent, please, if you'll excuse me, the Duke would very much like to resume your conversation.'

'One fucking minute,' I said, then turned back to my colleague. 'What about Albertine?' I asked furiously.

But Maggins didn't answer, and that was answer enough.

13

Nothing happened for a couple of days.

I mean, things happened. Babies were born, old folks died, lovers quarreled, addicts copped. Good men did evil and the occasional bad man stumbled his way into an act of virtue. The rich got a little bit richer, the poor scraped by as best they could, and the hoax took their end, as usual. It was as busy a week as it ever was in Rigus – but so far as things related to me, the Sons of Śakra and Black House, nothing happened for a couple of days. I made a point of enjoying the interim, knowing it wouldn't last.

Hume hesitated a moment in the doorway, a bruise against the afternoon sun. He wore the standard cut of his faction, a formless smock that made an extravagance of sobriety, a grim brown skullcap on top of it. The glare hid his face, but not his scowl.

Inside the Staggering Earl a handful of patrons stared back warily. The fanatics weren't much welcome in Low Town. It's not that welcoming a place. On the other hand, that sadly oversized segment of our clientele for whom an evening's entertainment meant getting blood on their knuckles wouldn't come in till later. The daylight drunks sprinkled about my establishment weren't in the mood to start trouble any more than they were to work an honest ten hours.

It was mid-morning, and I was sipping a cup of coffee at a back table. Adolphus was up at the counter, discussing the qualifications of the new High Chancellor with a pair of alcoholics. No great debater, our Adolphus, but he could hold his own against the collected wit of two hardened winos. It didn't hurt that his baritone bellowed out from a chest as broad as a bull's, nor that slumped against the counter he was half-again the height of his patrons.

'Hasn't been head of the Admiralty for eight months, now they give him the scepter? Don't make a copper's worth of sense.'

'He's part of Alfred's circle,' the first answered, jaw flapping beneath a nose like a burst tomato. 'Guess the King figures he's sharp enough to snort breath at orgies, he must be sharp enough to run the Empire.'

'Never would have happened when Good Queen Bess was alive,' his companion said. The first took a worn hat off his head and held it against his chest.

Good Queen Bess had been Old Queen Bess before she died. My countrymen are fools. So are everyone else's, of course.

Hume noticed me finally, walked over and took up a position at my table. 'May I sit?'

'I've got an eleven-thirty with the Patriach of Miradin, but if you think you can wrap this up before then . . .'

It took him longer than it should have to realize that was a yes. When he did sit he did so with the smallest possible modicum of grace, dropping uneasily on his stool, the long saber which completed his costume trailing awkwardly against the floor. He wore a brown coat over his gray tunic, and he was sweating through both, though it was mid-October, and the day far from hot. For some reason he seemed younger than he did during our first meeting, his forehead red with acne. Then again, everyone seems young at my age. I distrust the youth – there's no one more fanatical. Fired by the ardor of ignorance, happy to throw away life untasted.

'I confess, Brother Hume, it's a surprise to see you again. I'd have thought our last encounter would have been enough to set you off Low Town for a while.'

'You don't have a man waiting with a crossbow this time.'

'I didn't last time either.'

His eyes swelled up in his head, and to judge by his trouble speaking he might have swallowed something round, solid, and about the size of an egg. It took him about fifteen seconds or so to choke it down, and I was polite enough to let him do so in silence. 'My superior wants a meeting,' he said finally.

'I'm having the most overwhelming sense of *déjà vu*.'

'Do you think I like coming to see you?' Hume asked.

'Masochism is a surprisingly common feature of the human condition.'

'Do you like seeing me?'

'It's never been a particular passion of mine, of course.'

'If you find my company so unpleasant, then you ought do what you can to see yourself out of it. It's not as if you can't shave half an hour out of your busy schedule to come and hear what the Director has to say. You'd save yourself a lot of time and trouble if you'd stop acting clever and actually were so.'

I'd been waiting for Hume to come up with some sort of an argument to convince me to drop my reticence, feigned as it was. 'Fine,' I said, standing. 'Let me leak a puddle first.'

'What?'

'I'm going to go piss,' I said slowly. 'And then I'll come back, and we can leave.'

'Oh. All right.'

I strolled into the back, then up the stairs to my room. From beneath my bed I removed a black trunk, containing the small arsenal of weapons I'd kept from the war and added to occasionally thereafter. A throwing dagger went into a boot, a longer fighting dirk went into my belt. Thinking it over, I palmed one last blade, a tiny thing about the length of my middle finger, slipping it in place just above my wrist. If the Sons decided to search me I could give up the first two, but no one short of an engaged professional would find the third.

Hume was as I'd left him, rigid against the back of his seat, overlooking the Earl with exaggerated distaste. 'Dressed, primed and ready for the ball,' I said, and followed him out.

The main chapter house for the Sons of Śakra was a large building in the city center. In contrast to their usual aesthetic, it was actually quite lovely. White stone off a thriving thoroughfare, the facade an elaborate but far from garish depiction of the six daevas kneeling before Śakra the Firstborn. From the entrance, if you aimed your eyes right, you could make out the Palace, crystalline towers shooting above the skyline. A concrete reminder of how little there really was at stake in the current conflict, the fundamental similarities between the two sides. Which very rich person would control Rigus? It was of passing interest to most of the folk in my neighborhood, most of the folk in the Empire.

A pretty young woman in a homely frock sitting at a desk smiled when we came in. It was her job, smiling at people, but I think she turned it on particularly hard for Simeon. 'Hello Brother Hume,' she said. 'Is this your guest?'

'Directory business,' Hume said gruffly, stretching himself to his full height and trying to sound impressive. The girl blushed and stared at her feet. Hume blushed and stared at his. I kept my own eyes level – someone needed to keep a lookout for where we were going.

'I'm sorry,' the girl said after a moment. 'It's none of my concern, of course.'

Hume made this sort of choking noise in the back of his throat. I got the sense that speaking to women was not his strong suit. At this point I was having trouble figuring out what was. Scowling and rigid self-denial, but that will only get you so far. 'Stay here,' Hume said. 'I'll make sure the Director is

114

ready to see you.' He disappeared into the back, and the receptionist watched every step with bright eyes and a sad smile.

I leaned across the desk. 'Don't take it personal. He's under a tremendous amount of stress at the moment.'

'Of course,' she agreed.

'Really an extraordinary thing, a man so young tasked with such a grave enterprise.'

'He's an exceptional person,' she said.

'Most men wouldn't be willing to make such a sacrifice.'

'Brother Hume is very dedicated.'

'Of course, of course. Still, leaving Sarah and the children back in the provinces to come here and support the cause . . .' I clucked my tongue. 'Truly inspirational.'

She was so caught up with the tune it took her a moment to follow the lyrics. 'Sarah?'

'His wife, of course, and the mother of his five sons. Wait, no . . .' I snapped my fingers. 'Six sons. I forgot little Hieronymous. Born since he's been here in the city, you know. I'm sure he'd like nothing better than to be back in his hovel making more. But duty calls you know, and our Simeon is not one to shirk it. Are you all right, dear? You seem to have gone pale all of a sudden.'

'It's . . . it's nothing.'

'Maybe grab a drink of water,' I said. When she didn't respond I took a seat in the waiting area, happy to have done my good deed for the day.

After a moment the door opened and Harribuld walked out of it.

He'd aged, and not well. Muscle had long ago swelled into fat, and he'd allowed his hair to revert to its natural color of cobweb. He was dressed badly, for a man of his means – his suit was stained and sufficiently far out of date that even I was able to recognize it as such. It had been a long time since we'd seen each other, but the deliberate lack of attention he gave me, and the slow fade of his skin tone from fevered red to pale green, let me know he hadn't forgotten.

I could have told him, ten years ago, not to take my deal. That it was better to go toe-to-toe, take the risk of getting knocked out straight, than it was to spend the rest of your life being bled of everything you were. Once Black House got its hooks into you, that was the end, you were theirs forever. And it's an uncomfortable thralldom.

He waddled out into the street, an old man, well broken.

What was a Black House snitch doing talking to the head of security for the Sons? And more importantly, why had I seen him? One principle of running a covert operation is that you try and keep things – well, covert. Particularly for an organization like the Sons, for whom any slip would see them fall from legitimate political organization, secure under the King's peace, to terrorist radicals hunted to the ends of the Empire. The Sons had no way of knowing that I was once again working for the Old Man, but they had equally no reason to trust me. Was it simple incompetence that had caused such an avoidable scheduling error? If so, I couldn't figure out what the Old Man was so worried about.

I marked it down as something to chew over later, and turned my focus to the immediate. Brother Hume gave me a wave from the door Harribuld had just come out of, and I got up to join him. Inside was a stairwell, and a very serious looking gentleman with more than theoretical musculature.

'I'm afraid we're gonna have to search you,' Hume said, not sounding particularly fearful.

'No need.' I pulled the throwing knife from my boot and passed it over, then did the same with the dirk. Security put them in a nearby cubby, then looked over at Hume. He gave a quick nod, shortly after which I found myself up against the wall. It was a competent search, but I'm more than competent at hiding things. When it was through, the steel I'd secreted in my sleeve remained where it was. I didn't think I'd need it, but it was nice to know I was better at this sort of business than the Steps.

Hume nodded at a door at the top of the stairwell. 'The Director will see you.'

I climbed up, Hume following me close enough that I could

smell the oatmeal he'd had for breakfast. By the Lost One, even his eating habits were boring.

The room was the same color as the Steps' outfits. The walls were brown and the floor was brown and the desk was brown and so was the man sitting behind it. He stood to greet me as I came in, which was uncommonly courteous, under the circumstances.

'Cerial Egmont,' he said, offering his hand.

Cerial Egmont was dark, handsome and serious. His grip was strong, but the skin was soft – he might give the orders, but he wasn't executing them. I pegged him for a noble, something small but distinguished, the family recently titled or old but sunk into genteel poverty. High enough to know which cocktail fork to use at banquet, but low enough to have aspirations beyond spending his inheritance. Contra Hume, he was not dressed in the traditional frock of the sect to which he belonged. No surprise there – don't matter the organization, the top folk never need to follow the rules. He wore a set of bifocals that made his eyes seem larger than they were, pools of mahogany that urged you to trust him, that his interests were yours, and yours his, and whatever minor problems you had could be resolved amicably. He was doing everything he could to make himself seem older, but I'd have eaten dog droppings if he'd rung in his thirty-fifth year. That made him awful young to be in the position he held. Either the man up top was a fool, or he'd seen something special in Cerial. I'd have bet the latter, but then again I'm wrong a lot.

'A distinct pleasure,' I answered.

He waved at a seat across from his desk. I took it. Hume stood next to the door. Either he was trying to intimidate me or he thought repose a sin.

'I didn't bother to tell this to your man, because I don't suppose he's got his hands around the purse strings,' I began, 'but you want to talk to me, it'll set you back ten of the yellow.'

Hume sputtered. 'You're a common whore then, to sell your time for money?'

'You've got a very skewed conception of the economics of

prostitution if you think many of them are making ten ochres a session.'

'I don't visit whores.'

'Come around sometime, I'll introduce you.' I turned back to Egmont, who'd watched this back-and-forth without comment. He opened a drawer in his desk and counted out fifteen ochres with deliberate disinterest. 'There now,' he said, pushing the little pile over to me. 'I should be commanding your full attention.'

I scooped six months' labor at a mill into my pockets. 'Enough of it,' I said.

Egmont reached into another drawer in his desk, pulled out a pipe, long and black and well-crafted. Apparently tobacco was the one vice the Steps allowed themselves. He packed it slowly, lit it with a long match, made sure it had a good draw. It was boring and pretentious, but my pockets bulging, I wasn't in a position to call him on it. 'Do you know what I do for a living?' he asked.

'Look pretty?'

'I keep my eyes open.'

I spent a while staring into them, waiting to see if he'd blink. When he didn't, I nodded approvingly. 'You deserve a raise.'

'And I make sure a lot of other people keep their eyes open. Brothers throughout the city, from the corridors of the Palace to the grimiest dockside tavern.'

'I wouldn't think that last to be any place for a religious man.'

'Recently I've been receiving disturbing reports from your neck of the woods, reports of chopped up bodies, of savagery most foul.'

I put a hand to my breast, fluttered my eyes with horror. 'Violence? In Low Town? My heart's all a twitter!'

'Even by your rather . . . jaundiced standards, I would think that business with the dockworker and his wife would deserve notice.'

'The world's only getting less sane.'

'And that's coupled with word of a new drug on the streets, something they're calling the fever.'

'There's nothing you know about Low Town that I didn't know a day and a half before. I hope you're holding onto your high cards, because as of right now you just pissed those fifteen ochres straight down a sewer.'

He swiveled his chair to face the window, stared at the bustle of the market for a while. It's a funny thing, but somehow I already knew what he was going to say. It's not really so difficult, predicting the future. Assume the worst, you'll rarely be wrong.

'Does "Project Coronet" mean anything to you?' Egmont asked finally.

Like I said, I could make a pretty good living as a fortune teller. No, that's a lie – people don't get their palms read to find out their destiny, they go to get reassured. Happy ignorance has never been my forte. 'It rings bells.'

'I'd love to hear the note.'

I made like I was trying to recall specifics, playing for time. What did he know? Not much, I had to think. Coronet was top secret, only a half dozen people in the Empire had clearance even to hear the name, and Egmont wasn't one of them. But then, he had heard the name, and perhaps a good deal more. 'It was a project Black House was working on back in the day, personally overseen by the Old Man. It never came to anything, at least not before I was . . . retired.'

'Don't soft-pedal it – from what I hear, Coronet was to be the Old Man's crowning achievement, the ace in the hole that would ensure the permanency of his rule. That is, if it didn't have the unfortunate tendency to drive some of its recipients violently insane.'

'You're well informed,' I said. 'But I'm afraid I don't understand what any of this has to do with anything.'

'No? I'm thinking that the effects of this . . . red fever, are awfully reminiscent of Coronet.'

'Coincidence, nothing more. The project was scrapped a long time ago.'

'And you're certain of that?'

'Yes.'

'Why?'

'As you said – Coronet was meant to make sure the Old Man never lost his grip on the wheel. I know they never got Coronet to work for the simple reason that if they had, you'd be dead, and so would your boss, and so would everyone else in your organization.'

'An unpleasant thought.'

'Depends who's thinking it.'

'I hope you're right,' Egmont continued. 'I very much do. But I'm afraid the similarities are too strong not to take notice.'

'And this is where I come in?'

'Exactly. I'd like you to confirm what you think you know – find out who's selling red fever. Make certain that it has nothing to do with Coronet, that these . . . disturbing parallels are coincidence and nothing more.'

'And if they aren't?'

'We'll have to cross that bridge if we come to it.'

I sucked my teeth and scratched my chin. I squinted my eyes and shifted in my seat. I gave various other impressions that I was weighing his offer with great seriousness. 'I suppose I could look into it,' I said. 'But why would I want to?'

'I would think you'd have an interest in finding out why the good citizens of Low Town have taken to slaughtering each other without reason or preamble. Or do you enjoy watching serial killers spring up in your neighborhood?'

'Maybe I do, Egmont – maybe it's chocolate cake to me. Maybe I wake up every morning with my heart in my throat that today will be the day I get to walk in on a mother-made corpse. You don't know me well enough to be making any sort of assumptions about my character.'

I know you're a businessman, and I know that anarchy is bad for business.'

'Anarchy is the natural state of things in my part of the world. A little more chaos won't change anything.'

'It doesn't look good, bodies sprouting like weeds. I'd think it would be in your interest for you to tamp down on that sort of violence.'

'A few more corpses south of the river?' I shrugged. 'No one cares. Believe me, no one cares. I could start burning down city blocks and it wouldn't lift the eyebrow of anyone that mattered.'

'I'm surprised to find you so difficult to convince. My understanding is that your relationship with Black House is . . . less than amicable.'

'You don't avoid rattling the cage because you love the tiger.'

Egmont had an ugly laugh, one quick syllable that came out his nose. 'As it happens, we hunt tiger.'

'I don't see any pelts.'

'Come back in a few months, I'll have one stretched over the fireplace.'

'Confidence is the mark of victors. Also fools.'

'Do I seem a fool to you?'

'I don't make snap decisions,' I said.

He gave me a blank smile, like holding up a buckler. 'Putting aside the question of my intellect, for the moment – what would it take to peak your interest in the matter, as your sense of public spirit is insufficient?'

'Five hundred ochres.'

Five hundred ochres could buy a house in the Old City, or get you a fifty percent stake in a trading ship. Five hundred ochres could set a family up for life in the provinces, or give you a solid month of hedonism at a top-shelf brothel. Five hundred ochres could get enough men killed in Low Town to populate a cemetery, or get a blessing said in your name at the church of Prachetas every day for ten years. Five hundred ochres could do a lot of things.

'That's a . . . sizable sum,' Egmont said.

'For me it is. You could dig it out from between your seat cushions.'

'Perhaps not quite,' Egmont allowed. I didn't expect him to quarrel over the price, and he didn't disappoint me. Money doesn't mean much to someone like Cerial – nor women, nor booze. He was a junkie for straight power, like the Old Man, like I'd been. It's the most dangerous of all possible addictions, for the devotee, and for those around him. 'What would we be guaranteed in exchange for this honorarium?'

'You wouldn't be guaranteed anything. I'll talk to a few people that I know, follow along with what they say. They come through for me, I come through for you. They don't, you come through for me anyway.'

'It's not much of an arrangement.'

'I didn't invite you here.'

'No, I suppose you didn't.' Egmont made as if to think it over, though it was naught but play. We were acting out a previously constructed scenario. 'All right,' he said. 'I'll send it over. Brother Hume will be your contact. He'll stop by and see you in a few days.'

'It might be better if I wasn't constantly seen to be associating with you people.'

'Worried for your reputation?'

'I wouldn't want Black House to get wind of our arrangement.'

'I can't imagine your former employers are watching your every move.'

I supposed I didn't really care one way or the other – Black House obviously already knew what I was getting into. But it was foolishness on Egmont's part to be so cavalier about a piece he'd put into play. It was hard to square his evident intellect with such an obvious misstep, the second he'd made so far today.

'One thing you might want to think about, if you plan on going up against the Old Man,' I said from the doorway. 'He's always watching.'

Hume walked me out, past a pair of daggers shot from the eyes of the woman at the front desk.

'Good luck,' he said, before depositing me at the entrance.

'What fools call luck,' I said, 'wise men recognize as the will of the Firstborn.'

Said Firstborn had not gifted Brother Hume with the capacity to recognize sarcasm. He nodded seriously, then shut the door in my face.

Outside, I lit a cigarette and tried to piece together the half-truths I'd been eating the last few days. They didn't add up to a full meal – I'd just have to follow along with the program until I saw the chance to break something.

Of course, I already knew the answer to most of Egmont's questions. Uriel the Unredeemed was distributing red fever, though who he was getting it from and why they were giving it to him, I couldn't yet say. Regardless, there was no point in telling Egmont anything at this stage, not until I knew why he wanted to know it. I wouldn't get anything else from going straight at Uriel, not unless I had him tied to a post and a knife in my hands. Maybe not even then.

That only left Touissaint, and the cats. I hustled north.

14

The whiff you got coming in there, cat piss and sour milk, was enough to let you know you oughtn't go further. I gritted my teeth against it and waited while the door swung shut, the broken bells above me shaking faintly. The sign on the front read pawnshop, and I suppose there was nothing when you immediately walked in there to make you argue otherwise. If you looked a moment longer, you'd notice the place hadn't been cleaned in a long time, and a not altogether thin layer of dust had spread everywhere. You'd also realize there was no one up front to sell you anything, or buy anything from you. And finally, you'd recognize that the stock consisted entirely of tools of war, a contrived and bizarre menagerie of violence.

For my part I never understood why a person would sustain any particular attraction to an instrument of murder, want to adorn or, Firstborn save us, name it. Some of that's my history, I guess. During the war there was the odd fellow here and there who had some ancestral heirloom or just a strong inclination towards a particular shape of metal, but most of us stuck to whatever they handed out, and what they handed out was cheap, easy to make and ugly. Agents of Black House carry a short sword of the highest possible manufacture, but they're all identical, part of the uniform. In my current career the emphasis tends to be on things that can be hid under a coat, drawn and replaced quickly. Flash is no virtue for a potential murder weapon.

So I didn't really get the point of the collection, though it was one of Touissant's few passions. Weapons hung on every wall and overflowed off the shelves – foolishly impractical things, claymores a broad man couldn't have strapped to his back, let alone wielded. Matched sets of curved long blades, as if anyone had ever gone into battle holding two equal-sized weapons in front of him. It's astonishing, if demoralizing, to consider the sheer variety of objects humankind has crafted to what is ultimately a relatively simple end.

I spent a few moments avoiding resting against anything sharp. The shop was poorly lit, but here and there you could make out a curl of calico or a spot of bright red fur. Touissant's second love, even greater than that he held for edged weaponry, was for the ever-expanding clowder of strays that he accumulated and cared for. No doubt in the feline community he had a reputation for generosity and greatness of spirit in direct contrast to that which he enjoyed amongst his own species. Cats are famously counted amongst the cleanest of animals, though all that fur licking smacks of self-love to me, or at the very least an awfully concrete narcissism. Regardless, there were enough in there to repopulate the genus, and on those few occasions I visited they seemed to be well in the process of doing so, fat tabbies chasing snarling short-hairs around razored steel.

After longer than I'd have liked, Touissant's man came in from the back room and waved me in.

I'd known Craddock as long as I'd known Touissant, which was a damn sight too long. I disliked him inordinately, given that he'd never done anything particular to me. Mostly, he just stood next to Touissant and kept quiet, though his reserve wasn't exactly a choice. I wasn't sure what he'd done before he'd hooked up with Touissant, but whatever it was it had apparently pissed someone off enough to hold him down, wedge open his jaw and cut out the larger portion of his tongue. Most folk don't survive that – the rot gets into their mouth and kills them in a week or so – but Craddock was a tough son of a bitch, and he was, obviously, still alive. He had the unpleasant habit of tossing open his muzzle and showing off his deformity when he laughed, which was frequently, at any half-hearted jibe of his master.

I followed him down a narrow corridor into a small room. At least it seemed small, though a lot of that could have been the inhabitants.

Touissant was the biggest man I'd ever met, and I'm counting every inch of Adolphus twice. He was too big, his body a freakish, misshapen thing, more curse than blessing, a tower of meat that rose up from the floor and didn't stop till it brushed the ceiling. Thin strands of loose white hair trailed down past the neck he didn't have and onto shoulders wide enough to roll a cart over. His eyes were normal sized, which made them wildly insufficient for his face, two speckles of blue in a lagoon of pink.

If you asked the real old timers, that rare handful of folk who'd survived the plague and the innumerable petty wars since, they could tell you stories of a Nestrian who used to hire himself out as freelance muscle, an ogre with savage tendencies and the mass to enforce them. At what point he'd mounted himself onto his throne, a velvet-lined bench wide enough to comfortably facilitate an extended family of gluttons, I couldn't say – in the years we'd been acquainted I'd never seen him out of it. Regardless, during that period he'd made a reputation for knowing things he shouldn't have known, knowing things no one could know. Rumor credited him with a network of eyes that reached up to the foot of the Throne itself. Rumor credited other things to him as well – dark things, things spoken in hushed tones by men well used to sin. Course, that was all they were, rumors. The Firstborn knows they tell rumors about me – some of them ain't even true.

That said, looking at Touissant, his mammoth hands cradling a tawny kitten, there was no evil I wouldn't have believed of him.

'Come back to see us, yah?' Touissant began. He'd come to Rigus as a child, been here for something nearing a half century, but he still spoke with a barely comprehensible accent, wheezing vowels through the back of his throat. It wasn't any dialect of Nestrian I'd heard, and I'd heard quite a few during the war.

'Couldn't stay away.'

There was a third man in the room, though it took a while to notice him, distracted as I was by Touissant's bulk. Craddock was a constant, but the number three was always different – in the particulars at least, if remarkably similar in the archetype. Dark-haired and pretty was how Touissant liked them, and he'd picked this one according to the model. Pretty Boy carried a blade that was too nice to get blood on, a jeweled saber about the length of my right leg.

'Come closer, come closer,' Touissant insisted, a stilted whine I struggled to make out. 'An old man's eyes aren't so good anymore.'

'You don't look any different than the first time I met you.' This was true actually – something about the bubble of lard beneath his skin gave him a strangely youthful affect. Indeed, he looked like nothing so much as a giant baby, an oversized human whose limbs and shape remained locked into those of a toddler. Which is maybe more horrifying than it sounds.

Touissant burbled to himself happily. Strange, how long it takes vanity to leave a man. 'You always were such a charmer.'

'I do what I can.'

'What brings you around, Warden?'

'Beyond the pleasure of your company?'

'That doesn't need to be mentioned.'

'I need to know something.'

'I know lots of things.' The kitten seemed lost beneath the curve of his hands. 'Lots and lots of things.'

'There was a Black House project some time back, code name of Coronet.'

'This would be when you wore the gray?' he asked, gurgling

in his insipid drawl. Touissant liked to drop hints of your past into casual conversation, though it was hardly a secret that I'd once been an agent.

'The head of it was a man named Caroll – a dear friend, with whom I've sadly lost touch. I would very much like to speak to Caroll, for old times' sake. And I'd be willing to pay for the privilege.'

'What was the purpose of Coronet?'

'And here I was thinking I'd come to you for information. Course if you want to switch shoes, I'd be happy to take some of your money.'

'Suit yourself.' There was a squeal from the cat, pleasure at being stroked or fear of being crushed. Whatever it was, Touissant seemed not to notice it. 'I might still have a friend or two at Black House.'

'Amiable fellow like yourself, I'd think you'd have friends everywhere.'

He leaned the clean, bald globe of his head on one shoulder and batted his eyelashes. They'd been recently painted. 'This . . . Coronet,' he continued, 'I wouldn't suppose it to be widely known of, even amongst the ice?'

'I wouldn't think.'

'Special Operations?'

'Yup.'

He set the cat down on the table next to him. It skittered away immediately, evidence perhaps that its master's attention was less than appreciated. Touissant was busy scratching at the fat pink of his double chin with the fat pink of his hand. After an unseemly interval he said, 'It won't be cheap.'

'I'd hate to think I carried this bag of money here for nothing.'

His shoulders rose up around his ears when he laughed, flapping bags of flesh. 'We wouldn't want you to strain yourself carrying it all the way back.'

I handed Craddock the aforementioned bag. He looked inside and gave a low whistle. It was a shrill thing, split around the severed stalk of his tongue. Then he nodded at Touissant.

'I can't promise anything, of course. But I'll contact you in a few days either way.'

I'll eagerly anticipate it.'

No one bothered to walk me out, which I thought was quite rude, given how much money I'd left. Obviously I hadn't expected Touissant to violate his long torpidity, but at the very least I'd have appreciated spending a few more precious moments graced by Craddock's invaluable presence.

It wasn't until I was out in the street that I realized I'd stepped in cat shit. A minor detail, though it indicated the general tenor of the day. Week, month, take your pick.

15

The arrangement I'd made with the Old Man was simple. I'd put a potted plant out by the front of the bar when I had something to say, and four hours later a man with a blue cap would wander in, buy a drink, and wander out. I'd follow him wherever he went. It meant I needed to buy a potted plant, but other than that I didn't see a problem with it. I hit up a nursery on the way back from Touissant's, placed a rather sad-looking fern in the appropriate position, and stood myself to a drink. Four hours is a long time to wait around, but between my innate idleness and a selection of light narcotics, I managed it.

In fact, it was closer to four and a half when Black House's man came in for a quick shot of liquor. He seemed to know what he was doing, didn't look at me and didn't make any particular commotion. He was inside for all of about five minutes, but that wasn't in and of itself peculiar – it was early in the evening, and a lot of workers slipped in for a stiff one after their shift was over. Twelve hours at the mills, doing their best to avoid losing a finger or a whole hand, every spare thought occupied with those few inches of strong liquor – it's not an easy thing, working for a living. There was a reason I'd foresworn it.

Anyhow, Mr Blue Hat tossed his drink back and then headed out, and I followed him in a timely fashion. He lingered at the next intersection, but he didn't make it look like he was lingering. I wondered if he was an agent or just a stringer Guiscard had on budget. Probably the latter – once you put on the gray, you start to think yourself a little too good for this kind of work. Regardless, he knew his business. I walked a block and a half behind him for a mile or so, and no man alive would have known what we were doing.

He stopped in front of a small store in Wyrmington's Shingle, smoked a cigarette, then bailed back the way he'd come. That was as much signal as I needed. After waiting a minute or two to make sure he was gone, I slipped inside.

The store sold men's suits. Not particularly nice suits, but not the worst quality I'd ever come across. Unremarkable, would have been my description, and indeed this could have been the theme of the whole enterprise. A man stood upright in the main aisle, stub-necked with thick eyeglasses. He was the physical prototype of the image that popped into your head when you heard the word 'tailor'.

The place looked legitimate, and I figured it probably was. Once a month or so a man spent a few hours in the back office, took the occasional meeting, and was on no condition to be disturbed. In exchange, a gratuity was paid slightly in excess of the rest of the month's earnings. Back in the day, I'd kept a couple of these, for conducting business where my contact couldn't be seen entering Black House, or if I just didn't want the Old Man to know the particulars of whatever scam I was running. He always found out of course, but this gave me a little bit of time.

'Good day, sir.' The proprietor's voice was a rich baritone, thick as an oak-cask. 'Is there a particular cut you were interested in seeing?'

'What would you recommend?'

His eyes ran me over with professional diligence. 'With your build and complexion, I'd suggest something bright, but not overly so. How do you feel about light blue?'

'I had a suit like that, once,' I said. 'I didn't like it.'

He nodded sagely. The customer was always right, though at this point I suppose he'd figured I probably wouldn't be picking up any clothing. 'Of course, sir, of course. Dark Brown has been very popular, as of late.'

'Not my style either, I'm afraid.' I made a vague show of inspecting the merchandise. 'I don't suppose you have something in the back I might look at.'

He inclined his head. 'Of course, sir – straight on through. I'm sure you won't have trouble finding what you came for.' I followed his directions out of the main room and down a short, narrow hallway, ending at a door that I rapped on quickly before entering.

The first time I'd met Guiscard we'd nearly come to blows. More accurately, he'd nearly hit me – petty criminals did not, as a rule, strike agents of the Crown, not unless they wanted to find themselves losing the hand they'd raised.

He'd grown since then, or at the very least aged. Some men run to fat as they get older, others go in the opposite direction, burning through whatever limited allotment of excess flesh youth had provided them. Guiscard was the latter. I hadn't seen him in three years, and since then he'd lost a solid stone off a frame that was far from oversized to begin with. His coiffure had undergone a similar wasting process – initially he'd kept his white-gold hair in an exaggerated pompadour, better suited to wooing whores than chasing down suspects. The last time I'd seen him he'd shorn it away to stubble. Now I was pretty sure he'd just gone bald. He still had the classic Rouender nose, at least. That it had never been broken was evidence he hadn't put in his years at the bottom ranks of Black House. No honest agent made it six months without having someone reshape the tender portions of his face.

I disliked admitting it, because it ran against my ingrained sense that people rarely change and never improve – but I didn't have the hate for Guiscard that I'd once had. Back in the day he'd been as bad as anyone else that had ever married sudden power with self-righteous certainty. Now he was confused, tired and lacking in direction. He'd come a long way.

'You know when I was an agent,' I began, inspecting the less than prepossessing interior, 'we had a whole building for this.'

'It's still there.'

'Then why aren't we in it?'

'Given your recent activities, I thought perhaps it would be better if you weren't openly seen meeting with a member of the ice.'

'Don't refer to yourself that way – it makes you sound like an asshole.' I thought over what he said. That was an answer. A good one, even – but somehow I sensed it wasn't the actual one.

'What do you have to tell me?'

'Straight to business, eh? No casual pleasantries, no easy banter? It's been years, Agent. We've got so much to catch up on.'

'How's the Earl?'

'None of your fucking business,' I said, dropping into the chair that wasn't occupied.

In place of a laugh, Guiscard had an abrupt staccato snort, like he was ejecting a pea from his nostrils. 'So what do you have to tell me?'

'What did the Old Man tell you I'd have?'

He shook his head. 'That's not how this works. You're my stoolie, so you tell me stories. If I was your stoolie, the opposite would be true.'

'You've got an impressive grasp of spycraft.'

'You seemed to need a refresher.'

'Just trying to make sure I don't waste your time. No point in running over old news.'

'You're just trying to pump me for information. It won't work.'

It always had in the past. 'About eight hours ago I was called in to a meeting with the Sons of Śakra.'

'Represented by . . .'

'Director of Security, Cerial Egmont.'

Guiscard whistled. 'I guess they think you're more important than we do.'

'Thanks.'

'Egmont's supposed to be at the top of their seamy underbelly. Something of a prodigy when it comes to the skull-and-dagger business. How did he strike you?'

'He didn't seem a complete idiot. Then again, it was a short meeting.'

'What did he want?'

'You hear anything about this new drug that's been making its way around, called red fever?'

'No.'

'No, why would you – nothing that happens south of the Palace is worth being aware of. But Egmont appears a bit more globally minded. He's concerned about the similarities between the red fever and this secret project we scrapped a while back – Coronet, it was called.'

'Never heard of it.'

'No? Nothing? Not a peep?'

'That's what I said.'

'That's what you said.'

'You going to provide any specifics?'

'You want to know about Coronet, you can ask the chief about it. It was his baby.'

'I'll do that,' Guiscard said. 'So what did you tell Egmont?'

'I told him what the Old Man told me to tell him. That I'd take a look and see what I could find.'

'Interesting,' Guiscard said, though to judge by his expression I might as well have been reading a grocery list.

'So . . .' I began, 'did we scrap it?'

'I told you. I don't know anything about this . . . red fever. Nor about Coronet.'

'Does the Old Man?'

'The Old Man knows a lot of things I don't.'

'Would you lie to me?'

'Of course I would.'

'Are you now?'

'No.'

He seemed to be telling the truth. Then again, he made a living out of dishonesty. 'Fair enough,' I said.

'Anything else to report?'

'There is something else, in fact. I came into Egmont's office just in time to see one of ours walk out.'

Guiscard scrunched up his face in confusion – not altogether easy, given how little fat there was to play with. 'Who?'

'Alistair Harribuld.'

'No way; he's been feeding out of our hand since before I joined up. In fact – weren't you the one responsible for hooking him?'

'Which would suggest I'm unlikely to be mistaken on his identity, wouldn't it?'

'What was he doing there?'

'He didn't have his motive painted on his shirt, but it's hard to see what reason a Black House informant would have for meeting with the Director of Security for the Sons of Śakra. Apart from the obvious one, of course.'

'I'll look into it.'

'I would.'

Guiscard reached into the pocket of his duster and pulled out his tobacco pouch.

'I thought you quit?'

He didn't look up from his rolling. 'We can't all live your life of monk-like self-denial.'

That was worth a chuckle, I thought. After a moment he lit his cigarette, and smoke crowded the interior of the room, like a growing silence. If you didn't know better, you might even have thought that we liked each other. I did know better, however.

'You've moved up in the world, since last I've seen you.'

He shrugged. 'I've risen in the ranks, if that's the same thing.'

'Is it?'

He shrugged again. It was a habit he'd come to late in life – his earlier iteration was never uncertain about anything, and if he had been, certainly wouldn't have shown it. 'The Old Man won't be around forever. Somebody's got to keep all the pieces moving.'

'Do they?'

'I know your feelings on the subject – let the edifice crumble, right?'

Those weren't exactly my feelings, actually, but if that was the part he wanted me to play, I figured I might as well go along. 'Sometimes the rot goes too deep to paper over. You have to tear it down, and start from scratch.'

'And the people living inside?'

'A few nights in the rain never hurt anyone.'

'It's much prettier as a metaphor than in reality. The world is imperfect, I'm not unaware of that fact. Someone still needs to run it. Better us than a pack of brown-robed fanatics.' But the way he said it he didn't seem altogether sure, and he kept rambling on, trying to prove the point to one of us. 'It all sounds very nice, railing against corruption, calling for a more equitable society. What does it amount to really? Perpetual antagonism against the Dren, a sin-tax on everything they don't like. The instituting of their narrow moral viewpoint on a nation far vaster and more diverse than they can conceive. And if they ever did acquire power, what would they discover? Purity is no virtue in a King – compromise is the essence of rulership.'

'How noble of you to spare them such a burden.'

'You'd see no improvement in your lot, should the Sons succeed in their aims. They don't take so . . . nuanced a view on recreational narcotics as do we at Black House. Amongst their other aims is to re-institute the death penalty for drug dealers.'

'There isn't a country in the world that enforces all its own laws. Whoever ends up ruling in the Old City, I don't anticipate their suddenly concerning themselves with what we do in Low Town.'

'Is that the feeling? One monarch is the same as another? Seems awfully short-sighted.'

'I sell poison – it's a short-sighted way to make a living.'

'If the Steps come to power, it won't be business as usual. I'm under no illusions that we currently live in paradise, but I assure you, things would get much worse.'

'They generally do,' I admitted. 'All the same, I'll take your prediction with a grain of salt. You are not, after all, a disinterested party, but the heir apparent himself. I wouldn't expect you to throw away your patrimony.'

He didn't answer that for a while. 'You did,' he said.

I reached over and started on a cigarette from the supplies Guiscard had left on the table. I rolled it slowly, and thought about the past. 'It wasn't like that,' I said. 'Wasn't righteousness that brought me down, was foolishness. When I was in your spot I did whatever was required of me.'

Guiscard reached over and lit my smoke. 'That's all they ask of us,' he said.

16

There were five people in the room, but only two of us mattered.

The Old Man of course, looking like he always did, blue-eyed and smiling. He didn't wear the traditional agent garb, never did. A well-cut suit, modest and old-fashioned, served him better. And of course he never carried a weapon. Even the suggestion of physical violence was beneath him.

With Crowley, however, it was a virtual guarantee. He was short and squat as a cask of ale, with overlong arms and a head like a bullet from a sling. His eyes were black pinpricks set above a nose red from drink and bent from injury. His hair was shorn close to his skull, and his ice-blue uniform unkempt. Crowley wasn't much for vanity – he made up for it by doubling down on the other available vices.

Despite the way he looked, talked and acted, Crowley wasn't altogether worthless. He was a solid enough field man, and he had a blunt sort of cleverness that gave him a clear eye on the closest path between two points. That said, he wasn't there because he had much in the way of advice to offer or assistance to give. It was his little bonus – Crowley didn't care for money, and he didn't really understand what power was. He just liked to sit next to the Old Man, get his head patted, feel important.

Bohemond was the High Chancellor's chief aide. His presence in the room was a courtesy, and if no one went out of the way to express this to him, neither was his opinion given any particular weight. The High Chancellor back in those days was an old-blooded Rouender on whom the Old Man had enough dirt to cover six-square feet. The current High Chancellor is the same in all of these particulars. Although I don't know him personally, I'd be close to certain he has a fellow like Bohemond running about for him. A man whose job is to notice little and commit to less, who has the words 'plausible deniability' etched on the innermost chamber of his heart.

Raynald was the Old Man's second brain. He spoke five languages and could break code without a pen or paper. In a certain sense he was the smartest person I'd ever met, a veritable encyclopedia of trivia – but he was toothless, he didn't understand why people did the things they did and had never learned how to force them to do the things he wanted. In short, he was not the sort to steer the ship, though he was plenty useful in reading charts. He went and disappeared not so long after my own removal. I guess the Old Man decided to clean house.

And obviously, there was me. I'd been five years in Black House, the last three in Special Operations. My rise was nothing short of meteoric, to be commented on and railed against in the coffee houses and bars where my colleagues blew off steam. There were lots of theories to explain my rapid ascent. I was the Old Man's child from the wrong side of the sheets, one went – though anyone who knew him knew he didn't have time for anything as frivolous as sex. Another said that I'd saved the Old Man's life, and this was how he repaid me – though here again, a cursory knowledge of the boss's personality made it clear gratitude was no more in his make-up than lust.

The truth is, I was just better than any of them, and for all his catalog of vices, the Old Man could recognize talent. My existence simplified his, gave him an extra set of hands on his projects. I was competent, and ruthless bordering on amoral, and by the Old Man's way of thinking these were the highest traits to which humankind could aspire.

Between the five of us, which is to say the two of us, what needed to happen to ensure the continuation of the Empire, happened. Obviously not officially – the High Chancellor still served at the pleasure of the Queen, the Old Man at the pleasure of the High Chancellor, and me at the pleasure of the Old Man. And the obvious decisions, the things that made it into the broadsheet, the average, which is to say ignorant, man on the street thought were important – these were mostly taken care of by people officially slotted to do so. But the framework had been erected by the Old Man, and was kept standing by our continual machinations.

The meeting, slated for two hours, was stretching past its third, and my head was starting to hurt. I poured myself a cup of lukewarm coffee from the spread on the table, and examined the handful of stale pastries that sat beside it with a critical eye. The Old Man could say a word and a diplomat on another continent would wake up tomorrow dead, but he was unable to ensure us an edible working lunch. It's a strange world.

'I just think it's crucial that the niceties be observed in every detail,' Bohemond was saying. His voice oozed out of his throat like syrup from a tapped maple.

'Of course,' the Old Man responded with equal unctuousness. Not quite equal. Close.

'It is a delicate situation, after all – the Nestrians are still our allies.'

'Bosom brothers,' the Old Man answered.

'We wouldn't want to do anything to jeopardize our relationship.'

We were in the process of making the decision to plant dirt on a Nestrian official who was giving us some trouble. In fact, the decision had already been made, it was just a question of allowing Bohemond, and by extension the High Chancellor, to feel as if he had some role in making it. Actually, this accounted for perhaps sixty or seventy percent of our time in these things. One of the many facets of the Old Man's genius was that he operated absolutely without ego. So long as his decision was ultimately carried out, he cared very little who received the credit. In fact, I think he preferred to work through intermediaries – easier to cut them loose if trouble came up.

'The furthest thing from my mind,' he answered pleasantly. 'So it's decided.'

The committee was informal, there was no roll call and no official vote of any kind – the thought of ever having to take responsibility for his decisions was a concept that threw Bohemond into a cold sweat. All decisions were by custom unanimous, the Old Man first amongst equals, stewarding the discussion, but not imposing his will. It was a polite fiction, but one that we all upheld.

'While we're on the Nestrians,' the Old Man switched topics glibly, 'where are we on identifying this . . . operative they seem to have planted in our midst?'

Counter-intelligence was primarily Crowley's department, and he was well suited to it. He was dogged and thorough, and he didn't care about being hated, a necessity when your job largely consists of investigating your own people. Nor did he mind putting a person to the question, if he thought it would get any information. He didn't really seem to mind putting a person to the question regardless, if we were to be honest.

'We're close,' he said.

I whistled tunelessly. Crowley snapped his gaze over to me. 'We are,' he insisted.

This was before my simmering rivalry with Crowley had turned into open hatred, which explains why we were able to sit across from each other without him trying to stab me with a fork – though even at the time our relations were frosty bordering on glacial. Crowley didn't like the fact that I was smarter than him, that I'd usurped the position that he thought should be his.

Beneath that, he didn't like the small confidences the Old Man offered me, the perceived closeness between us. That the Old Man could no more bond with another human being than he could grow wings and take flight seemed not to have occurred to Crowley. For my part, I disliked him for being a brutal, thuggish oaf, with a propensity for violence bordering on the unprofessional. He was also very easy to provoke, an activity I enjoyed participating in for its own sake.

'As close as you were last week? And the week before that?'

'He's out there, dammit, I can smell him. The frog-eaters have been a step ahead for too damn long. They're getting an earful from somebody.'

That we were allied to the Nestrians, had backed their fading horse against the Dren, had given them a share of the spoils after they'd bailed out of the Great War early on account of general incompetence, did not alter the fact that they ran operatives within the Empire proper. Deep cover, often as businessmen or within their legitimate diplomatic apparatus. We had the same on their end of course, a ring of spies led by a quiet, uninspiring figure who owned a shop selling used books in their capital, spoke in perfect regional dialect and ran a network so efficient we knew what King Louis ate for breakfast by dinner. Said operative was picking up some disturbing chatter the last season or so – that the Nestrians had someone high up in our ranks, ferreting out crucial bits of information before we were able to act on them. I wasn't sure I believed him, to be frank. The primary purpose of any organization is to perpetuate its own existence. Deducing, or inventing, a threat like that would be proof against budget cuts for years to come.

'Three months you've been telling us you've got a line on the Nestrians,' I said. 'Six months you've been running around like a bull with the scent of blood, knocking into actual opera-tions in the misguided belief you're on the way to something solid.'

'They figured out we had our hooks into their archduke, and they rolled up the network we were setting up in Barruges,'

Crowley said, referring to two recent reverses. 'That's no fantasy of mine – how the hell do you explain that?'

'Maybe the mail boy's been kicking out our secret memos. Maybe Śakra the Firstborn visits the dreams of King Louis every evening and tells him our innnermost plans. I have no fucking idea Crowley, because it's not my question to answer. I'm not in charge of counter-intelligence, you are. But if our positions were reversed, I can assure you that I wouldn't come in here every week promising that next week's meeting would be the one where I finally did my job.'

The Old Man watched over our feud without a dip in his smile. It served his interests to have his numbers two and three at each other's throats. He would have encouraged our enmity if it hadn't developed naturally. 'So that would be a "no" then, on whether any progress has been made in ferreting out our mole?'

Crowley grunted.

'Lovely. Our next order of business would be . . .' The Old Man turned to Raynald.

Raynald took out a sheet of paper from his folder, though I was certain he knew the details without looking. 'Lood De Burg, former colonel in the Army of the United Dren Commonwealth, forcibly retired along with most of the rest of his comrades since the armistice. He's founded a political party called *Het Eenheidsfront* that seems to be getting some traction.'

'We let them have political parties?' Bohemond asked, an attempt at humor.

The Old Man laughed politely, then nodded at Raynald to continue.

'It's the usual pot of revisionist bitterness flavored with conspiratorial nonsense. They claim the war was lost by traitors on the home front, a fifth column which overturned their efforts. By this they appear to mean the Commonwealth's population of Asher and Islander. Their platform consists of curtailing the rights of the aforementioned, an end to payment on the war debt and a policy of rapid rearmament.'

'He sounds like a lovely fellow,' the Old Man said. 'What exactly do we want to do with him?'

'I'd like to give him a few thousand ochres,' I said.

There was silence. 'Would you now?' the Old Man asked eventually, mostly out of politeness. The Old Man was very polite, something he'd developed to hide his lack of empathy.

'Through intermediaries, of course. It would go pretty firmly against their policy to get in bed with us openly. But we've still got a few Dren nobles on the payroll. I think it's time one of them becomes De Burg's silent backer.'

Bohemond scoffed. 'You want to get into bed with these . . . zealots?'

'No – I want to fuck them.'

'I'm afraid I'm having trouble following,' Reynald said.

'Let me lay it clean to you – sooner or later, the Dren are going to realize that there are five million more of them than there are of us, and that they might have better luck on a second go-round than they did the first. But right now they don't know that, or at least they can't see it. It would be best to keep them in this state of ignorance for as long as possible – in fact, I would go so far as to say this is the primary foreign aim of this office.'

Bohemond made as if to clean out his ears. Bohemond had a rather broad sense of humor. It was one of the many things I disliked about him. 'If your purpose is to keep the Dren from starting a second war, then why in the name of the Scarred One would you want to encourage the growth of an organization trying to do just that?'

'The armistice prohibits any nationalist party from holding seats in congress. The current government will be forced to crack down on them.'

'So?' Bohemond asked.

Crowley growled in the corner – even he'd managed the thread by this point. 'So they can't very well make war on Nestria if they're caught up killing each other.' He gave a quick jerk of his skull. 'I like it.'

'It's risky,' Reynald said. Everything was too risky for Reynald, he had the balls of a schoolmarm. 'What if the Dren government gets wind of our support?'

'Who would believe them? *Het Eenheidsfront* in the pocket of their most hated enemy? A conspiratorial fantasy, meant to undermine the good work of De Burg's minions.'

'And what if . . .' the Old Man began unexpectedly, 'your plan succeeds?'

'Perish the thought.'

'I'm quite serious. The men currently running the Commonwealth are . . . pliable, if nothing else. This one, by all accounts, would not so comfortably acclimatize to our wishes.'

'Exactly. Fanatics don't gain power. He's too rigid, he won't be able to broaden support beyond his base.'

'Don't underestimate the willingness of any large group of people to leap off a cliff.'

'It won't happen. Even the Dren aren't that mad.'

'And if they are?'

'De Burg wouldn't be the first person who didn't live forever.' The Old Man chuckled. 'No, I suppose he wouldn't.'

'I still say it's too risky,' Reynald broke in.

'Yes, we heard you,' the Old Man answered, gracing his secretary with a smile that shut his mouth before turning back to me. 'Two thousand ochres will be deposited in the usual slush fund. You're to dispose of it as you see fit.' He folded his hands. 'Is there anything else?'

'Just one outstanding piece of business,' Reynald turned over the next leaf in his file. 'Coronet.'

The atmosphere strained noticeably. Bohemond began to look extremely uncomfortable. Concrete knowledge of anything was anathema; he'd made a career out of not noticing things. 'Shouldn't someone from the Bureau of Magical Affairs be taking part in this conversation?' Forced out of active ignorance, he preferred to dilute responsibility to as many parties as possible.

'They know what they need to,' the Old Man said.

'I'm going to go out on a limb here and guess we've yet to see results?' I asked.

'Carroll insists we're close,' the Old Man answered.

'An objective observer, if ever there was one. This is a waste of our resources.'

'It won't be if it works.'

'It won't work.'

'Carroll seems to disagree.'

'What's he going to say?' I asked. '"Sorry, you've pissed away five thousand ochres in the misguided belief I had any idea what I was doing"? Guarantees don't mean anything. Results are what we're looking for – looking for in vain, I might add.'

'But the possibilities . . .' The Old Man trailed off, smiling.

'It's possible my next shit will be twenty-four-carat gold, but the bank won't take it as security for a loan.'

'Your vulgarity is laudable, as always. That said – we've come this far. It seems reasonable to see if something more will come of it.'

'I could introduce you to any number of vagrants with similar investment strategies. And besides – there are costs here beyond the financial.'

'Oh?' He batted his eyelashes, waiting for me to continue, innocent as a schoolboy.

I gritted my teeth. 'Carroll is as frugal with his test subjects as he is with our money.'

The Old Man nodded at this slowly, his baby blues depthless. 'The costs are . . . unfortunate. Honored volunteers, their suffering to the greater good of the Empire.'

'You can't volunteer for suicide.'

'In point of fact – several hundred thousand of you did, during the war.'

I'd have struck a different man for saying that, though it more or less echoed my own feelings on the conflict. 'Death is a possibility one reasonably ought to foresee in joining the army,' I said, 'not when signing up for a supposedly harmless medical experiment. Death,' I added, 'and worse than death.'

To my left Bohemond was growing steadily grayer, if we kept at this much longer he'd have been vomiting on the table. I'd violated protocol by speaking so openly in front of him. The Old Man rapped a hand on the table, a casual gesture, but nothing he did was ever less than deathly serious. 'That's what makes their sacrifice so noble.'

I was a fool to have even mentioned the casualties. They meant nothing to him, I knew that. All I'd done was demonstrate weakness. 'Do whatever you want,' I said abruptly. 'It's not coming out of my ends.'

'I think it's important to reiterate that the Chancellor could never condone doing anything that might injure a subject of the Throne,' Bohemond said, as if the specifics of Coronet were new to him. 'I think it's important that that point be made clear.'

'Of course he wouldn't,' the Old Man said, smiling. 'Neither would any of us. Coronet doesn't exist – it never did. My friend and I are having a theoretical conversation, engaged entirely in the abstract. It affects no concrete reality that the Chancellor will ever encounter.'

Theoretical. Abstract. He wasn't wrong. Somewhere along the line people reduce themselves to numbers in a ledger, and at that point you're truly damned. It's a rather concise definition of power – when you no longer need to look at the names.

'Now, I do believe that takes us to the end of our list for today. Thank you all for coming, and for your hard work.'

Class was dismissed. Four men started for the door with as much speed as age and dignity allowed. The fifth was the Old Man, and the Old Man, as a point of pride and principle, did not hurry anywhere, for any reason.

'If you could allow me just one more moment,' the Old Man said, halting my egress.

Crowley didn't like that. More than anything else, it was the fact that I'd edged him out of the chief's favor that he really held against me. Odd, but no matter how high you rise in the halls of power, it's impossible to escape the conviction that our collective fates are largely determined by the petty jealousies of overgrown adolescents. He didn't argue though. No one argued with the Old Man except for me, and even then, unsuccessfully.

The two of us were left alone, staring at each other from opposite ends of the table, over the picked carcass of the lunch tray. He'd asked for a word, but he didn't offer one, just sat there beaming at me. It was like looking into the sun: do it long enough and you start to get a headache, do it longer and you go mad. I broke first, but then someone had to. The Old Man would have happily continued at it till we both dropped from dehydration.

'What exactly can I help you with?'

'Regarding Coronet – it's important we remain on the same page,' he said.

'Of course.'

'Any concerns you have, these would best be shared between us and us alone.'

'I understand.'

'There's no need for Bohemond to be exposed to anything which might make him . . . anxious.'

'I'm sure he'd agree.'

'Then we understand each other?'

'Hand in glove,' I answered.

'Very good,' he said, standing and ushering me out. 'And do give my best to Albertine.'

Hearing her name in his mouth made me faintly nauseous. But I smiled through that and followed him into the hallway.

My promotion to Special Operations had brought with it a shitty little office crammed into a corner of the third floor. It was hot in the summer and cold in the winter, but it smelled of mildew and old paint regardless. The window was stuck, had been since my arrival.

There was a stack of papers on my desk that needed looking at. There was perpetually a stack of papers on my desk that needed looking at, as if at night elves materialized from beneath the floorboards and undid everything I'd finished during the day. I spent twenty minutes in my chair, chain smoking and pretending I was about to get to work. Then I gave up, stuffed out my butt, locked the door and left. It was almost quitting

149

time, anyway. I figured I'd stop off and see Albertine. Catch her before she left work, take her out to dinner.

The desk sergeant flattered me as I walked out, and I nodded and took it as my due. Spring was shaking off winter's hold, my coat was an encumbrance. The Old City is beautiful at dusk, or at least I found it so that evening. It was a long walk over to Albertine's office, and I smiled all the way through it.

17

The guard came in early the next morning, sweating despite the autumn chill. Part of that I attributed to the fact that he was, in the grand tradition of the hoax, carrying around a few toddlers' worth of excess weight. The rest I assumed was a function of his presence being an implicit violation of the agreement I had with his superiors. Which was, in essence, that I saw the guard once a week, during which I gave them money they didn't deserve, and in exchange I spent the rest of it inured against any unexpected visits.

He shuffled nervously from one foot to the other, like a child waiting to piss. It seemed I would have to take the initiative.

'Good morning, officer. Is there something I can do for you?'

'The Captain was wondering, if you ain't got nothing going, maybe you could stop by and see him?'

He was new to the force, his age and the fact that I didn't know him were enough to confirm that. I made a point of at least recognizing by sight every member of the city guard working in Low Town or its immediate environs. It was good policy, insurance on top of the cut of my operations I gave to them. The worker ants, they'd never know the specifics of the deal I'd made with their superiors, and I doubted they were getting much of a percentage off the one I kicked up. A free beer, a friendly word – these can get you more than a cart-load of ochres on the back end.

I don't have any more against the hoax than I absolutely have to, and less than I probably ought. Even as a child, when I'd roamed the streets little short of a savage, I felt kind of bad for them. Dragging twenty-pound suits of mail in hundred-degree weather, having to duck and bend to every two-copper crime lord that paid that week's tithe. It's not their fault that the Crown doesn't care a sweat stain for what goes on in Low Town, nor that the native population would sooner slit their throats than give them the time of day. You can't blame the croupier because the game is rigged – they're just playing their part, like everybody else.

'You're from the fourth district, right?'

'Yessir, that's right.'

'Didn't I pay you this week?'

'Yessir, you did, last Tuesday. Ain't about that – no problem with the tax, I mean. The Captain would just like to see you at your,' he paused to remember the wording he'd been given. 'At your earliest possible convenience.'

'Captain didn't say what this was about, did he?'

The guardsman shook his head.

'No, I guess he wouldn't. How long you figure this is going to take?'

'Not long,' he said promptly, happy that I wasn't going to make an issue out of it. 'Just a couple of minutes.'

I finished my coffee and got my coat. When bowing to the inevitable, it's best to do so low, and quickly.

It was a sunny morning, and the walk over was almost pleasant enough to justify the errand on its own. I reminded myself that it was an inconvenience and stitched a scowl across my face.

The Fourth District guard station was not a sight that inspired much by way of civic pride. It could have been mistaken for a budget whorehouse if it hadn't been for the two hoax sitting on the stoop outside. Not that the presence of the city's elite brotherhood of defenders was unknown amongst Low Town's brothels. Far from it – most of the pimps I knew paid their weekly tax out in kind.

The Imperial flag hung limply in the still morning, halfway down its wooden pole. 'Who died?' I asked.

'Some noble, Harriben or Harrison or some such. A big hero during the war, they say.'

In his mind at least. By the Scarred One, but Black House worked quick. Double-agents tend to have short lifespans, but I couldn't quite see what the rush was in stamping out Harribuld.

The reception hall was quiet. A guardsman sat yawning at a counter. Apart from him, there was no one else to be seen. I guess there wasn't any crime happening in Low Town that day. To judge by the efforts of the hoax, we seem to be an astonishingly law-abiding community. My escort fell quickly into conversation with another officer, and I was left to find my way to their boss on my own. A glaring lack of hospitality, but then I was a frequent guest.

Captain Kenneth Ascletin was a sight to make a whore's heart flutter. He was tall enough to take notice, but not so much as to make an issue out of it, and though he wasn't broad, the meat he had was well-muscled. His hair was dark and his eyes were dark and he had a bright smile that he gave without much prompting. 'Warden, good to see you.'

Between the way he looked and the fact that he came from a branch of the minor gentry, Kenneth's future in the guard was assured. His stint south of the Old City would be brief, a year or two until he could secure a more respectable position. He'd taken over after old Captain Galliard had choked to death on a herringbone one evening. Credit to Ascletin, he took his responsibilities, to use the term loosely, more seriously than most of his confederates. His men were always well clad and in reasonably high morale. A few months back he'd even managed to solve a case, picking up some lowlife that had been molesting housewives over by Brennock. I'd put an extra few ochres into his cut that month, a reward for good service.

'How's trade?' I asked.

'I'll tell you, it's a strange time. We've got Ling Chi's people near at war with the Tarasaighn, we got random civilians going after each other with rusted metal, and it's looking very much like the remains of the Bruised Fruit Mob is going to turn on each other to see who gets to be king of shit mountain. And heaven forbid I try to get any back-up from the Old City – with these fanatics running around stirring the waters, Black House is too busy to worry about the occasional rape or murder.'

'Black House has never been real concerned about the occasional rape or murder.'

'True,' he conceded, 'but this still feels different, somehow. Like there's no rudder anymore, if you can follow?'

I followed exactly. 'So what did you call me in for?'

He nodded regretfully. 'Sorry about that – hope it didn't cause you any trouble.'

'I always have time for the law,' I lied. 'That said, I do have a man I've gotta see about a thing, so if we could get to the root . . .'

'Of course, of course. I just thought you'd want to know, on the offchance you hadn't heard already – the Gitts took a swing at Uriel last night.'

'Did they now?'

'Started by ruffing up a dealer, Kitterin Mayfair.'

'How's he doing?'

'That depends. Do you think there's more to life than lying in bed and staring motionlessly up at the ceiling?'

I thought about that a while. 'Yes.'

'Then I'd have to say he's doing poorly.'

'That's a rough break – I'll send condolences to his wife and kids.'

'He's got neither.'

'His favorite whore, then.'

'Apparently inspired by their handling of Mr Mayfair, the Gitts proceeded to lead a raid on one of Uriel's gambling joints. Trashed the place, roughed up some patrons.'

'Disrespected the wait staff?'

Kenneth gave a perfunctory chuckle before breaking serious. You could tell he was serious because his mouth swelled regretfully, and his deep brown eyes grew pregnant with meaning. In the eyes, though in little else, Captain Ascletin reminded me very much of a con man I'd once known, made his ochres swindling rich widows out of their fortunes. One got wise to it, threatened to make issue, and he panicked and buried an ax in her head and her head in the garden. Black House has a pretty strict policy about killing the wealthy, and he didn't remain a free man for very long. Last I saw of him he was tangoing in mid-air, those bright eyes warped with blood and fear.

Back in the present, Kenneth sighed and made an expansive gesture with his hands. 'Look Warden, we're happy enough to let you boys blow off some steam once in a while. The nature of the business, the occasional broken bone or disappeared body. But there's limits. I have people to answer to, same as everyone else.'

'I'd think the Crown would have more to worry about than an unaffiliated button man getting worked over in an alleyway, what with the country a stray match away from inferno.'

'That's Black House's set of worries. My set of worries is that this recent unpleasantness will be the opening salvo in a gang war that's going to consume everything east of the docks.'

'That's a concern,' I agreed. It was one of Kenneth's many distinguished qualities, that he felt some faint sense of duty to his territory, even if it was born of nothing more than a practical consideration for his own career.

'I'd consider it a favor if you could do something to squash that trouble.'

'If I've given you the impression that the underworld went and voted me king, let me set you straight . . .'

'These other boys, they respect you. Respect what you represent.'

'Some of them did, once. Maybe. But things ain't like they was.'

'Not in anything,' he agreed.

I scratched at what was becoming a beard. 'I'll run over to Uriel's when I get the chance, see if I can't head this thing off at the pass. But if I was you, I'd start thinking what you're gonna tell the people you answer to. Cause the Asher are hungry, and I doubt there's much I can say to lessen their appetite. And as for the Gitts . . .'

'I know about the Gitts.'

'You know about the Gitts,' I agreed.

The Captain spent a moment silhouetted by the sunlight coming in through the window. He looked good, but then, he'd put in a lot of practice.

'While we're running things past each other, what's your take on the Steps?' I asked.

'You aren't getting mixed up in politics, are you?' As if I'd suggested we strip naked and go bathing in a sewer.

'I'd hope you knew me better than that.'

The Captain eased back in his chair, vaguely apologetic. 'Sure, you're right. Crazy times is all.' He rubbed his chin with his index finger. 'Well let's put it that way – for a pack of zealots, the Steps know what they're doing. They talk fierce, and they're never without steel – but they stay on the right side of the line, careful not to do anything that might give Black House an excuse to pounce.'

'Black House doesn't generally need one.'

'Special situation. The Sons aren't some collection of anarchist dockworkers. Monck's line is old as mud, he's a few steps from the King himself. There are plenty of other folk wearing brown hats that could come up with a few hundred thousand ochres in the bank, and the right to interrupt the King at dinner time. Folk like that – well, you can't just go making them disappear cause they speak unpleasant truths at cocktail parties.'

'Tell me more about this Monck character.'

'I don't know anything beyond the common knowledge. He's high born, like I said. Served in the war, not in the trenches of course, but still, supposedly he made a good enough showing. He's been a member of parliament for a solid ten years now, sits with the radicals but doesn't always talk to them.' He crossed his eyes. I noted with watered-down envy that he was capable of making even this motion captivating. 'Why are you so interested in the Steps all of a sudden?'

'I'm thinking of helping them overthrow the state.'

'All right, all right. Close to the chest, I wouldn't expect anything else.'

No one ever believes me – I guess I don't have an honest face.

'Well, like I said,' Kenneth began by way of an ending. 'I'd owe you a solid if you could do anything to keep the city from killing each other.'

'You don't owe me nothing,' I said, standing. 'My life won't get any easier if I have to start stepping over corpses going to market every morning.'

Outside of the building I went to roll myself a cigarette, realized I'd left my makings back at the bar. One of the guards lolling about was kind enough to provide a substitute – it wasn't much as far as a return on my investment, but I appreciated the courtesy all the same.

18

I was hauling myself towards Alledtown with a bag full of pixie's breath when I noticed him shadowing me. Shadowing me was too strong, gives the impression that he wasn't trying to be seen. And he was, very much – indeed, I suspected me seeing him was the point.

Of course, if he had been shadowing me, he wouldn't have had much luck. One upside of having carved up Crowley's face like a pumpkin – he really stood out in a crowd. You didn't need to see him to know he was there, you could watch the reaction from passersby, nervous wavering, sidelong looks at his deformed flesh. Children wept and moaned, pregnant women miscarried – you get the idea. Not that stealth had ever been Crowley's forte, even back when he'd been whole. He didn't need it, or he thought he didn't. Brute force and open intimidation had been Crowley's favored tactics, and I didn't suppose the six-inch cut I'd made from the top of his cheekbone past his incisors lessened their effectiveness. For twenty years Crowley had been the mailed fist to the Old

Man's velvet glove. Brutally competent, if thuglike – the cudgel as opposed to the stiletto.

The other upside of carving up Crowley's face like a pumpkin was that doing it was the most fun you can have with your pants on. Not for him, obviously.

He noticed me noticing him and waved. He was smiling, which was bad news. Violence made Crowley happy, the nestled shrieks of pain from people that weren't him. If things were going good for Crowley, it meant they were about to go damn bad for someone else. Under the circumstances, it was hard not to suppose that someone would be me.

I crossed the street into a little cafe. The waiter, a smiling Kiren in western garb stopped quickly by the table. I ordered a cup of coffee and waited for what was coming.

I didn't have to wait long. Crowley cruised through the doorway, then came and sat down quickly across from me. He didn't say anything for a while, just sat there, smiling. The waiter came back with my coffee. Crowley waved him off with a friendly nod, which worried me more. By habit Crowley was cruel to those beneath him, and he had a particular and not entirely unearned hatred of Kiren. That he had neglected to demean this one meant that he was in a swell mood indeed.

I figured I'd do my best to puncture it. 'Remind me – the last time you followed me into a bar, how did it go for you?'

'Good to see you've kept your sense of humor.'

'That and a whole face.' His eyes wavered, gnats hovering over pig shit. 'I'll tell you honestly, Crowley, I'm impressed.'

'Yeah?'

'Normally you don't come to visit without a crew of thugs backing your play. Your pair drop since we last met?'

'Just a friendly call – it's been such a long time since we've seen each other.'

'Did you miss me?'

'Every day,' he said with more than a hint of madness. 'Every motherfucking day.'

I ran my hand down the length of my face, mirroring

the discolored line on Crowley's cheek. 'That itch much?' I asked.

His smile went away in a furious intake of air. His eyes gleamed madly. Below the table I let my knife fall out of my wrist sheath.

Then he laughed, and blinked away homicide. 'It's good to be reminded.'

I slid my weapon back up into my sleeve, not without regret. 'Of what?'

'Of what you did to me.'

My failures and mistakes, duly collected, would fill an encyclopedia. In the midst of such a catalog, leaving Crowley breathing when I had the chance to snuff him out ranked somewhere in the middle – nothing to be proud of, but far from the worst decision I'd ever made. And truth be told, like many of my errors, I didn't regret it. I was afraid of Crowley, only a fool wouldn't be. But I hated him more than I feared him. And if I'd killed him, he'd just be dead, a corpse, and you can't do nothing to torment a corpse. Leaving Crowley alive I'd planted a seed into the bottom of his soul, an ugly little bur that had taken root and flowered into the cold thing that kept his eyes from meeting mine.

I had taught Crowley fear. Of course, he wanted to kill me for it, but he'd wanted to kill me long before, so nothing had really changed.

The window of potential violence closed, and now Crowley was all smiles again. He even signaled to our waiter for another cup of coffee. We waited silently until it came. Crowley dropped an argent into the bewildered server's hand. He was very grateful, and I had to sit through about ten seconds of bowing and scraping before I could get back to making threats.

'I understand that as a government employee you're full up on empty time. But I've got a lot on my plate at the moment, so if we could skip ahead to the reason you're here?'

'You busy?'

'I am busy, I'm extremely busy. I just said I was busy. Frankly, I'm too busy to be repeating myself.'

'Still running drugs?'

'Still asking dumb questions?'

He sort of laughed. Not at what I was saying, but at the situation. Despite my urgings, he seemed very little inclined towards hurry, or indeed, motion period.

'If I was you – and daily I thank the Firstborn that I'm not – I wouldn't make a point of trying to run into me. I'd think it would dredge up bitter memories. Like running into an old girlfriend, if said girlfriend had left you for dead in an alleyway.'

'If I was you, I wouldn't be so quick to crow about what you done. Might make me lose my temper.'

'But you aren't going to lose your temper, you're just going to bluster for a while before heading home. You're at the end of a short leash. The Old Man finds it useful for me to continue breathing, and so long as that's the case, you've got no play. You'll gnash your teeth and pout, but you'll back down. Unless you want to go off-book – and that didn't end well for you last time.'

He sipped at his coffee. For a lunatic, he was showing uncomfortable self-possession. 'You're about half right. It's true the Old Man likes keeping you in his pocket. But then, he thinks you're being a good little boy, pumping poison into that cesspit you run, keeping the rest of the trash in line. And what if you wasn't? What if you started making your own moves – what if you'd decided to throw your hands in with the enemy?'

'I find hypotheticals rather dull.'

'More than a hypothetical.'

'Is it?'

'You've been sniffing into things you shouldn't, for people you shouldn't.'

'Your problem Crowley – apart from the face – is that you have aspirations beyond your station. Today's no different than twelve years ago. You don't know what's going on because you aren't smart enough to follow the thread of it, and the Old Man don't tell you anything because he knows that's the case. Go back to Black House and talk to someone above your paygrade.'

'What would they say?'

'They'd say keep your mouth shut, and leave me the hell alone.'

'Maybe they would say that. Maybe they'd say that exactly. So I'm not gonna ask them. I'm a representative of the Crown, sworn to hamper anyone who seeks to bring harm to the Empire. I find any evidence that includes you, and I'm not going to waste time kicking it up the chain. I'll deal with you myself. Afterward I'll be very sorry for what happened. I might even get a stern talking to.'

'You muck up the Old Man's game, he'll wipe you right out of your shoes.'

Crowley was a man of ravenous appetites. He could eat a whole duck in a sitting, down a quart of vodka and walk off steady. He brought his mug of coffee up to the hole in his face, and when he set it back down it was all but empty. 'The Old Man won't live forever.'

'He's made a pretty good run at it so far.'

It was starting to rattle me, how little success I was having in rattling Crowley. He was not a man renowned for his sense of self-discipline, and I'd gotten off a zinger or two, if I said so myself. And he had good reason to hate me, several of them. If I knew Crowley, and to my chagrin, I did, he should have been near to murder. But instead he just sat there sneering, off-color teeth mashed crooked against each other.

'Better men than you have gone broke betting on the downfall of the Old Man,' I said. 'And by "gone broke", I mean ended up dead. You oughta know – you've killed most of them.'

'Times change,' he said. 'Don't nothing last.'

It was rare that I found myself in agreement with Aldous Crowley. It made me uncomfortable – water running uphill, cats and dogs lying down together. 'You might be right. But even so, you'd be wrong.'

'Oh?'

'I'm sure you tell yourself that the Old Man's protection is what's kept you from coming after me these last six years – at times you may even believe it, you're so fucking pathetic.' I took a sip of my coffee. 'But of course, that isn't it at all. I'm not under the Old Man's aegis, not really – you are. If you ever decided to come at me again I'd snap you up, Crowley, snap you right up. That the boss won't sanction a move on me is a polite fiction that lets you pretend you're still a man. But it's a lie, you can tell that by a look in the mirror. If the Old Man falls, you do the smart thing and you get as far out of Rigus as you possibly can, because if someone else doesn't come knocking on your door, I'll go ahead and do it myself. And this time I won't stop at cutting you – though I'll sure as hell start there.'

It had taken me a while, but I'd finally managed to do for that smile of his. Crowley's face went white and his eyes went mad. The hand holding his glass tensed, and then there were shards of glass on my lapel and blood running onto the wood. Our waiter reacted with admirable celerity, approaching with a rag in hand to do for the spill – but a quick look at the two of us must have convinced him that customer service took second place to self-preservation, and he scuttled back to his perch.

My shiv was out again, my heart fairly leaping at the prospect of using it. There was something about Crowley that made me not ever want to see him again, that wanted to make certain of that fact and was unconcerned about what would come after. I didn't suppose the public murder of a Crown's Agent would be something Black House could casually overlook. Nor was I entirely certain that I'd be the one left standing if the two of us threw down. But at that moment, neither of those things mattered to me. My breath was rapid, my throat dry, every muscle tensed and waiting for release. We'd been hating at each other too long – it starts to eat into a man.

It was an uncharacteristic display of self-control on Crowley's part which saved one of our lives. He wrapped a napkin around his wounded hand, tying it tight while keeping his eyes firm on me. 'We'll see each other again soon,' he said, standing.

'Make sure you bring some friends by, help keep your spine straight,' I returned, by way of a parting shot.

The problem, of course, was that he would do just that. For all my talk, I took a back way out of the restaurant, and I kept my head swiveling during the walk east.

19

This time the two men outside of Uriel's house decided to make me wait. I wasn't sure if that was meant to indicate my stock had fallen with their masters since my last visit, or if they'd just decided to upgrade security now that open warfare with the Gitts was in the air. When they saw me round the corner they started muttering back and forth in their native tongue, a fierce-sounding song appropriate to the race that owned it. Then one of them disappeared into the building, presumably to square my arrival with the boss. I tried to strike up a conversation with the one that remained, a square-jawed stereotype with thick muscle over fat, but either he didn't understand Rigun or he just wasn't interested in anything I had to say. Eventually his comrade returned and nodded me inside.

Uriel was normally as composed as granite, calm as a running stream, and even now he was far from what you'd call addled. His suit was a pleasant cream color, perfectly cut and unwrinkled. A cut flower peeked out from a button in his lapel – hothouse grown, I assumed, as it was far too late in the season to pick them wild. Not that I could see Uriel picking a lot of wildflowers at any point in the year. He'd combed his hair back in a slick wave, and nary a stray curl broke from formation. But the hand holding his mug of tea was taut, like he was being careful not to spill it, and a few beads of sweat had leaked down his forehead. In a normal human being, this was the equivalent of a state of derangement rarely seen outside of an asylum.

His brother was doing a pretty good impression of a caged bear. He huffed and puffed and throttled his silk scarf in his hand. He was wearing a bright purple suit, and he looked like a two-day-old bruise.

'My sincerest apologies for keeping you outside,' Uriel said. 'Can I get you some whiskey? Perhaps a twist of vine?'

'I'd love a cup of tea,' I said. This was a lie – I hated tea, but I wanted to see what a little push would do.

'Qoheleth, make the man a cup of tea.'

'Fuck the tea – and fuck the man. You're in here a week ago promising bright skies and easy sailing, now the swamp-dwellers are busting up our operations and murdering our people!'

'Make the man a cup of tea,' Uriel repeated, and though he didn't raise his voice there was enough menace in it to propel his flesh and blood up out of his seat and into the back room. Once he was gone, Uriel said, 'You'll have to forgive my brother. He's not much of a diplomat.'

'Already forgotten,' I assured him.

'Of course, he has other virtues.'

'I'm sure.'

'The Asher believe that every man needs to be trained in blade, bow and spear. It's akin to religious instruction for us – our priests teach that the One Above demands we give a good account of ourselves if we wish to meet with him.'

'I was in the war,' I answered. 'The Asher units were . . . well regarded.' Feared would be a more accurate term, ranks of

166

black-robed men with the stink of death on them, crawling over each other to volunteer for suicide missions.

'Back when we were still within the fold, Qoheleth was considered the most talented swordsman in the Enclave. Something of a prodigy, in fact. Our instructor was heartbroken when we left – would have been at least, if my brother hadn't killed him.'

One thing I appreciated about Uriel, in contrast to most of the bully boys with their swagger and cheap talk – he could make a threat quietly. Not that there was much subtlety in that last one. 'To live is to suffer disappointment.'

'Quite,' Uriel said, nodding. 'And while there's no excuse for my brother's outburst, surely you can understand his ill temper.'

'Can I?'

'He's just overcome with grief regarding the recent injuries to our organization.'

'You ever think that maybe he's got too soft a heart for our business?'

'I make up for him.'

'That's the good thing about a solid partnership, you even out the other man's flaws – leveling passion with reason, as it were.'

'In the abstract, I agree with you. But in this instance, as it happens – I'm also overcome with grief regarding the recent injuries to our organization.'

'Surely you don't hold me responsible?'

'Oh, the culprits are very clear.' He made a face like he smelled something foul. 'They made no effort to hide their involvement.'

Qoheleth came in from the other room, a mug of tea in his mitt. He spilled most of it onto the table setting it in front of me. Then he dropped back into his chair, crossed his legs, then his arms, and began to chew over his lips in a manner that brought to mind a rabid canine.

I took a sip of what was left. 'Got any sugar?'

Qoheleth stayed where he was, but his neck swelled bright red around the polka dot of his collared shirt.

'You know our door is always open to you, Warden,' Uriel

continued, 'and there's nothing I enjoy more than the occasional back and forth. But I have to say, today we're a bit busy for a casual chat, so if we could get to the main dish.'

'I had assumed my reputation as peacemaker had preceded me, but if you need a formal explanation – I'd like you to forgo any violence against the Gitts. I'd like you to agree to a sit down in the next couple of days, on my territory, with me guaranteeing security. And in the interim I'd like you to forgive the recent raid on your enterprise.'

'I'd like a handjob from Queen Bess, but it ain't gonna happen,' Qoheleth ruptured.

I shrugged. 'Everyone's got their own thing, I suppose.'

'While I hesitate to express myself in terms as . . . profane as my sibling, I'm afraid I regard your proposition with equal lack of enthusiasm. I don't need to explain to you what happens when someone in my line of work loses his reputation as a person who looks out for his own. Were I to allow this attack to go unanswered, it would be seen as weakness – a misimpression I wouldn't want getting around.'

'It's a simple question of business, you say.'

'Exactly.'

'Ochres and argents.'

'Yes.'

'The hard bottom line.'

'As I said.'

'If that were really the case, then you'd do every fucking thing I just asked you, and you'd do it without giving me any more trouble. Because I assure you, however busy you think you are today, I've got you beat by a long shot – and it don't mean a thing to me personally if you and the Gitts decide to massacre each other. I'll shed no tears on my pillow, not for you, not for your half-lunatic brother, not for that inbred pack of fuckwits living east of the walls. My being here is a kindness to you, and you'd be wise to recognize it as such.'

Qoheleth was ready to open me up, slice tendons and break bone. I was certain that I didn't stand a chance against him, so

I didn't bother trying to defend myself, preferring to take my chances with his brother's good graces. And indeed, Uriel kept that same even face on, and put his arm across his sibling, easing him back down. There was a moment when it looked like Qoheleth might throw off the burden of fraternal loyalty and mash me into something less pretty, but it abated.

With Qoheleth back in his chair, Uriel spoke quietly. 'We very much appreciate you taking time out of your schedule to stop by and clarify the situation. Perhaps, having been so kind already, you might go so far as to explain yourself further.'

'I had a meeting yesterday with Captain Ascletin, of the city watch.'

'Did you? I have a meeting with him once a week, during which I give him a pouch of yellow. In exchange, he leaves me to make my own decisions during the rest of it.'

I shook my head back and forth, chuckling vaguely. 'You new kids, you're always so quick to shit on the hoax.'

'I didn't realize you held them in such esteem.'

'I wouldn't walk a mile in that direction. But I recognize their role, and the difficulty of it. Middle-management is a bitch. So let me clarify a point that you seem to be hung up on – the hoax don't work for you, they just take your money. The hoax work for the Crown, which means they work for Black House. Most days, Black House doesn't give a damn what we all do to each other, and the hoax is happy to follow their lead in apathy. Today is not one of those days.'

'Of what interest could our little disagreements with the Gitts be to the men upstairs?'

'Maybe you've noticed the brown-robed fanatics hanging around every intersection in the city, passing out fliers and generally making a ruckus?'

'I notice lots of things.'

'Maybe you've heard their complaints about the incompetence – indeed, even the corruption of those forces sworn to uphold Crown Law south of the Old City.'

'Terrible, the way these rumors get around.'

'It would be worse if anything happened to confirm them.'

'Meaning?'

'The word from up high is this – no one gets to kill each other this week. Next week, next month maybe, you can start hanging people from lampposts – but right now, today, the peace gets kept. The hoax don't like to work, but they'll take it up if the alternative is answering to Black House. And as close at Ascletin is with the Gitts, who do you think he's going to decide to bring his weight on?'

'I hadn't realized that the good captain is on the Gitts' payroll.'

'The good captain is on everyone's payroll, as you observed – but he's a little more on the Gitts', if you follow me. Things keep going in the direction they are, you're going to get a visit from the hoax that you won't enjoy. Or, hell, maybe the Old Man will decide to cut out the middlemen, send a squad of hitters over to your house in the middle of the night, slit your throat in front of your kids.'

'I don't have kids.'

'But you have a throat.'

Uriel's eyes widened about an eighth of an inch. To cover up for such histrionics he pulled the nosegay out of from his shirt and held it beneath his nostrils, as if warding away a foul odor.

Even Qoheleth, with his dim sense of consequence, seemed slightly taken aback. He settled into his seat, his scowl suddenly less threatening and more petulant. 'Black House don't mean shit to me,' he muttered, though the fact he couldn't quite speak aloud went a ways towards undercutting the sentiment.

The Old Man was the bogie beneath the bed of every criminal in the city, and the stick I'd been using to beat the underworld into submission for more than ten years. If he hadn't existed I'd have invented him. But he did exist, sadly, and the reality was far more terrible than anything I could have dreamed up.

'Well,' Uriel said after a while, and for a monosyllable it held a lot of meaning.

'Yeah.'

'When would this meeting take place?'

'A couple of days. I'll let you know – I've still got to square accounts with your erstwhile enemies.'

'You came here first?' Uriel asked, faintly incredulous.

'I figured you were the injured party. And I figured you were smarter, so I'd start with the easy job.'

'That's very kind of you.'

'Don't mention it.'

Qoheleth's brief flirtation with composure hadn't taken, and he was back to reminding us all of how loud he could talk. 'You're not actually considering this nonsense, are you? We're just supposed to let these swamp-dwellers step all over us? What the hell kind of message is that gonna send?'

'Now, now, brother,' Uriel admonished him faintly. 'There's no harm in listening to what the Gitts have to say. You can keep your blade in its sheath a little while longer. It's the least we can do for our friend here, whose commitment to peace is so admirable.'

'When you've been doing this as long as I have, Uriel – you recognize stability as the good from which all others derive.'

Uriel raised his mug back up to his mouth, nodding slowly as if he was listening to me. I'd been paying close attention to the attention he'd been paying his cup, and I was starting to think that he never drank from it, just held it to his lips before bringing it down again. There was no other way to explain how he could sip all afternoon from something half again the size of a thimble without ever needing a refill. Of course everything Uriel did was affectation, he couldn't take a piss naturally. He reminded me of the Old Man in how little he reminded me of the rest of our species.

'It's interesting that you bring that up, actually. Your . . . extensive experience, I mean.'

'Is it?'

'To me at least. There's something I've always wanted to ask you.'

'I quiver in suspense.'

'Mad Edward – did they call him that because he was angry, or crazy?'

'Both, most of the time.'

'All my life, I've been hearing these stories about Mad Edward – what a savage, frightening character he was. How he killed off his own line to take over Low Town. That he once cut a man's throat for bringing him coffee without cream. It's fascinating to be able to have a conversation with someone old enough to remember him.'

'So few people these days have an appreciation for history.'

'History – yes, exactly. Ancient history. And now that we're on the subject, there's actually something else that I've always wanted to ask you.'

'Anything I can help you with.'

'What happened to Edward? There are so many . . . rumors, and so little in the way of hard facts.'

'He joined a cloister, if memory serves.'

'He's a monk?'

'Or he might just have taken a vow of silence. At the very least, you won't be hearing from him.'

Uriel laughed his cocktail party laugh. It was perhaps the one expression that he'd yet to master, there was something false and cloying about it. 'It was bound to happen at some point, right? I mean, no one sticks around forever. You get old, you get slow, you can't keep what you have. Best to get out while the going's good, I imagine. Leave the game to people young enough to play it.'

I did my best to match the gleam of his smile, though I have fewer teeth, and the ones left are yellowed with age. 'Good advice, indeed.'

'A fraction of the wisdom I've received through your tutelage.'

'It swells my heart to think I've had some role in mentoring the next generation,' I said, standing. 'I'll send a message over in a day or two with specifics on the meet.'

'Assuming you can convince my counterpart.'

'I convinced you, didn't I?'

'You did indeed,' Uriel said, rising to bid me farewell.

Qoheleth didn't bother to move from his seat, just dirtied up his grimace and eyeballed me down the stairs. Out front the two guards eyeballed me out to the main thoroughfare. The passing Asher eyeballed me back to Low Town, not for any particular reason so much as an expression of the general contempt everyone has for people that don't look exactly like them. By the time I was out of sight of the Enclave I was getting pretty damn sick of eyeballs.

Still, the whole business was wrapping up well enough. And it had been nice of Uriel to give me that warning. I could have passed him one in return, if I was as kind. Never give notice that you're going after someone. You plan on killing a man, you'd best aim for his back.

20

At fifteen the substantive core of my being had already more or less hardened into the shape it would remain – which is to say that I was abrasive in speech, quick to violence though slow to anger, unattractive and little inclined towards honesty. A melange that would have landed me in prison amongst the middle classes, this was a cocktail in high demand in Low Town, and I was thought of as something of an up-and-comer, a bright youth of which great things were to be expected. If by great things you meant thuggery and petty crime – which was more or less the neighborhood's working definition.

This was nine or ten years after the plague, and Low Town had stumbled back to about where it had been before the red fever turned it into something little better than a charnel house. Trash lined the roads, the roads were dirt tracks, the guards didn't give a shit about anything and the only law was enforced by those outside of it. But at least there were people there to fill the damn place – for years after I'd been orphaned a turn off the main streets would take you past rows and rows of empty houses, rotting wood floors and broken windows, burned-out husks where families had once lived.

In time though, folk trickled back in. Immigrants mostly, hicks from the provinces and that smattering of foreigners so desperate to leave their own country that they were willing to risk months on a ship to come to what was widely considered the most horrible spot in the Empire. There weren't many still around that could remember the place as it had been. Those the plague had spared were not, understandably I suppose, in any hurry to return.

With the gradual influx of newcomers came the syndicates, like rats in a grain barge. Low Town never had any money, but if you owned it you owned the docks, and if you owned the docks you could move anything you wanted in and out of the city proper. More or less worthless by itself, this fact alone made it of interest to the rest of the city's powers. Back then Low Town was still in play, and there were four or five major syndicates with a finger in the pie, all looking to snap up the whole pastry if given half a chance. The Rouenders were hanging on, albeit by their fingernails. Big Noel still owned most of the whorehouses and cribbed protection money from whoever he could force to pay. The Islanders held to their spot at the Isthmus, but they tended to fight too much amongst themselves to expand effectively. The heretics weren't major players yet, it would be another ten years before Ling Chi managed to break the back of his fellow countrymen and reforge them into a force to be feared. The Tarasaighns were the top dogs. They had more or less tossed the Rouenders out during the First Syndicate War some years prior, a particularly brutal affair which had seen the swamp-dwellers expand their holdings at the cost of everyone else. They controlled most of the docks, and the greater share of the bookmaking trade. Choke wasn't yet the moneymaker it would come to be in later years, but they controlled that to.

Even by Low Town's standards, it was a violent time to be walking around. When you've got one guy sitting on top, however ugly he may be, things tend to run well enough. Small crimes, random acts of violence, these are rare and swiftly punished – it's in the big man's interest to make sure that the rules run clear, and that he and his are the only ones who get to break them. The trouble comes when no one knows who to answer to, when every half-wit with a rusted knife gets to thinking he might make himself king. One of the many things my childhood taught me – any order is preferable to none.

Still, the chaos made it wide open for a young man of talent. At that point I'd gig for whoever paid me, and they all did. Not much, I was still too untested to be given anything serious, but I had a talent for making myself valuable. I kept my ears open and my mouth shut, and that's the sort of thing that will endear you to anyone.

Christiaan Theron was just one of a half dozen would-be neighborhood tyrants, kingpins of a few square blocks. But he'd been that for a long time, had owned his territory before the fever, and returned once the Blue Crane's great working ensured he wouldn't end his days choking on a line of lesions running up his throat. He was short and fat. At one point he'd been stocky, powerful even, but now he was mostly just fat. He'd always been short, of course. Christiaan had something of the old guard about him – he used to pay widow's rents, pass out candy to children, that sort of thing. It was all bullshit of course, whatever coppers he gave out he was cutting from the ochres he'd stolen, but it was more than his successors would ever provide. And he seemed to enjoy it, liked to think of himself as a man of the people. He had a certain superficial good humor to him, but that was as far as it went. He wasn't decent, or upright, or honest. He was just friendly, and in the grand scheme of things that barely passes for a virtue.

Christiaan had set up operations in the back corner of a sweet shop, a small table that he sat at for ten or twelve hours a day, drinking strong coffee and eating through his stock. It was a pretty terrible confectionery, nothing but stale caramels and day-old croissants, but it was the only game in Low Town,

Christiaan having encouraged any potential competitors to enter a less cut-throat enterprise, like selling wyrm. I'd brought him a message from somebody over something, and he'd taken a pause from waiting around for people to bring him money to spend a few minutes boring the shit out of me.

'When I got it back to Low Town,' he was saying, 'I sold it for a full eight ochres.'

'Wow,' I said.

'Damn right wow!'

'That's quite a story, Mr Theron.' Actually it was an incredibly tedious story, had been the first time I'd heard it, and hadn't improved with repetition.

Christiaan hemmed and hawed, as if I'd had to pull the monologue out of his nose, rather than sit still while it was spewed on me. 'I thought you might learn something from it. If you keep your eyes open, check for the angles, you can make money anywhere.'

It is astonishing the degree to which people are not listening to you. I remember I'd known that even then. No one cares about your opinion, they're just waiting for the opportunity to offer theirs. Once you understand that, it's pretty easy to make someone like you – give them free reign to discuss themselves until they tire of it, and you've won a friend for life. It's a simple enough trick to master. Mostly it demands nothing beyond your presence, and even then only physically. Should some encouragement be required, just repeat their last few words back at them in question form.

'Of course the Islanders love me, always did,' Christiaan continued.

'Love you, do they?'

'I've been good friends to them over the years. Some people, they'll tell you they don't trust the darkies, won't do business with them. But I don't hold with that.'

'Don't hold with it, huh?'

''Cause it takes all kinds, you see. You need all kinds.'

'That right? All kinds?'

178

'That's the glorious thing about Low Town,' he said, waving one pudgy hand expansively. 'Seems like a rough place, don't it?'

'Seems that way.'

'But there's more to her than that – you look after her, you treat her right, she'll give it back to you. But then, I've lived in Low Town my whole life,' he laughed. 'The old girl owes me something!'

'Not your whole life.' It was out before I realized I'd said it.

Christiaan seemed equally surprised by my interruption. And maybe there was something in my eyes that I shouldn't have let show, because he cleared his throat and straightened up in his chair. 'That's right – you were here during the plague, weren't you?'

I made a noise in my throat that could have been taken as confirmation, or denial, or anything else that suited your fancy.

'Must have been a rough time.'

My pitch varied, but the meaning stayed the same.

'Go grab me another shot of coffee, will you?' His cup was still half full, but he wanted to remind me of where I stood in the pecking order.

'Sure, Mr Theron,' I said. I always said sure to Mr Theron. I grabbed his mug and went into the small kitchen in the back of his shop. The water had grown cold during our chat, so I set it back on the stove and stoked the fire, waiting around for it to warm. The chime above the front door rang, and I heard the footfalls of a small group of men – three, I thought, but wasn't certain. 'Good morning, Uncle,' a voice said.

'Edward,' I heard Christiaan say with deliberate, perhaps exaggerated, enthusiasm. 'What a pleasure. Sit down, sit down. Can I get you something? We've got some fresh jelly doughnuts, just out the oven.'

There was a long pause, longer than it should have taken for Edward to decide he didn't want any fried fat. Something told me to keep quiet. I went ahead and listened to it.

'I'm not really in a doughnut mood, Uncle,' Edward said finally.

'Maybe some hard candy? Or a sweet roll?'

179

One of the men snickered.

'I'm not in a sweet roll mood either,' Edward said.

I crept to the edge of the doorway and chanced a peek. My ears had not deceived me. Three men stood in a rough semi-circle around the still-seated Christiaan. Two of them I'd never seen before. The third would, after that day, come to claim the sobriquet Mad Eddie.

Edward was ugly, acne-scarred and balding, but he made up for it, or thought he did, by dressing himself in the latest fashions of the Old City, gem-encrusted rings on his fingers, a scarlet coat lined with ermine fur. If he'd been wiser he'd have known that fashion is a tool to make the beautiful more so. The plain, and in particular the homely, are better off considering dress as a form of camouflage, avoiding anything that draws attention – it won't improve your chances of getting laid, but at least no one will point and laugh.

But then, Edward wasn't wise, only clever. Though, in fairness, he had enough of this last to have expanded on his uncle's holdings substantially, and at an impressive rate. Indeed, it was Edward's moves these last few months – brutal, sudden, and with little concern for any implicit or spoken arrangements which had heretofore curbed violence in the area – that had led to his Uncle's preeminence amongst the small group of petty criminals that claimed Low Town as their turf.

'Fine, fine,' Christiaan said too loudly. 'Sit down then, we've got business to discuss.'

But Edward didn't sit. The difference in size between them, substantial had they stood back to back, seemed vast. 'Of course, Uncle.'

'I want you to pay a call on Samhael Eirrson,' Christiaan said, naming one of his direct competitors, a Valaan based out of the east corner of Offbend. 'Word is he's trying to set up a choke house on Alisanne Street.' Christiaan slammed a fist against the table. His arm fat jiggled. 'That's our territory, and you damn well need to let him know it.'

'I paid him a call last night, Uncle,' Edward answered in a quiet voice.

'What?'

'We had a long discussion. He'll make sure to keep to his own end in the future.'

'That's . . . excellent,' Christiaan said, though something in his voice seemed to indicate he wasn't entirely certain this was the case. 'Very good,' he turned to face the others. 'The perfect deputy – you know what I need without me even asking it.'

Neither of Eddie's boys laughed. That was one of the ways you could tell they were Eddie's boys, and not Christiaan's.

Eddie didn't laugh either, but his smile should have given his uncle pause. 'You know, I think I've changed my mind – actually, there is something I'd like.'

'Of course, of course,' Christiaan said. He gestured towards the display case and started to stand. 'Whatever you want.'

Edward put a hand on his uncle's shoulder and settled him back into his chair. 'I don't want a pastry.'

Uncle licked his lips. 'What then?'

'Everything,' Edward said in a quiet voice. 'I want you to give me everything.'

Looking back now, I don't think Christiaan ever had the grit to keep his hands on what was his. What he had he had because he'd gotten in early, taken his cut of Low Town before the bigger players realized there was a meal to be made. And he should have seen what was growing in Edward, it wasn't hard. No one likes being second on the chain, not when they're doing the work to be first. Perhaps it was familial loyalty which had kept Christiaan from recognizing the viper at his breast, but I suspected it was just age. No one keeps an edge indefinitely.

'I don't understand,' Christiaan said finally, though at this point he should have, and probably did.

'What you have,' Eddie began, still speaking in his low, soothing, serpent voice, 'I want. Protection, the whorehouses, your share of the rackets. The breath and vine you've been bringing in from the docks. Even this shitty little sweetshop – I want it. I want it all.'

There was, obviously, very little to say to that. If it had been me sitting there I'd have gone for Eddie's throat, done my best to bring him down before his associates sent me to meet She Who Waits Behind All Things. But it had been a long time since Christiaan had done his own work. He'd lost the spark of violence that a man on the wrong side of the law needs to keep forever nursed. 'I've been . . . meaning to make some changes to the organization. Do something to recognize all the valuable work you've been putting in. Maybe deal you a percentage.'

Edward still had his hand on his uncle's shoulder. Seen from afar there was something intimate in it, even paternal. He leaned over as if to whisper something, but when he spoke it was loud enough for me to hear. 'Don't embarrass yourself.'

The fat man's jowls trembled. 'What happens to me?'

Eddie shrugged and stood back up, letting his hand drop to his side. 'What happens to all of us.'

'You don't mean . . .'

'I do mean it, Uncle. I mean it very much indeed.'

'You wouldn't . . .'

'I would.'

'It's not necessary. I'll disappear – I'll leave tonight, right now. You'll never see me again. I won't be a problem.'

'Where would you go? Who would want you? You're a fat old fuck who talks too much and drools when he eats. And besides – Low Town needs to know I'm serious.'

Most people, at the last gasp, when they see they don't have a way out, react to their imminent demise with some last surge of nerve. The rest break completely, weeping and smearing snot on your boots. Christiaan, at least, was one of the former. 'You're a vile son of a bitch,' he said. 'You always were.'

Eddie put one hand to his breast, as if shocked by the profanity. 'That's your sister you're talking about,' he said. Then he nodded to one of the boys.

I turned away.

There was a wet sound, an ugly sound. Then a few short seconds of burbling as the life leaked out of Christiaan Theron. Then silence.

The whistle of the kettle broke it, and spurred me into motion. The best thing to do was to play it strong, bull right on out of the place. Edward wasn't trying to keep what he'd done quiet – on the contrary, he wanted word of his ruthlessness to carry. There wasn't any reason to do to me what he'd done to Christiaan, so long as I didn't give him one.

All the same, my sudden appearance was something of a shock to the assemblage. There would be no consequences for the murder of Christiaan, the hoax were not called that because of their high level of efficiency, and obviously his family wasn't going to declare a blood feud. But no one likes being surprised mid-murder. One of the boys tensed up when he saw me, the one who'd done the deed itself, to judge by the freshly painted knife he was holding. The other made a quick move for his own piece of steel.

Eddie was the only one who kept his cool – Eddie and me, I mean. 'Christiaan seems to have had an accident,' I said.

The one with the knife laughed. Years later, when I had him killed in the street, I remembered that chuckle and felt good about myself.

Edward didn't laugh though. He leaned down till he was just about eye level, and took a slow look at me. 'You got any notions of revenging him?'

He had a half foot on me, would for a few more years. But I didn't look away from no one, not then, not ever. 'I don't give two shits about Christiaan. He was a man who paid me. I don't imagine he'll be the last.'

Eddie seemed to like that. He smiled and stood back to his full height. 'You're a smart boy,' he said, and gave his men a quick head shake that meant I wouldn't be following Christiaan into the next world. Then he waved at the front door. 'You can see your own way out.'

But I didn't. 'Your uncle owed me two copper, for carrying a message from the hoax.' Actually, I'd already collected my pay from Christiaan, but I didn't see any harm in collecting it twice.

Eddie nodded towards the corpse on the chair, wide-eyed, a

crimson semi-circle seeping into his shirt. 'I don't imagine he'll be able to make good.'

'It's your set-up now, ain't it? That means it's your debt as well.'

'Shut your fucking mouth kid, before you get it shut permanent.' This from one of the hoods – not the one holding the knife, though I figured he had one on him somewhere.

Eddie didn't answer, just kept staring at me. After a pause he reached into his pocket and came out with an argent. I reached over to take it and he grabbed my arm. 'Smart boy, like I said. You ever feel like moving up from this petty-ante bullshit you've been doing, come see me. We've always got work for smart boys.'

He let go of my sleeve. I shoved the argent into my pocket and hoofed on out.

I stopped running errands for the syndicates not long after that. I was getting to the age when people started to expect you to make a commitment, and even then the idea of having some trumped up choke pusher tell me where to walk wasn't my cup of brew. Besides, at the time I'd had dreams of being more than another Low Town thug. The foolishness of youth, but there it was.

Killing his uncle was only one step in Eddie's positioning himself at the forefront of Low Town's underworld. He was still a running dog for the Rouender interests, not much taken seriously in the city proper. But for the rest of his life he called the shots in Low Town, as much as anyone could claim to control the bedlam that reigned north of the bay and south of the Old City.

In the months and years to come, the reign of Christiaan Theron would come to be seen as a halcyon period in Low Town, and false memories of his charity and benevolence would spring up every time Eddie raised rents or brutalized a bystander, both of which he did with unfortunate frequency. Eddie was something very close to an animal, as killing his uncle had been meant to showcase. It was just as well, really. I'm not one for nostalgia, and in truth I think I preferred Eddie to his uncle. Evil is best served without a patina of hypocrisy. The man mugging you doesn't need to offer false sympathy.

Despite his banter, despite his age, Christiaan didn't understand Low Town. Nobody did, not like me. Because when Christiaan and Eddie and the rest of the city had taken shelter in the provinces, wetting their beds against the thought of the plague following them, I'd snuggled tight against her bosom. Fed from her effluvia, nested amidst her bones. Listened to her whispered secrets in the still hours of the night. The rest were summertime lovers, quick to show when times was easy and as hard to find when the day turned cold. Only I had stayed faithful to her.

So I could have told Christiaan something about Low Town, could have told all of them. She is a hateful bitch – without loyalty, without affection, ever eager to turn against your hand. To possess her is to take a wolf to bed, and to forget that fact is to be lost.

21

I kept a bottle of whiskey in a closet in the back, near where Wren sleeps. It was ten years old when I was given it ten years back, partial payment from a distributor who'd decided liquor wasn't enough for him, gotten pretty heavy into me for daevas honey. That night, after the trade had left and Adeline had gone to sleep, I pulled it out and cornered Adolphus at a back table he was cleaning.

'I've had a thought,' I told him, taking a seat and gesturing him down.

He obliged me. 'A rare occurrence,' he said, his smile ugly but honest.

'And one that deserves commemoration.' I poured us each a few fingers.

'Your health.'

'Yours.'

We clinked glasses.

'By the Lost One, that's good stuff,' Adolphus said.

'I'd hope so – I took it in exchange for like two ochres' worth of ooze.'

He sucked his teeth. 'It's not that good.'

'No.'

'This was from that guy who owned the distillery?'

'Yeah.'

'What happened to him?'

What had happened to him? I chewed over lost memories. 'I think he ended up offing himself.'

Adolphus took a long look at the amber-colored liquid he was sipping. 'That's pretty terrible.'

'Yeah,' I agreed, and gave us both another shot.

The fire cracked and snapped in the corner. On the surface it was like a lot of other nights we'd had, hundreds, maybe thousands going back to when we'd opened the bar. There wouldn't be many more like them. It's only at the end of things that you come to any appreciation for what you've let slide by.

'This thought,' Adolphus began, 'I don't suppose it's a happy one?'

'Depends on whether or not you go along with it.'

He finished off his end of the whiskey, wiggled his glass for more. I dutifully refilled it. 'I'm listening,' he said.

'We've had a good run,' I said.

'That's all you've got?'

'Pretty much.'

'We've had a good run,' he repeated. 'In the past tense.'

'Yes.'

'And what are we set to have now?'

'A bad one,' I said, and finished my own drink. 'We're getting ready to have a very bad one.'

'Care to elaborate?'

'I've gotten caught up in something.'

'This is you elaborating?'

'It's still a little hazy – suffice to say things have gotten awfully knotted.'

'You've unraveled them before.'

'I'd be a fool to mistake luck for skill, and twice over for thinking it'll last forever,' I said. 'You know that bum, sometimes see him begging for change around Crossed Street Market?'

'Not really.'

'He's always screaming about how the world is gonna end? Sometimes holds a sign up to that effect?'

'Oh, that one. Sure, I know him.'

'I guess you don't pay him much attention.'

'Not really,' Adolphus said, with an exaggerated show of patience. 'Because he's a bum holding a placard saying the world is gonna end.'

'Understandably – he's always been wrong before.'

'Exactly.'

I set my hand on his, both gnarled, both wrinkled, one twice the size of the other. 'But he won't always be wrong. You wait around long enough, you'll wake up to see everything turned to ash.'

'This is all a little abstract.'

'You want me to put it simple?'

'We ain't all so sharp as you.'

'I think the Empire is on its last legs. I think Queen Bess was the last thing holding us together. Sure, she was nothing but an inbred hag eating off solid gold saucers while the rest of us scraped for dinner – but she'd been around so long we'd all grown attached. With her dead, the fissures are bound to start showing. There isn't enough of everything for everyone that wants it, and ain't nobody interested in sharing.'

'This sense of impending doom,' he said, 'it have anything to do with that Step you met up with?'

'In part.'

'What's the other?'

'Black House.'

'How long they gonna have you on a chain?' he asked, shaking his head in sympathy. Despite everything we'd seen, there was still some part of Adolphus that was disappointed the powers that be weren't honest.

'Until the day I die, obviously. Though in fairness to the Old Man, I sort of . . . volunteered for this one.'

'You haven't volunteered for anything since you joined the army, and you've been complaining about that ever since. What possibly prompted you to work for Black House?'

He deserved to know the truth. I wouldn't tell him the truth, of course, but he deserved to know it. 'Albertine's back in Rigus.' It near choked me coming out.

He put a hand the size of my chest to a brow the size of my hand. 'Śakra's swinging cock, how long you gonna hold a torch? She's poison.'

'I know.'

'She's wyrm.'

'I know.'

'You don't truck with wyrm. It's kind of your thing, as I remember.' That was one thing about Adolphus – he could back-hand you, but still cut it with sugar.

'I don't have any notions of reunion.'

'Then what's the point?'

That was a very good question. I really ought to have had an answer, at least one to give myself. Adolphus was kind enough not to push me on it.

'It's not about her,' I said finally. 'And it isn't even about me. We're heading towards a cliff, all of us, the city, the whole fucking Empire. A month, three, maybe six at the outside. But when it comes, it's going to make the red fever look like tummy ache.'

'You're talking about civil war?' He seemed faintly incredulous. Even the best of us don't like to look at what's in front of them. 'Between Black House and the Steps?'

'The Steps are a symptom of the rot – they aren't the cause. What's left propping up the edifice? Nationalism? That burned out in the war. Religion? Lip service aside, nobody important ever took the daevas serious, and that's unlikely to change. Money is the glue that's been holding us together. So long as the man on the street could afford a new coat, a new bed, a new house, he wasn't much concerned with what had to happen for him to get them. You turn off the spigot, you see how quick he gets to counting his rights. And the well has run dry, my friend – we've gorged ourselves on the wealth of the colonies and reparations from the Dren for fifteen years, but that's done with. People get angry when they can't buy new shit, and they start looking around for things to break, and listening to anyone who gives them a decent excuse to do so.'

'It's not the first time that Black House crushed a revolt.'

What Adolphus had failed to mention was that he'd been a part of the last rebellion, and paid dearly for it. I, of course, saw no percentage in pointing out his oversight. 'The Old Man isn't infallible. Don't no one retire from life undefeated.'

'You think the Sons will win?'

'I think we'll lose.'

Adolphus settled back into his chair, the wood groaning uneasily at his bulk. He'd pushed aside his glass and moved straight to the bottle. I didn't say anything, but it hurt my heart to see him absent-mindedly putting away whiskey that had cost me a full jar of daevas honey.

'Where do we go?'

'The Free Cities. The Empire doesn't have much pull over there, and they'll have less by the time things settle.'

'Won't be cheap, setting up a new life.'

'I've got enough stashed away to take care of us for a while. It won't be easy, but . . .'

'Ain't never been,' Adolphus answered, then brought the neck of the bottle up to his lips, choking down the dregs. 'When do we move?'

'As soon as possible. This week, the next at the very latest.'

He shook his head. 'That's impossible – there's no way in hell I can sell the bar that fast, not at any sort of a price.'

'You won't be selling the bar. You won't be packing a bag, or telling a soul you'll be going. You won't be doing anything that would deviate from routine. Neither will Wren, or Adeline. Neither will I.'

'I've got a life here,' Adolphus protested. 'Customers, suppliers. I can't just disappear.'

'Everyone that matters will be coming with us.'

Adolphus is well liked because he likes well, because he's garrulous, and openhearted. Near twenty years behind the counter at the Earl, he'd raised a small army of well-wishers and half-friends. I'd been in the city twice as long, and could count my intimates on two hands with my thumbs down.

'Believe me – they'll have more to worry about than the whereabouts of their favorite publican. The way things are going, they'll have a lot more to worry about. We wait around much longer and so will we.'

He thought this over for a while, then shrugged uncomfortable agreement. 'We'll need something to tide us through – pay our way out, set us up once we get there. I figured what we'd make off selling the Earl would be that. As it is, my hoard isn't exactly what you'd call vast. I don't fancy the idea of making it to the Free Cities and starting over as a fucking beggar.'

'This should cover our initial expenses.' I dropped the note I'd gotten from Egmont onto the table. Adolphus picked it up and whistled. 'What are you doing for the Sons of Śakra that's worth five hundred ochres?'

'Betrayal.'

'Whose?'

'That's the question, isn't it?'

22

Wren slept in the back, on a bed by the fire that Adeline built for him every night and dutifully removed each morning. It was the warmest spot in the bar, and the most comfortable – a distinct cut above the small room I occupied on the second floor, which was drafty, cramped and had the tendency to leak rainwater onto my forehead. On the other hand, it afforded the boy little in the way of privacy, or protection from passersby. He'd come to adopt the sleeping habits of a wintering bear; without forcible interruption his repose often extended well into the center of the day.

Which is a very long way of explaining that I had to put a boot into his side to wake him, and even then it took a solid forty-five seconds for him to blink into consciousness.

'What was that for?' he said finally, shoving my toes out of his armpit.

'I'm a mild sadist,' I said.

'Mild?'

I thought that was pretty cute given that he was still wiping sleep out of his eyes. 'Get dressed. We're going for a walk.'

'Where to?'

'Not to catch the early worm, I can tell you that much.'

'What?'

'We're going to see Yancey,' I said. 'So put on some fucking pants.'

He nodded and waved me off – indeed seemed by all outward signs to be rousing himself to full attention. All the same, I spent another half hour sipping black coffee and scowling before he finally managed to make an appearance. And even then he was moving at something less than half-speed, yawning and scratching himself.

When Wren had joined our little commune, six years prior, it had taken three months to convince him to spend the night beneath our roof. For a long time after that he'd snap awake any time anyone passed by, wary of letting sleep get too firm a hold on him. I looked at the well-fed youth in front of me, trying to make out the ghost of the wild thing he'd been. There wasn't much. A certain sharpness in the eyes, a speed of hand you rarely saw amongst the settled. But by and large he'd been pretty well domesticated.

For some reason that thought made me angry. 'What time is it?'

'I don't know. Ten? Eleven?'

'Twelve.'

'If you knew the answer, why'd you bother to ask?'

'A lot of things happened, during the first half of the day.'

'Do tell.'

'Adeline was eaten by a passing gang of cannibals. A giant eagle came for Adolphus, swooped down from the sky and carried him back to the nest. A cadre of courtesans slipped by looking to pleasure you, but they left when they found you asleep.'

'Sounds like a busy morning.'

'How the hell would you know? The building could have burned down around your ears, you'd have woken up in the next world, paying for your sins.'

'Good thing I've led a life of such firm moral rectitude.'

I stretched my shirt down off my shoulder, revealing a patch of mottled pink skin, the scar long faded but still unpleasantly visible. 'You see this?'

He leaned over to inspect it. 'Yeah.'

'One night, a long time ago, when I was a little younger than you, I found my hands on a bottle of rotgut. I guess I hadn't had much experience with liquor by that point, because evening found me passed out beneath the Mast bridge.'

He chuckled.

'A couple of the neighborhood fiends stumbled through, hopped up on choke, saw where I'd laid my head. Decided to have some fun.' I pulled my shirt back up.

'So what did you do?'

I didn't answer for a while. 'I suffered, Wren. I suffered.'

Now it was his turn to be silent. Not for long of course – you'd need to stuff a rag in his mouth to keep him quiet for more than half a minute. 'I don't imagine anyone's going to knife me in the back room of the Staggering Earl,' he said, as if to close the conversation.

I've often found the importance of a lesson can best be emphasized via some small display of physical violence. My fingertips found the pressure point in Wren's shoulder and I pulled him in closer to me. 'You think like that long enough, someone will come by and prove you wrong. And that's the thing, boy – you only gotta be wrong once. You ain't safe here. You ain't going to be safe anywhere you ever find yourself, dig? Not till they wrap you in a shroud and set you in a box. This side of that, don't ever get so comfortable that you let a man sneak up and touch you while you sleep.'

One thing about Wren – he'd stare back at you. Always had, even when he'd been a child weighing less than a solid bowel movement. 'All right.'

I let my grip on him slacken, and went back to my coffee. 'And quit sleeping till midday. You give the rest of the world a six-hour head start.'

'All right,' he said.

'All right,' I agreed. 'Now make yourself something to eat, and let's get to rolling.'

We left later than I would have liked, but one upside of my trade is that it doesn't require a fixed schedule. The half-junkies that bought from me could wait a few hours. They didn't think so, obviously. I'm usually a step removed from the real casualties, nails bitten to the quick, scratching themselves till their skin bled, but a fair few of my dealers were known on occasion to dip into their stash. Not that I was one to judge, mind you.

It wasn't raining, but it was that sort of damp that got into your bones and your lungs, that made you cough up phlegm and chatter your teeth. Wren was overbundled in his winter coat, a thick woolen burden that would have kept him comfortable in a blizzard. I was wearing the duster I'd picked up shortly after I'd left Black House, a leather thing, black at one point, long turned the color of apathy. Its primary purpose was to offer some camouflage for the various illegal things I was carrying, and as insulation it had little to recommend it.

So I walked quickly, to try and keep myself warm. Wren, taller and lankier, kept pace without breaking sweat. 'The other night,' I started. 'You were telling me that you wanted me to give you something real to do.'

'Yeah.'

'You still interested?'

'Yeah.'

'You're going to become intimately familiar with the nocturnal movements of Captain Kenneth Ascletin. Between leaving work and the sweet release of sleep, his life will be an open and well-thumbed tome.'

'All right.'

'It goes without saying that the good Captain will be unaware of your attentions.'

'If it goes without saying, then why did you need to say it?'

'Emphasis, my dear child. And because I savor the sound of my voice.'

196

'That's a lovely quality.'

The rest of the journey was made in relative silence, occasionally broken by the chattering of my teeth. I was happy enough to see Yancey's house, and its promise of respite from the wind.

'There was one other thing I wanted to mention to you,' I said to the boy as we climbed the stoop.

'Which was?'

I knocked twice, and waited to answer until I heard footsteps from inside. 'We're leaving Low Town at the end of the week, and we're not ever coming back.'

The door opened in time with Wren's mouth.

Ma Dukes was getting ready to call me what I was, but when she saw the boy she seemed to decide against it. This had been one of the reasons I'd brought him. 'Been a long time since I seen you round here.'

'He keeps me locked up in the basement, most days.'

She gave me a look which would have brought sleep to an injured man. 'It wouldn't surprise me.'

The house smelled of rot and endings. The drapes were closed, though little enough light would have entered anyway, given the weather. And it was cold, almost as cold as it had been outside. In my memories Yancey's house had always been warm and loud, drum pulses rocking the walls, cooking smells wafting from the kitchen.

Mrs Dukes seemed to see me seeing these things, and bristled slightly. 'I'll make you some tea to warm you up,' she said, aiming herself narrowly enough at Wren to make clear the offer was only to the one of us. 'You know the way.'

In contrast to the rest of the house, Yancey's bedchamber was hot to the point of stifling. The air was bad, saturated with the excreta of the room's inhabitant. It seemed it was no longer possible to expose the Rhymer to a chill, even if doing so would cut the stench. A candle on the bedside table provided the sole source of illumination, flickering and feeble. All to the good. I didn't need a better view of what was happening to my friend.

He had gotten closer to death in the last week. I suppose we all had, but with Yancey you could really make it out. He was paler, and respiration had ceased to come natural – he labored to breathe, willing each gasp of air in and out of his lungs. When he saw Wren though, he lit up a bit, even managed a weak smile. That had been the other reason I'd brought the boy.

It was months since they'd seen each other. I'd made no secret of Yancey's illness, but it was one thing to hear about it and another thing to be confronted with its reality, with the way that the body can decay right in front of you, go from a tool that expresses your will to an anchor dragging you down to hell. To his credit, Wren didn't grimace, made little outward show. But it ballooned up in his eyes, quick as he was to blink it away. 'How you been handling yourself, Rhymer?'

'Ain't nothing to it,' Yancey answered. 'You here to protect him from Mom?'

'I protect him from everything,' Wren said, puffing out his chest dramatically. 'If it wasn't for me, he'd get knifed on the way to the outhouse.'

Yancey laughed, though it cost him something to do so. 'What you been keeping yourself to?'

'Women and sweet wine.'

'Chores and cheap beer,' I corrected.

'How your studies going?'

Wren shrugged, all cool nonchalance, but he started to speak strange words in a low voice, and his eyes took on the glazed half-stupor that befalls a practitioner when he initiates a working.

The candle sparked to life, the flame rising higher than its source would merit, melting through the wax rapidly. It produced smoke apace, but the exhaust remained in a tight ball rather than dissipating into the gloom. Wren kept up his muttering, then brought his hands up in the shape of an hourglass.

The mist answered his direction, forming into the outline of a woman, inhuman but somehow quite alluring. She stood in place for a moment, offering herself to view, hair curling trails of vapor, an ample chest and full spectral buttocks. Then the apparition rose one ephemeral leg over Yancey, straddling his

198

body beneath the covers. Another moment and she leaned over and set her lips down onto the center of his forehead.

Wren stopped chanting and blew softly, and the vision evaporated into the ether.

Yancey laughed and clapped and laughed and clapped until I began to worry he would exhaust himself in celebration. For fifteen or twenty seconds he lost all awareness of his imminent demise, of the pain he was in and the pain he would leave behind. I reminded myself to give Wren a pass the next time he did something that made me want to smack him.

'Where you send her!' Yancey asked once he finally tired of exertions. 'Things was just getting interesting!'

Wren smiled and inspected his fingernails.

'Yes, we're all very impressed,' I said. Though actually I was pretty impressed. 'You head back downstairs now, boy. Keep an eye on Mrs Dukes.'

Wren didn't like being kept out of anything, though in this particular case I think he was happy enough to turn the sight of Yancey's shell into an unpleasant memory. 'I'll get back at you soon, Rhymer,' he said, then slipped down the stairs.

I wasn't sure if he knew it was a lie. Yancey knew it, though.

Neither of us spoke until we heard Wren's footfalls down the steps. We didn't speak for a while after that, either. All of the energy and good humor seemed to have left with the boy.

'He's come together,' Yancey said.

'He's getting there,' I half agreed.

'You done a good job.'

I sniffed and shrugged. 'Adeline deserves most of the credit. Adolphus gets the rest. All I done is taught the boy vice.'

'No one needs any help with that. What you here for?'

'I need you to do something for me.'

It was not the first time I'd said this to him, and the low, sickly chuckle Yancey offered seemed to acknowledge it. 'Done – so long as it's within reach of the bed.'

'I'm taking your advice.'

'A rarity indeed. Which bit?'

'That piece about getting out of Low Town, and not ever coming back.'

I'd been thinking about finding passage out of the city since before I'd discussed the possibility with Adolphus. I'd been thinking about finding passage out of the city for about thirty-five years, if we were being honest, but the last few days had calcified this vague wish into a viable reality. In theory, finding my way to exile should have caused no great difficulty. The Free Cities, as their title would indicate, welcomed any newcomer who could pay their way, and the Empire had no legal claim to my presence. In practice, there were eyes on me, even before I'd found myself embroiled in this latest business with the Sons. Signing my name to the manifest of a passenger ship, waiting on the quay with the rest of the pilgrims – let's just say there were a whole host of folk who might have wanted to drop by and make sure my goodbye was permanent. Nor did I imagine the Old Man would allow me to slip his grasp, remove myself from the board at the height of his game. The surest way out was to do things sly – which is more my custom anyway.

The Islanders were the best sailors in the Thirteen Lands, as even the ugliest-minded neighborhood drunk would acknowledge, albeit after he'd spent ten minutes on a list of their perceived vices. They were also the best merchants and as such, the best smugglers. Indeed, to the Islanders, there was little distinction between the two – their aversion to customs duties was virtually an inherited trait, one lamented by port officials throughout the known world. Yancey of course had never been a sailor, never been anything but the best damn musician in the city, which was more than enough. But his brother had been a coxwain in the Navy, before he was lost to a storm a year or so back, and he knew plenty of people that had stuck to tradition.

There were other ways to find my way out of Rigus. Merchants that owed me a favor, ships' captains that could be bought or frightened. If we were being honest, in some strange way I thought it might be good for Yancey. If you care about someone, let them do you a kindness. It would be the last in a long line he'd done me.

It took a moment for the news to sink in. 'All right,' he said. 'Good. Fucking great.'

'Me and the boy and his folks. One of the Free Cities – I've heard New Brymen is nice, but frankly the where's not so important, as long as it ain't here.'

'When you looking to move?'

'It would make me very happy not to be in Rigus in a week's time.'

He thought that over slowly, going through the contacts he'd accumulated in a lifetime of being well liked. 'I think I can handle that,' he said. 'Won't be cheap.'

'Doesn't need to be,' I said. 'But it needs to be quiet – can't anyone hear about it before it happens.'

'I'm not so far gone you need to explain me that.'

He seemed pretty far gone. 'I know you're not in the best way right now,' I said. 'If you ain't up to it . . .'

'I'm up to it,' he snapped, and I almost smiled at the burst of energy. 'You know Isaac Gaon? Runs a galleon for one of the big trading houses?'

'By reputation.'

'He and my brother used to be in the Navy together. He's solid as they come, and happy to do me a favor.' He nodded to himself, the pieces settling in a comfortable line. 'Isaac Gaon would be perfect.'

'You'll put a word in his ear?'

'Today, and I'll make sure he gets back to you with speed.'

'That would be grand,' I said. 'Just grand.'

And then we fell into our second uncomfortable silence, one that lasted longer than the first. This close to the end, patter seems disrespectful. Words carry extra weight, you strive to make every sentence a summation of some great truth.

'Am I going to see you before you split?' he asked.

That was the question right there. 'Absolutely,' I said, though I was far from certain this would be the case. 'But I'm not sure when. I've got business needs taking care of, before I cut and run.'

'This business would be why you're so desperate to leave?'

'It would.'

'Make sure it don't take care of you.'

'That's certainly my intent,' I said.

It was time to beat a retreat, but here again I faltered. I ran through all of the normal salutations, found each absurd, even insulting. 'Farewell' – he would not be able to do that, it was clear. 'See you soon' – perhaps, perhaps not. Our language has yet to develop a proper send-off for leaving a close friend's deathbed.

He saved me. 'Stay loose, old man.'

'As best I can,' I answered, before bending down to wrap his frail body in an awkward embrace. He returned it to the degree that he was still capable. I wrinkled my nose at the overpowering smell of carrion, and felt miserably guilty for doing so.

Wren and Ma Dukes sat across from each other at the kitchen table. I couldn't make out what they were discussing, but I heard her laugh, buoyant and bright, like her son's. It was the first time I'd seen her laugh in a long time, and I didn't get to see it long. She snapped her jaw shut when I came into the room, narrowed her eyes against any further levity. Belatedly, I wished I'd lingered longer in the hallway, given her a few more minutes of simple cheer.

'We're moving,' I said.

Ma Dukes turned pointedly towards Wren. 'Stop by again soon,' she said. 'I'll make you a proper lunch.'

'Soon as I can,' he answered, though if you were looking you could see his eyes falter. He'd need to get better at lying.

Wren stood up from his chair and pulled on his coat. I jerked my head towards the exit, and he tipped his head to the matron and followed in the direction I'd indicated.

The door slammed shut. Ma Dukes grabbed a cigarette off the counter behind her. I couldn't remember her smoking, back when she'd allowed me to be in the same room with her for more than a moment.

'Is there anything I can do for you?' I asked.

'Can't nobody do nothing for me.'

'How you fixed for coin?' The Rhymer had been keeping his mother afloat these last years, signing over the greater part of his earnings even when they'd begun to dry up.

Her sneer cut across her face like a wound. 'I wouldn't take a copper from you if I was dying of hunger.'

I'd held out some hope for reconciliation, here at this final stage, when it wouldn't much matter anyway. But things don't really work like that – Ma Dukes was held tight in despair. Her trials had left her with a full skin of bitterness, and I was a convenient, even deserving, target.

I didn't mind, if it made her feel any better. I doubted I did. 'I'll stop by again in a couple of days.'

She grunted and turned her attention towards the far wall. I joined Wren out in the street.

I spent the first half of the walk home figuring out a way whereby some of my money could go to Mrs Dukes without her being the wiser. I didn't have much time – it would need to be taken care of before we split town. And I'd have to be slick enough to make sure she didn't smell my hands in it, or she wouldn't take a clipped copper. Her pride wasn't for my benefit, she had a spine stiff as an old oak. A familial inheritance, though one it seemed that would die out with her.

I spent the second half of the walk home thinking about this last, about the funeral I would never attend, and a good man taken before his time. The second half of the walk home, and a good while longer.

23

I dropped the boy back at the bar and spent most of the rest of the afternoon catching up on my rounds. Generally I'm one or two steps up above direct hand-to-hand transactions, which is to say that I sell things to people who sell things to junkies. The upside of not having anyone work for me is that I don't have to pay, trust or talk to anyone. The downside is much of the grunt work falls on my shoulders. I could pawn it off to Wren, of course, but in general I preferred not to have him carrying anything that could set him up for five years in the poke. The hoax knew not to bother me of course, and Black House generally didn't display much interest in anything as petty as a narcotics transaction, but then again, you never knew. If a rival decided to set me up for a fall, or there was just some rookie guardsman who hadn't learned who staked his retirement fund – well, Adeline would never let me hear the end of it.

It was two or three chilly, not particularly interesting hours padding my way around Low Town. A few dozen bartenders and street hustlers, the occasional pimp and fixer. Most of them meant nothing to me, cogs in the mill, the end product a few tarnished pieces of gold. One or two I would have gone so far as to call passing acquaintances. Yancey had been right, they wouldn't miss me when I was gone, nor would I lose any sleep when I made it to the Free Cities wondering whether Tam Half-Eyed was still able to pass out joints of well-cut dreamvine to deaden his patrons' wits while his tame whores ran through their pockets. All the same, I went through the motions with particular meticulousness. It wouldn't do to give anyone the sense that this was the last time they'd see me, that anything was any different from the hundred other times they'd scored off my stash.

I came back to a slow late afternoon at the Earl. The place was almost deserted, two old men playing a confused game of chess beside a roaring fire, a handful of other drunks sipping their way into nostalgia.

Wren sat at the counter, picking the burrs out of a suspiciously familiar looking bag of dreamvine. Next to him sat the rest of his makings, fine leaf tobacco, a twist of paper. He knew what he was doing – I'd taught him well. Or badly, depending on how you looked at it.

Adolphus leaned against the other side of the bar. He started when he heard the door open, his face guilty enough to get him hung in front of the most impartial tribunal in the Thirteen Lands. Adolphus was not strong on deceit – I made up for his slack, though.

'She'll be at market for hours yet,' Wren said, trying to calm him, voice smooth, fingers nimble. 'She's got to buy dinner for the rest of the week. Sit down, try and enjoy yourself.'

Adeline endeavored to keep her household inviolate despite the sea of iniquity in which she swam – which is to say that Wren wasn't allowed to smoke dreamvine, and Adolphus was strongly encouraged to similarly abstain. I was a lost cause of course. Like any wise ruler Adeline measured severity with leniency – Adolphus and Wren were never to indulge in narcotics within the Earl's confines, and in exchange Adeline committed herself to not making sure of that fact between the hours of roughly three and five on Sundays.

I thought it a broadly sensible arrangement, one our actual authorities might look into introducing on a wider scale. Adolphus worried about it every week, just the same.

Wren finished rolling the joint, brushed the refuse onto the floor and lit it off one of the candles leaking gold light into the air and melted wax onto the bar. He had that pleased sort of swell the youth get when breaking laws, however mild the offense or rash the motive.

Adolphus took the spliff between fingers the size of blood sausages, and brought it to a mouth that could have swallowed a suckling pig in one bite. He coughed like it was his first time – twenty years with me, the man still didn't know how to smoke correctly. Puffed his lips out like a monkey, and held in each lungful of vine till he near choked. When he handed it over the tip was wet with saliva.

I took a puff. 'Did you get this from my stash?'

'Yes,' Wren said.

'At least you're honest in your dishonesty.' Since it was technically my joint, I resolved to sit on it for a while. Adolphus didn't mind, despite his bulk a few pulls were all it took to set him on his posterior. If it bothered the boy, he had sense enough not to say anything about it. I watched the fire spark in the corner, and tried not to think about the chaos that eddied around me.

Wren ended that quick enough, quicker than I'd have liked, certainly. 'You put in a solid day?' he asked.

'We didn't all spend our afternoon stealing from people we live with.'

'Full day, then?'

'Full enough.'

'I guess it's overtime.'

'What's that mean?'

'Your Step is in the doorway,' Wren said, 'and he seems excited.'

I didn't bother to look. Wren's smirk was sufficient to let me know he wasn't lying. Why exactly the child took such pleasure in seeing the world make trouble for me, I'd never understand.

'You all right to handle him?' Wren asked. 'He hasn't made you yet – you could probably still slip out the back. I'll run him around for you.'

This was somewhere between insult and challenge, and I didn't bother responding to it. I took another hit, let the vine spackle over the cracks in my mind. Then I contorted my face into a grimace, turned suddenly and rushed over to greet our new arrival.

'There you are,' he started. Likely would have continued even, if I hadn't grabbed him stiffly by the arm and hustled him into the back corner.

'Are you out of your mind, coming here?' I asked him, swiveling my head back and forth as if inspecting the walls for peepholes. 'What could you possibly be thinking?'

He was at a brief loss for words. 'I . . . I thought . . .'

'Do you have any idea the heat you could bring down on me if anyone saw us together? How fast my throat would be cut, and yours twice as quickly?'

'I was here last week.'

'That was different!' I said adamantly. 'That was last week! Last week isn't this week! These are two different weeks we're discussing!'

'Then your efforts have yielded success?'

'Absolutely!'

'Of what fashion?'

'Of what fashion?'

'What developments have you to tell regarding . . .' He cut himself short in an admirable display of subtlety. As if to make up for it, he initiated a spastic round of facial jerks and low whistles meant to replace the object of his prior sentence. One of the old men playing chess looked over.

'I get it,' I said.

'Well, what have you been doing about it?'

'What have I been doing? What have I been doing?' What had I been doing? 'I've been running down every lead from every contact I could frighten, buy or cajole. This Coronet thing goes deep, Simeon, right to the bone. There are men, powerful men, who'd give everything they have to stop us from finding out the truth!'

'So you've learned something?'

'You think this is a game, Simeon?' I was enjoying this whole thing more than I should have been. Normally dreamvine affects me very little, a garnish of good humor to set off my well-spoiled personality. But that moment I was really feeling it – I had to work not to giggle. 'Do you think this is a game?'

'No,' he said. 'Of course not.'

'Good – just so you know it's not. It's not a game.'

He nodded seriously – we were clear on that much at least. 'What have you found out?'

I stared into his eyes for a solid five-count, my own pupils wide as a mad man's. Then I shrugged. 'What have they told you about Coronet, Simeon?'

He rearranged his skullcap. 'What I need to know.'

That meant nothing. 'You're a lucky son of a bitch. I wish I was in your boat, wish I could reach right into my brain and scrub it free of knowledge, scour my skull till it was as empty as yours.' It seemed to occur to him dimly that this was not a compliment, so I plowed on before the realization fully overtook him. 'But I can't – you can't do that with brains, you know – it's not like washing laundry.'

I could see the inner processes of his mind functioning on his face, knew that somewhere within a line of truth had been indelibly etched – *A Brain Is Not Like Laundry*. Next to it read, *This Is Not A Game*.

'I need you to tell Egmont something – but only Egmont, no one else, do you understand? You can't imagine Black House's reach – they've got ears everywhere, in every closet and cranny, the drawers of every night table, the bottom of every chamber pot.' That last might have been a little much, but if so Hume seemed not to have noticed.

'No member of the Brotherhood would ever stoop so low!' He had one hand tightened on the pommel of his rapier, the other raised up against his heart.

'You cannot conceive of the duplicity of Black House, a decent, honest, simple soul like yourself. There is no perfidy of which they are incapable, no path too crooked for them to have designed it. The Old Man is as bent as a cheap nail, sharp as a saber and cruel as grim death. As sure as I'm sitting here, they have men in your organization.' All of a sudden I'd stumbled into truth. I switched paths quickly. 'Don't trust anyone with what I tell you. Not your best friend, not your confessor. If your mother comes by tonight and asks what you've been doing today, you were sick and didn't leave home, you understand?'

'My mother's dead.'

'And we all deeply mourn her loss. But at least now she cannot betray you, as so, so many of your closest allies are no doubt, at this very moment, waiting to do.' I looked around conspiratorially, then leaned in close to him. 'You cannot trust the people you trust.'

'Then how can I trust Egmont?'

'OK, Egmont you can trust. No one else though.' Adolphus was puttering about behind us, clearing tables and repositioning chairs. I played it up for his benefit. 'Oh, would that I didn't need to involve you in this, Simeon – to think of the danger I'm putting you in, simply by whispering this in your ear.' I shook my head, as if overcome with concern at the thought. 'It's a terrible burden I'm placing on your shoulders.'

He strained to meet it. 'The Firstborn sets ahead of us what challenges he sees fit – we must meet them with stout heart and even eye.'

Adolphus made a little face behind his back. I could appreciate the sentiment, though I thought it best not to echo it. 'Good man, good man indeed.' I leaned back against the wall and closed my eyes, as if gathering my will for the next effort.

It was a surprisingly comfortable spot, a few feet down from the fire. I could have kept at it a while, maybe eased into a nap. But Hume was anxious as a virgin at a whorehouse, and refused to allow me the comfort. 'Well? What's the secret?'

I blinked myself back into the afternoon, took one last look around for spies peeking out from cracks in the walls, then leaned in close and whispered, 'I know who's selling red fever.'

'Who?' he near shouted, then looked around nervously and repeated in a tone so hushed I could barely make it out, 'Who?'

'Uriel Carabajal.'

'Oh,' Hume said, as if the name meant anything to him.

'He's an Unredeemed crime lord, owns a slice of land near the Enclave.'

'Śakra-damned black robes!' I supposed that was as close to profanity as Hume allowed himself. 'Is there no blasphemy to which they won't sink!'

'Forget about Uriel,' I said. 'He's just the front man.'

'For whom?'

'I'm not sure yet – but it's beginning to seem that I might have been speaking prematurely, when I called Coronet a failure. Black House is looking very hard in my direction, all of a sudden.'

'How so?'

'They put a tail on me – the Old Man's top enforcer, name of Crowley.'

Hume hunched his shoulders down over the table, then took a wary look around the bar. 'Is that him in the corner?'

It took me a while to realize he wasn't joking. 'No – not here right now. Tracking me generally.'

'Oh,' Hume said, a little disappointed. 'I'll let Egmont know.'

'You'd better get a move on. If Black House sees you here it'll be drapes for the two of us.' Not that the Old Man needed to put me on surveillance, given that I was stooling for him. 'And while we're on the subject, next time you come visit me, do it in your civvies.'

He looked down at his brown garb. 'I guess I stand out a bit,' he acknowledged.

'That, and your sect's brand of moralizing doesn't jibe so well with the natives. The local youths might decide to roll you and drop you in the canal.'

He spent a moment contemplating the feces-to-water quotient of our primary estuary. 'All right,' he said unhappily, then stood. 'I'll contact you once I've spoken with the Director.'

Maybe it was the vine – probably it was the vine – but before he could leave I broke out of my seat, grabbed him by the shoulders and pulled him into a rough embrace. 'Be careful,' I hissed, then released him. 'Keep one eye on your back, and two on your best friend.'

'That's three eyes.'

'You'll need four to survive what's coming,' I said.

Adolphus coughed to cover up his laugh. Anyone other than Hume would have noticed, but happily the Son was too busy trying to work out how to grow another set of peepers to pay attention. The operation proved too much for him, and he nodded frantically, then exited the Earl at a dead sprint.

I rejoined Wren and Adolphus at the counter. The boy was halfway through a second joint. I took it from his mouth and put it to my own.

'What spooked him?' Wren asked.

'High strung, these religious types.'

'You think you overplayed your hand?' Adolphus asked.

'I don't imagine Egmont pays much attention to Hume's reports. Gotta do something to shock him out of apathy.'

'If he doesn't trust the man, why's he got him following you around?'

'That's an excellent question.'

It had been a fun way to spend a few minutes, but there was one thing nagging at the reaches of my mind, kept me from fully enjoying the high I was cocooning myself into. I had obviously not been running about the city, roughing up informants and digging up secrets. There was no need to. I'd seen the connection between the fever and Coronet before Egmont had pointed it out to me, seen it that first day when I'd picked up a tin of narcotics from the house of a dead man. And if most of what I'd just served Hume had been the most errant nonsense, in one critical regard, I'd been as upfront as a priest – if Black House had started up Coronet again, and at this point it looked very much like they had – we were all in a fuck-load of trouble.

24

Guiscard's man in the blue hat was quicker in coming than he had been the first time. I was at the counter, consciously not drinking. He stood a man off from me and ordered quietly. Adolphus brought over a bottle and used it to fill a glass, then moved on down the line.

'Nice whiskey here, yeah?' I said. 'Worth the trip?'

He rolled his eyes and shook his head about an eighth of an inch back and forth. 'You're a dick,' he mumbled out of the far corner of his mouth.

I couldn't argue. At least, I didn't argue. I reached over and poured him a second shot, then did the same for myself. He put it down with the same ease as he had the first, dropped a coin on the table and walked out. I waited half a minute, then drank mine and followed him.

Outside a bleak afternoon had turned into an ominous evening. It's easy to put your mood on a place, read your temper in the pedestrians and passersby. Summer and youth and maybe a pretty girl on your arm and the whole berg sings your praises. We were a long way from summer and I was a long way from youth. The city itself seemed to have some half-formed sense of what was coming, and had passed the notion on to the creatures that lived in it. Mothers pulled their children tight as you passed, old men scowled from stoops, young men with ravenous eyes congregated in the alleys. Also, I'd forgotten to wear a coat.

Idinton is mostly factories blotting the sky and choking the air, but out towards the walls there are a few sections that could give Low Town a run for its money in terms of just generally being a shithole. Maybe not quite. Blue Hat tightened his step when he got there, scowling indecipherably, making himself a part of the scenery, a graffiti-stained wall, a stretch of rubble. Everybody who moved south of the Old City had a similar outfit. I pretty much never took mine off.

Finally he stopped and lit a cigarette. I got the feeling Blue Hat didn't smoke regularly, that he just used it as a prop. It seemed more task than pleasure. But then I imagined he was like that with everything, eating dinner in a workmanlike fashion, plowing his wife with all the enthusiasm he would a field. He stepped off finally, and I wasn't sad to see him go.

I spent a moment looking over the building I'd been tipped to. I was pretty sure I knew what it was, and felt a mild surge of shame as I knocked at the door. It was the sort of neighborhood where people made a point of not noticing things, but still, I had a reputation to uphold. Not that there was anything for it – I was going inside.

After too long shivering in the cold the madame opened the door. Madame makes it sound too classy. Old whore would be more accurate. Hers was the breed of prostitute which succeeds from persistence and affordability, rather than through any natural gifts. I'll spare a more detailed physical description. There's no need to be cruel – she had a living to make, like everyone else. 'Yeah?' she said in a voice appropriate to someone with her history.

'Good evening, I'm here to contract a rotting malady from an ill-fed illiterate.'

She was choked out of her mind, tiny little bug eyes struggling to make sense of what I was saying. 'What?'

'I'm here to see the man in the back.'

'Oh,' she said, dully aware that this was not, in fact, what I had said. 'Come in, I guess.'

The parlor was cut in half with a sheet nailed to the ceiling, more space to do business, though thankfully at this particular moment the chamber was not in use. I struggled to form an image of a person so desperate for human contact as to patronize the establishment, as well as with the realization that there were apparently enough of them to warrant an expansion of the premises.

'I'm rarely in a place where day-old wyrm fumes are the least offensive odor,' I said.

'What?' she repeated, sort of angrily.

'I said it's a lovely spot you have here!'

'I don't get you at all, man,' she said.

'Genius is never understood in its own time. Where is he?'

'He's . . .' she waved her hand down the hall. 'That way.'

I was torn between not wanting to spend a single second further in the woman's presence, and the fear that if she didn't clarify Guiscard's location I might walk in on something unfit for innocent eyes. She solved the difficulty for me, though grudgingly. 'Last door on the left.'

I considered giving her a gratuity, but decided I didn't want to touch her hand. I felt similarly about the handle on the last door to the left, though in that case I managed to man up.

Like in the back of the tailor shop, it appeared that Guiscard rented out the room infrequently, and that it was put back to its regular purpose when he wasn't in attendance. Which is to say that the bed was . . . well used. It was also the sole piece of furniture in the room, except for a small table and chair that had been pulled up against the back wall. Guiscard sat at it, going through a thick stack of papers with impressive single-mindedness, given the setting. From a room over, a loud squealing could be made out with no great difficulty, indisputably masculine, but of a strangely high pitch.

'Don't look now,' I said, 'but I think there might be some illegal activities going on around here.'

'It's clear you've kept your keen investigative sense.'

'There wasn't a free room in an abattoir you could rent?'

'No one would think to look for me here.'

The moaning from the other room increased in volume. 'I wonder why?'

Guiscard closed the folder he was looking at and gestured for me to sit. 'I'm afraid there isn't another chair – you're welcome to a spot on the bed.'

'I'll stand, if it's all the same.'

'Suit yourself,' he said. 'I hadn't expected to see you again so soon. Fast progress, then?'

'In fact, no – the situation with the Steps is more or less at a standstill.'

'Just fancied a stroll?'

'I guess I was wondering what the anus of the world looked like.' I inspected the environs studiously. 'I thought it would be cleaner.'

'I'm surprised to find you so squeamish.'

'Feather pillows and silver plates, that's how I roll.' The moaning rose suddenly, and I had to match it to make myself heard. 'I had an interesting visit from an old friend yesterday,' I nearly yelled.

'Did you?'

'Perhaps "friend" is the wrong way to phrase it. Nemesis would be more accurate, though I think it gives the man too much credit. I'll settle on a homicidal ape with a Crown's Eye and a fervor to see me a corpse.'

'You're talking about Crowley?'

'I hope that description doesn't apply to anyone else you know.' Though I was fairly certain it did. 'He seemed quite knowledge-able about the range of activities you've engaged me in.'

'I didn't tell him anything.'

'Well someone seems to have, cause he's pretty well in the loop.'

'The loop right now consists of you, me, and the Old Man. I

haven't broached the subject, and as far as the chief goes . . .
he's not exactly the loquacious type.'

Guiscard didn't have any reason to lie to me that I could think
of. I thought harder.

'What did he say to you?'

'Suffice to say the effect was unfriendly.'

'You did cut him up pretty good.'

'Did I? I'd completely forgotten.'

'I'd advise you not to underestimate the man – just because
he came off second best during your last encounter isn't a reason
to forgo worrying about the next one.'

'I don't need to worry about him. You're going to worry about
him for me. It's bad business to let your people get murdered by
your own side.'

Guiscard ran a hand over his scalp. 'He might be a problem.'

'I know he's a problem. You're the answer, that's why I'm here
yelling at you.'

'I mean he might be a problem for me. Things at Black House
are . . . loose right now.'

'What the hell does that mean?'

'It means that an order from me might not be one that Agent
Crowley chooses to obey.'

'Are you the Old Man's number two or not?'

'I am.'

'Then you should be able to bring his number three to heel.'

'I'll talk to him.'

'That's not good enough – not near good enough. You'll put
him in line, or you'll put him in the ground. The second would
be wiser – and more certain.'

'He seems to really hate you.'

'We go back a ways.'

'I mean that he might hate you more than he fears the Old
Man.'

That was a disturbing thought. 'Then it's up to you to remind
him of what a frightening character he works for.'

'I'll have the Old Man speak to him. It might do some good.'

'If overwhelming concern for my well-being isn't enough motivation, bear in mind I can't very well keep tabs on the Sons of Śakra with the ice dogging my every step.' I rolled and lit a cigarette, hoping the tobacco might do something to block out the odor. It didn't. I'd have been better off using my match on the bedding. 'This is a shitty safe house.'

'Thank you.'

'All the resources you've got, we couldn't meet in the back of a nice coffee shop?'

'I'll try and arrange more comfortable surroundings next time.'

'Or I could just swing by Black House. I'm all for secrecy, but at the rate we're going I'm worried our next meeting will be in the side corner of a cesspool.'

'I told you – so long as you're bait for the Sons, we're not going to risk them knowing we're running you.'

'The fanatics don't have a plant on me. Besides, I learned to drop a tail when you were still sniffing your sister's panties.'

'What does it matter where we have our conversation?'

'It matters if all the secrecy is because you can't trust your own people.' It was a shot in the dark, I was as shocked by his reaction as he was at my guess. 'Śakra's cock, that's it – the Sons have people in Black House.'

'The Sons have people everywhere,' he said quietly.

It was a sign of how much that shook me that the bed briefly seemed a comfortable spot to regain my equilibrium. 'You shouldn't have told me that.'

'You figured it out yourself.'

'I didn't need it confirmed. How the hell did the Old Man let that happen?'

'We think they inserted some of their people into the Academy, years back. They've been playing the long game, and playing it for a while now. The slots are mostly filled by nominations at this point, favors for people's kids. The Steps count a lot of nobles in their ranks.'

'Nepotism bears bitter fruit. What are you going to do about it?'

'We're running background checks on everybody,' he gestured at the stack of papers on the desk and grimaced. 'Everybody. It's slow going – we don't know who to trust to figure out who we can't trust.'

'How many rats you got in the house?'

'We're not sure – Egmont has two men that he knows we know about, and one we think he doesn't. What's your take on the Director of Security?'

'Ten minutes ago I would have told you he's out of his depth, but you guys don't seem to be swimming so well yourselves.' I was shocked to find there was some part of me that still associated with Black House enough to be horrified at the thought of it falling into such a state. 'When I worked the shop, we tried to keep a pretty firm monopoly on the gathering of internal intelligence.'

'They had outside help – funding, training.'

'From?'

'The Nestrians. They're pretty pissed about our dialing down tensions with the Dren, and they know the Sons are strongly opposed to anything that smacks of rapprochement. A regime change would be in everyone's interest.'

'Probably not everyone.' I didn't want to go any further in this direction. Guiscard, predictably, was happy to drag me.

'In fact, our source says they've gone ahead and sent along an adviser. The top of her craft. Something of a legend, I'm told, on their side of the pond. It's a bit rich, you griping over our failures, when yours was the most celebrated leak in the history of the office.'

'No point in being second best at anything.'

'Don't worry, we still keep the extent of the disaster under close wraps. There aren't five men in all of Black House that know the truth of the matter. Even the Old Man was surprisingly coy about it. In fact, if I didn't know him any better, I'd be inclined to think he found the whole situation regretful.'

'The wolf regrets your death while gnawing on your shinbone.'

'That was why I qualified it.' Guiscard was pretty openly smirking now. In his smile I could see the man he'd been a half decade before, the man I'd disliked to the point of violence. 'She must have been something extraordinary, to have played you with such facility. I mean that quite sincerely – I have the utmost regard for your talent.'

'How kind.'

'They say she was very beautiful.'

I ground my cigarette into the floor. The Firstborn knew it wouldn't make the place any worse. 'It would be very much a mistake, Guiscard, if you were to imagine that our business association offers you any personal liberties. It might be the sort of mistake that ends with you getting your throat cut, bleeding out in a copper-an-hour whorehouse with cum on the carpet.'

'I can't imagine you'd do something so contrary to your own interests.'

'It would be an even worse mistake to overrate my sense of self-preservation.'

Guiscard bore the threat stoically. The moaning had stopped, replaced with the steady pounding of what I assumed was the next-door bed against our adjoining wall. The house was typical slum construction, the barrier between us and the happy couple about the width of a fingernail. It didn't seem out of the realm of possibility that our overactive neighbor's exertions might bring the whole place tumbling down. I decided the time had come to end our conversation, rather than face such a humiliating obituary. 'Figure out your leak and plug it. I'd thought the Sons little more than amateurs, but at the moment they seem to be very much ahead of both of us.'

Guiscard didn't say anything on the way out. The proprietress had collapsed on a couch in the main room, staring at the wall as if somewhere in the warped wood was the secret of existence. I considered joining her, but decided against it. A man can only stand so much unvarnished truth, and I less than most.

25

'So you see, my young friend, she's played you.'

We were in the Old Man's office, me, Crowley and the chief. The Old Man's office is small even by the standards of Black House, famously so. That was part of the mystique, that he made the world run from a space the size of a noble's shoe closet. It was cramped with the three of us – the Old Man and I at opposite ends of the desk, Crowley's squat bulk wedged behind me. He didn't need to be there, had little enough to add – it was an object lesson in humiliation, knocking me down a peg. All the way to the bottom, in fact.

In front of me sat a folder containing the confessions of a handful of low- and mid-level Nestrian spies, stringers and feeders. I hadn't had time to read it through in detail, but scanning them seemed to suggest that what the Old Man had said was true. As astonishing as it was to admit it, Crowley had been right. The Nestrians did have a man on the inside, a deep plant scanning the innermost secrets of Black House. Her name was Albertine, and we'd been fucking for nine months.

I'm not usually one at a loss for words, but try as I might, nothing came. I pulled out the makings of a cigarette and got to making them. You weren't allowed to smoke in the Old Man's office, but I figured a little tobacco wouldn't get me in any deeper than I already was. The Old Man didn't call me on it, which was out of character verging on shocking. If nothing else, he was a stickler for the rules.

'Pretty quiet now, ain't you? Not so clever, all of a sudden?' Crowley was enjoying this inordinately, seeing me in agony.

The Old Man was a distinct contrast to his subordinate. He was not a sadist *per se* – the pain of others was a byproduct of his drive to maintain power, not a goal in and of itself. He watched both Crowley's glee and my own sudden misery with that sense of detachment which was his defining quality. Both emotions were a bit too potent for his refined tastes. He cleared his throat and continued.

'Initially we were quite concerned that perhaps the fair Ms Arden had co-opted your loyalty, that you were an active participant in her plot. That will, incidentally, explain the condition of your apartment, which I'm afraid suffered some . . . damage, during the search.'

'I might have taken a shit in your bath,' Crowley said, the height of wit as always.

Crassness was something the boss could not abide, and Crowley's love of it was one of the many things that would keep him from ever rising above enforcer, albeit of the first rank. 'Agent,' the Old Man said stiffly, 'your good work is much appreciated, and would best be continued in your own office.'

Crowley was so caught up in riding me that it took him a moment to recognize this as a dismissal. His face fell, and he shot the chief a pleading look, like a child hungry for more dessert. A wasted effort – the Old Man was not one to be swayed by sentiment. Crowley moved to the exit, pausing to blow me an air kiss before closing the door behind him.

'An occasionally unpleasant individual,' the Old Man said, 'though he has his uses. As I was saying – initially there was some concern about your loyalty to the Throne, but our investigation revealed no evidence to that effect. Moreover, I put some . . . mild stock into my ability to read people – it's clear from your reaction today that your involvement was . . . unintentional. I believe the correct word would be, dupe?'

Dupe. Mark. Fool. There were different ways to put it.

'Clearly this . . . Albertine is a cagey operator. In particular, our work with Coronet seems to be of common knowledge to our competitors across the bay.'

I didn't bring my work up in casual conversation, and certainly had never discussed any of the details of our operations with Albertine. It would have been the furthest thing from my mind – when I was with her, the point of being with her, was that I didn't think about work. I did, however, often bring files back to my home office, left them there overnight, sometimes longer. I had a small safe built into one of the floorboards, kept a coffee table on top of it. I had imagined I was being very careful.

'Still, if there's one thing I've learned in my time in this business, it's that there is no misfortune that cannot be turned into an opportunity. Your Ms Arden would be a . . . treasure trove of information, I'm quite sure. Will be, once we have her in our safekeeping.'

No doubt. Didn't matter how tough a person was, no one stays quiet, not forever. A few hours, a day or two for the very strong. But the Questioners were skilled in what they did, had far more practice inflicting pain than anyone had in suffering it.

'This is where you come in, my boy.'

It took me a while to realize that this required a response. 'What?'

'We have to be careful not to spook her – no doubt she's prepared a side exit for herself, and of course, if she had to she could take shelter at the Nestrian consulate. What's required here is a light touch – the assistance of someone close to her. Your assistance, in fact.'

I knew on some level that I ought to be listening to him very carefully, for the sake of my own immediate future. I was not listening to him, however, or at best only distantly.

'You have made a terrible mistake, my young friend. A terrible mistake. But there is still the possibility for redemption, to in some way salvage what you have bungled. Crowley was . . . forceful in obtaining some of the confessions you've just read. I imagine we have about a half day before Ms Arden discovers her contacts have gone quiet. In that time, you will ensure she is delivered into our care. I leave it to you to determine the specifics.'

There were other ways to do it, ways that didn't involve me. Detailing a squad of men to grab her when she walked out from work would have been easier and more certain. No sadist, as I said, but still. Transgression required punishment.

He got up to leave. 'Take a few minutes,' he said. 'Calm yourself down, and figure out how you're going to make this situation right.' He draped his coat over his arm, and took his hat off a hook next to his chair. Then he hesitated – I remember it very distinctly because the Old Man didn't hesitate, never balked or stuttered. He moved through life as if his path had been marked out by the Firstborn himself.

'It'll be fine, my boy – you'll do it, and it'll be done. And when it's done you'll understand, like I do. You'll understand how . . . small a thing, are these affairs of the heart. You'll understand what it is that really matters. What really matters.' He opened his mouth as if to say more, but seemed to think better about it. He put his face back on, nodded and stepped out of the room.

Looking back, I think it was the only time I ever saw any evidence the Old Man and I were members of the same species.

I'd rolled another cigarette before realizing the first still smoldered between my teeth. That seemed as good a sign as any that it was time to leave. The agent at the front desk gave me a respectful greeting. It would be the last time he'd have any reason to try and curry favor with me, though of course he didn't know that at the time.

The walk seemed to take place in between thoughts, one moment I was outside Black House and the next I was in front of my building. I owned a two-story row house in one of the nicer neighborhoods in the Old City, a few blocks from the Palace gardens. It had cost something, but then I'd had it to spend.

As promised, it had been quite thoroughly wrecked. I made my way down a hallway littered with refuse and overturned furniture, up a stairwell with a broken bannister and into my bedroom. Inside, the shelves had been torn apart, books and knick-knacks scattered across the floor. Some portion of the ruin could be justified as part of a vigorous search, but most of it I chalked up to Crowley's attempts at revenge. Though given what else I was going through it was hard to imagine what effect he hoped to produce by breaking my armoire into kindling.

In fact, I was surprised at how little I was affected by the destruction of virtually the entirety of my possessions. I'd read the books already, and everything else was just shit to fill space in a house I was unlikely to be holding onto much longer. It turned out I could not count materialism amongst my vices. Megalomania, viciousness and blindness, however, I had in spades.

I sat down on the bed we'd slept in the night before. I could smell her in the sheets, and the throw pillows she'd insisted I purchase though they seemed to be utterly without purpose. My cigarette was doing nothing to cut her scent. I ashed onto the quilt in absent-minded bitterness.

Fragments of the last nine months ran through my mind, scraps of memory banging at the door. I was finding it very hard to breathe, though that didn't stop me chain smoking with a determined single-mindedness, as if to fill the sudden hole I'd discovered had taken over the bottom half of my torso. It was more than humiliation at the discovery I'd been so easily deceived, that I'd been used without scruple. It was as if some fundamental underpinning of existence had been upended. Like I'd woken up to discover that fire had ceased to burn, ice to chill.

Snap out of it, you can wallow after you take care of the

situation at hand. Emotion is a luxury, not to be rashly indulged. Now wasn't the time for the past – I needed to deliver Albertine into the Old Man's clutches in the next few hours, or say goodbye to everything I'd built, and my skin along with it.

She worked at one of the Nestrian trading houses, oversaw a fleet of merchant ships plying the channel. No, I reminded myself, in fact she did not work at one of the Nestrian trading houses, did not oversee a fleet of merchant ships plying the channel – she worked as the chief of Nestria's intelligence service here in Rigus. Also, her name was almost certainly not Albertine. Also, she had never loved me.

This woman who was not named Albertine and who had never loved me nonetheless kept a tight cover at one of the Nestrian trading houses, and as part of that cover she'd still be at the office for another hour. Or perhaps she wouldn't, perhaps the times I'd met her at work had been nothing but an elaborate put on. Perhaps she stopped off in the morning and filtered out at night, and in between was running an identical scam on a half dozen other men as foolish as me, bankers and parliamentarians, merchants and naval officers.

I realized I'd crushed my cigarette between my fingers. I tossed it away and rolled another.

I'd picked her up at her office before, she'd still be there unless something had happened to tip her. If it had then she was long out of the country and I was dead in the water, so it was best to assume she hadn't. We were supposed to meet after work at a little Nestrian joint near the house. Our favorite, in fact, family-run, the owner from the same province Albertine had been born in. Said she'd been born in. They'd chatter away in their native tongue, and I'd listen to the rhythm and watch her blue eyes in the candlelight.

That didn't matter, stop thinking like that. Best to keep our appointment, lead her out the door and into the waiting arms of the ice. She wouldn't suspect anything – no doubt she'd begun her work with the utmost care, vigilant for any hint that her cover had been penetrated. But no one stays like that forever, after nearly a year of wrapping me around her pinkie she'd have dropped her guard. It would be easy.

The closet had been ransacked, a line of my suits thrown onto the floor. I'd given her a shelf a few months back – we'd laughed about it, like it had meant something. They'd tipped those over as well, black lace panties pushed into the carpet. The thought of Crowley's animals running through her underthings made me want to hit someone.

If for some reason I didn't meet Albertine for dinner, of course, she would be spooked. No matter how complacent she'd grown, still my absence would be enough to at least get her thinking. She'd stop by my house next, I'd given her a set of keys six months back, longer maybe, almost as soon as I'd met her. A peek in the window would reveal the devastation, and from there she'd be off.

So I needed to meet her for dinner.

They would be cruel to her in Black House. The questioners were cruel men. The thought of Albertine at their mercy, of Crowley laughing and watching over it all – I felt my stomach seize, swallowed the urge to spill my lunch onto the carpet.

But what was there to do? I'd get the same if I didn't offer her up. My conduct amounted to the most extreme negligence, and in a position as important as mine failure was tantamount to treason.

And why did I care what happened to her? There wasn't anything between us, it was a con. I'd allowed myself to buy into it but the truth was clear now. I ought to have been grateful to the Old Man. He'd be doing me a favor.

The Old Man was right. I thought about that for a while. What that meant, if the Old Man was right.

They found me about six hours later, passed out beneath the table of a Low Town dive bar. I woke up in a cell beneath Black House from a bucket of cold toilet water, and Crowley was very quick to take advantage of my sudden reversal. The next few days were . . . long.

But the Old Man hated me too much to kill me. After it was

over, after they'd beaten me raw and shattered my Eye, they dumped me into an alley and left me to it. I'd planned on being dead by that point, and had struggled to figure out what to do upon discovering I'd been granted a reprieve. I guess I've been struggling ever since.

26

My second visit to the Gitts' domain was a good deal less enjoyable than the first, and I'd taken no particular joy in that one. Sipping my morning coffee and looking out the window, it was clear we'd see rain – but I had hoped it might hold off until my return. What's there to say? I'm city-bred. I can tell which end of Low Town I'm in by the stray graffiti on the walls, know how to get from Brennock to Estroun without using a main road and can cuss a fellow out in six separate languages, but my weather sense is for shit.

I hadn't left sight of the walls before the clouds decided to empty themselves. The roads, far from excellent under the best of circumstances, quickly became practically impassable. After a half mile of trudging through mud the likes of which I hadn't seen since I'd left the trenches, I gave up and flagged the next wagon that went by, slipped the driver an argent to let me ride beside him. It was something resembling robbery, but I was happy to pay it.

Not even the offer of another silver, however, was sufficient to convince him to take me to the Gitts' doorway, such was their reputation for petty vandalism and unwarranted violence. I had to hoof it the last quarter mile, up the winding track, cursing the mire which had coated my boots and the lower third of my pants.

Calum's pigs were loving it, however, rooting about loudly enough to drown out the falling rain. Our reaction to mud is one of the few differences between our two species – though looking at the handful of Gitts' children sitting on the uncovered stoop, pale flesh and black grime, it was hard to grant even that distinction.

'Is your father-uncle-cousin in?' I asked the eldest.

He crinkled up his face in confusion. 'What?'

'Nevermind,' I said, stepping through the knot of unwashed bodies.

Boyd sat on the couch inside – sat suggests more effort than he was putting forth. Draped would be more accurate. His eyes were open but they didn't see anything, and his breathing had that even, rhythmic quality that generally accompanies sleep. A long-handled wyrm pipe sat on the table, and explained its owner's condition. I was debating the wisdom of trying to wake him when Cari came in from one of the side quarters and saved me the trouble.

'Boyd!' she screamed. 'We got company!'

This was enough to bring the man awake, though it was another twenty seconds before he managed to fix his eyes on me in a way that betrayed recognition. I'd have to wait around a hell of a lot longer if I hoped for anything resembling intelligence.

'Hey, Warden,' he said finally. 'We ain't been expecting you.'

I hoped if he had, he wouldn't have smoked himself into a coma to celebrate my arrival. 'Don't trouble yourself to stand, Boyd,' I said, though he had done nothing to worry me on that account. 'I'm just here to have a few words with Calum.'

'He's around,' Cari said warily. 'I'm sure he'll be in eventually. You can tell me what you need to in the meantime.'

I didn't say anything to that, but my eyes registered disapproval. There was no reason to outright explain to Cari that she was no more running this ship than I am the back side of the moon. But nor was I going to waste my time discussing the situation twice. 'I'll wait.'

Cari dropped down beside Boyd. Hers was an ample posterior – I feared for the structural integrity of the sofa. It held, but barely.

Time passed. I got the impression I was not so welcome as I had been last time. Boyd at least forewent promising future sexual liaisons with members of his immediate family. For her part, Cari went at her wyrm pipe for the better part of ten minutes without offering a puff. I was insulted – really hurt.

Calum arrived finally, filtering in from a side room. Artair followed in his wake. The bulge of his esophagus had not shrunk since last we'd spoken.

'Hello, Calum,' I said.

'Howdy.' This time he didn't offer me his hand.

'I'm sorry to drop in uninvited like this – I figured it would be better if we spoke sooner, rather than later.'

'You always welcome out here,' Boyd hiccuped from his perch on the coach. 'Y'all know that.'

Calum didn't bother to agree. 'It's a long walk,' he said.

'Ain't short.'

'And in the rain at that.'

'Is it raining?'

'I don't suppose this is a casual visit.'

'I'm not a casual person,' I said.

Calum nodded. 'Me neither.'

There had been another couple of chairs when last I'd visited, but they were gone now, broken up for kindling or for the simple joy that accompanies destruction. Except for Calum's rocking chair, of course, which sat untouched in the corner. Even the Gitts' renowned sense of recklessness wasn't enough to do any damage to the throne. Calum worked himself into it with a barely audible sigh. Artair dropped down onto the ground, apparently unconcerned that he now rested in the grime tracked in from outside. He took a wavy, wide-bladed knife from his waist-band and started gouging flecks out of the floorboards with an enthusiasm that seemed to indicate personal enmity.

'You here to talk about Kitterin Mayfair?' Calum asked.

'I'm here to talk about what he means.'

'He means the black robes know we ain't gonna bend over and take it,' Artair said.

'Last time I warn you to be quiet,' Calum responded promptly, though with seeming dispassion.

'And yet he isn't altogether wrong. Mayfair's unfortunate fate, not to mention the wreckage you made of Uriel's gambling house, has indeed caused something of a furor out near the Enclave.'

'Some days,' Calum said slowly, 'I find you really tiring.'

'Imagine how I feel.'

'I don't see what the big fucking problem is,' Artair said, still picking away at his home. 'The Asher are flesh and blood, they die the same as anyone.'

Calum wasn't exactly a quick man, and he had to get up from his chair to throw the punch. So Artair could see the blow coming, even managed to let go the knife and raise his hands in a rough defensive posture. It didn't do a copper worth of good of course. He could have had a week to prepare, built a barricade and covered it with wire, and it wouldn't have mattered. Calum's fist busted the right side of the boy's face, sent him sprawling into the center of the room.

Cari and Boyd looked in opposite directions. It wasn't the first time one Gitt had slugged another. If Calum decided to go further, break the little runt's head into the ground with a few treads of his boots, they might speak up. Or not. It wouldn't have been the first time one Gitt had killed another, either.

'I warned you once – you keep your fucking mouth shut when grown folks are speaking,' Calum said. 'All you want to do is talk and talk and fucking talk, show everybody what a big man you is. If you wasn't my sister's boy I'd put you in the ground myself, dig the hole and dump dirt on you while you was still wriggling.'

Artair groaned something that could have been taken as an

apology. After a moment he spat a tooth straight up into the air, like a fountain. I suppose that could have been taken as an apology also.

Though his nephew had been the subject of the lesson, I wasn't so slow as to miss who it had really been aimed at. Calum was breathing like he'd run a marathon, his sunken passivity washed away in a tide of fury. He seemed to realize how far gone he was, blinked twice and forced himself back into his chair. Almost reflexively his hands went about cutting a hunk of chew, but his eyes were still wild, and I decided to wait for him to start.

'I hate the taste of pork,' he said finally, after he'd worked his way through half the plug. 'Did you know that?'

'I did not.'

'Can't abide it. Makes me sick. So why do you think I keep hogs?'

'I look forward to finding out.'

'Cause they eat anything you put in front of them.'

'I've heard rumors to that effect.'

'Ate Kiren, back in the third syndicate war. Ate Islander and Valaan. I imagine, it comes to it, they'll eat Asher just as easy.' He spat onto the floor, near enough to Artair to splatter his supine body. 'This been Gitts territory since my daddy's grandaddy came up from Kinterre. I'll be damned if some trumped up black robe is gonna take it out from under me.'

Like I said before – we are what we are, no point in hiding it. Calum was bigger than his people, stronger and smarter. But blood tells, you wait long enough – and Calum was a Gitt down to the white of his bones.

'I wasn't operating under the impression you made your money through livestock – but there's still time to see this end without any more violence. Uriel says this whole thing is a misunderstanding. Wants a sit down, wants to clear things up.'

'All due respect, Warden. I think we're past conversating.'

'Don't let the fact that they haven't responded to Mayfair lull you. These are not soft men.'

'I'm not underestimating Uriel,' Calum said. 'It's cause he's dangerous that he's got to be taken care of now, while it's just him and his brother and a handful of others. In a year they'll have enough men on the rolls to swamp us outright – with what they must be making selling that fever, they could hire half the Enclave. I don't step into this lightly – I didn't go after Uriel because I'm hell bent on puffing out my chest, like my idiot nephew.' He nodded towards the boy on the floor. Artair hadn't moved in a while. Either he was sleeping or he was on his last sleep. No one else seemed concerned about it. I wasn't particularly concerned about it either, if we were being honest. 'I did it because if we don't fix the Unredeemed now, they'll swallow us outright in eighteen months.'

Calum was not wrong. Uriel was only getting stronger. It made sense to step on them now, before they swelled their ranks. But it didn't make sense for me, so I kept on talking. 'You think about the war much, Calum?'

'I try not to.'

'A wise policy. Still, there are lessons to be learned, unpleasant though they may be to remember. Were you at Anquirq?'

'Yeah.'

'So was I – we held a stretch of trench next to a company of Asher. Three long months, until the Dren rolled us back.'

'I remember.'

'I say us, but of course, I don't include the Asher when I speak of our retreat. I was one of the last there – too stupid to get moving, I guess. You know how certain moments are clear as day, no matter how long ago they happened? You can bring them up in your eye, like you was staring at a portrait.'

'Sure.'

'That's one for me, one burned into the back of my head good and permanent. Cause the Asher didn't run, Calum. Not while the trenches around them were emptying of soldiers like worms after the rain. Just stood there, still as statues, swords unsheathed, identical rows waiting for the slaughter. When we retook that segment we found a thousand rotting Asher corpses. You know what else we found?'

I waited a while for him to answer. When he didn't I continued ahead anyway.

'Dren. We found a hell of a lot more Dren than we did Asher, Calum. You think on that, when you eat dinner tonight. You look around at your family, and you think about how many are going be sitting there in a month, if you go to war with Uriel and his people.'

Calum cut out a plug of tobacco big as a child's heart and set it into one corner of his mouth, chewing over it slowly. For once Cari and Boyd had the good sense to keep quiet. Artair kept quiet too, though he had less choice in the matter. 'Where'd we be sitting down at?'

'My turf. I'll handle security, make sure things stay square. There's still time for an amicable resolution – nothing that's gone down between the two of you can't yet be squashed.'

He nodded slowly, acknowledging my words but not agreeing with them. 'I got no interest in blood for blood's sake,' he said finally. 'If this can be cleared up without making bodies, I'm all for that. But if it can't . . .' He spat a stream of juice out onto the floor. 'Them hogs is always hungry.'

27

'The Director is very concerned. He needs to know what progress you've been making. It's important you get your hands on something concrete, as soon as possible.'

Brother Hume and I were huddled together in a back booth at Edgar's, which was a shitty little diner in Offbend. The coffee was cold and the pie was stale, our waitress looked a few years shy of her centennial and someone had ashed a cigarette into the bowl of stew I'd ordered. For years I'd been trying to figure out what Edgar's was a front for, if they were moving choke out the back or if it was a tax dodge for one of the syndicates. Eventually I'd come to realize that it was just, in fact, a shitty little diner, and the incompetence and hostility of the help not cover for anything. By that point I'd grown sort of attached to the place, and I patronized it more than it warranted, particularly when I was with people I didn't much care for.

Not that Hume gave any signs of being unhappy with the

quality of the fare. He'd consumed the greater portion of the mutton sandwich he'd ordered, though our conversation had lasted all of about five minutes. A piece of wilted lettuce rested unnoticed on the lapel of his shirt, would remain there in all likelihood until the next time he changed clothes. At least the faded greenery wasn't staining the dark brown robes he normally wore – he'd taken my earlier admonishment to heart. It had been wise counsel, though almost everything else I'd been telling him was sheerest bullshit.

'As soon as possible.' I shook my head back and forth in slow bewilderment. 'Does the Director imagine my task an easy one, Simeon? Does he think it's just a question of strolling into Black House, knocking on the Old Man's door and asking him to reveal state secrets?'

'I'm . . . I'm sure the Director doesn't think that.'

'I've got heat on me like you wouldn't believe. Half the city is trying to kill me, and I'm getting chewed out because I'm not moving fast enough?'

'You're not getting chewed out,' Hume was quick to tell me. 'The Director is impressed with your work. We all are,' he added. 'He just wants to make sure that you're proceeding with reasonable haste.'

'Haste and carelessness go hand in hand. This isn't a game we're playing.'

He nodded solemnly. He'd remembered that much from our last go round.

The one big unknown in this whole situation was what exactly the Sons thought they were getting out of me – this Coronet thing stank to high heaven, and I didn't buy Hume as anything other than a convenient dupe. I needed to get another crack at Egmont, and to do that I needed to work Simeon into a tizzy sufficient for him to kick me further up the line. I was considering how to stir the pot further when I saw Crowley peering in through the windows which took up most of Edgar's front wall.

My first reaction was shock, and something in the direction of distress. But that faded quickly – nothing ever goes the way you think it will. You've gotta be ready for unexpected eventualities, and willing to roll with them. And in fact, following on the heels of surprise, so closely they're almost intertwined, is excitement. Opportunity is the flip side of disaster. Crowley might be just the thing I needed to convince Simeon of the seriousness of our situation.

I played off my initial instinct, let my jaw drop, my face go pale. Even Hume, no great observer of the human condition, managed to figure out that this didn't indicate anything positive. He dropped the remains of his sandwich onto his plate, and contorted his neck in the direction that I was looking. I grabbed his lapel and jerked him back to face me.

'Stand up, follow me out the back, and don't say a fucking word,' I said, with all the gravity I could muster.

'But—'

I cut him off. 'Not a fucking word.'

He'd swallowed the hook deep enough at this point not to argue, though he looked far from happy. I deliberately stumbled over my chair as I stood. It gave Crowley an extra second to identify me, and he took it. I watched his grin widen, heard him shout something I couldn't make out, threats or directions to whomever he'd brought with him. Filtered through the glass he seemed more than usually monstrous, his mouth oversized and distorted, strange flickers of color mottling his face.

The alley outside was cluttered with refuse from the restaurant, half-eaten scraps and the rats that feasted on them. It was not an environment which encouraged discussion, which was all to the good as we were in quite a hurry.

'That's Agent Crowley,' I said after we'd reached the main thoroughfare, answering the question Hume had been repeating non-stop since I'd pulled him out of his chair. 'The Old Man's bulldog, maybe the most dangerous man in the Empire. He can follow a salmon upriver, track a gray wolf across a hundred miles of snow-covered tundra.' I'd never seen the tundra, nor a wolf, nor did I think that Crowley could actually do any of these things. But the spirit was moving through me, and Hume didn't object to the pastoral imagery. 'If he's on our tail, we must really be on to some-thing serious.'

'Where are we going?'

'Somewhere that Agent Crowley isn't,' I said, stepping up the pace.

'I've never run from anyone in my life,' Hume said, indignant but still moving.

'Then this should be very exciting for you.'

The streets were quiet – the portion of the population making their living honestly were still engaged in doing so, while the portion of the population making their living stealing off the first generally don't shake out of their holes till nightfall. It was easy for Crowley to follow us given the lack of cover, and easy for us to make him out, him and a handful of boys moving at a brisk pace a short ways back. Every so often I'd make a quick detour, but always within sight of our pursuers. Despite what I'd told Hume, Crowley's play had actually been surpris-ingly weak. He'd blown the trap early, hadn't even been sharp enough to station anyone outside the restaurant. I figured I could lose him, even with Simeon in tow. But it was important to give Brother Hume a good scare, let him see who we were playing with, hope he'd pass it to his bosses.

After a few blocks I came up with what I figured was a pretty good means of satisfying both of these requirements, wearing away at Hume's nerves while giving Crowley something to occupy his time, and I broke north through an alleyway, Hume close on my heels.

In the square outside of the Enclave the full body of the Asher had congregated, perhaps ten thousand strong, a sea of black robes and unsmiling faces. The men were short, stocky and vicious looking. The women were dowdy, dark-haired and dark-eyed, not pretty and not trying to look so. Scrupulous attention to hygiene is not a characteristic of the Asher – it displays an attachment to the physical which is frowned on by their god. Most things are frowned on by their god, as far as I was able to tell.

'Heathens,' Hume muttered behind me. I turned and cut him

short with a quick chop of my hand. The Steps were not popular amongst the Asher – contradicting fanaticisms tend not to mix well. And while Simeon's fervor for the Seven daevas might incline him towards being beaten to death by a mob of black robes, my own sense of piety didn't extend nearly so far. Outsiders in general were not welcome near the Enclave, not that day of all days.

Because today was the Eve of the Anamnesis, the highest holiday on the Asher calendar – something like our Midwinter, though the two have about as much in common as a handjob has to a swift kick to the balls. At the end of each autumn, as the last gasp of color gives way to the grim emptiness of winter, the Asher gather to pay homage to god in their own curious fashion.

'What is all this?' Hume asked, no keen student of comparative religion.

'This is the day the Asher commemorate their damnation,' I said, 'and resign themselves to its continuation.'

Philosophers and poets break themselves against an implacable truth – existence is bitter and uncompromisingly cruel, and no entity responsible for its creation and upkeep could be called decent. That it is, in short, impossible to imagine a divinity who is at once absolutely powerful and absolutely good.

The Asher have a simple explanation to this thorny problem. Their god does not love them, quite the contrary. The pain and bitterness of human life, their own suffering in particular, is not a flaw in the system – it is the very purpose of it. Life is not a gift, it's a punishment. Their affinity, one might even say affection, for physical violence is a direct consequence of this belief. A sharp death, dearly bought, was an Asher man's sole shot at evening up accounts with the almighty. The female equivalent, I am told, is death in childbirth.

It had a certain something to it, I had to admit. Logical, at the very least. Of course, the Asher do not accept converts – not that there's any great swell of folk looking to join – so I never had opportunity to explore the particulars in detail. Also, black is not my color.

241

I cut through the crowd as best as I was able, making sure Hume was close behind. Wouldn't do to have him fall back and be caught by Crowley. The Asher made no particular effort to assist our passage, standing in tightly packed ranks, scowling when they bothered to notice us at all. That was fine – any trouble they gave us I figured would go double for our pursuers. At first it was impossible to make out the centerpiece of the event, but as we muscled our way towards the far end of the square I got a better look at what exactly everyone else was staring at.

A line of Asher children, seven or eight years of age and not yet wearing the traditional black frocks, stood in solemn procession before a bonfire. The girls carried a range of toys: dolls, wooden carts, the occasional book. The boys held almost exclusively practice weapons: mock swords, ash spears.

At the front, nearest to the flames, stood two of their holy men, white-bearded and shirtless, well-muscled despite being past middle age. The first, older and with wilder eyes, held a book open in his hands, a fat black tome that looked primordially ancient. The other carried aloft a naked blade, the glittering sickle-swords that are the inheritance of the Asher race.

Without warning the elder began speaking in a foreign language, the tongue the Asher had taken from their homeland two thousand years prior, before the cataclysm that had made them permanent exiles amongst the Thirteen Lands.

'Once there was a people,' his adjunct repeated in unaccented Rigun, the sword steady.

The first continued his unintelligible chatter.

'A happy people,' the second priest said. 'A proud people. A strong people. A people made so by the blessings of the One Above.'

The assembled children stared fixedly, and unmoving, at the scene in front of them. From a distance they could have been mistaken for intricately wrought stonework. Such attention would have been uncanny in adults. In children I found it little short of disturbing.

'An arrogant people. A foolish people. A people who turned their back on what they had been given.'

The high priest's melody was constant and discordant. He seemed never to pause for breath.

'When the One Above saw what had become of his children, he grew angry, and he spoke: "I will break the back of my children, and I will leave them to crawl in the dust, and to beg for mercy that shall not come, no, not until the moon comes to the sea, and the sun submerges into the last dark."'

The adjunct continued his oration blandly, as if reading a shopping list. His blade remained perfectly still, and his chest was thick with sweat.

'We remind ourselves that we do not deserve the kindnesses we have received. That we are unworthy of the gifts we possess, of the joys we experience.'

The high priest finished his last line, and fell silent.

'Till death redeems us,' his second said.

'Till death redeems us,' the assemblage echoed.

The first child stepped forward. Rare amongst the boys, his gift to the flames was not a fake weapon, but a simple toy boat, brightly painted, a red bow and a purple cloth sail. He ran his fingers over it almost unconsciously, his eyes fixed on the pyre in front of him.

The priest nodded.

The boat went into the flames. It was a small thing, but the fire seemed to surge in response. The child knelt down before the conflagration. 'I ask forgiveness from the One Above.' His voice was high but clear.

'In his name, we refuse it,' the priest said.

The second brought the sword down so swiftly that for a moment I thought the ritual would end with a head rolling into the dust. But the blade halted just short of decapitation, a slight cut on the back of the boy's neck the only evidence of how near he had been to death.

The child nodded and slipped into the crowd. Another took his spot.

He had not flinched, the little boy with the boat. It occurred to me that it would be unwise to bet against Uriel in his coming conflict.

The press of the crowd eased off slightly. I managed to weave my way forward, Hume in tow. The priests continued with their ceremony, destroying the beloved objects of small children.

We stopped at the outskirts of the square. I boosted myself up onto an overturned fruit crate, and scanned the back for our pursuers.

Crowley was easy enough to make out, the only one of the multitude not wearing black. He was flanked by a few of his boys, themselves surrounded by a group of Asher. He was yelling at someone, and that someone was yelling back. He didn't notice me, attention taken up with the fight he was starting. Crowley was very good at starting fights, though not quite so talented at finishing them.

If Crowley was smart he'd back off and try another day, but he wasn't smart and I was pretty sure the afternoon would end with him the victim of a pretty solid beating, and his boys maybe worse. The Asher weren't so foolish as to kill an agent of Black House, but you don't go mucking about in a badger's den and leave unmarked. All the same I dropped off the crate, grabbed Hume by the shoulder and pushed him ahead, the two of us sprinting west towards the Old City.

I kept it up as long as I could, until forty-plus years of bad living caught up with me and I staggered against an alley wall. Hume looked well winded, but little short of that. It does ugly things to a man, seeing the youth with life they haven't earned still full in them. 'I guess we lost him,' he said.

'For how fucking long?' I asked, gasping for air. 'I can't go around dodging the Old Man's heavies indefinitely. The Director wants proof that Black House is behind the red fever? How about the fact that I've got Agents of the Crown trying to kill me just for asking questions about it!'

'I'll set up a meeting with Egmont,' Hume said. 'If they want you this bad, you must really be on to something.'

'Good – do it quick. I've only got but so many tricks in my satchel.' Though you've yet to see half of them.

He nodded, rested his hand on my shoulder for a moment, then bolted off towards the Old City.

I spent a while waiting for my lungs to forgive me. Eventually they decided we were quits, and I rolled a cigarette to spite them.

I imagined Crowley would be too busy licking his wounds to want a rematch, at least for the moment, but all the same I decided the rest of the day was best spent away from the Earl. I headed towards an apartment I keep in Brennock. It was a long walk in the cold, but I didn't mind – really the afternoon had gone better than I could have anticipated. Hume was firmly in my camp, an ally though he didn't realize it. Crowley would want to kill me even more, but this was no great alteration to the *status quo*. Crowley had been trying to wipe me out for almost fifteen years. Another beating wouldn't get him any angrier.

28

It was snowing, that's one of the things clearest in my memory – not the worst winter we'd ever had, but a bad one, a damn bad one. I'd taken to wearing a thick wool coat and a pair of heavy fur gloves over top of the usual ice blue duster. It sort of killed the effect, but it was better than freezing.

Crispin thought the same way, or I supposed he did since he'd taken the same precautions. We didn't see each other much by that point, our partnership had officially ended a few years before, after I'd bumped myself up to Special Operations. He had stayed where he was, chasing after people who'd actually deserved it, rather than just those unfortunates who'd stumbled in the way of the Throne. That he was there that day was coincidence, or fate if you're apt to see things in that fashion. I was apt to see it as coincidence.

We'd been killing time in Black House, drinking bad coffee and waiting for something important to happen when Crowley's messenger had come in. A low-ranking agent, new to the force, pleased as a puppy. His boss had cornered a Miradin spy cell in north Offbend, wanted back-up before he went in. The messenger was too stupid to recognize that my grimace did not signify happiness with this development, but Crispin wasn't. Though foreign affairs was strictly the business of Special Operations, he'd offered to come along and I'd taken him up on it. I'd also grabbed a handful of department heavies, thick mugs waiting around to jump on people, and we'd hauled ass west.

These days that part of Offbend has long become overrun by businessmen and merchants from the Old City, a gentrified enclave of refurbished townhouses and eateries with exposed brick walls. But back then, the burgeoning upper class that now populate it wouldn't have come within a dozen blocks. There was nothing but crumbling tenements and immigrant teenagers sneering at you from the shadows.

The messenger led us to one of these faded multistory apartment buildings, but I could have guessed it was our destination by the half dozen agents surrounding it, and from the dead body that lay in the snow in front of the door, leaking red into the jet white.

There was a tiny restaurant directly across from the scene, and Crowley had requisitioned it in the peremptory fashion which makes law enforcement so beloved by the population they are sworn to serve. He sat at a chair by the window, kept warm by the fire and a strong sense of superiority.

'Who set up the cordon?' I asked by way of greeting.

'I did,' Crowley said happily. He looked exactly the same as he did twenty years later, save the scar of course. He had the same black eyes and the same stupid little smile on his face, like he'd figured out everything worth knowing and further conversation was a waste of his time. 'Caught one of them buying information off a broker I've been watching, followed them back here. Guess I must have spooked them,' he said, grinning like this development was of no consequence.

'Guess so.' I took off my gloves and laid them on the table. 'Whose body was that in the snow?'

'That was the one I tailed. They must have figured he'd sold them out, or maybe they just wanted to show how they dealt with fuck-ups.'

'An admirable policy. A policy worth adopting.'

He didn't know what that meant, but he kept talking anyway. 'They've taken the rest of the building hostage. Say they've got two kegs of black powder stashed in the basement, and they'll blow the whole place to hell if they so much as see a glint of ice blue.'

'They say.'

'But I don't buy it. We go in full force, before they get the chance to entrench any further.' He'd been drinking from a cup of coffee, the mug half empty on the table next to his flipper-hands. It was a heavy thing, ceramic. I picked it up and finished the dregs. His sunken eyes followed me, confused.

I doubt very much it was the hardest blow Crowley had ever sustained, but certainly it was one of the least expected. One minute he was upright in his chair, smug as an eldest son. The next he was on the ground, picking bits of clay out of his hair.

Not that we'd ever been friends, but I imagine this was the moment where Crowley developed his particular dislike of me.

'You stupid fucking dog you,' I said, watching the trickle of blood inch down his scalp. 'You worthless rag-picking monkey.'

Crowley was not the type to allow an injury to go unreturned, but the suddenness of my attack and the fact that I was technically his superior kept him quiet.

'Do you have any idea how long I've been watching this cell? Nine months. Nine months of my time. Nine months coaxing them into the open, nine months inserting people into their operation. I was about to find out who they were reporting to.' I followed up this revelation with a solid kick to his gut. 'Once I flipped him we'd have had a real asset, a straight line back to Miradin.'

Miradin had been our nominal ally since before the Great War, though that didn't stop their intelligence services from operating in our capital any more than it did ours theirs. The critical difference being the people that I had ferreting out information were professionals, hard men and women, sure, but worker bees. Not so the other end. Miradin was a strict theocracy, the Emperor holding the absolute reigns of secular and spiritual power, their Black House equivalent at once a civil and religious authority, arresting pickpockets and holding *auto de fe*'s. One imagined that the larger part of their population held as much truck with the priests as necessary to avoid being burned at the stake, but those involved in the secret service were true fanatics. The Emperor was Śakra's direct representative, every order he gave a command from the Firstborn. Death in his service was the greatest glory imaginable, a bolthole to paradise everlasting. It meant I'd had to be especially cautious when I'd picked up on this cell, moving slowly, never allowing my presence to be noticed. It also meant that Crowley's impetuousness was likely to result in the death of everyone in the building.

'I didn't . . .' he began, stuttering, still on the ground but starting to pick himself up. 'No one told me.'

'No one told you because you didn't need to know, and you didn't need to know because you don't fucking matter. Let me break it down for you, so there's never another mistake – knowing things is my job. Your job is to kill people that I point at.' He was most of the way to his feet, but I hooked him by the ankles and sent him sprawling back to the earth. 'I swear to the Scarred One, Crowley, you forget again and I'm gonna pull you apart with my fucking teeth.'

Back then, before ten hard years of crime and breath, I didn't find myself getting angry so easy, always tried to make sure I kept my temper hanging on its hook. But right at that moment I wanted to beat that ape-looking bastard into the ground, shut him down permanent. He was a nice substitute for my real problem, which was that I didn't see a way out of this without a lot of random folk dead. Images of my heel on Crowley's throat, one short jerk – the Old Man would give me his disapproving look, but that would be as far as it would go. The Old Man didn't shed a lot of tears.

I blinked away thoughts of easy murder, walked back over to the table and pulled on my gloves. There was a shuttered window looking at the Miradin hideout. I undid the latch and peeked through.

'What do you figure?' Crispin asked. He'd remained silent while I'd worked over Crowley.

I sucked my teeth and glanced over the tenement building across the street. 'In this weather they've only got one play. If it was summer they might ask for passage out – we wouldn't give it to them, but at least we could string them along for a while.'

'You think about going to the Mirad ambassador?'

'Even if he knew about them, he'd never admit it – an unfortunate crew of miscreants, of no concern to the Emperor or to the great nation of Miradin.'

'Hostages?'

'They've got them. Probably corralled the rest of the building's unfortunates into the basement somewhere.'

'And the black powder?'

I wasn't sure about that one – the man I'd had inside hadn't ever said anything about it, but he might not have known, or he might have been saving it to sell me special. A keg of black powder was hard to get, no one in the underworld would have been foolish enough to provide it, and even the army made a vague point to see that they didn't fall off the back of any wagons. But they might have smuggled it in from their homeland, a last-ditch defense in case of this exact situation. And if they did have it, it meant they could level the whole building and half the block. 'We have to assume so.'

'What's the plan?'

The plan, the plan. The plan had been to get someone in there that they trusted, have him follow the chain up. They had to have a man this side of the channel, a merchant or ambassador backing their play, the brains of the operation, who would book passage on the first ship back to the old country once he heard about this fiasco. I snapped my head back into the present. 'Negotiation isn't an option – what they want can't be provided this side of the afterlife. We go in hard, and fast, and we don't leave anybody alive.'

'And if they've got black powder?'

'Then we better get to them before they get to it.'

'The plan sounds distinctly similar to Crowley's.'

'Don't think that doesn't gall me. But we aren't exactly full up on options.'

'I'll take care of it,' Crowley interrupted from the floor, blood streaming down his nose.

'I wouldn't trust you to take out the fucking trash,' I said, but not angrily; I'd put my rage aside. He was yesterday's problem, and tomorrow's. Just then I was focused entirely on today's.

'We'll need an edge, if this has a shot in hell of working.'

'Couldn't hurt.'

'One of us will have to buff up, break through a side window. Give the rest a chance to come in through the main entrance.'

'I had a similar line of thinking.'

'I'll do it,' Crispin said.

'It's my operation – my responsibility, my fault for letting things get as far as they did.'

'Now's not really the time for self-pity.'

'There's always time for self-pity.'

'Like you said, it's your operation – you'll need to lead the rest of them through the front, need to be there for clean-up if something goes off.'

He was right. It made more sense for someone else to take point. 'You buffed yourself since the Academy?'

'No,' he said. Crispin wouldn't tell a lie, even when a lie would have been more convenient, more comforting. It was one of the things I liked about him, and, also, very much detested. 'Have you?'

'Twice.'

'Those are two more reasons it should be me.'

I spent a moment trying to find a chink in Crispin's thinking, but there wasn't much time, and it was pretty sound. 'All right,' I said, liking no part of it.

'You and the rest of the squad post up near the entrance. I'll be a minute or two – when you start hearing screams, come in full force.'

'Don't worry about us – you just take care of yourself.'

He nodded and skulked off.

I called him back for one last word. 'Crispin – be careful. It feels good, real good, better than anything. Don't burn yourself out.'

'I'm not exactly a hedonist.'

'That's what worries me – you're unused to succumbing to temptation.'

He gave a nervous smile and disappeared through the door and out into the snow.

The Crown's Eye can do all sorts of extraordinary things. It can compel obedience, breaking a strong man's will into splinters. It can overcome wards and basic runes, rendering magical protection void. And finally, perhaps most impressively, it can supercharge the body, make it capable of feats of speed and strength far beyond that which the human organism was normally capable.

It took months to learn how to do any of that, part of what they drilled into you as a cadet, the instructors rough men, quick to repay failure with abuse. Once you learned you never forgot it, it was too much fun to forget. The best drug you could imagine, better than anything else I'd ever tried, and I'd tried them all. A shot of pixie's breath might make you feel like a god, but the Eye . . . well, the Eye turned you into one.

Like any drug of course, there was a price, one commensurate with the benefits. The Eye was meant to replicate the workings of a practitioner, allow us a tiny fraction of their power. But we weren't practitioners, didn't have their strength to draw on, whatever pool of energy was theirs by birthright. Anything one did with the Eye was fueled by your lifeblood, by the breath in your lungs and the strength of your body. Every second Crispin spent buffed was an hour off his life, a day, maybe a week, there was no way to know exactly. It was why we didn't do it for fun, didn't do it just to cross the street or impress strangers. Didn't do it during the course of a normal operation, even when violence was called for. All but the most callous of agents had some appreciation for what they spent when they used the Eye.

I'd brought three men besides Crispin, serious hitters, near on useless for any actual investigative work but exactly the sort of ogres you wanted carrying your play in a situation like this. I drew my sword with one hand, the mid-sized weapon we all wore, longer than a trench blade, prettier and more versatile. 'Agent Crispin is going to buff up and go through the back – once he's made his presence known, we follow in double quick. They've definitely got hostages, and at this point we have to assume a stash of black powder as well, probably in the basement. When we get inside, I'll go downstairs, the three of you head up to take care of any stragglers. Remember – most of them are just in the wrong place at the wrong time – you leave off of anybody not carrying steel.'

They all nodded, though I wouldn't have given my pension for the lives of any unlucky civilian in there with the fair skin and dark hair common to the Mirad. They drew their weapons to match me. That was as much preparation as we were able to make.

'Keep your heads up,' I said, my last word of pep talk. 'I'll see you on the other side.'

There was a scream from the building, and I nodded at the foremost of my soldiers. He put his foot in the door and followed in after it. He came stumbling back almost as quickly, a bolt in his stomach and a dazed look in his eyes. I thought he was probably not going to live but there wasn't anything to do about it, not until we had the rest of the building clear. I sprinted over his body, praying to Meletus that there weren't two men guarding the doorway. He chose to grant my prayer – the Scarred One has always been kind to me. There's just the one fanatic, working to reload his weapon. Foolish – a bolt-thrower takes a competent man thirty seconds to rewind, and he was far from that – fingers trembling, eyes on me instead of his machine. I flicked the point of my sword through the hollow of his throat and kept on moving. It was a quicker death than he deserved, but it would have to do.

There were two men in the next room, pale and wet-eyed, each holding a curved scimitar, impractical given the size of the interior. They ought to have waited for me to come to them, but they didn't, excited by the prospect of dying nobly. That was the one upside of dealing with fanatics, as opposed to professionals, who tend to have a strong attachment to their own existence, and to take what measures they can to prolong it. The first one followed a feint I made at his chest, and found himself unprepared for the boot I put into his shin. It was supposed to be his knee, but I'm far from perfect, and it ended up against his shin. It worked though, slowed him down long enough for my back-up to take care of him. I bulled past him and into the second one, sending both of us to the ground.

I've met plenty of men better than me with a sword, faster hands and better footwork. But up in close, flesh against flesh, when you can feel the other man's breath on you, when his blood sprays up into your hair and your mouth and your eyes – well, daevas forgive me, that's where I always excelled. I fish-hooked the Mirad with three fingers on my left hand and he started to scream, the sound mutilated by what I was doing to his mouth. I had a knife in my sleeve – I always had a knife in my sleeve back then – and I managed to get it into my hand and saw it across his windpipe.

I brought myself quickly to my feet, grabbed my sword and chanced a look behind. The Mirad was on his last legs, courtesy of the agent following me, bleeding heavily from wounds on his hands and stomach. I didn't bother to give any help – the thought of a keg of black powder somewhere in the basement was imprinted into my head.

They'd prepared the next room for their last stand, a makeshift barricade and the forces to man it. There were three of them, big, vicious fellows, blades out. They had the dream of death in their eyes, like the Asher I'd seen in the war, religious mania raised to the pitch of madness. I had a dagger in one hand and my sword in the other, and I knew they wouldn't be enough. I raised them both anyway – best to go out swinging. Best not to go out, but if you got to, best to go out swinging.

All of a sudden, the backmost one didn't have a head.

At least that was how it looked from my perspective. In one instant, he stood upright, a scimitar in his hands, ready to see me dead and himself just as happily. Then the crux of his corpus was flying through the air, a trail of blood following behind it.

A sudden swirl of movement and the second and third were dead at the same instant. Logic told me that this was false, of course, that there must have been some interlude between the two men collapsing onto the ground, but my eyes were unable to detect it.

I didn't take the time to marvel at the miracle I'd seen – there was an open door behind the corpses leading downstairs, and I sprinted through it, well behind the blur that I assumed was Crispin. He must have been fading out of it, slipping back down into humanity. There were two doors at the bottom of the steps and he took one and I took the other.

It was cramped, dark. There were some things on the floor, bundles I didn't have time to pay attention to – my focus was squarely on the dark-haired man with the curved knife, and with the young girl squealing beneath its edge. His back was turned and I could see him struggling to finish his work, watch the muscles and his shoulder strain against resistance. Either he hadn't heard me or he was too fixed on the slaughter to pay attention, but either way he made no move to defend himself, nor even to turn and face me. My first stroke severed the tendons in his shoulder, and with my second I took off the top of his scalp, careful to make sure I didn't do damage to the innocent he was holding.

The child saw all of it, watched me savage a man and enjoy it. I imagined it would be a fixture of her future nightmares, though in truth she was lucky she'd be having any.

'All clear,' Crispin said from behind me, mumbling the words out in between heavy breaths. 'They had the fuse going, do you believe that? Those sick sons of bitches. If I'd have been a few seconds later we'd be meeting She Who Waits Behind All Things, us and half the block.' His hair had gone gray, I realized suddenly, just the tips but they'd been black ten minutes before. Were those lines around his eyes new, I wondered? I wasn't sure – who takes the time to inspect everyone you meet, every time you meet them?

Whatever he'd given he was smiling, though this last dripped off his face as I turned away from the door. 'What?' he asked. 'What's wrong?'

I didn't answer. I wished he hadn't followed me in there, after what he'd sacrificed today he deserved better news than I had to offer. The bundles on the floor were bodies, four of them, three children and a fat mother. The fanatic had already begun his business by the time I'd intervened. The youth I'd saved was cowering in the opposite corner, surrounded by the corpses of what I presumed were her family. She began to scream, then. I imagined she would go on a long time.

29

Touissant's had not changed. Same mess, same stench of cat piss. Same stupid selection of weapons on the walls, same horny tabbies chasing each other through them. I had to wait the same length of time for Craddock to show up, and when he did I wished he hadn't. For once his back-up remained unchanged as well, the pretty young thing whose name I didn't know and didn't care to learn sneering at me as I came into the back room.

Touissant was as grossly vast as ever, though this time he wasn't holding a cat. On his lap was a silver tea service, barely larger than his wide pelvis and thick, cordlike thighs. He sipped from a cup that seemed built for a doll in his hands, and a selection of brightly colored macaroons sat half eaten next to the pot.

I grabbed the seat in front of him. Craddock angled himself a few feet away, but off to my right, in the blurred region of my vision. I could hear pretty boy take up a spot behind me.

'Warden,' Touissant opened in his grating sing song, my *nom de guerre* four extended syllables by the time he was done with it. 'To what do we', pause to shove a cookie into his mouth, and lick one oversized digit clean of crumbs, 'owe the pleasure.'

'Tardiness.'

He laughed that awful little laugh of his, his moon face beaming down on all of us. Craddock laughed as well, the stump of his tongue wagging at me. Pretty boy was too pretty to laugh, though I thought I could feel him smirk.

'I'd expected some sort of word from you by now, Touissant. A crack operator like yourself, four days and nothing?'

'I told you it might be a while before I found anything out. It's not a light matter that you've deputized me to look in on.'

'Indeed – it's a very serious matter, Touissant. Immensely serious. Critical, even.'

'Then it's a good thing you gave it to someone so capable.'

'And trustworthy?'

Touissant was munching loudly, however, and couldn't quite make it out. 'What?' he managed between bites.

'I said, "and trustworthy".'

He giggled like a schoolgirl and put another cookie into his mouth. 'You look tired, old friend.'

'It's been a long few days. I had to get up and walk around some – standing really puts me in a foul mood, if you can appreciate it.'

'I can!' he said gleefully. 'I can appreciate it exactly! And I'm very happy to report that this last trek, at least, was not a waste of your effort. I've just recently received some information that might interest you.'

'I'm interested in information that might interest me.'

'I've got a location on this Fourth Sorcerer Carroll that you mentioned.'

'That's lovely, Touissant. I'm happy to hear you've earned your pay.'

The feint towards relevance proved brief. 'Do you like cats?' Touissant asked.

'No,' I said. 'Not at all.'

'Why not?'

'I figure I feed something, I got a right to expect gratitude.'

'Cats are too clever for loyalty. They don't care about what you done for them, only what you can do. They're like people that way.'

'I don't particularly like people either.'

He laughed uproariously, spewing pastry flakes into the ether and onto my leg.

'Still waiting on that address,' I said.

He crammed the rest of what was on the tray into his mouth, ground it down between the thick white squares of his smile. 'I've done a lot of good for you, over the years, would you say?'

'You've been well-compensated for your services.'

'Fair enough, fair enough – but you'd agree at least that I've executed these tasks capably?'

'I'll give you that much.'

'I appreciate it. And I was all set to deliver again for you on this one, really I was. But then I got to thinking.'

'A dangerous pastime.'

'It was just such a strange request. Why would the lord of Low Town want to dig up something so long buried? You never seemed to me the sort to obsess about the past.'

'You'd be surprised.'

'I'd always heard strange things about you from my people in Black House. That there was a no-touch order on you, straight from the top. It's an open secret that you still have contact with the Old Man. Why, I could tell you some of the wild rumors I've heard – that you'd been planted into Low Town to assume control over the underworld, that your fall had been ginned up as cover. I know none of that's true, of course – your impulse for self-destruction is too sharp to be anything but authentic.'

'You've a keen insight.'

'Thank you, yes. It's a job requirement after all. Anyhow, something fascinating happened when I brought your name up to my friend at Black House. He's very interested in you, my friend. Asked me to see if I couldn't figure out from whence came your sudden interest in history. And what did I find? Would you believe what I found?'

'Lay it on me.'

'Treason!' He shifted himself towards me, his excitement so great as to override his instinctive dislike of motion. 'It seems that members of the Sons of Śakra have been seen in your bar, openly discussing Crown policy!'

'I guess those drunks were paying more attention than I'd thought.'

'Even more shocking, you yourself have been seen at the Step's chapter house. I must say – I've thought many things of you over the years, but I'd never have credited the suggestion that you'd work against the Throne.' He shook a finger at me, the fat on the last joint wiggling up and down. 'For shame.'

'This man you have in Black House – he wouldn't by any chance be named Crowley, would he?'

Touissant puffed out his baby cheeks and clapped his hands together. 'Right in one!'

'And you figured, while you were making money off me one way, why not see what you could get from another end?'

'Don't take it personal, Warden,' he was near to giggling. 'I'm not the sort to leave ochre on the table. I'd ask for a counteroffer, but we both know I wouldn't hold to my promise.'

'We do indeed!' I said, a sudden moment of elation.

On paper it had been a mistake to allow myself to be buttressed by Touissant's pair of heavies, but in practice allowing someone to think they have an advantage is sometimes worth putting yourself in a hole. Craddock had a smile to match the fat man's, and it didn't go anywhere, even after I'd set my knife into his skull, even as blood began to bubble from his ears. I'd palmed it out of my sleeve a few sentences earlier, a little thing, three slender inches, barely enough to reach his brain pan.

But barely would do it.

Touissant began to scream then and didn't stop for a while – I guess those rumors about him being muscle back in the day weren't based on much, or maybe he'd just gone soft in the chair. Regardless, once I heard him squeal I knew he wouldn't be anything to worry about, and while Craddock opened and closed his mouth like a wriggling fish, I turned to deal with his partner.

Back during the war I saw every kind of hand weapon you could think of, and a fair number of things your imagination likely isn't cruel enough to conceive. It's all well and good to carry your claymore around on a pack animal when you've got the time to prepare for a battle – but all the steel in the world don't mean shit if you can't get it out its sheath. Pretty boy was realizing that now, fumbling at the jeweled hilt of his curved sword. When it came down to it, he wasn't much – Touissant had chosen pretty boy for the same reason pretty boy had chosen that saber. It glittered, and was pleasant to stroke.

I had my hands wrapped around his shapely neck and I squeezed until little bubbles of blood erupted in his irises. There was another knife in my boot but once I got started it seemed best not to risk letting go. Craddock's near-corpse continued its stream of babble and half-words, his brain slow to catch on to his demise. The whole thing took a while – I've killed men that way before, and it always surprises me just how long it takes. If Touissant had grabbed a weapon or just uprighted himself from his throne and fallen on me, things would have gone different. But he didn't – he was cracked down through to the middle.

Once it was done I brought myself to my feet and readjusted my coat. Craddock's eyes stared against the far wall unblinking, and though he'd lost the capacity for speech his mouth was still bobbing, open and shut, open and shut. I pulled my knife from his brow and he fell forward onto the table, like a marionette clipped of its strings. For some curious reason it was this event that finally quieted Touissant, who had been shrieking uninterrupted for a solid minute and a half.

I wiped Craddock's blood off on Craddock's shirt, then jammed the knife into the table. I had knocked my chair over in the commotion, and I turned it upright and sat down.

'There's something about the smell of death that puts me in

need of a smoke,' I began, and started rolling it.

By the time I was done Touissant had managed to mostly pull himself together, though his eyes were shot through with red, and snot pooled beneath his nostrils. He held his hands between the crook of his thighs, as if to keep them warm. The tray lay overturned on the ground next to him, broken pieces of his tea service scattered across the floor.

'You ever feel that way?' I asked, lighting my cigarette with a match.

He didn't answer, but then the question was more or less rhetorical.

'Last I remember you were telling me that I didn't have much to offer you.'

His eyes had grown wide, each as big as an ochre piece, finally of size to fit his face. 'I don't see what's changed,' he answered.

'Really?' I asked. 'Don't see a change?' I swiveled my head back and forth, taking long, deliberate looks at the two bodies I'd made. 'I'm going to have to disagree with you there.'

'Whatever I tell you, you're gonna kill me.'

'Things do seem to be shaping up that way,' I agreed.

'So there's no point in giving you anything.'

'But you've still got so much left to lose, Touissant, so much more than just your life. For starters – if you don't tell me what I want to know, I'm going to find every kitty you've got in here, and I'm going to unpeel them and hang them from the rafters, one by one, if it takes all fucking day. And when I'm done killing the things you love, I'll start on you. By that point, I'll be well practiced.' I pulled the knife I'd used on Craddock out of the wood, holding it in the air between us. 'You'll talk, Touissant – believe me, you'll talk. It's just a question of whether I'll need to show you your insides before you do.'

I stepped out of the pawnshop a few moments later, Carroll's address in my pocket, whistling into the brisk autumn air.

30

After a bath and a strong cup of coffee I was standing at the location Touissant had died trying to keep from me. Seventy-eight Saint Paul Street was a lovely two-story stone house, unattached, in one of the less gaudy outskirts of Kor's Heights. It was a pretty neighborhood, the sort of place you'd want to raise a family in, if for some reason that endeavor appealed to you. Looking at the rows of pleasant suburban hamlets made a fellow think about founding a dynasty. The yards were verdant, the autumn foliage rich above them. I heard the laughter of children from a block over, voices carrying in the early evening.

Carroll had been one of the worst people I'd ever met in my life. It made sense that he would rise to a position of prominence.

I wiped my feet on the mat, and knocked twice on the door. A fat woman with a pinched face opened it. She scowled at me, but I didn't take it personal. I got the sense that she scowled at everybody.

'Good evening – is Mr Carroll available?'

'Fourth Sorcerer Carroll,' she snapped.

I did my best impression of an ingratiating smile, but I'm an ugly person and I think I only succeeded in frightening her. 'Fourth Sorcerer Carroll, of course, please forgive me. Is Fourth Sorcerer Carroll available?'

'He just got home from work.'

'The demands of such an important position – it's regarding work that I'm here, in fact.'

'Who's calling?'

'I'm afraid my name wouldn't mean anything to him. Could you tell him it's an old acquaintance from Black House?'

'If you're from Black House, why aren't you in uniform?'

'It's at the cleaners,' I said. 'They only give us the one, you have to get it pressed every few days.'

She thought that over for a while. She had a pushed-in nose and a mouth that hung half open, like one of those fish that sift along the bottom of a riverbed. She also reeked of alcohol, bathed me in it when she exhaled.

'I guess I'll have to ask him,' she said, as if hoping I would talk her out of it.

'That would be extraordinarily generous.'

She grunted and slammed the door in my face.

A few moments passed while I inspected the garden. It was really quite lovely, the grass newly cut, the hedges appropriately trimmed. I imagined Carroll paid someone to do it. He'd seemed the sort of person who found physical effort somehow distasteful, and also I couldn't see him lavishing care on anything living that wasn't him. It was a quality I was sure had made him a fine father.

I heard the door open, but preferred the view of Carroll's lawn to Carroll's wife. 'You can wait in the kitchen,' she said, her tone indicating she felt this fact to be something close to a tragedy.

I took a wistful look at the evening I was about to leave, then followed her inside.

The kitchen was well-designed and infrequently used. On a

266

table in the middle of the room a two-thirds empty bottle of wine sat next to a half-smoked cigarette. Mrs Carroll dropped into the seat next to them. There was an open chair, but she didn't offer it and I didn't ask. A single pot bubbled on the stove, emitting odors too bland to be actively unpleasant.

'It's a lovely home you have here,' I said.

She made a sound somewhere between a grunt and a snarl, strangling a cigarette between thin lips. As it burned down near the end she reached into a drawer and grabbed another from a ready supply. One hand stubbed out the casualty while the other, in near synchronous union, fitted and lit its replacement. At no point did her dull, half-sober eyes leave their perch on the wall.

'Is that table oak?' I asked.

There is a creature they say exists in Low Town, an amalgamation of hundreds of rats bred in such fetid proximity that their tails become inextricably entangled, and they function as a single organism – the rat king, they call it, unimaginatively. My long association with the city's rodent population has yet to confirm its existence, but it's a potent image, one brought to mind with the sudden arrival of the Carroll children.

Their entry was preceded by roughly twenty seconds of screaming, a duet that grew louder as they approached. There were two of them, a boy and a girl to judge by the harmony. Physically, they took after their mother, which is to say they'd never win any beauty contests. I got the sense they took after her in spirit as well, which is to say they'd never win anything. Such was their dedication to the battle that neither noticed my presence. I resolved not to do anything to interrupt their single-mindedness.

They stopped doing each other violence long enough to raise the issue with the magistrate. 'Mom,' the girl began, extending the word to about seven syllables. 'Junior stole my sweetie.'

Junior could go without eating a sweetie. Could have gone without eating dinner or tomorrow's breakfast as well. Really, the entire household would have been well served dedicating themselves to a few weeks' fast.

'That's because she broke my dolly!'

It occurred to me then that perhaps I'd misjudged Junior's sex, not at all an impossibility given that apart from a slight difference in height the two siblings were virtually identical, down to the hideous bowl-cut some sick bastard with a barber pole had chosen to inflict on them. I made a more concrete effort to ascertain the genders of the children in front of me, and came away confirming my initial conclusion. Junior was a boy, and had a dolly, or at least had had one in the recent past. Which was none of my business, of course, I mean I didn't know a damn thing about raising a child. My toys when I'd been his age had been a well-used knife and a set of lock picks that I had, ironically perhaps, stolen.

Mom did not seem overcome with worry at the violence of her progeny, seemingly more concerned with the discovery that her carafe of wine was not inexhaustible. She held the neck over her glass for a firm five-count to make sure, then groaned her way to her feet and over to the cabinet for a second bottle. The children recommenced fisticuffs in the interim.

I was saved by Carroll's arrival from the second floor, tromping down the stairs with something less than enthusiasm. Mrs Carroll would only be saved by the arrival of grim death, but that was her burden to carry and not mine.

Fifteen years had changed Carroll very little. He was still that dull brand of plump which can't quite commit to obesity. His eyes were flat little slits in his face, his nose too small, his mouth far too large. He'd grown bald since I'd seen him last. Maybe he'd always been bald, I couldn't remember. I hadn't spent that much time looking at Fourth Sorcerer Carroll. There wasn't much to see. If he hadn't been an Artist, he would have been nothing. As it was, he was pretty close.

He didn't recognize me, but then it had been a while, and there was really no reason to think that Coronet had represented a pivotal point in his development, any sort of critical nadir. Likely he'd continued on the same path, going in to work every day, putting his hand at whatever abomination the higher ups asked of him, coming home every night to his fat wife and ugly children. 'I suppose this conversation would best be conducted in my study.'

'I suppose it would.'

'Call me when dinner's ready,' he told his wife with forced ease.

Mrs Carroll poured herself another glass of wine. I followed her husband into the adjoining corridor and towards what I assumed was his office.

The hallway was lined every few feet with tables displaying frilly decorative pillows, cloying strands of doggerel sewn into them. The walls were hung with paintings of things adolescent girls believe beautiful – pink posies, smiling kittens and the ilk. How to fit the décor with the woman who had presumably instituted it was a puzzle beyond my ability to solve. In our short acquaintance Mrs Carroll had shown herself to be a person well stocked with vice, but honesty bids me to add that sentimentality did not seem one of them.

I've always wanted an office, hardwood bookshelves and the bound volumes to fill them. Sadly, it was an affectation incongruous with the career I'd ultimately assumed, nor was I ever exactly sure on where it would fit in with the Earl's established floor plan. Carroll's was, give him his due, a lovely manifestation of the ideal. Small but well stocked, the volumes mostly history and, strange to say, poetry, arranged alphabetically by author. A comfy-looking armchair sat next to a small end table, and Carroll fell into it. It was the only seat in the room. Apparently Carroll did little entertaining. 'I don't understand why we need to go over this again.' His voice was hollow as a dead tree.

That was a very curious statement, I thought, but continued forward as if I'd expected it. 'You don't need to understand why we do what we do. You just need to do what we tell you.'

'Yes,' he stammered. 'Yes, of course.'

'Run through it again. From the beginning.'

He threw his hands up in the air. 'I owed the man money, a lot of money, great smacking gobs of it. Coronet was my out. I knew it could be re-purposed into something the addicts would go mad over.' He shrugged. 'There's nothing more to tell.'

'The man?'

'Uriel Carabajal, obviously.'

The human mind is fabulously successful at recognizing patterns in the chaos of existence, piecing together seemingly random strands into a coherent whole. Sometimes it works too well – you get to forgetting that at bottom there is no grand conspiracy, no web tying everything together. Just an endless number of small, petty, foolish men, each grasping desperately for what they want and damn the rest.

Carroll apparently recognized my surprise, because all of a sudden there was a sheen of grease on his forehead and plump beads of wet falling off his nose. 'I remember you.'

'I'm flattered.'

'You don't work for Black House – they threw you out!'

'They did indeed.'

He groaned rather theatrically. 'I'm a dead man.'

'It sounds like you dug your grave a long time ago.'

'I can't tell you anything. They'll kill me if I tell you.'

'Well, Carroll, here's the thing about "them" – "they" are an abstract collection of agencies and interests. They don't have a home that I'm sitting in, or a wife and children within reach of the knife in my boot.'

'Sakra the Firstborn, who sits above, have mercy on a poor sinner,' he intoned.

'Given your history, I wouldn't think you'd want to be calling the attention of any higher powers,' I said, taking out the aforementioned knife and pointing it at him. 'And if it's mercy you want, you're better off aiming your requests a sight lower.'

It's a narrow thing, breaking a man, especially one as weak as Carroll. You push them too fast and they're likely to go catatonic, piss themselves, weep until they can't speak. So I gave him a moment to regain some semblance of composure before asking my next question.

'What happened to Coronet?'

'They shut it down. They shut the whole project down, years ago, just after you left. Said there was some sort of leak, scrapped the whole thing.'

'What happened to the test subjects?'

Carroll looked away from me. 'I can't remember.'

'Try harder.' I said, and I put some edge on it.

'I seem to recall something about the Children of Prachetas Sanctuary.'

'So if Coronet is shut down, then how come you can buy it on half the street corners in the city?'

'There were two parts to Coronet – implanting a command into a subject required use of the Art. But to get the subject into a receptive state we used a powerful narcotic, made in-house, no relation to any of the more common drugs. It induced a potent sensation of bliss.'

'And occasionally drove the user violently insane.'

'Not everyone,' he insisted. 'A fraction, a small fraction only.'

'Does Uriel know?'

'Of course he knows. The money he's making, you think he cares about a few corpses?'

'So then all of this – the murders in Low Town, the city ready to tear itself apart at the seams – all this has happened because you got into hock with the wrong people?'

'The Unredeemed are savages. I had to give them something – this house, all my property, it's in my wife's name. They said they'd kill me if I didn't make good, I had no other choice. It was all I could think of.'

I'd seen enough men in his position to understand how it worked. You're drowning, you grab on to whatever lifeline's offered. You don't worry about who threw it or where it leads. 'Where you been cooking it?'

'We've got a lab set up in Alledtown.'

'What's the address?'

He ducked his head down into his shoulders, shook it back and forth.

'There's only so many times I can threaten you before I gotta

271

make good, or lose all sense of self-respect,' I said, wagging the knife at him. 'We're getting very close to that number.'

'There's a warehouse at the corner of Classon and Brand,' he said. 'In the basement.'

'Must be slow going, just you there to oversee it. Uriel force an apprentice on to you?'

He scoffed. 'Do you have any idea how complex the process for creating the fever is? No ignorant black robe could pull that off. I'm the only one who knows how to do it.'

'When did Black House come to see you?'

'Three days ago.'

After I'd told Guiscard about red fever. 'And what did they say?'

'That they knew what I was up to. That I was to keep going doing it, unless they told me otherwise.'

Carroll ceased then to be of any interest to me, I turned my mind to what this new information indicated, tried to slot it into the picture as a whole. The reprieve I gave seemed to breathe some life into the half-man in front of me.

'You've got some nerve coming in here, playing the hero.'

'Oh?'

'You know what they used to call you?'

'Well-hung?'

'The Old Man's pet. You were in it as deep as I was, reading over those reports, licking your chops at the thought of what we were making. The collateral damage didn't bother you then, you'd have traded a thousand lives if you thought it would get you what you wanted. How are you any different than me?'

'I'm holding the knife.' And I thought very much of using it just then, because Carroll deserved it and because what he'd said had gotten to me and because despite all the blood I'd shed so far that day I hadn't yet quite had my fill. There was a second, standing in front of that sallow-faced monster, where it was a coin flip whether there would be two of us walking out of the study.

But finally I put the blade back into my boot and stood. 'You aren't worth the clean-up,' I said, and meant it. 'If Uriel finds out that I've been here, he's going to kill you. He's going to kill you anyway, once he figures out your process, but he'll kill you right off if he finds out I've been here.'

'I'll keep my mouth shut,' he said. 'I'm not a fool.'

'You are the very definition of a fool, Carroll. If you had any brains in your head you'd off yourself tonight, rather than let things string out another month or two. Cause whether it's Uriel or the Old Man, I can promise this much – when they come for you, you won't die easy.'

I closed the study door behind me, traipsed back through the kitchen. The kids were gone off somewhere, but Carroll's wife remained, finishing off her next bottle of wine. If she had a wonder about what I'd done to her husband, she didn't voice it to me.

31

Brother Hume picked me up at the Earl next day around noon, and he was back in his usual outfit. The brown cap which was the hallmark of his half-cult was too big for his skull. He was adjusting it constantly – it made him look more like a schoolboy than normal.

We spent the walk in relative silence. If Wren was following the order I'd given upon waking him up rather brusquely a few hours earlier, he was dogging our steps. I knew I wouldn't see him either way.

The receptionist at headquarters sniffed when she saw us and crooked her neck to face the wall. She had a lovely neck, as Hume seemed to notice, staring at it with undisguised longing. They didn't make me wait this time, just ushered me into the main office.

Egmont was nowhere to be seen. His chair was though, and I thought about sitting in it just to needle Hume's strict sense of propriety. But Hume seemed awkward enough as it was, standing in the doorway and not blinking. 'The Director will be with you shortly,' he said.

'I'll count the seconds.'

Hume remained there a while longer, then said, 'I'll go look for him.'

'Take your time. I think I'll stretch out on the desk and take a nap.'

The door closed. I waited about ten seconds, then stood quickly and started to rifle Egmont's desk.

Even before I'd been a professional snoop I'd been a pretty excellent amateur one. Still, I had my work cut out for me. The bureau was a big oak number with enough drawers and chambers to lose a newborn in. I tried the big ones, found the first three locked and the fourth one open. Beneath a quarter-inch of seemingly meaningless notepaper, I caught a glimpse of an unlabeled leather folder.

Inside were three pages, most of them written in some sort of code, lines of doggerel and unfamiliar acronyms. I didn't bother with them. Didn't need to in fact, because I figured I had a pretty good idea what I was looking at from the one section that wasn't in cipher, a list of names towards the end of the document.

Danie Cronje
Torcvil Barclay
Edward Corolinus
Petier Maggins

I'd never heard of the first three, but I knew the fourth well enough. It was hard to imagine my old subordinate shilling for the Steps, he was too dispassionate to throw in with their cause and too dull to succumb to any vice they could blackmail him with. But then, we hadn't spoken to each other since I'd been stripped of my Eye, and things change.

By all appearances, I had found the list of double-agents the Steps had planted into Black House. I memorized the names quickly – tried to at least. My mind isn't as sharp as it once was, though it's an open question whether drugs or time did more damage. Then I put the folder back into the drawer, the drawer back into the desk, and my ass back into my seat.

Five minutes closer to the grave and the door handle jiggled loudly. Egmont was having a great deal of trouble getting into his office. He managed it, finally, though it took him longer than it should have.

With the door at last open, Egmont entered briskly, took his seat at the opposite end of the table. Hume came in after him, but remained standing behind me.

'It's lovely to see you again Director, a real thrill. Thanks for providing it.'

Egmont grunted. He did not seem to return my enthusiasm. 'Brother Hume tells me the two of you had something of an . . . adventure yesterday.'

'That's one way to describe it.'

'I appreciate you ensuring that he made it back to us safely.'

'Don't worry about it. He's kind of growing on me.'

'Well,' he said, pleasantries completed. 'I've other duties to attend. Might we get straight into it?'

I saw no point in doing that. From inside my duster I pulled out my tobacco and started rolling a cigarette. 'I went ahead and earned those five hundred ochres.'

'Did you now?'

'Figured out who's selling red fever, figured out why. Shaded in all the blanks and whatnot.'

'Don't leave me in suspense.'

'Coronet was a two-part operation. First, the subject was given a specialized narcotic. While they were under, we'd have one of our practitioners implant a command into their brain – a kill order on a specific target. The subject would wake up and not remember any of it. Continue about their business as normal. Then, one day, we'd have a man walk over to them, whisper a few words in their ear . . .' I snapped my fingers. 'The perfect sleeper agent. You can appreciate the enthusiasm the project engendered in Black House.' I lit my cigarette, took a draw.

'Except that it never quite worked. Something about the narcotic drove a small but not insubstantial portion of our test subjects crazy. Not the chase-butterflies-around-a-park kind of crazy either. The cut-up-your-neighbor-and-bath-in-their-blood kind of crazy.'

'I follow.'

'So we shut it down. The long-term goal of Coronet was that it could be used on potential enemies of the state – foreign dignitaries, belligerent nobles, that kind of thing. But its side effects made that impossible. If the chief ambassador of Miradin kills his wife and kids, people are going to start asking questions.'

'I suppose they would.'

'A month and a half ago, a crime lord named Uriel Carabajal started selling something called the red fever through a series of small-time dealers and middlemen. It's become quite the hit. So far, no one has made the connection between its arrival and the sudden uptick in violent crime. Or if they have, they don't much care.'

'Yes, Hume told me. So far, I'm not hearing anything I didn't already know.'

I ignored the rebuke. 'Needless to say, this red fever is the same narcotic we were using for Coronet. So I took a meeting with Uriel, tried to rattle his cage a bit. It didn't do much good – he's not one to be rattled. But ever since I saw him I've had heat like you wouldn't believe, Black House Agents stalking my every move.'

'And you ascribe this attention to the inquiries you've made into red fever?'

'Fits, doesn't it?'

'Not entirely. Why would Black House choose to put Coronet into the hands of this . . . black robe?'

'I can only surmise.'

'Have at it.'

'We scrapped Coronet because we were losing too many test subjects. The Old Man's not one to blink over a little collateral damage, but he loathes attention. Even Black House couldn't keep a lid on it indefinitely.'

'What changed?'

'You all, if I had to take a guess. I imagine the Old Man started thinking that this would be an excellent time to have a secret weapon in his back pocket. So he thought it over, came up with an idea. There's an entire population living south of the River Andel happy to pay for the privilege of consuming a substance that might kill them. No different than wyrm, or even breath, if you think about it. Why not offer them the opportunity to test out this exciting new narcotic? Once the great minds at Black House figure out a more stable version of the compound, they'll stop selling it as a drug, and start using it as a weapon.'

A thin sheen of sweat beaded on Egmont's broad forehead. He wiped himself down with a folded handkerchief, then put the handkerchief back in his breast pocket. 'That's a very interesting hypothesis. But it hardly amounts to firm evidence.'

'What do you want? A signed confession from the Old Man? Whispers and innuendo, that's the way this works. You piece it all together as best you can. Or are you too new at the business to understand that?'

'If your goal is to insult me, you're wasting your time.'

'My goal is to live as long as possible. I assume that's your goal as well, in which case I have to say, you're doing a shit job. Do you understand what will happen once they get a functioning version of Coronet?'

'Yes, of course I do.'

'No, you obviously don't, because if you did, Director, you wouldn't be sitting calmly in that chair answering my questions.'

'I pride myself on my composure.'

I turned my head and blew little circles of smoke over to Hume. 'There's a thin line between equanimity and torpor. Be careful not to straddle it. Coronet can turn anyone into an assassin.' I pointed over at Hume. 'A few drops of it in his drink, a whispered word from a cut-rate practitioner, he'd slit your throat and not stop smiling.'

'I wouldn't!' Simeon protested, horrified even at the hypothetical.

'You would. You'd hear the words, and you'd reach to your belt, and you'd pull out your dagger and you'd put it in the Director's throat. Afterward, you'd look at the blood on your hands and on your shirt and you'd wonder, "how the hell did that get here?" You'd feel very, very bad about yourself, and the Director would still be very, very dead.'

We sat silently while Egmont decided whether or not to buy my line. A lot of what I'd said wasn't true, but it was all plausible. Most importantly, it played into his preconceptions – the dastardly Asher, the Old Man masterminding it all.

Egmont started tapping a rhythm against the desk. His fingers were long, and his nails were polished. If all you'd seen were his fingers, you'd have thought him a woman, and a pretty one at that. 'I'll look into it,' he said.

'I looked into it. You should go ahead and do something about it.'

'And what would you suggest I do?'

'Fear,' I said. 'As a verb.'

'That's comforting.'

'I'm not the Director of Security for the Sons of Śakra. I'm a man hired to find out a specific piece of information. You're the man who determines how that information is best used. My job is all but completed – perhaps it's time you start taking care of your own.'

To judge by Egmont's increasingly uneven beat, I'd shivered a little paranoia into him. I figured it was best to end on that note, hope that things played out the way I'd planned.

Hume opened the door but didn't say anything to me, didn't even look at me, which I thought was a little odd. There it was, I'd just about saved his life not two days back, and now we were all but strangers. Of course, I'd been the one who'd put him into danger, but he didn't know that.

The receptionist sniffed and turned as I walked out. Either some of her anger at Hume's fictitious transgressions had spilled over onto me, or she just had the good sense to recognize trouble when she saw it. I leaned against the desk until she finally deigned to notice me.

'What is it?' she asked.

'I forgot to tell Brother Simeon – Joyanne keeps asking for him.'

'You said his wife's name was Sarah?'

'His wife's name *is* Sarah. Joyanne is his favorite whore.'

The woman who would never speak to Hume again opened her mouth wide enough to trap a spider, then closed it rapidly.

'Was his favorite whore, I mean. She's missed him these last weeks, talks my ear off on the subject, if I'm being honest. Sure, he was paying for it, but a man comes to see her twice a day every day for a month, she gets to expect something.'

'Twice a day?' she asked, horrified or excited.

'Three times on Sundays,' I said, then nodded and left.

Once you start tipping things over, it's hard to stop.

32

The Step had been staring at me for about five minutes, trying to work up the nerve to approach. I was sitting on a bench near the docks, burning a twist of dream-vine and killing my way through the afternoon. It was chilly, turning towards cold, but what the sun refused in warmth it made up for by basking the wharfs in bright light, throwing every tiny detail into fine relief. Workers like ants marched off and on the anchored caravels and galleons. From a distance it gave the impression of happy industry, though that would have been dispelled at closer inspection. It was a fair enough substitute for my usual spot at the Earl, though Adolphus had a pretty strict no-proselytizing policy, which would mean the conversation I could see coming wouldn't have happened.

He was young, a little older than Wren maybe, though in terms of life experience I suspected my adopted ward had a couple of decades on the rosy-cheeked child trying to entice passersby with the sheaf of fliers he held gingerly in one hand. He was having little enough luck, the pedestrians hustling back and forth from the wharf fixed on their business, in no mood to be derailed by an overeager missionary. Perhaps that was why he settled on me, at the very least a captive audience.

I studiously avoided eye contact, hoping that might be enough to earn a reprieve. No such luck. He took a deep breath, centered his crooked skullcap and crossed over to meet me.

'Excuse me, Brother,' he began in a tolerably earnest voice. 'Do you have a moment to think about eternity?'

By his accent I took him to be fresh from the provinces, a farm boy who knew no more of Rigus than that it was the epicenter of all mankind's sin. So we agreed on that much, at least. 'I'll have eternity to think about eternity, won't I? There's really no reason to get a jump on things.'

He worked through my addition. 'By the time eternity comes, your fate will be settled. It'll be too late to change it.'

'How could it be too late? Eternity lasts forever. That's what eternity means,' I explained, puffing smoke into his direction. 'Forever.'

'No man knows when his last hour will be,' he said worriedly, concern for my immortal soul etched onto his face. 'Eternity can begin at any time!'

'I'm rarely punctual,' I admitted. Maybe it was the vine, or maybe it was that up close the poor boy seemed even younger, less capable, but some part of me felt bad for him. I nodded to the empty half of the bench and he plopped down onto it, happy for the meagerest slice of encouragement.

'The Sons of Śakra believe that all men are meant for salvation,' he said, as if this information was both relevant and exciting.

'What about the half-witted?'

He blinked rapidly. 'What?'

'The half-witted, the retarded, what about them? They can't read the holy texts, can't commit the prayers to memory. Some of the more unfortunate can't even swallow the sacrament.'

He stuttered a while. 'I suppose . . .'

'What you're saying is that objectively, the Firstborn is uninterested in the salvation of the retarded?'

'I'm not sure,' he said after a while. 'I guess I never really thought about it.'

I shrugged accommodatingly. Some perverse instinct bade me offer him a toke off my joint, and I followed it down into the abyss.

He sniffed at it for a moment, then shook his head. 'I don't smoke tobacco.'

'It's your lucky day my friend, cause this isn't tobacco.'

'Oh,' he said, crossing his eyes together. 'What is it?'

'An herbal concoction of my own making,' I sort of lied. 'Try it, you'll like it.' That at least was true.

He shrugged and took a little puff. He coughed it out immediately afterward, along with some of his lung.

'The coughing means you're doing it right,' I said.

By the time Wren arrived I had pretty well convinced the poor fellow that there was no point in human existence, and his best plan of action was to give up his calling and become a professional catamite.

'If the Firstborn didn't want you fucking, you'd have a smooth patch of skin between your legs,' I said. 'And if he didn't want us to hurt each other, he'd never have given us hands. Or pointed things. Or rocks. Think about it,' I said, standing. 'This has been great, really enlightening – thanks a lot. You ever fancy another hit of my special blend, stop by the Staggering Earl and ask for me,' I said. 'But don't come at night – some of the locals are a little unfriendly.'

I left a very confused young man sitting there. He'd recover at some point, or at least he'd be more careful about approaching strangers on park benches, which is a good lesson to learn regardless.

'Corrupting the youth?' Wren asked.

'Expanding my customer base.'

We walked north towards the Old City. At one point Wren started to say something but I shushed him quiet. It was better to get the whole report straight, in a situation where I could mull it over comfortably. I pulled into a bar a few blocks down, one of a line that had been spreading south these last few years, along with refurbished townhouses and overpriced grocers. Which is to say that in contrast to the drinking establishments a mile towards home the floor was not lined with sawdust, and the bartender didn't keep a truncheon below the counter.

It also had a *maître d'* instead of a drunk passed out on the doorstep. The place was near empty, but he seemed little happy to see us just the same. 'Dinner?' he asked in a tone hinting it would be of little concern if we never ate another meal again.

'Drinks,' I said with equal good humor.

He sniffed and waved a hand towards the sea of open tables. 'Take a seat.'

We grabbed two. After a longer wait than seemed appropriate given that there wasn't anyone in the joint, a server came by, left again, came back a second time with a bottle of whiskey.

I poured Wren a shot, reward for the last several hours of work. He nodded thanks and drank it quickly. I let him finish before poking at him.

'Break it down for me.'

'A few minutes after you left, a man matching the description you gave me of Director Egmont walked out.'

'By himself?'

Wren nodded. 'No back.'

'Continue.'

'He messed around the Old City for a while, ducking into shops and whatnot.'

'Did he spot you?'

'There's no reason to be rude.'

Vanity, vanity. 'You figure he was just being careful?'

'Yeah.'

'What then?'

'He disappeared into a merchant house off Aniseed Park. One of the smaller ones, you wouldn't have heard of it. I got dinner at a cafe across the street, with a good view of the front exit. You owe me three copper, by the way.'

'I'll deduct it from this month's rent. Continue.'

'Your man split after about an hour. I let him go, like you said. Closing time saw a mass exodus of worker bees, but nothing that rang out as suspicious.' Wren wiggled his glass for another shot. I refilled it dutifully. He was enjoying having me on the hook, liked feeding out bits to my growing sense of anticipation.

'Until?' I asked.

'About an hour after the rest of the building left, two out-of-uniform Steps escorted a woman to a guesthouse a few blocks past.'

'You sure they were Steps?'

'They walked like they needed to shit but couldn't find a chamberpot.'

I finished what little remained in my glass.

'So what was the point of all that?' Wren asked.

'Egmont's getting help from Nestrian intelligence. Money, advice. I figured I'd shake him up, see if he wouldn't lead us to his contact.'

'Correspondence with a foreign agent – sounds illegal.'

'I imagine Black House would be extremely interested in the address you just gave me.'

'You going to tell them?'

I shrugged, poured myself some more whiskey. Wren did the same, sipped at it for a while. 'You've never told me why they threw you out of Black House.'

'You've never asked.'

'I knew you wouldn't tell me.'

'Smart boy.'

'But I asked Adolphus, years ago.'

'And?'

'He told me that you were betrayed by a woman.'

'I was betrayed by my own stupidity,' I said. 'The woman was the agent by which the daevas brought me low.'

'Albertine?'

'Now that you mention it, yes – I think her name was Albertine.'

'I've never known you to get out of your head over a piece of tail.'

'Once bitten.'

'Adolphus told me that she was back in Rigus – that part of the game you set up with the Steps is to get back at her.'

'Adolphus should learn to keep his mouth shut,' I said.

'Do you want to talk about it?'

'If you had to take a guess whether or not I wanted to talk about it – what would you think my answer would be?'

'Probably you don't.'

'Smart boy, like I said.' But after a few more fingers of whiskey I found my mouth opening against itself. 'How did she look?'

'She was tall, blonde. Pretty I guess, if you like them old.'

I went silent again for a while, sifting through lost memories, trying to find them, trying to hide them once I'd found them.

'What was she like?' Wren asked.

'You ever swallow a razor blade?'

'No.'

'That's a good policy. I'd go ahead and stick to it.'

'She must have been something special, if she had enough to hook you.'

'I guess I thought so at the time.'

'You must have really loved her.'

'Love,' I repeated, taking my time over the word, stretching the single syllable till it fit a sentence. 'Don't ever fall in love, boy. Don't ever love nobody. The balladeers and poets are lying to fill their purse. It makes you weak, and it makes you stupid.'

'You love Adolphus.'

'I tolerate him.'

'More than that.'

'I'm far from perfect, as I'd assumed you'd picked up on by this point.'

'This . . . philosophy you claim to follow seems like a recipe for an awfully pointless existence.'

'It's extraordinary, the depth of understanding you've acquired at the tender age of eighteen.'

'All right.'

'Absolutely unprecedented. Precocious, that's how they'd describe it, this insight of yours.'

'I just did you a favor – you ought to watch how you repay me.'

'You did your job,' I said. 'You don't get a pat on the head for it. In fact, isn't now about the time you should be shadowing Captain Ascletin, rather than sitting in a bar and pissing me off?'

'Suits me fine,' Wren said, standing. 'You want to wallow, you can do it on your own.'

'My preference as well.'

The place was starting to fill up, young businessmen and their wives or lovers or paid accompaniment, well-dressed, happy or at least competently faking it. I felt distinctly out of place, or would have if I'd cared at all what these people thought of me. I stayed around longer than I wanted to, just to shaft it to the server. But after a while the pleasure started to seem awfully petty, and I paid my tab and split.

I hadn't told Wren what I'd wanted to tell him, hadn't made the warning stick. Because it's a lit fuse, love – you light it yourself, and you stand around the powder keg afterward, grinning from ear to ear.

33

Crispin was late in arriving, which was rare for him. He was scrupulously punctual. He was pretty much just scrupulous period. I liked him in spite of it.

At that particular moment, I was happy for his uncharacteristic tardiness. It had been one of those weeks where sleep was hard to find and uneasy when it came. The Minister of War, a quiet, corrupt figure we'd long had in our pocket, had made the sudden and unexpected decision to buck the company line, backed a bill to re-arm against the Dren. We figured the Nestrians were behind it, had something on him that we didn't. I'd spent three days trying to figure out what it was, then three more trying unsuccessfully to bury it. Point being I was happy to spend a few minutes in the back corner of a quiet bar, with a warm fire not too distant, and a pull of good strong stout even closer at hand.

He came in eventually, and I was half regretful for the interruption to my repose. Crispin was handsome, dignified and decent, all things I wasn't. He looked good in the ice gray we both wore, striking, maybe even noble. I looked dangerous, and despite my best efforts otherwise, faintly disheveled.

'Sorry, sorry,' he said, setting his coat on a hook next to the booth and dropping in across from me.

I waved away his apology, and signaled to the bartender for two more. When they came we drank them in happy silence, and if that's not friendship, I'm unfamiliar with the term.

Ours was an unlikely thing – Crispin was about half a count, would be the whole thing once an uncle he strongly disliked found his way into the next life. You could see affluence rolling off of him in waves – if he'd ever have come to Low Town out of uniform someone would have rolled him before he'd walked five blocks. Someone would have tried anyways, though they might have found that for all his airs and fine speech, Crispin was a bad man to set upon in an alleyway. I didn't like the fact that he'd been born in nominal ownership of more land than all the city south of the Palace, but he didn't rub your nose in it. And he'd served in the war; really served, not just pushed papers across a desk. That could forgive a lot. And back then I hadn't entirely acquired the loathing for the upper classes I later would. In fact, at the time I'd been mostly concerned with joining their ranks.

We'd been partnered up with each other straight out of the Academy. I knew little, and he knew less – but we were smart, and anxious to learn, and having spent most of the prior five years in the trenches this new gig seemed like a fair slice of heaven. And it was easier then, you had a clear sense of what you were aimed at. A body would show up somewhere where it usually didn't, we'd head over and try to figure out who put it there. Sometimes we failed, but not often – we were smart, like I said. After a while we got detailed to looking in on the syndicates, making sure none of the players got big enough to eat another, crumpling up the particularly brutal or stupid ones.

But a while back I'd transferred into Special Operations, reward for betraying an old friend, and since then we hadn't seen much of each other. We'd both been busy, I told myself, and it wasn't a lie but it wasn't really the truth either.

'How you been?'

'All right,' Crispin said, though he didn't look it.

'Working a case?'

'Yeah, a doozy. You know Big Noel, the Rouender kingpin?'

'You know this real bright thing in the sky, they call it the sun?'

'We caught one of his top lieutenants at a brothel near the Isthmus.'

'Stop the presses.'

'One specializing in young girls.'

I whistled through my teeth. Even by the syndicate's reprobate standards, that was pushing it.

'We got him stashed in a safe house outside the city, been working him over since Monday. Think he's about ready to flip. I mean what other choice does he have? We let him back out on the street, he'll be sporting a second grin before sun up.'

'Black House – making the world safe for pedophiles.'

'I'm far from thrilled with it myself – but the man's a gold mine. With what we'll get from him, we can roll up Noel's whole operation, top to bottom.'

I clicked my glass against his. 'Good luck to you.'

Course, luck had nothing to do with it. The lower you are on the pole, the more events seem to be governed by chance. Climb up a few steps and you realize that there's an order to the whole thing, the dice are loaded and the cards well marked.

Rumor in Low Town had long been that Big Noel had support from Black House, but even the most jaded conspiracy theorist wouldn't have had any idea of just how high it went. The gang was, in effect, a lever of the Old Man. Their nominal leader, Crispin's nemesis, was in no greater control of his destiny than a marionette. He pounced on who we told him to pounce on, moved what we told him to move where we told him to move it, and in return we assuaged any of the legal concerns which might be expected to occupy a man in his position. I didn't have the heart to tell Crispin, but his informant wouldn't make it to next week, let alone see the inside of a courtroom. Crispin might not know what the other hand was doing, so to speak, but I would put an ochre down against the promise of copper that somewhere on his team there was an agent who took orders straight from the head of Black House. All supposition of course, I was concerned with foreign affairs, the syndicates weren't in my balliwick anymore – but a well-informed hypothesis all the same.

'You hear about this business with the Minister of War?' Crispin asked.

'I might have.'

'Madness. Doesn't seem like he'll be around much longer.'

'You never know,' I said, though I did.

'Figure he'll retire?'

'No,' I said, 'I very much do not expect him to retire.' Because about two hours ago the Old Man and I decided things would go smoother for all of us if the Minister, overcome with remorse at a lifetime of poor decisions, drank a thimble-full of widow's milk. There had been some debate, in fact – I wanted to turn him, figure out who'd set him against us, maybe get an eye in the foreign camp. But the whole thing had already started to bleed, and in the end it seemed safer to tie it off.

'How are things on your end?' Crispin asked.

'Not bad,' I said. Prolixity was little encouraged in Special Operations.

'Nothing exciting to report?'

'I got a tooth pulled last week.'

Crispin reached over to his coat and took out his tobacco pouch. He started on a cigarette. His fingernails were clean, and his motions sharp. 'Not much leaks out of your end of the shop, but all the same I've been . . . hearing things.'

'Nothing bad, I hope?'

'Depends on how you look at it.' He patted his pockets for a match.

I found one in mine, leaned over and lit his smoke. 'And how do you look at it?'

'They say you walk in the Old Man's footsteps. That you're waiting with a handkerchief when he blows his nose.'

I laughed. I'd never been liked in Black House, not when I was coming up in the ranks, not now that I'd reached the top. That was fine – I didn't care particularly about being liked. Respect was what I aimed at, or at the very least fear. 'And?'

'And they say it quietly, because beyond having the Old Man's ear, you're known as a person that it's unwise to cross.'

'Does that sound like me?'

'What's it like working with him?'

'It's all right.'

'Learning a lot?'

'You can quit riding me whenever you feel like it. I know you thought it was a mistake, me getting in with Special Ops.'

'I did. I still do.'

'But it's my hand to play. Thus far I've managed things well enough.'

'Thus far,' he repeated. 'Don't trust the Old Man.'

'I don't trust him. I trust that he's good at his job. And I trust that he knows I'm good at mine. The Old Man and I . . . we understand each other.'

It shames me now, to think how true that was.

We had pretty much this exact conversation every time we saw each other, which was likely the reason that neither of us had made much of a point of staying in contact. I'd done what I'd done, there was no going back.

Our dialogue trailed listlessly for a while, asking over people neither of us cared about, shared acquaintances and not quite friends. And then she walked in the door, and I stopped listening to him entirely.

The streets of Low Town were not an environment which encouraged a sense of romance. I'd had my first woman at twelve, mainly so the other neighborhood toughs would quit ragging on me. A whore of course, unwashed and more than plump, though tender. It had been my introduction to what the saps called love-making, and I admit it might have given me something of a mercenary attitude towards the whole endeavor. Sex was a necessary bodily function, like shitting, to be completed briskly, without guilt or fuss. There was no point in imbuing it with any special meaning.

Five years on the front lines had reaffirmed the lesson. Anyone who'd come into the trenches thinking they'd stay true to their sweetheart back home stopped thinking that right quick. There wasn't much point in getting hung up on monogamy when the morrow would likely as not see your lifeblood running into your boots, your woman half a world away, bored, young and lonely. Nor had my time in Black House done much to convince me as to the merits of true love. We got half our intelligence from the paramours of powerful men, pulling information between bed sheets, rifling through drawers once their mark was safely asleep.

In short, my experiences in the realm of honest affection were rare, bordering on nonexistent. Few women not turned off by the fact that I was, in the kindest of estimations, quite homely, weren't likely to overlook the fact that I was a bit of a bastard as well. There were a handful of high-class working women I visited infrequently, none for long enough that sentiment could accrue on either end. If we were to be honest, I would say I thought it was a weakness, getting hooked on a pair of bright eyes.

Time would prove me more correct than I could possibly have imagined. In retrospect, it might well have been better if I'd spent my youth chasing after dames, like a gallant in the ballads. Perhaps having my heart broken a few times would have given me some understanding of the singular deceit which is the sole province of the female sex. Probably not, though. If we had any idea what we were in for when we let another person touch us, the human race wouldn't last beyond the next generation.

She was beautiful. Too beautiful. I should have known looking at her. In truth, she was more than beautiful. I'd seen beautiful women before, laid with them, all paid for but so what? I knew the touch of a long limb, the feel of ripe breasts against my chest, the slender curve of a thigh. And I knew how little any of that meant, when you light a candle and have to look into their eyes. But somehow her beauty seemed to speak of something beyond the superficial. She looked like someone . . . she looked like someone you wanted to see again.

Hell, I don't know.

Watching her move across the floor, float I would have said, I was over-conscious of my unkempt hair. Of my torn ear and asymmetric eyes. Of the scars I'd accrued over twenty-nine years of barely surviving things. I smoothed the folds of my suit unconsciously – it was well made and fit correctly, but it did little enough to improve the body inside of it. I wouldn't have had the courage to speak with her. That was another sign, though of course I wasn't interested in seeing it.

She ordered a drink at the bar. The keep was quick in bringing it to her. She spent a languid few moments draped over the counter, sipping a glass of red wine. Eyes watched her, mine amongst them.

'Quite a beauty,' Crispin said, a smile on his face like he'd beaten me in chess.

I shrugged and turned my gaze pointedly towards a wall. 'She's all right.'

'Just all right?'

'Not really my type.'

'Then you shouldn't have any trouble.'

'With what?'

'Her rapid approach.'

I half thought him kidding, was shocked to look back to the counter and discover that she wasn't there, and more shocked to recognize in the mass of flesh directly in front of me the most perfect creature I had ever seen.

'Albertine Arden,' she gave me her hand. I held it too long, but she didn't seem to notice, or she didn't seem to mind.

I turned to introduce Crispin and discovered he was on the other side of the room, covering our bill at the counter. He was a good friend, Crispin. If he'd been a better friend he would have struck me across the back of the head with a beer bottle, dragged me forcibly back to my home.

'I was to meet a colleague here,' she said. 'But she seems to be slow in arriving. Perhaps I might wait for her?' Her Rigun was perfect, better than a native's. She had the barest hint of an accent, but only with certain words, and you strained to hear it, like the scent of a subtle perfume.

After a moment I realized I hadn't answered. 'Of course,' I said, nodding at the seat Crispin had vacated. 'Please.'

She angled one leg over the other. Distantly, I was aware of the attraction, but my eyes remained locked on her own. 'This pretty outfit you wear,' she said. 'It means you are someone important?'

'I'm the second most important person in Rigus,' I said. It was only mostly a joke.

'That must be very tiring.'

'I drink a lot of coffee,' I admitted. But what I wanted to tell her was – I run the secret side of the secret police. I'm important and only getting more so, and it's worth your time to talk to me, I promise you, despite what I look like and what you look like. Albertine was a very good spy, because she rarely needed to do any spying. You came right out and gave it to her.

For the moment, however, I managed to keep my mouth shut. 'And you? What do you do?'

'I am an importer in a merchant house,' she said. Her eyes hung on mine, but her finger curled with the sunlit straw of her hair. 'It is quite terribly boring, but at least it offers the opportunity to spend some time in your city.'

'How do you find it?'

'Lonely,' she said.

There was a lump in my throat.

'Have you ever been to Nestria?'

'Three years,' I said, 'but probably not the same places you have.'

'You were in the war?'

I nodded.

She shook her head in false sympathy. 'Such a terrible thing, what men do to each other.'

Nothing compared to the cruelty of a woman – but I didn't appreciate that at the time.

'Did you learn any of my language?'

'I did.'

'Won't you say something to me?'

I laughed. It was the first in a long line of chuckles, snickers and guffaws that she'd draw out of me over the course of our ill-fated relationship, banter as practiced as a surgeon's hands. 'I didn't learn the sort of Nestrian appropriate for tender ears.'

Her smile seemed full with promise. She laid her hand atop my bicep. I resisted the urge to flex, but it was a close run thing. 'I am not so easily shocked.'

We left for my place shortly after that, her suggestion, accompanied by a slight, trembling blush that made you feel she didn't make it often. Later I would come to recognize that blush as something she could call on command, one of an arsenal of artifices that she had mastered, perfected over long sessions in a mirror or on other poor fools like myself.

I spent the next nine months cocooning myself in pleasant falsehoods, looking left when anything that smacked of truth exited stage right. Of course it was also the happiest period of my life.

Like I said – I should have known it looking at her. Because at the bottom, when it was just you pleading your case to logic, that cold, implacable and resolute force, women like her did not fall for men like me. Birds do not swim, nor fish fly. The sun gives heat, and the night steals it, and I would no more be loved than I would wake up one day to discover I'd grown a pair of eagle's wings.

Life is what it is – but by the Firstborn, sometimes you just want to pretend.

34

The first half of the next day was uneventful. I spent it in the bar, running through the weave in my mind, gradually transitioning from coffee to beer. Things were starting to move too fast, it was hard to keep track of the particulars. More than once I found myself reaching into my satchel for a quick hit of breath, then forcing my hands out again. I didn't do that anymore, I reminded myself. That I still very much wanted to was proof my decision to quit had been a wise one.

In short, I guess I wasn't paying much attention. I know I wasn't, which was why by the time I noticed Crowley he was already inside and walking towards me. He was flanked by two men whom I strongly suspected were not priests. They stood a few yards off, and let the scarred man take the seat in front of me.

'These all you got?' I asked.

Crowley had a bruised lip and a freshly blackened eye. The

Asher had gone easier on him than I'd expected. 'Those two Mirads at the bar with steel crowding their jackets,' he said, nodding towards a pair of men who matched that exact description. 'And the Valaan pretending he can't see me in the corner.'

'He's doing a terrible job.'

'I didn't hire him for his acting. I hired him because he likes to break heads,' Crowley smiled that smile I'd come to loathe. 'And he's good at it.'

I guess he'd been seeding men throughout the place all afternoon. If he'd come in with a squad of thugs I would have noticed whatever mental state I was in. 'Black House don't have shit on me,' I said. 'And our little back-and-forths have long gone from frightening to tiresome.'

'I had something,' he said. 'I had a witness that said you were sticking your nose into accounts long closed, and doing it for the benefit of the Steps.'

I craned my neck over my shoulder, then peeked beneath the table. 'Is he around here somewhere? I'd love to meet him.'

'You've met him already. You killed him.'

'He's a dead man then, your star witness? What's that they say about dead men – that they like to tell tales?'

He brushed a few crumbs off the table, then rubbed his hands together. 'You're right, I don't have anything. But I'm gonna ace you, all the same.'

'The Old Man won't like it.'

'I'm not so much in his graces these days anyhow,' he leaned his weight to one side and farted loudly. 'Besides, the Old Man won't be around so much longer.'

'You so sure of that?'

'He's slipping – I've been tagging after him for twenty-five years, I can tell. He ain't what he was.' This made Crowley sad, in the dim way that he was capable of feeling anything more complex than lust or sadism. He shook it away uncomfortably, and came to his feet. 'It don't matter anyhow – whether I'm right or wrong, whatever might come of me doing it – it's going to get done, right now. You're going to stand up, and follow me out, and you ain't going to make any trouble, not one peep, or my crew runs roughshod. And the first one to drop will be the boy,' Crowley said, and something cool leaked out my temple. 'I forgot to mention, I've got a man over by him as well.'

Wren was serving drinks at one end of the counter, laughing, oblivious to the danger. Near enough to throat him, a pale bravo in a black coat pretended to drink a beer.

I took a long, slow look at the inevitable. 'I walk out with you, and the boy gets left alone.'

'I don't give a fuck about the kid. Once you're out the door the rest of my men follow me. You've my word.'

Worth less than a bag of nightsoil, but I didn't have any other option. I finished off what was left in my glass, tried to enjoy it as much as I could. That I'd be chasing it with blood seemed all but certain. I stood. Crowley did the same, took the spot in front of me. His men took the rear.

I kept my eyes on Crowley's back, made sure I still had a blade up my sleeve, martialed my resources for the move I'd make once we were outside. If I was lucky I might get to bring Crowley along with me to the other side. If I was very lucky, I might even have a shot at escape. And if I was very, very lucky, I might stumble over a big bag of ochres during my flight. Pipe dreams, all of them. Crowley hadn't waited this long just to blow his shot at offing me. The best I could hope for was to make enough trouble that they had to kill me quick.

'Where you off to?' a voice said. A loud voice, booming even. I looked up to see our path obstructed by Adolphus, and there was no doubt what had earned him the sobriquet 'Grand'.

'Black House business, fat man – get out of the way,' Crowley bowled forward, used to these few words acting as a panacea for any trouble he got in.

But Adolphus didn't move, and Crowley found himself stopping short. There was an awkward pause, during which Adolphus inspected the smaller man with elaborate deliberateness, 'Where are your uniforms?' the giant asked, placidly. Foolishly, one might have said, if one were oneself a fool.

'What?'

'If this is Black House business,' Adolphus said again, loud enough so that others could hear. 'Where are your uniforms?'

The crowd had started to perk up by then. If in the past I had given the impression that our usual patrons are friendly, or law-abiding or clean, let me rectify that. They are none of those things. If you were to count up the collected felonies committed by the ale-swillers growing old in my establishment, you'd hit three figures before you'd gone ten steps.

At a table near us sat a knotted Tarasaighn named Dougal, known within the neighborhood for his excessively large knife collection. 'Yeah, why ain't you in uniform?' he asked, and if you couldn't hear a threat in that you were deaf as a fucking post. Dougal didn't have nothing for me, but with a pint or two in him he'd fight his mother over a half-eaten sandwich. For the first time in my life, I was happy we were in the same room.

'Don't look like no kind of agent I ever saw,' someone else called out.

'Looks like some fat thug thinks he can come in here and muscle us around,' that was Wren's voice, and I was grateful for it.

Somewhere in his dim simian mind, Crowley recognized danger. He held his hands up in the air, away from the sword at his side, then began to move one slowly towards his coat.

Adolphus cut that short. 'You put your hand into your pocket, and I'm going to break you straight in two.'

'My Eye is in my pocket,' Crowley said. 'I'm going to show it to you, and you'll know I'm here on Crown business.'

'So you say. But I might decide you're going for a blade, and if I decided that was the case, I might have to make sure I'd stop you.'

'My boys wouldn't like that,' Crowley said, remembering now that he was a man not unaccustomed to violence.

'Nothing your boys could do before I got my hands on your throat,' Adolphus said, but not threateningly, more like he was trying to explain something complicated to a simpleton.

'And once that happens, there ain't enough men in the world to stop me before I kill you. Besides,' he continued, 'I've got a boy or two here myself – and they don't take too kindly to people impersonating the Crown. Since we're speaking plainly, even if you were who you say you are, my boys don't take too kindly to the genuine article, neither.'

The bar was all but silent, and in it you could hear dangerous men getting ready to ply their trade, knives unsheathed, brass knuckles slipped over fists. Copernicus Sweetroll took up position behind Adolphus, a squat Valaan with a high-pitched whine who'd killed two men I knew of for commenting on it. Out of the corner of my eye I saw Red-Handed Annie slip a stiletto from a strap on her thigh – that she had the biceps of a dock-worker and the temperament to match hadn't stopped her from stepping out as a working woman for twenty odd years. The occasional trick inclined towards cruelty had discovered quick enough that Annie was similarly disposed, and more skilled at it. There were the occasional honest tradesmen who frequented the Earl, decent people, mill-workers and men plying the docks. But in that particular moment, one would have been hard pressed to recognize them.

Crowley's instinct, as always, was to move straight to violence. It was one of the things that made him good at his job, actually – that the line for him was so thin that he didn't need any time to force himself into action. But even Crowley's disproportionate self-respect couldn't convince him he stood a chance in hell of going toe-to-toe with Adolphus, and drawing open steel would be tantamount to starting a riot.

'I won't forget this,' he said.

Adolphus leaned in close to Crowley's face, but didn't say anything. Just gazed at him, running his one eye back and forth over the smaller man. Then there was the sound of a thunder clap, and Crowley was spinning backwards, on his feet but barely.

'Not now.'

It always amazed me how good Adolphus was with his hands. Blood trickled from the corner of Crowley's mouth that still functioned, and he seemed dazed, slow to move. When he finally managed to shake it off his eyes were little pinpricks of rage, and his hand trembled near the hilt of his sword. But that was as far as it went. After a moment, he wiped crimson off his scowl and dipped out the exit. The rest of his boys followed him, and not slowly either.

At bottom, Crowley was hollow, as the scar I'd given him proved. The very embodiment of the void when he was on top, weak-kneed and piss-yellow once his stack got low.

A handful of times in my life I'd come face to face with She Who Waits Behind All Things, made my peace with the thought of entering the next world. A handful of times I'd been brought back from the brink, given another chance to make the same mistakes. And in those first moments, as you stutter back from the edge, things look different – not better, but more vivid, the muted wood of the walls brighter, the smells wafting in from the kitchen more pungent.

'Drinks are on me,' I said, and the place erupted, the mood swift to turn from homicidal to jubilant. Adolphus and I were all but carried back to the counter, the crowd overwhelmed by our victory and the promise of free booze. I managed to get a word in to my partner before he was forced to the taps.

'You shouldn't have done that.'

Adolphus shrugged. 'A man only gets but so far on wisdom alone. Besides, we won't be around long enough to pay for it.'

'Pray you're right – Crowley isn't one to forget an insult.'

'I'll keep my eye out,' he said.

That last was all but lost by the swelling chorus, our patrons excited to get to the drinks that I'd pay for and Adolphus would serve. I had to yell to make myself heard over the commotion. 'I figure it would make sense for me to sleep somewhere else tonight.'

'Sounds wise.'

'Adeline and the boy ought to do the same. Send Wren over to Mazzie's for a couple of days, and stash Adeline somewhere.'

'I'll do that.'

'You'd be smart to lie low as well.'

Adolphus's grin was uneven and about as wide as my fist. 'I've got customers to serve.'

I figured as much – Adolphus wasn't one to back down from a fight, not with victory fresh under his belt. 'I'll be back around in a few days, to pick y'all up and get the hell out of here.'

'Watch yourself till then.'

'I will.'

I was about to leave, Adolphus turning to the tap, accepting the backslaps and good wishes of a crew of roughnecks that had been willing to die, or at least kill, for him a moment past. Before he was lost completely I stepped back and put a hand on his shoulder, made sure to get his attention. Once I had it though, oddly, it took me a few seconds to say anything.

'Thanks,' I said finally. It wasn't enough, wouldn't ever be, but it was all I had to give him, and I think he understood.

Adolphus winked his one eye – homely, fat, the best man I'd ever known. 'Don't mention it.'

35

Earlier that morning I had decided to eschew all this cloak-and-dagger nonsense, just sent Guiscard a message consisting of an address, a time, and one extra word – *urgent*. Despite that last exhortation he was late, unhappy to have arrived at all, and not slow to let me in on his feelings. 'I don't understand,' he said, wind whipping at his gray duster, 'why we couldn't have had this conversation somewhere else.'

'It's not a whorehouse, but I thought you might enjoy the fresh air.'

'It's raining.'

'It's drizzling.'

'Water is falling on me,' he said rather testily. 'Can we get to it?'

'You got somewhere to be?'

'Beyond the weather, and the fact that it seems unwise to risk the chance of us being seen together, you are not, in fact, my day's sole concern.'

'Do tell.'

'Last night the High Chancellor resigned his badge of office.'
I whistled. 'Two weeks, huh? Gotta be some kind of record.'
'Monck's block no-confidenced him on the tariff bill.'
'Gosh.'
'That's all you've got to say?'
'Golly?'
'That means he can stop the nomination of the next one as well, leave us without a rudder. It means he can cause a crisis whenever he wants, use it as a pretext to raise the city.'
'I can see why that would be of some concern to you,' I said.
He scowled. 'Where the hell are we?'
We were in Wyrmington's Shingle, well north of the Old City, in the foothills where Kor's Heights begin. That was obviously not what he meant, however. 'I thought you might want to know before I gave word to the Steps – I found the end result of Coronet.'
He took a longer look up at the building that was sheltering us from the wind. It was old, and had been pretty once, though it was hard to make out when. The stone facade was crumbling and weather beaten. It was also a frequent target of vandalism, graffiti stretching across it in layers. A patient excavator could have discovered a decade plus of abuse from neighborhood wits. 'Here?'
I banged loudly on the door in answer. It was a while before the eye slit opened. 'The blessing of Prachetas upon you this morning,' a woman's voice said. 'Mr Chamberlain, I presume?'
'That's me.'
The panel closed. After a moment the door opened. 'Sister Agnes, at your service.'
Sister Agnes was homely and old. The gray habit she wore was too big, seemed to swallow her up. Only her hands and face showed, and these were mottled, the result of some sort of skin condition. She looked tired – she looked like she had been tired for a very long time. Still, her eyes were clear, and they didn't blink as they looked us over.
She didn't offer her hand – her order had strict rules regarding

310

physical contact between the sexes. I inclined my head in substitute. 'Forgive our lateness – my associate had some difficulty finding the place.'

'Not at all,' she said, stepping aside to allow us entry. 'With lunch out of the way, there's little enough to occupy us.'

The corridor was made of the same stone as the front, though it had been cleaned more recently. 'Welcome to the Children of Prachetas Sanctuary, gentlemen.' She seemed to belatedly recognize Guiscard's garb, and thus his importance, and she stood up straighter. 'Good afternoon, Agent.'

He nodded respectfully. 'Sister.'

She turned back towards me. 'I'm afraid your message didn't specify what organization you're representing.'

'I'm head of the Low Town Business Association.' And had such a thing existed, I probably would have been. 'With Midwinter approaching we're considering what charitable institution to sponsor in the coming year. One of our members brought your asylum to our attention.'

For a moment her face showed something that might have been pride, but she chewed that down into the steady solemnity that was her constant expression. It was one that allowed for neither excitement nor satisfaction, that expected disappointment and prepared to meet it without regret. 'We're a small facility, dedicated to the care of only a few poor souls, their numbers dwindling every year. All the same, any kindness you could do for us would be greatly appreciated.'

'Who keeps the lamps lit?'

'The Order provides what assistance it can,' she said. 'But there are many in the land that need the help they can offer. We are primarily funded by a private endowment. It's enough to pay for our food, though sadly little else.'

'Provided by?'

She shook her head. 'The endowment is anonymous, granted to provide care for our wards. I don't suppose you remember, it's been so long, but it was quite a scandal at the time. Two dozen souls, seemingly healthy, all going mad within the span of a few days. The broadsheets had a field day of course, blaming it on one thing or another. After a while they lost interest, as they tend to.'

We kept to Sister Agnes's speed, which is to say it took us about five minutes to make it out of the entrance way. Finally, we stopped at a heavy wooden security door, a little brass bell hanging on the wall next to it. Sister Agnes tapped the ringer lightly. The pleasant chimes that echoed out were discordant, laughter at a funeral.

'Since Sister Rajel passed, Mr Amar and I are the only full-time staff. A novice used to stop by from time to time and read stories, but . . .' She looked more than normally regretful. 'There was an incident.'

I didn't press her on the specifics. It was another moment before I heard the sound of the locks on the other side being undone.

The man who opened the door was an Islander of advanced age, snow white hair and jet black skin. He was a large man with soft eyes. I supposed those were the most important traits for someone in his position. The strength to sit a patient down when you had to, and the decency not to enjoy it.

'Thank you, Mr Amar,' Sister Agnes said.

Mr Amar gave Guiscard and me a clean once over, weighing our intentions and hinting at theoretical consequences. Then he nodded languidly and dropped back into his chair.

'This way, please,' Sister Agnes said, leading us onward at her interminable pace.

As a youth I'd done a stint in a reform school run by the Order, after I was stupid enough to get caught doing something I'd done a thousand times before. During my brief stay one of the Sisters had taken badly to my lack of manners and poured a half-pot of tea over my upper arm. I had found it unpleasant, if memory serves. That pretty much soured me on both public education and the church.

It was hard to hold any of that against Agnes. I've found that people who work in institutions tend to do so because they find their charges easy victims, incapable of escape or retaliation. Clearly the Sister did not fall into this category. It was difficult to square with my general worldview, the idea that a human being might dedicate themselves to another without hope of gain.

'I must warn you gentlemen – our wards can be . . . difficult for outsiders to see.'

'Agent Guiscard and I are not easily disturbed.'

'Nor am I certain as to how our patients will react to your presence – should it upset them, I'm afraid we'll have to end your visit early.'

'Of course. The last thing we want is to cause any trouble.'

Sister Agnes looked at me for a time, into me I might say. One advantage of the frock is that certain basic social conventions – for instance, the prohibition against staring at someone for an unbroken thirty-five seconds – can be comfortably ignored. I wasn't so foolish as to ascribe any particular prescience to the Sister, and it had been a long time since I'd thought of the daevas as being more than names to curse by. All the same, I was happy when she turned and opened the door.

A dozen-odd folk sat in varying positions inside the room, some on hard wooden chairs, some crouched down against the wall. Two of them were playing cards, or more accurately with cards, the arrangement betraying no sense of order that I could perceive. Some were knitting, sewing strips of cloth together. Most seemed incapable of even these activities, staring at the walls and chewing their lips like cud.

'This is where we keep the quiet ones,' she said. 'We try to give them something to do, to take the mind off their . . . situation. The Order frowns on games of chance, but I can't see the harm in it.' Though to judge by the vague sense of shame she seemed to exude, she wasn't certain. 'You don't see any harm in it, do you Agent?'

It took Guiscard a beat before he realized the question had been addressed to him. 'No,' he said. 'Not at all.'

I thought it humorous, under the circumstances, that Sister

Agnes thought of a member of Black House as having some sort of moral authority.

'We used to allow dice, but the rattling agitated some of the more nervous ones. The knitting is a recent introduction of my own, gives them something to do. Of course, you have to be careful with the needles.'

A very thin man with wild eyes stood up from his post and approached us. 'Mother? Mother, is that you?' For some reason he fixed his attention on Guiscard, took his duster between both hands. 'Mother? You've come back to see me?'

Guiscard turned his face towards the wall.

Sister Agnes gently hushed the man into silence, then led him back over to his spot. 'He was a student, back before the madness took him,' she explained. 'I brought a book in once, to see if it would trigger anything. He tore the paper up and ate the binding.'

We stood there for a while, though it was little enough edifying. Eventually I stopped looking at them, just sort of rested in my peripherals. Sister Agnes didn't follow my lead, however. The entire time we were in there she kept her eyes on her charges. That she'd been doing it for fifteen years and could still see them, that they remained people to her, rather than bipedal cattle, well – let's just say I found myself admiring the Sister enough to wish my pretext for the visit wasn't entirely fraudulent.

'I'll be back around in a little while,' she said eventually. 'Dinner is sausage and onion pie.'

One of the men fiddling with the cards looked up at her, eyes tight, trying to make out what this message could mean. Failing, he shrugged and went back to his deck, rapidly turning four cards face up, then back over, then face up again. The rest remained silently fixated on whatever was directly in front of them.

Sister Agnes closed and locked the door behind us, then headed further down the hallway. It was grimier than the entrance. The mortar in the brick walls was green and thin, and I could hear the steady drip of water coming from the ceiling. At the end of the corridor a spiral staircase descended to a lower level. It was narrow and crooked, and I found myself worried that Sister

Agnes might trip, though of course this journey was one she'd done ten thousand times before.

The subterranean level made what we'd seen so far seem quaint, even homey by comparison. Strange sounds echoed through the heavy stone, distorted and off-putting. The hallway was dark and narrow, not enough room to walk abreast. We moved in silent single file, and didn't bother with conversation till we reached the next door.

'This is where we keep our more . . . difficult cases,' Sister Agnes said. 'It would be best to prepare yourselves.'

The chamber was bigger than a coffin, though not much. A small cot took up most of the room. The man inside seemed quite harmless, to the degree that a stone is harmless, or a tree stump. All the same he was weighed down with heavy chains, thick links of iron attaching from the wall to a collar at his throat, and to cuffs on his arms and legs.

'I do so hate to keep him bound,' she said. 'But the last time we removed them, he chewed off two of his own fingers. Didn't make a sound, poor dear. Would have bled to death if we hadn't come by with dinner.'

The Sister's voice seemed to bring him out of his stupor. His eyes darted manically about the room, then locked on the three of us in the doorway. With surprising speed for a madman who'd been living in a box for fifteen years, he broke to his feet and launched himself in our direction, atrophied muscles firing into motion. There was a snap as he reached the ends of his bonds and was slammed backwards against the ground. He lay there for a moment, then began to laugh, loudly and hysterically. Or perhaps it was weeping. I wasn't sure.

Agnes closed the door with a sigh. 'There are three more with quarters down here,' she said. 'Mr Hammond here is the most stable. I don't think it'll do them any good to see you,' she said, then turned and nodded back the way we came. 'I don't suppose you'd mind if we called the tour short.'

Neither Guiscard nor I minded. We followed the Sister back down the corridor, up the stairs and towards the exit.

'As I said, anything your organization could do would be greatly appreciated. Our stipend covers the monthly costs, but nothing on top of it – it would be very fine if we could refurbish the interior, the foundations in particular are in a quite hideous state. Perhaps even buy them new clothing, bedding . . .' She trailed off, as if even these modest hopes were too audacious.

'I'll let you know as soon as I can,' I said, shamed to think that she'd never hear from me again. Though in the grand scheme of things it was far from the worst act I'd ever done – today had reminded me of that very clearly.

'Good day to you then, Mr Chamberlain. Agent.' She nodded.

Next to the door was a small alcove with an alms box inside. I put two ochres into it. Guiscard surprised me by doing the same, before stumbling outside. The Sister smiled her thanks, and closed the door behind us.

Guiscard took a seat on a low stone wall across from the asylum. It offered a pleasant view of the city below. I rolled a cigarette, lit it and handed it to him. He took it without saying thanks, puffing rapidly but without enthusiasm, eyes lost on the horizon. I started rolling another.

'It was Carroll's idea to use volunteers,' I said. 'Normally we test these things on criminals first, but he was worried that their tendency towards violence might skew the results. Honest citizens is what we were looking for. Upright, law-abiding. I believe we paid an ochre a head – quite reasonable for a few hours' work. Enough to buy a year's worth of books for a hard-pressed student. Or Midwinter's gifts for a single mother. Gave them a cup of tea with two drops of our house brew in it, had a practitioner come by while they were stoned near catatonia to give them their commands. They wouldn't remember any of that of course, not until they'd been given the command word. Then . . .' I snapped my fingers. 'They'd take care of whoever you wanted. We never did get to that part, truth be told. They took the drug, went home, and woke up a few days later broken as a spiked cannon. Not all of them, but enough.' I lit my smoke. 'The stipend must come from the Old Man. I'm surprised he remembers.'

I wasn't sure if Guiscard heard me. The cigarette I'd given him had gone out in his hand. To judge by his pallor, he seemed close to vomiting. I made sure to move a few feet away from the potential blast radius before asking my next question.

'Why haven't you moved on the Sons?'

Guiscard blinked twice, then looked up at me. 'What?'

'Why haven't you moved on the Sons?'

'We can't very well cut off the head of anyone who doesn't like the Prime Minister, can we? A certain amount of opposition is required for the system to function.'

'An illusory opposition – an opposition you can control. I'm afraid the Steps have long since grown beyond that. For the last few months I've been watching them take shots at you and wondering, why doesn't the Old Man crush them? What is he waiting for? It's a measure of my . . . respect for him that the obvious answer didn't seem so.'

'Meaning?'

'His position isn't strong enough. He no longer holds the reins.'

'The King doesn't like him,' Guiscard said after a long pause. 'Never did.'

'That speaks well of our Alfred, though I hardly see why it's relevant. The dirt he must have accumulated all these years? It was a cottage industry, back when I first joined Special Operations – you spent a month following around the Crown Prince's latest paramour, see what humiliations she got him into.'

'We've got more filth on the King than you could find knee deep in a sewer, but what would we possibly want to do with it? Alfred doesn't like the Steps any more than we do, thank the Firstborn. If we weaken his position, we weaken ours along with it.'

'Where does the army stand?'

'Hard to say. They're generally not for change of any kind, but they're damn unhappy about the rapprochement we've been working towards with the Dren.'

'Of course they are – if we're not expecting to go to war with the Dren, there's no reason to maintain their third of the annual budget.' I smiled toothily. 'And I don't suppose your having killed the leader of the Veteran's Organization enamored them to you particularly.'

'Perhaps not.'

That had been my doing, though Guiscard had never realized it. 'Still, you don't get four stars on your lapel by rocking the boat. They'll probably stand aside until they figure out who is going to win.' I started working it out in my head. 'The city will declare for the Steps – not because they're actually for them, but because they hate Black House, and they're bored easily, and they like to riot. You'll have the provinces though, I imagine, and if you can hold out the few weeks it'll take them to raise the militia, you might be able to weather the storm.'

Guiscard's silence suggested he'd followed along with my prediction.

'Of course, that's if the King stays with you.'

'Why wouldn't he?'

'Why would he? He'd have the chance to throw off the yoke his mother accepted, perhaps rule on his own, rather than as a cat's paw for the Old Man.'

'You think Monck has any intention of allowing him to make policy? He'd be trading one master for another.'

'Then maybe he just prefers brown.'

Guiscard sniffed. 'Did you bring me here, show me this – just to soften me up for interrogation?'

'That was part of it,' I admitted. 'But not everything. I wanted you to see what you're fighting to prop up. I wanted to give you that opportunity. It's easy to lose sight of it from where you are – I know that better than anybody.'

He waved backwards at the asylum. 'This isn't everything there is.'

'Of course not – there's also mansions in Kor's Heights, and humming factories in Brennock, and fat, happy, smiling children getting presents on Midwinter morning. But this is what it rests on, Guiscard, and don't you ever forget it.'

'Coronet was your project.'

318

'And I'll burn in hell for it.'

'It isn't on me. I didn't know it existed until last week.'

'And what did you do about it?'

'What?'

'When I told you about the connection between red fever and Coronet, what did you do? Did you try and shut it down? Did you make sure that no more of this poison leaked out into the city?'

He didn't answer, or if he did it was too quiet to make out.

'No, you did the opposite. You traced the leak to Carroll, and you made sure that he knew that the *status quo* was to continue unabated.'

'It was the Old Man's decision. We needed to keep you close to the Steps, and that was only possible if Carroll's operation was still a go.'

'Today, maybe tomorrow, maybe next week, someone is going to wake up from a stupor and discover they've killed their parents, or their kids, or both.' I tossed my smoke into the gutter. 'And that will be on you, Guiscard, have no single illusion on that score. Every day this continues means another patient for Sister Agnes.'

Guiscard turned and looked back at the hospital facade. 'I'll take care of it.'

'Carroll shrugs off this life of toil and pain, and he does so in the immediate future.'

'Carroll dies,' he agreed, then went back to staring out over the skyline.

Our vantage point provided an impressive view of Rigus – the crystalline towers of the Palace, the winding stone streets of the Old City. Evening was descending, and far below people were hurrying out of work, quick to get home or to their favorite bar. From up high they looked like ants. Sometimes they look like ants to me even from close in.

'The Old Man,' Guiscard said finally. 'He's going to screw you. He knows about your safe houses. The apartment in Brennock, the one above the tea shop in Offbend, that hovel near the docks.'

'How?'

'He's got someone in your camp, whispering your next moves.'

'Who?'

'He wouldn't say.'

'As it happens, I have a piece of relevant information for you as well.'

'Yeah?'

'I picked up a secure communication from Egmont's desk last time I was in there. It detailed the operators he's planted inside Black House.'

This was enough to break Guiscard out of the lethargy that had overtaken him since we'd left the asylum. He leaped to his feet, ran his hand over the stubble on his scalp. 'You didn't think this was something you should have mentioned to me earlier?'

'Not particularly.'

'Why not?'

'Because it's bunk,' I said. 'You're being played. We all are.'

36

Later that evening I was watching Wren smoke a cigarette across the street from an old stone building in the seedier section of Brennock. If you weren't paying particular attention you'd have just said he was smoking a cigarette on the street in the seedier section of Brennock, but we'd been doing this long enough that I could read his shorthand. I didn't like that he'd taken up tobacco, but then I wasn't in a situation to say much about it. I'd be happy if it was the worst of my vices he'd adopted. I made myself quiet in an alley a block or so back from where he waited and burned my own. When it was done I pulled up the collar of my coat and went to join him.

'He's in there?'

Wren nodded. 'What's the plan?'

'Follow in after me, and try to look tougher than you are.'

The door was neither unlocked, nor made of tissue paper. But you can break anything if you know where to aim. I planted the center of my boot a few inches from the handle and it flew open.

There was a glimpse of pale flesh beneath silk covers, but Captain Ascletin was up from the bed with admirable celerity, moving for a chair in the corner where he'd hung his sword and neatly folded his pants. I had a steady lead on him though, and it was easy enough to hook his foot and send him sprawling. I regretted the violence – it would only put his back up. But then I couldn't very well let him make it to his blade. The gentleman below him hadn't Kenneth's reflexes, nor his nerve, and his best attempt at resistance was to pull a corner of the sheet up over his face.

I waited a minute for it to sink in, happy I'd gotten lucky with the timing – they were deep enough in to be incriminating, but not so far along as to make things awkward. Kenneth spent the interval scraping himself up off the ground. I hoped the fall hadn't bruised any of his more tender areas.

Wren was damn near as surprised as the Captain. I'm not altogether clear on what he thought we were busting in on, but it apparently wasn't this. He watched the spectacle with something close to revulsion, as if Kenneth's dalliance was the worst thing he'd yet to lay eyes on. In some ways he was still a child.

'What the hell are you doing here?' Kenneth demanded once he finally managed to get himself to his feet. He maintained an impressive degree of imperiousness, given that he wasn't wearing any pants.

'The question isn't what I'm doing here, Captain, because no one cares about me. I'm a small-time hustler from Low Town. You, on the other hand, are one of the shining stars of the city guard, a man with promise, a man with a future. Your whereabouts would be of concern to any number of people. Your superiors at the watch, as an example. Your family would also, I imagine, have concerns about what brings you to such a disreputable part of town at so late an hour.'

The spirit went out of him pretty quick at that point, not that I blamed him. It was a lot to take in.

'Sit down, Captain. Let's chat.'

'Let me get dressed at least.'

I shook my head. The thing worked better with him flaccid and cringing. 'We're all adults here. No reason to get modest.' I gestured at the foot of the bed. There was a pause during which he examined his options, determined correctly he had none, and went ahead and followed my command. I took a chair from the other end of the room, turned it towards him and sat as well.

'You know, it's a funny thing,' I began, carefully shaking out a smoke. 'What people care about. If I'd broken in here and found you knee deep in a half dozen Kiren prostitutes, it wouldn't have meant nothing to nobody. If I'd come in here and found you say, beating a suspect with a length of pipe, that wouldn't get an eyelash batted neither. But the suggestion that Captain Kenneth Ascletin, stout of heart and broad of chest, gets his jollies playing rat-in-a-hole with a clean-limbed stranger . . .'

'No one would believe it,' he hissed.

'Of course they'll believe it – people like believing things about other people. Hell, they'd believe it even if it was a lie. That it's true is just icing on the cake.'

His shoulders slumped. He seemed to sink further into his perch. His lover reached out to touch him but Kenneth snapped his shoulder away. 'I've never done this sort of thing before,' he said, all of a sudden quite desperate to convince me of this obvious falsehood. 'It's . . . I'm not . . .'

I waved that away. 'You don't need to sell me on nothing, Captain. As far as I'm concerned this little assignation barely ranks as vice. But then, as we've already established, I don't matter – and the rest of the world is, sadly, a good deal less understanding.'

'I thought we were friends.'

'We're still friends. We're better friends. We're such good friends that I'm going to raise your take an extra two ochres a month – how's that for friendship? And now that we're so close, I feel comfortable asking for a small favor.'

'What do you want?'

'I want an active civic presence in your area – I want the brave men of the guard to perform the noble duties demanded of them by their position. In particular, I want the brave men of the city guard to perform their noble duties tomorrow morning at nine, in a warehouse at the corner of Classon and Brand.'

Kenneth was a sharp enough character, but this was a little hard to follow for a man who'd been mid-*coitus* less than five minutes earlier. 'I don't understand.'

'At the intersection of Classon and Brand, you'll find a warehouse. Tomorrow morning, at nine, a squadron of men under your command are going to enter that building. In the basement, they're going to find a laboratory making red fever. They'll destroy said laboratory, and any of the drug they find. They'll be very thorough – I think a small fire wouldn't be out of order.'

'Classon and Brand? That's Uriel's territory.'

'You know, I think you just might be right.'

Something clicked behind his eyes. 'This trouble between the Asher and the Gitts – you're behind it, aren't you?'

'I wouldn't go that far. Two groups of homicidal criminals, each bumping up against the other. The powder was already dry, if you get my meaning. I just struck the match.'

'I won't do it,' he said. 'No two-copper slinger is going to come in here and muscle me into submission.'

'I admire your spunk. But you will do it – if you take a moment to think about it, you'll realize that you will do it. Because the Gitts don't mean anything to you, and neither do the Asher – not anything against your future, against your reputation. You'd weigh your own good against a whole pile of strangers' corpses and not need to double check the scale.' I waved off his protest with the hand that wasn't rolling a smoke. 'Don't take offense – I'd do the same. Everyone would. And once you realize that, you'll realize that the only thing that's stopping you is pride. Nothing wrong with a little pride – keeps a man's spine upright, keeps his walk steady.'

I offered him the cigarette. He refused it. I stuck it between my teeth, and turned my head back on Wren. 'What did I say – pride.'

Wren didn't respond. He didn't seem to be enjoying this as much as I was.

I rounded on the Captain. 'Just don't take pride's counsel too closely. Right now it's telling you to buck – throw a punch, tell me to go fuck myself. But pride will be cold comfort in two weeks when you're busted down to private for suspicion of buggery, I can assure you of that.'

Kenneth was smart, and angry – but anger goes away after a while, and smart sticks around. He muttered something that I knew to be assent, but I needed him to say it to me straight. 'What was that?'

'I said all right, damn it.'

'I knew you'd do the smart thing.'

There was no point in hanging around and humiliating the man any further – in truth I did like the Captain. On some level I regretted getting him involved in this, though that part of me that felt bad for using people was pretty well atrophied. I signaled to Wren, and he slid out into the darkness. Then I got up from where I'd been sitting and went to join him. Kenneth made a frantic dash for his pants, pulling them on with impressive speed.

'No reason to sprint out so soon,' I said. 'The damage is done, you might as well enjoy yourself.' I stopped in the doorway. 'But don't get too wrapped up in your recreation. Business comes first, after all, and you've got responsibilities to take care of – tomorrow at nine.'

'Tomorrow at nine,' he agreed, everything that made him what he was drained out onto the floor.

'Good man,' I said, and stepped into the night.

37

We walked a few blocks east in silence, then moved into a small bar, taking a seat in the corner. Wren was holding back bile, but it had soaked out on to his face, plain as print. He'd need to control himself better if he wanted to follow in my footsteps. But then, after the night's work, I didn't think that was in the cards.

I ordered a bottle of whiskey. The bartender took a long time bringing it over, but that was fine. I wasn't particularly excited to begin the conversation that was coming.

'You didn't need me for that,' Wren said.

'Not really,' I admitted.

'Why'd you take me along?'

'Ain't you been asking to take a step up in the ranks? Tricks of the trade, my young apprentice.' I poured us both a shot, clinked my glass off his and threw back the shot. 'Cheers.'

Wren kept his hands at his sides, didn't touch the drink in front of him.

'Don't make yourself ill over it. No real harm done. The Captain is better off in my pocket than he was out there all alone, stirring up trouble.'

'He seemed real appreciative,' Wren said.

'Some people have trouble displaying gratitude.'

'You've never said anything bad about the Captain.'

'I've cut the throats of men I liked more than Captain Ascletin,' I said honestly. 'Wasn't anything personal in what we did tonight.'

'What you did.'

'What we did,' I repeated. 'I'd never have found him if it wasn't for your capable shadowing. And if you think he'll forget the face of one of the men that broke him, I can assure you, you're thinking is incorrect. No, my young friend – morally and practically, we split culpability straight down the center.'

Wren took a while to swallow that, and he needed the assistance of the whiskey I'd poured for him. 'Tomorrow the Gitts and the Asher will go to war.'

'Looks like it.'

'Gonna be a lot of bodies.'

'Couldn't happen to a nicer set of people.'

'You're always saying that violence is bad for business.'

'I do say that.'

'That only amateurs solve problems with a weapon.'

'And I stick by it. Professionals solve their problems with other people's weapons.'

'That was why you had me run that stash of fever over to Kitterin Mayfair.'

'Calum knew Uriel was behind the red fever. If he found someone selling it on his territory . . . You didn't need to be a Scryer to anticipate a reaction.'

'If there's open war in Glandon, it'll filter into Low Town.'

'Won't be the first war I've lasted through.'

'Why'd you do it?'

At the table in the corner, two amateurs were engaging in a very thinly veiled drug transaction. Alledtown wasn't the sort of place where the guard were likely to go about hassling anyone, but all the same, it offended my sense of professional pride. I took another swig of whiskey. 'I didn't raise a fool. You can't put the pieces together when they're all laid out, I got no help for you.'

He sat with uncompromising stillness for several slow heart-beats. Then he ashed his cigarette onto the floor. 'Uriel,' he said finally.

I gave him a slow clap, though he seemed not to enjoy the attention. 'How long before he and his boys look my way and start seeing a meal? This gives them something to think about for a while. And as far as the Gitts go – the world sees no shortage of hillbilly wyrm-junkies, so far as I know.'

'Who's going to win?'

I smiled something that might have been savage. 'I will. I always win.'

'If you wanted them to get going, why'd you set up this peace conference? Why work so hard to try and head it off?'

'Because it makes me look reasonable. The guards say to themselves, that Warden, he's a decent character, the sort of person you can talk to. And the other powers, they tell themselves that Warden's a good bloke, not interested in more than he's got, and he's just the one fellow, and we could take it from him if we really wanted. I'm the best-liked criminal in the city, and my hands are clean as a nursemaid's.'

'That's . . . horrible.'

I made as if to pick something out of my ear. 'A stake in the enterprise, if I remember your words correctly. What did you think that meant? You think it's just vialing breath, tossing out a few sticks of dreamvine?' I knocked back the shot and poured another. 'How do you think I hold onto what I got, me all by my lonesome? The world's full of hard men, razor boys hopped up on breath, heretics who'd slit their mothers' throats and walk over the corpse. You can't never be tougher than everyone – but by the Firstborn, you can be meaner.'

'That's what you are, then?'

'Damn right. Low Town is mine – bought with my blood and

sin. I'll hold on to it till I'm propping up dirt, and I'll put any man to sleep who gets to thinking otherwise. Put him to sleep before he gets to thinking it. That's the job – you talk fools into killing each other. They generally don't require much persuasion.'

Wren was looking at me like he hadn't never looked at me before, bitter and disappointed. That what I'd said wasn't exactly true, that maybe I had better reasons for lighting fires than just to see things burn – there wasn't any point in him knowing that. This was an object lesson – let him see it isn't a game, let him see what he'd be in for if he kept going the way he was.

But still, it hurt to have him look at me like that.

'Ain't so pretty, is it boy? This is what pays for the clothes on your back, lessons with Mazzie. You want to eat the meat, you gotta skin the buck.' I put the shot to my lips, then slammed the glass against the counter. 'Now get the fuck out of here. You're breathing my air.'

He left a copper on the counter. I picked it up and put it in my pocket. After that I got very drunk. It was a short walk back to my flophouse, but I barely made it.

38

'It smells like a set-up,' Mad Edward said, about five minutes before I killed him.

'It's too late to back out now – Hayyim is already in there. We don't show he'll figure we played him, and then it's back to knives in the alleyways.'

It was a quiet night in early spring, the first quiet night Low Town had seen in a while. We were in a side street towards the northernmost end of the docks, surrounded by row after row of bleak warehouses, all shuttered windows and boarded up doors. I was trying to convince Eddie to walk into one of them.

He was nervous. He had reason to be. 'Who says we aren't still at open war? Who says he doesn't have a handful of thugs waiting to introduce me to She Who Waits Behind All Things?'

'I've been over every inch of it myself. It's him and two of his people, and they're not carrying, just like we agreed.'

He sniffed petulantly. 'Still smells like a set-up.'

My feelings about Mad Edward, or Eddie as we called him

– his nickname was strictly to be whispered, lest he reaffirm its origins on your person – had remained steady since I'd known him as a child. The fifteen years since he'd come to power hadn't done much to make him any worse, but then there wasn't much room to fall. Of course, my not liking him had nothing to do with his imminent demise – we could have nursed from the same bosom and I'd still be doing what I was doing. He was in my way, that was as far as it went.

'None of this makes a damn bit of sense,' he said. 'Ten years I've split Low Town with Hayyim, ten years and no serious trouble. They had their ends and we had ours, and if there were any problems we settled them without going to steel.'

'Then it should be easy to get back to the *status quo*.'

'What made them start up in the first place?'

'I wouldn't hazard a guess,' I said. 'And anyway, it don't matter – we are where we are, and where we are is the end of our fucking rope.'

I was five months out of Black House, and they'd been busy ones. The last three, anyway – I'd spent the first tumbling my way into a vat of alcohol, and the second climbing my way out of it. But you can only go at self-destruction for so long. At some point you've gotta open a vein or move on. Once I decided not to do the first, there was nothing for it but to go out and find myself a job. Five years in the army and five more with Black House hadn't prepared me for anything more productive than killing people and causing trouble. Happily for me, though perhaps less so for the city and world, this was a skill set in high demand.

Eddie didn't appreciate the suggestion that the last several weeks of slaughter had been anything less than an unbroken series of victories. 'I wouldn't go that far.'

'Go wherever you like, just don't expect to have anyone following you, cause they're all fucking dead. We don't have the muscle to keep this up any longer. We lost Amos and Niklaas when they raided our wyrm den last week. Obadiah is still filling a bed at Mercy of Lizben Hospital – whoever spiked his pixie's breath knew what they were doing. If he ever wakes up again, it'll be too damn late to do us much good. Of course you know what happened to Deneys . . .'

Eddie smashed his hand against his palm. 'I still can't believe that bastard sold us out!'

It had come as some surprise to Deneys as well. 'He paid for it. Not worth putting any more thought towards.'

It hadn't taken me long to work myself into Eddie's good graces. I was a local boy – that didn't mean anything to Eddie, parochial loyalty was one of the many virtues he lacked, but still it looked good to the rest of the neighborhood. More important was I'd been someone in the real world, and it made Eddie feel special to have me getting his coffee. His last lieutenant had been cut down in the early days of the conflict we were about to bring to an end, cornered in the street and sliced apart by a team of Hayyim's heavies – a calamity, real tragic. I'd sent flowers to the funeral and taken over the responsibilities he could no longer fulfill. Once I'd gotten my in with Eddie, it was no great effort to gain the ear of his rival. Hayyim was quick to believe that Eddie was waiting to pounce, and quicker to recognize the virtue of striking first, especially with me pointing out easy targets. After that, the whole thing ran pretty predictably.

'I've never left an enemy alive. Leaves a foul taste in my mouth, this negotiation business.'

'Another month of this and you won't have an organization. We're bleeding, I don't need to tell you that.'

'They've got their share of corpses.'

'Plenty of them – so what? We don't make corpses for a living, we make money. People don't fuck whores, or smoke wyrm or toot breath if they're worried they're going to get sliced up walking down the street. Our cash flow's cut to a trickle. And how long you thing the hoax is gonna let this go on? They've got to at least pretend to do their job, and that's not easy when every night brings a fresh massacre.'

'Fuck the guard – they've been eating off my table since before

I popped my cherry. They can keep their eyes on their feet for a couple more weeks.'

'Ain't just the guard.'

Something very like fear passed behind Eddie's eyes. 'Black House?'

'They won't let this go on indefinitely. I'm hearing chatter from people back at the shop. Things don't quiet down soon, they're going to have to go ahead and bring the silence themselves.'

The entirety of Low Town could walk into the bay with rocks in their pockets for all the Old Man cared, but Eddie didn't know that. Nor did he know that I didn't have any more sources in Black House than I did on the other side of the fucking planet.

I put my hand on his shoulder. 'Today isn't tomorrow – we're hurting right now, and this is our only out. We rest up and re-arm, keep the peace until we got enough men to break it. In six months, when Hayyim's sitting fat and happy, we'll take another look at the situation. For right now, we dip our heads or we lose them.'

Credit where it's due, Eddie was a cagey son of a bitch – he wouldn't have kept his grip so long otherwise. He could smell something was off, had a dim notion that there was another hand in the mix. But he was old, and he was scared, and between the two, he made the quite fatal mistake of thinking me his friend.

He nodded slowly. 'You're right.' Decision made, he puffed his chest out and exited the alley at a good clip. At the mouth of it stood Duncan, practically the only soldier still alive, one half of the contingent of bodyguards Eddie was to take into the meeting. Duncan would do a poor job of it, but I hardly blamed him – I was the other half of Eddie's protection, and I would do a damn sight worse.

'You coming?' Eddie asked, when he saw that I hadn't followed him.

'I'll join you in there,' I said. 'I'm gonna do one last sweep.'

He nodded like he'd thought of the idea, then snapped his fingers at Duncan and headed into the meeting. I waited till they were both inside, then started off at a brisk pace.

Attached to the back of the warehouse was a small guard

shack, long out of use. Inside I'd stuffed about a pound and a half of black powder, one-third of the supply I'd smuggled out of the war. It was worth its weight in ochre, and if I'd had to I could probably have figured out a cheaper way to bring the joint reign of Mad Edward and Hayyim the Half-Islander to an end.

But this way was a statement, the start of the legend that would echo out my name. The exact circumstances would remain secret, a hallowed and well-discussed bit of neighborhood lore. But the message would be clear, clear enough to make sure that future generations of Edwards – rough and wild, looking to grab their own and more – would take a gander at Low Town, shake their heads and keep walking.

I struck a match and held it to the fuse, then dipped on out. A block later an explosion left my ears ringing, but I didn't bother to turn around and look.

39

'It's good to see all of you here today,' I began. 'It shows character, real character.'

The next morning found me in a small restaurant in the west side of Low Town, the opposite end from the docks, as far away from our disputants' territories as you could get and still be in mine. It was owned by a man I owned. Normally it makes enough for him to pay the monthlies on a debt he'll never escape. When it doesn't, he does me little favors. I'd told him to unlock the joint at nine and not come back before twelve. I was hopeful he would still have an establishment to run after lunch.

The deal had been two men apiece, but Calum had the good sense to come solo. He was worth a second by his lonesome, and the folk he had backing him wouldn't be much use over a negotiating table. Uriel had brought his brother. It would have been wiser if he had followed Calum's lead, but he probably wasn't as sure of himself up close as was the Tarasaighn. Besides, Qoheleth did not seem like the sort to be left out of a party.

We were sitting around a big circular table, the two groups as far apart as circumference would allow. I'd contracted security out to a crew of Islanders from the Isthmus. They fit the bill, being large, frightening, and unaffiliated with either of the two parties. There were a small handful of them outside, smoking dreamvine and making sure we weren't disturbed. Two more stood at the door, big men with steel weighing down their winter coats. They'd searched us all thoroughly when we'd come in a few minutes earlier.

'Obviously, you two have had your difficulties. We aren't here to relive them. We aren't here to make you best friends, or allies. We're here to make sure that we all keep making money – that's the point of this, not to figure out whose dick is bigger. Keep that end in mind, I'm sure we can reach a reasonable accommodation.' Things were moving nicely; at this point it was all over but picking up the pieces. I was anxious to reach that stage, and having difficulty keeping my mind on the proceedings.

Events were slowed by Uriel's strong attachment to the ring of his own voice. 'First I'd like to take the opportunity to express my deepest appreciation to our host, whose wisdom and good humor are an . . . example to all of us.'

I inclined my head.

'And, as he said, the issue at hand here is not the broken body of our compatriot, although we have not forgotten that. Nor the disrespect shown in injuring a member of our organization – the issue at hand is of course, how we can divide the territory east of the docks in such a fashion as to ensure that the aforementioned provocations are the last of their kind.'

'Warden's a man got words,' Calum said. 'You sound like you the same. Words is just loud breathing, far as I'm concerned. Glandon is ours. Was yesterday. Be tomorrow. Anyone thinks otherwise . . .' he trailed off, as if he couldn't be bothered to end the threat.

'We've no interest in your ancestral domain. But Glandon's boundaries, last I checked, did not extend to Brennock, nor Nestria, nor the entirety of the bay.'

338

I found my fingers dribbling a beat on the table, forced them into repose. I ought to have been at least pretending like I was interested in the proceedings, for all that I knew how things would end. What came next was still in doubt, I supposed, which of the men in front of me would be alive in a month, which of their families. The Asher knew how to brawl, no doubt about that. But Calum's folk weren't any less slow to draw steel, nor use it. I figured it'd play itself out into a bloody stalemate – Calum aside, the Gitts didn't have enough on the ball to take down Uriel – but nor could I imagine the Asher and his brother leading a team into the Gitts' territory and burning out their shacks. Of course, it wouldn't really matter – even if Uriel ended the conflict victorious, his organization would come out battered and broken, easy prey for any of the other mobs that had been watching his rise with displeasure.

For some reason I found myself going over yesterday's meeting with Guiscard, and his warning about the Old Man having a spy in my camp. At first I'd figured he'd meant Touissant, but looking at that now it didn't add up. Touissant was Crowley's creature, if the dead giant had been reporting directly to the Old Man then Crowley would have gotten called off before things had come to a head.

Back on the main stage they were hammering out the details, specific pushers to be protected, which avenues and thoroughfares were whose, the boundaries of each enterprise.

'Your wyrm den on High Street isn't big enough to hook in the whole neighborhood,' Uriel was saying.

Calum spurted tobacco juice from between closed lips, then leaked a response out through the same. 'Been doing well enough so far.'

If not Touissant, then who the fuck was in the Old Man's pocket? I don't know that many people – well, I know a lot of people, but don't many of them know me. The circle of folk who had any idea what I was doing next was small enough to keep on one hand.

So I counted them out. Should have done it the day before,

but I hadn't. Adolphus, Wren, Adeline – obviously they weren't whispering anything to Black House. Uriel broke me out of contemplation with a question I missed the specifics of.

'It depends on how you look at it,' I said.

Something else from Uriel.

'I can see both sides.'

The conversation I wasn't paying attention to was interrupted by a commotion from outside, an angry back and forth between the Islanders and a newcomer. After a moment the door opened, and a member of my security peeked in. 'Ay, Warden.'

'Yeah?'

'We got a black robe out here, says he wants to talk to the ones inside.'

The tension in the room rose a notch. 'What's this about, Uriel?' I asked.

Uriel looked at Qoheleth, who shrugged his shoulders. 'I'm not sure,' he said.

'That wasn't the deal,' Calum said, and it was hard to miss the note of menace.

'Whatever it is, you'd best figure it out quick,' I said. Uriel nodded, and I nodded at my security.

The door opened, and one of Uriel's men came inside. He took a wide route around Calum, circling the table before bending down and whispering something into his boss's ear. Uriel listened without speaking, without blinking, without breathing. Message delivered, the Asher took a few steps backwards.

Uriel didn't say anything for a while.

Then he was up from his seat, up like a shot. The table we were sitting at was a big round oaken thing, and Uriel's fist went through it with enough force to send splinters spraying in my direction. He must have broken half the bones in his hand, though he didn't seem in the mood to notice it.

'You inbred son of a bitch!' Uriel screamed. He'd pulled his hand out from the hole he'd made, brought it instinctively down to his hip. The realization that he wasn't carrying a weapon didn't slow him down, if Qoheleth hadn't wrapped him up in a bear hug I think Uriel would have climbed across the table and gone at Calum with his teeth. 'You traitorous, backstabbing cocksucker!' Uriel continued, bucking furiously in his brother's arms. 'I'm going to cut you till you beg to die! I'm going to lick your blood off of my fucking fingers! I'm going to slice your heart out and shit in the hole!'

It had taken some doing, but I'd finally managed to ruffle Uriel the Unredeemed.

The two Islanders stationed at the door got off it quick enough, pulling swords and double-timing it over. I held up a hand to keep them from using their weapons. The rest of their brethren heard the commotion and were inside a moment later. 'Nobody is doing nothing to nobody. Not so long as you're in here. What the hell is going on, Uriel?'

The half dozen Islanders with drawn steel were enough to bring Uriel down a notch, but barely. He said a word to Qoheleth in their native tongue, and his brother released him rather grudgingly. 'He had his tame Captain raid our shop! Didn't you, you sister-fucking sack of garbage. Talk peace while you've got a man cutting our throats! I don't know how you found out about it, and I don't care – it'll be the last victory you ever enjoy, I swear on the One Above. I'm going to gut you and play with your insides. I'm going to murder every living thing with a drop of your blood in their veins!'

I was never exactly sure what Calum thought about the situation. He didn't have a tame Captain on the payroll, and he obviously wasn't responsible for destroying Uriel's factory. But on the other hand, we were clearly beyond the point of explanation or excuse. And it was like I'd told Wren – these were violent men. They didn't need much of a push.

'I'll remind you of all that,' Calum said, standing, 'when I've got you strung up next to your brother.'

Uriel responded in kind, though I barely noticed him. Something had finally clicked in my head, something that reminded me the immediate goings-on were far from the largest of my concerns. I'd wasted too much time on them already. There was one person who had known of my plans but wasn't a part of them, whose guilt I hadn't even considered because it seemed so pointless and far-fetched.

'Boys, come on now, let's not have things end this way,' I said – wasted effort, even if I'd meant it. Calum had a smile on his face that would have set a child to screaming, and he walked out through the door without taking his eyes off Uriel and his brother. They'd be out the back soon after, off to headquarters to plot out the next round of violence. It was everything I could do not to hurry them out.

I needed to see Yancey the Rhymer. I needed to see him very badly.

40

I waited in the rain across from the Rhymer's house until I saw his mother leave, then quickly slipped across the thoroughfare. The lock should have been easy, a thin piece of tin worth maybe half an argent. But my hands were unsteady, and it took longer than it should have. Thankfully the weather kept traffic to a minimum, or I might have had to give an uncomfortable explanation as to why I was breaking into the house of a dying man at midday.

The foyer was dark, but I didn't need the light to find my way up to Yancey's room. Years and years I'd been coming here, years of friendship with a man I trusted, whose imminent loss was a wound I tried not to think about, who had betrayed me to my worst enemy.

Yancey's jaw was slack, his face turned up at the ceiling. He didn't notice me when I came in, or he didn't bother to react.

'Hey, brother,' I said.

'Hey.'

'I told you I'd be stopping in to say goodbye.'

'Is this that?'

'One way or the other.'

'You figured?'

'I guess that was why you only did six months for tagging that noble.'

He went on a coughing jag that lasted a very long time. 'Where's Mom?'

'I paid a boy to come by and tell her the priest at the church of Lizben had a message for her. I figure we've got another twenty minutes before she realizes he doesn't.'

'You gonna let me see the end of it?'

Walking over, waiting in the alley outside of his house, I'd wondered how I'd react to seeing him. Anger, bitterness – what was the point of any of that? Death was coming for the Rhymer, a cruel one, crueler than I'd have wished despite everything. 'Seems a little pointless.'

'Pointless,' he agreed.

'But I need to know the particulars.'

'A freeze came in to see me my second month in the cage. Said he could make all my problems go away. Said he knew the two of us were friends, said all I needed to do was keep my ears open, and pass along what went through them. I told him to go fuck himself.'

'But he came back,' I supplied after a long moment of silence.

'Once a month, every month. I was already getting sick then, I could feel it in my bones. I knew I wouldn't outlast my sentence. I thought it was prison, I thought maybe if I got out in time I could recover.'

'Why you still talking to them? Black House can't give you any more time.'

'Mom,' Yancey said, and somehow he managed to look even worse. 'They said if I didn't stay snitch, they'd go after my mom.'

And there, at raw bottom, was why there was no point in trusting anyone. Yancey wasn't a punk, wasn't a rat, hadn't sold me out for money or power. Honor, virtue, these are abstractions

344

– what do they mean set against the warm touch of a spouse, the thousand remembered kindnesses of a parent, the pregnant hopes for a child? Yancey would have done almost anything for me, but he would have done anything for his mother. And how much hate could you hate him for that, really? You don't break a man by his vices, you break him where he's the most decent. You find what he loves, and you kill him for it.

'What did you give them?' I asked.

He shrugged, then winced – it was a painful effort to raise his shoulders three inches. 'What they asked for. Haven't had much to tell them this last year though, other than the color of my wallpaper and how much it hurts to breathe.'

'They know about the berth you booked for us?'

He turned his face to the ceiling, blank eyes and an open mouth. 'Yeah.'

That was salvageable. There were plenty of other ways out of Rigus. In fact this might work to my advantage – so long as the Old Man thought he knew what my escape route was, he wouldn't spend any time looking for another.

'That's not so bad,' I told him. 'That's nothing that can't be fixed.'

'That's not all they know,' Yancey said, with a grim certainty that made me extremely uncomfortable.

I thought hard then, about the last three years, about my collection of sordid deeds, petty crimes and mild treasons. The Rhymer knew about my dealing of course, had helped set up many a buy – but the fact that I sold drugs was open knowledge, hardly the sort of thing to interest the Old Man. Mostly there was very little about me at this point that would have interested the Old Man. My evils were so far beneath his as to be barely worth notice. And I don't make a point of unveiling myself, not even to people I trust. But still there was something, a nugget of fear that grew to envelop me once I finally found my way to examining it.

'Mazzie,' I said, and as I formed the word I knew I was right. 'By the Firstborn, they know about Mazzie.'

I didn't bother for confirmation, nor did I stop to say goodbye. I was out of the room and down the stairs as quick as my feet would carry me.

'I'm sorry,' Yancey said to my back, struggling to raise his voice. 'I'm sorry!'

So was I, but it wouldn't do neither of us any good.

41

I t was too far away to sprint to. At my age a lot of places are too far away to sprint to. I kept a rapid clip through the drizzle that echoed in my chest. By the time I'd made it to the Isthmus the cloud cover had evaporated, the sun doing its best to undo the work the rain had put in the last half day. In a few hours the mud would be dirt, but just then it sucked at my boots like you'd pull a lover back into bed.

There was no concrete reason to think that the Old Man had moved on Wren, but then, fear is better than certainty. These swarmed around me, mocking my stupidity and sluggishness, taunting me with thoughts of Mazzie dead and Wren dead with her, dead or locked up below Black House, which was as bad, which was worse. All my clever maneuvering had been for shit, I'd lost the only thing in the Thirteen Lands that meant anything.

I found the first agent a half block from Mazzie's shack, face down in a puddle, motionless, drowned in three inches of water. Two more were staggered in the narrow bend of the last curve, alive and wishing otherwise. One was deep in a fit, seizing violently, head doubling back to reach his ankles, and I very much think he would have screamed if he could have. The next stared up at me, not at me, not at anything really. His eyes blinked fearful and furious, the blood frothing over his lips a sure sign that he had bitten through his tongue.

A standard Black House kill order is carried out by six men, brutes hand-picked from the lower ranks. The Old Man always has his eye out for talent, and it's never hard to find someone happy to make money doing violence to strangers. Six men are enough to kill damn near anyone, if they're armed and trained and willing. Six men would have been enough to kill me a couple of times over.

Six men were, apparently, not enough to kill Mazzie.

The latter half of the unfortunate sextet lay scattered across her front yard, face down, like parishioners at worship. The object of their exaltation sat on a tree stump, thick haunches straddling the wood, isolated by the sunshine. A fat cheroot was nestled in a corner of the smile that took up most of her face. She surveyed her fief, the little plot of upturned mud, the men she had made into bodies – and she found it to be good.

I should have been happy – Wren was safe, my enemies slain. But in fact I was only frightened. I've seen a lot of people die before, but damn few die worse than the men expiring slowly behind me in the midday sun. 'Hey, Mazzie.'

She didn't hear me. At least, she didn't react.

'Mazzie,' I said a second time, louder than the first.

Mazzie swiveled her smile over to me, nodded faintly. 'Nice to see you again,' she said.

'What happened?'

It was a minute before she answered, so occupied was she by her moment of bliss. 'Men come to take Mazzie away,' she said. 'Men came to take Mazzie away before. Mazzie got the scars to prove it, scars on her back and between her thighs. Mazzie been waiting for men to come back a second time, waiting to show them what she learned.'

Mazzie had the rather grandiose habit of referring to herself in the third person. Under the circumstances I was little inclined to call her out on it. 'What did you do to them?'

'Who, them boys?' She waved vaguely in the direction of the men she'd worse than killed. 'You tell me once, never teach Wren nothing of the void. I kept my promise – he's pure as a virgin.' She took the cigar out of her mouth and leaned forward. Her eyes were holes in her head that went back as far as you'd care to look. 'That don't mean Mazzie had nothing to teach.'

I shivered through the warmest day in a month. 'Wren here?'

'He in the hut. He would have helped, if I'd let him.' She put her smoke back between her teeth. 'I didn't need it.'

Behind me one of the agents recovered the capacity for speech, though not movement, staring up at the sky and shaking back and forth. 'The worms the worms the worms the worms the worms the worms the worms the worms the worms the worms . . .'

'You hush now,' Mazzie said. 'Mazzie be getting to you in a minute.'

Whether on her order or by coincidence, the agent fell silent. I couldn't help but wonder what he was seeing, and to be grateful that I'd never find out for certain.

'They're after the boy,' I said. 'Trying to get to me through him.'

'Yeah.'

I tilted my head at the soon to be carrion. 'You've made the list as well. They'll be back, and back soon. Best not be here when they come.'

Mazzie was lost in days long gone, head cocked absently up at the sky, and it was a minute before she answered. 'I ain't going nowhere. Men want to come look for me, they'll find me here.'

'Black House has practitioners on the payroll – whatever you can do, they got people who can do worse.'

She shrugged, unimpressed. 'I can do some awful things.'

For which we had ample evidence.

'You take the boy out the back,' she said. 'He don't need to

349

see nothing. You tell him to do right by what he got inside him. You tell him to think kindly of me.'

'I won't need to.' I stood there for a minute, a minute longer than I ought to have been standing there, given how much I had to do, and a minute longer than I wanted to be standing there, given what I was looking at. But I figured that I owed Mazzie another crack at saving her life. 'It's not like you've got so much here worth holding on to. We're heading out tomorrow, for the Free Cities. I can arrange an extra berth.'

There was a long pause, though I didn't get the sense that Mazzie was giving any particular thought to my suggestion. More that she'd forgotten I was still in front of her. 'I ain't going nowhere,' she said a second time.

That was what I figured. I made for the doorway, stopped when she started speaking again.

'You ain't going nowhere, neither.'

'I told you, I'll be gone tomorrow. I've got nothing keeping me here.'

She turned her attention away from what she'd done, looking at me with something like pity. 'You ain't never leaving Low Town, child. They gonna stick you in the dirt, same as Mazzie.'

There was nothing to say to that. I peeled apart the canvas curtain and walked inside.

Wren was keeping it together well enough, given everything. He sat in one windowless corner of the hovel, and he was very pale.

'You all right?' I asked.

He nodded.

'We're getting out of here.'

'What about Mazzie?'

'Mazzie can handle herself.' He opened his mouth to protest and I shook my head quickly. 'There's no time to argue – she's made her choice. You know as well as I that there's nothing either of us can do to change it.'

He nodded at his shoes. 'Where are we going?'

'You're going to the docks. Adeline is there already, you can hole up with her until I come for you.'

'Where are you going?'

'I'm doubling back to the Earl, to pick up Adolphus. I shouldn't be long.'

Wren stood up from his seat. 'Time's wasting.'

It was indeed. We hustled out the back door, down a side path leading north. A few yards down there was a little gap between the hovels, and I took a last look at what we'd left behind.

Mazzie was bent double over the body of an agent. One hand held his head up by his hair, the other pressed an oversized carving knife against his throat. She hummed tunelessly. There was a flash of sun against upturned metal, and then a bright spurt of blood.

I turned away. It was the last I would ever see of Mazzie of the Stained Bone – and for all the good she had done me and mine, I can't say I was sorry for that fact.

42

Adolphus was as large in death as he'd been in life, six and a half feet of cold flesh splayed across the floor. He had two bolts in him, and a half dozen wounds from knife and sword.

Two men joined him in permanent repose. The first stared up at the ceiling with unblinking eyes and an indention several inches square intruding into his brainpan. The second lay in the corner, his skull swiveled backwards. I recognized the one that was still recognizable as being a member of the party that had intruded on the Earl a day earlier. Crowley was not a sentimentalist – it hadn't been worth the trouble to move his people from where they fell, let alone ensure their return to the dirt.

I closed Adolphus's eye. I took a seat at a nearby chair, one of the few still standing. I smoked a cigarette, watched the fat man on the floor begin the slow process of decay.

I made a decision.

Upstairs in my room I cracked open my arsenal, buckled on

my old trench blade and made sure of my daggers. I had a crossbow I'd bought from a crooked quartermaster a few years earlier, and I stuffed that into a sack and took it along also. From the false bottom in my closet I removed a dozen vials of pixie's breath and slipped them into my coat.

Down at the bar I grabbed a bottle of rotgut, took a swig, winced at the taste, took another. I found Wren's bed, unmade as usual, and poured out the rest of the bottle on top of the matting. Then I lit a match and walked out the front.

I pulled a vial of breath out from my pocket, inspected it for a moment, the pink mist flecked with gold. I undid the top, felt the old movement come back natural, though it had been three years since I'd popped one for recreational use. The first hit and I couldn't remember why I'd ever stopped.

The Earl took a while to get going. I was through my first vial by the time the fire started to show, flickers of orange through the front windows, a faint but perceptible rise in the temperature. I cracked open another and watched my home burn.

Guiscard was careful to make a lot of noise as he approached. It was a good time to be wary around me. I was looking for an excuse.

'I wouldn't think it wise to show up here, under the circumstances,' I said, resting my hands on the hilt of my trench blade.

'I'm here alone,' he said. 'And I didn't have anything to do with your man's death.'

I reached over and pulled at the lapel of his duster. 'They don't let you hold onto that, if you retire. I should know.'

'This wasn't Black House.'

'Crowley don't work for Black House?'

'I told you before – Crowley's writing his own ticket.'

'And the team you sent after the boy? You're going to tell me Crowley had nothing to do with that?'

Guiscard wouldn't meet my eyes. 'It was an insurance policy – once we realized what Crowley had done, the Old Man wanted something to bring you to heel.'

My bedroom window burst from the heat, and the fire pulsed

out, reacting to the sudden rush of air. 'How does that seem to be working?'

'The Old Man doesn't want this to affect the situation with the Steps.'

'Even the Old Man don't always get what he wants.'

'He's willing to forgive the dead agents.'

'How kind of him.'

'And he's willing to do whatever else he needs to square accounts.'

'You've got nothing can balance the ledger.'

'Crowley's holed up at one-forty-three Stamford Avenue. Whatever happens to him is no longer our concern. He'll have some people with him, how many we're not exactly sure. You want me to detail a hit squad as back-up, that can be done.'

'I'll take care of it myself.'

'That's what I figured.'

I could feel the breath spreading out through my sinuses and into my brain and into my lungs and into my soul. I forced myself to cap the vial, then put it into my pocket. Three years off the stuff, my tolerance wasn't what it had been. Today wasn't the time for an overdose. Tomorrow, maybe. 'How you feel about all this Guiscard?'

He didn't answer.

'Does this have the flavor of a man with a strong hand on the tiller?'

'There's still time to salvage things – if you're willing to think logically, and not act on impulse.'

'How long have you known me?'

'A while now.'

'Have I given you the impression of a man willing to forget an injury?'

'No,' he said.

'How smart are you, Guiscard?'

'Not as smart as I thought I was.'

'That you can recognize that is a point in your favor.'

Karl came out from the house next door. I hadn't seen him

since that first day, hadn't been looking for him particularly. He took in the growing conflagration, then sprinted over to where I was standing. As close to a sprint as an old drunk can manage, at least. 'Your bar is on fire!' he yelled. We were about two feet from each other, but he yelled anyway.

'That would seem to be the case.'

'Aren't you going to do something about it?'

'I am doing something about it,' I said. 'I'm smoking a cigarette.'

His mouth quivered indiscreetly, fat lips surrounding a partial collection of yellowed teeth. A few seconds of that and he turned to Guiscard. Guiscard didn't look at him. Guiscard wasn't in a position to do anything for anyone, though it took Karl a while to realize it. Finally he turned and ran off, presumably to alert the city guard. I didn't think they'd do much for him either.

'Are you smart enough to know which way the wind's blowing?' I asked.

'What does that mean?'

'The Old Man is gone, he's done. He's had a good run, or maybe a bad one, but either way it's one that's coming to an end. The Steps are going to put him down, and I'm going to help them.'

'Why are you telling me this?'

'Because you're going to help me.'

I'd been working at Guiscard since before I figured what I'd need him for, since I noticed that little worm of self-doubt had taken root inside him. That's what I do really, chisel at weak links. Of course, he wasn't going to bend just like that. He'd need to be shivved into it. 'I've spent ten years in service to the Throne. You think I'll betray Black House like that?'

'The place ain't going nowhere – you'll just be in charge of it. And when you are, what looks like treason will be revealed as preemptive loyalty. Who exactly do you imagine you're betraying? The King? He'll be fine, the Steps will need a figurehead, same as ever. The country? It hasn't exactly flourished in the hands of our current tyrants. The only person who loses out in this is the

356

Old Man, and I can't imagine even you're so foolish as to think you owe him anything.'

We watched the fire burn. Fire does that.

'And what?' Guiscard asked. 'Trust my future to the good graces of the Sons?'

'Why not? Today, a man like you swapping sides, that could tip the balance. You kick them the Old Man, you tell the rest of the force to stand down – some of them won't listen, but some of them will. You're a noble, and high ranking – the Steps are going to need someone to tell the old guard the new one's arrived. You'd be as good as gold to them.'

'And what about tomorrow? What happens when I'm not so useful, when they've got the whole thing sewed up?'

'If I was to be worried about tomorrow, I'd be worried about one wherein I threw my weight behind an aging monster without the strength to keep his grip. The Old Man will not hold the city another month. You stand with him, you'll fall with him, and I can promise you the drop will be steep.'

'The Steps are fanatics. They're trying to destroy the Empire.'

'No, they're just trying to steal it. Line up early, and you can get a place at the table. You think the Sons of Śakra won't need a secret police? Hell, they probably won't even make you wear the hat.'

Guiscard had gone silent, staring into the flames.

'Take this as your fair warning, and one you don't deserve. I'm bringing it down, all of it, the whole damn thing. You'd best not be standing beneath it when it goes.'

At the end of the day, Guiscard wasn't any worse than anyone else, and better than most. But we're all pretty attached to our own skin. I might have exaggerated the degree of certainty with which I predicted the demise of the present order, but it was a plausible enough scenario. And when it came down to it, who had any real loyalty to the Old Man, or the world he had built?

The bonfire threw his face into sharp relief against the coming night. 'Even if I were to . . . consider something like that – how would I go about doing it?'

'You're running security for the Old Man, yes?'

'Yes.'

'Stop running it.'

'It's not that simple. The Old Man doesn't trust anyone, and he isn't the sort to stick his neck out on my say so. He's holed up deep – you want to lure him out, you'll need bait.'

'I'll get it.'

'You'll get it,' he repeated. 'Care to tell me what it will be?'

'You'll know when you need to.'

A scrap of fire jumped from the roof of the Earl onto Karl's house. The city guard was also responsible for putting out fires, though they took as much interest in that as they did locking up criminals. If Karl had been wiser he'd have spent his time pulling what few possessions he owned outside into the street, rather than running off to alert the hoax. They'd come eventually, too late to save the bar of course, though probably in time to stop the rest of the block from going up with it.

'Did it occur to you that the fire might spread?' Guiscard asked.

I flicked the end of my cigarette into the inferno that had been my home. 'It had very much occurred to me,' I said.

43

Enjolras could see there was something off with me, and was doing his best to take advantage of it. It had been a while since I'd had any breath in my system, and it was having more of an effect than I'd anticipated. My teeth edged against each other, my mouth was dry and pinched. Beneath the table I clenched and unclenched my fists compulsively. Aside from my fidgeting, the simple nature of the request was enough to tip him to a desperate situation. No one asking to be smuggled out of Rigus on the next morning's tides is operating from a position of strength.

I was starting to get very antsy. This was the least of what I needed to get done, and I had little enough time to do any of it.

'Five ochres,' he said, 'and that's the last number I'll quote.'

'Three.'

'Four,' he said, making a liar of himself very quickly.

For four ochres you could sleep in the Captain's bed on a caravel, and eat like a noble besides. It was closer to rape than robbery, but I was over a barrel. I'd have paid twenty ochres to get Wren and Adeline away from what was coming. I'd have paid forty. I'd have given every copper I'd ever owned.

We were in a little shithole tavern by the wharf, wedged tightly into a booth in the back. Though as the entirety of the establishment could have fit comfortably into some of the nicer outhouses I'd been in, the back was near the same as the front. At the counter the bartender stared out his open door, wiping the counter numbly. He'd been wiping at the same spot since we'd come in. It was the only clean spot on the bar, but that hadn't yet occurred to him. I was pretty sure he'd taken a dose of Ouroboros Root, though the effects of that hallucinogen are often indistinguishable from simple idiocy. The only other occupant was the resident whore, fat-faced and fat-thighed, the first painted up like a doll, the second on display below the skin-tight skirt she wore. After a futile few moments of trying to attract our attention she'd given up and gone back to her spot at the window.

Enjolras was one of the many petty smugglers that worked the Kinterre-to-Rigus route, had a junk called *Kor's Bitch* that he held together with turpentine and string. He brought in wyrm and dreamvine and sometimes the occasional unfortunate girl, destined to live out a short life in one of the brothels his countrymen ran. Rigun was his second language, the first being a sort of gutter Tarasaighn all but indistinguishable from gibberish. He'd worked for me a few times, hustling in product. He'd always played square, but then in the past the stakes had been considerably lower.

I counted two ochres out from my pouch and handed it to him. 'You'll get two more when you're in Kinterre.'

'All right.'

'You leave tomorrow before dawn.'

'Before dawn.'

'And they're your only human cargo – no other passengers. Four ochres buys out the rest of the vessel.'

'We don't generally carry travelers. But there's a cabin in the back they can have. It's small, but cozy.'

His 'cabin' was a few square yards by the bilge, covered over with old foodstuffs in case the authorities decided to search it, and usually filled with contraband. But it would do for ten days' sail to Kinterre. Anyway, I wouldn't be using it.

I hadn't touched the beer I'd bought when I'd come in, and it wasn't because I didn't want a drink. I desperately wanted a drink. I more than wanted a drink, I was pretty sure I needed one, like a weed in the desert. I just didn't want this one, because it smelled distinctly of piss. 'They tell stories about people in your position, who decide once they're out to sea that there's no point in keeping the promises they made on land. They figure they'll steal what they can off the corpses they make, and they won't need to worry about retribution, since anyone who might offer it is stuck a thousand miles away.'

Enjolras spat onto the floor but didn't look away. 'People tell all kinds of stories. Most ain't nothing more than that.'

'People tell stories about me, too.'

'Yeah.'

'Every one of them is absolutely true. The boy and his mother don't show up at Kinterre in ten days, won't nothing happen to you right away. But one night, long after you've forgotten this conversation and what you've done, you'll answer a knock at your door and men you've never seen will be standing there. And then they'll do things to you, Enjolras – terrible thing, vile things, things that no man should ever have done to him. And as you suffer, and shortly before you die, you'll wonder desperately what could possibly have possessed you to set yourself up for such a . . . horrific end, just to have carried around a few extra ochres in your pocket.' I let the pause build. 'But you won't get no answer.'

By the time Wren and Adeline did or did not make it to their destination I would almost certainly be dead. There was, of course, no need for Enjolras to know that. And if I were to live out the next few days, and if Enjolras was to have betrayed me – well, then my threats would have been far from empty.

He went white and drank the rest of his shitty beer before

speaking. 'By Śakra the Firstborn and his consort Prachetas, by Lizben the Kind, by Kor who watches over sailors – your people will be in Kinterre in ten days' time, or my junk will be in the bottom of the ocean.'

I let him sweat for a while before speaking. 'You didn't swear by me.'

'I swear by you, Warden. I swear on your name.'

That wasn't near good enough, but it was all I'd get. I nodded and stood. 'Till tomorrow, then.'

'Till tomorrow,' he agreed.

Adeline had been keeping her head down at an inn called the Half-way Home for the last two days, and I'd sent Wren to join her after I'd picked him up at Mazzie's. It was a short walk, a half dozen blocks, but during it I took the opportunity to finish off another vial of breath.

The Half-way Home was also a shithole. There are very few establishments near the docks that cannot claim that dubious distinction. Adeline's room had a back entrance, and I climbed up the narrow wooden staircase that led to it after making sure no one was following.

She was nervous, understandable even from what little she knew of the situation, but she was holding it together. I locked the door behind me. Would have bolted it and shoved a chair against the handle, if there had been a bolt to shove, or any furniture apart from the crumbling bed Adeline was sitting on. Wren stood at the other end of the room, staring through a little window at the slums and the bay beyond.

'There's been a change of plans,' I said.

Adeline nodded.

'We aren't going to the Free Cities next week on an Islander caravel. You're going to Kinterre, tomorrow at first light, in the bilge of a Tarasaighn junk.'

'You said "you",' Adeline noted.

'Because I'm not coming, not right now, and neither is Adolphus. We've got to stick around for a little while, make sure some things here work out a certain way. We'll follow in a couple of days, should be right behind you. But don't wait for us – you get a berth on the first ship heading to the Free Cities. If we don't see each other in Kinterre, we'll meet up across the sea.'

'Where is he?'

I'd been mentally preparing myself to lie for the last forty minutes or so, but I froze at the moment of truth, had to play for time by fiddling with my cigarette. In short, it was not my best performance. 'He's at the Earl, I'm going to pick him up after I'm done here.'

Adeline was all but impossible to lie to. What took a Questioner an hour and a selection of sharpened metal to learn she could pick up in a second-long glance. Generally she tempered her insight with an astute capacity for not asking certain questions. I wished she hadn't asked this one. 'What are you two going to do?'

'We're going to handle some things that need to be handled. I need someone to watch my back, just for the next couple of days. Don't worry about us – the things we've been through, this barely qualifies as a scrape. You'll be listening to his stupid jokes before you know it.'

I think she must have known this was a lie; my story was full of holes big enough to drive a wagon through. But she didn't call me on any of them. Perhaps some part of her mind – that bit below full consciousness which is concerned only with self-preservation – perhaps it knew that to inspect my claim too deeply would make it impossible for her to keep going. 'All right,' she said finally, though of course it wasn't that at all.

I counted ten ochres from my purse and handed them to Wren. They represented most of my current stash, but I was pretty sure I wouldn't be needing money much longer. 'This is hers,' I said, 'but I trust you to hide it better. Two go to the Captain, once he drops you in Kinterre – two and not a damn copper more. There's an account drawn up at the Ormando banking house, in New Brymen.'

'How much?'

'A little north of a thousand ochres.'

363

Wren released a thin intake of breath, though by my way of thinking it was an awfully paltry sum for a lifetime ill spent.

'I don't trust the men taking you there any more than I trust anyone else outside of this room, and you shouldn't either. Lock the door, sleep in shifts. The first hint you smell of anything you ace the captain, and you do it public like, with the Art – you can do that, right?'

'I can do that,' he said, nodding fiercely.

'They'll be pissing themselves to think they've a practitioner aboard, and that should keep them honest for the rest of the voyage. But don't kill more than two of them, or there won't be enough people left to run the ship.'

'I got it.'

'I mean don't kill anyone if you don't have to. That would really be best.'

'I got it,' he repeated, aggravated.

That was all I had to say to him. Actually I had much more to say to him, hours and hours of monologue, but that was all I did say to him.

'Adolphus will join us soon,' Wren said or asked, I wasn't sure.

'I don't have the time to repeat myself. You'll see him in Kinterre in two weeks, or in the Free Cities in a month and a half. Find yourself at the *Kor's Bitch* tomorrow morning before dawn. Don't leave the room till then.'

That was the end of it, there was no point in a dramatic farewell, both because I was still pretending this wouldn't be the last time we'd see each other and because I'm just generally not one for melodrama. Adeline isn't either, but I suppose she's further in that direction then I am, because before I could bolt out the back she stepped forward and took me into an awkward embrace.

I didn't want a hug from Adeline. I was about to start doing some things for which being human was a distinct liability, and the smell of her hair and the feel of her fat arms holding me were sharp reminders of the few steps I still was away from monster. I squeezed her back and tried to keep my mind off the twenty years I'd known her, the meals she'd made me, the confidences we'd shared. Of what she'd meant to the best friend I'd ever had, that she'd been mother to the boy who was nearly my son.

Then it was time for Wren. My mouth was dry and I had a pretty bad headache, the pixie's breath the cause and the remedy. Wren was watching me with an intensity that made me want to look away, so I didn't look away, I looked back at him, harder, till he slid his eyes off mine. I reached my hand out. He took it after a moment, squeezed it harder than was really necessary. 'Look after yourself,' I said.

They weren't much for last words, but they were all I could find right then. I left by the back exit, flinching when the door closed.

44

I huffed breath till my head was the size of a watermelon, then went to kill a man. A lot of men, most likely.

The address Guiscard had given me was in the far east corner of Offbend, a half hour's walk through some of the city's less savory boroughs. I had daggers in my belt and my boot, and my trench blade swinging at my side. The crossbow hung on my back, more bolts than I'd need in my pouch. I moved at a rapid clip, steel rattling with every step. The carnivores looked away as I passed, made sure to give me a wide berth.

One-forty-three Stamford Avenue was a detached two-story wooden house at the end of a street of slum tenements. It was bigger than I had anticipated, which was worrisome. Crowley had brought six men when he'd come looking for me last time, minus the two Adolphus had taken care of meant four that I knew about for certain. It was best to assume there were more, that he'd re-upped after the fiasco at the Earl, that he knew I was coming for him and was well prepared.

It didn't matter. Crowley could have had a dozen men in there, two dozen, a hundred. The end was imminent, and I was bringing it to them.

I needed to get the attention of the men on the inside, focus them in my direction. A warning maybe, except that I didn't want any of them taking heed of it and making a break. I settled for a statement of fact, though if you didn't know better you might have mistook it for a threat. 'Every man here is a corpse!' I screamed. No one said anything, but from inside I could hear the bustle of movement.

I never had much use for crossbows. They break easy and they're slow to reload, and they're inaccurate as hell, or at least I am with them. But they're powerful – a bolt will go through an oak door like it was paper, and come out the other end bloody. It was a good opening, which was why I'd taken it out from my stash.

I'd taken something else out as well, a cloudy jewel in a silver setting. Crispin's Eye, the same one I took from his body after I'd gotten him killed six years earlier.

But first things come first. I nocked a quarrel to the crossbow and settled along the sights. This was one of the newer versions, a simple trigger as the firing mechanism. I hadn't used one since the war, was unprepared for the kick against my shoulder that would swell into a bruise if I survived the next few minutes. The bolt spiraled towards the door, and I quickly forgot about it.

The Eye was warm in my off hand, warmer than a normal stone would be, and I concentrated on that warmth, let it roll through my palm and down my arm. Let it go deeper, coasting with my blood as it pumped into my body, down into my chest and somewhere deeper still. Swam in it, let it overtake me, breathed it down in place of air. It felt like I was under forever, though I knew from previous experience that it had lasted only a fraction of a second.

When I opened my eyes it was on a new world. A horsefly fastened around the discharge of a nearby outhouse, and I could count the beat of its tiny wings. The bolt I'd just fired spun lazily through the ether, and if I wanted I could have numbered each bristle of its feathers. I could have reached out and grabbed it in flight, sprinted ahead and beat it to the target.

Instead I dropped the crossbow, its descent slow as a feather's, then sprinted around the back. By the time the bolt reached its destination I had reached mine, though I heard its effects with uncanny clarity – heard it puncture wood and rupture flesh, heard the sharp intake of breath and the scream that followed.

I made the second-floor terrace in a single leap, grabbing the balcony with an outstretched hand and swinging myself up after – an impossible feat, but then I wasn't human any longer. The back door was locked and barred. I touched it with the palm of my hand and it burst like a ripe blister, splintering wood through the interior.

Inside were two men, very much not expecting to die. Their heads were turning towards me, swiveling in surprise or terror, it was never quite clear, because before sentiment could manifest on their faces I did for both of them, two strikes with my trench blade, the hardened steel cutting through flesh as easily as air.

I was into the next room before their bodies bounced off the ground. An injured man lay groaning on a bed in the corner. His face was wrapped tight with cloth, Adolphus's handiwork presumably, and I took a thin sort of pride in thinking of my old friend's strength. I finished what he had started, one quick severing stroke doing for the man's body and the bunk he lay on top of.

Three down in less time than it took to finish a sentence, four if you counted the one downstairs, screaming his short way to death. I was burning through my future quickly now, sunny afternoons in the shade and cool autumn evenings, but I didn't expect I'd ever see them so there wasn't any point in being miserly. There were more men than I'd thought there would be, I could hear them shuffling below – but what did numbers matter? Stack the deck all you want, I had the high card stuffed into my cuff.

Down the steps and there was one in front of me, and then there were just parts of him – a hand clutching a sword in the corner, a half-shorn head in the other, lips still quivering. The next one was faster, or maybe the buff was starting to wear off, whatever it was he got his sword up to parry. My movements were too swift for the steel to take it any longer, and my blade shattered, fragments flying off in all directions. I was too quick for this also, ducking beneath the shrapnel, but my opponent was just a man, and he screamed as the cloud of metal entered his face and his neck, leaving him blind and disfigured and well on the way to death.

I thought about grabbing a weapon off a corpse, but decided there wasn't any point. My hands were a personal introduction to She Who Waits Behind All Things. In the front room a man rolled on the ground with my bolt stuck in his chest, two others standing over top of him. The first had his back turned and I could hear his spine shatter as I set my foot against it, internal organs rupturing into pulp. The second had his sword out, a long saber that he tried to keep between us, an admirable if useless tactic. I slipped past his guard like he was a stone statue, brought my fist up to his cheek, watched his head rotate halfway around his spine.

There was a noise from behind me and I whirled in time to catch Crowley burst through the door. It took me a second – not really a second, it felt like a second but it wasn't that, wasn't a tenth of that – to realize that we were moving at the same speed. It made sense – we'd both gone all in at this point. He started to draw his weapon, the gleaming, beautiful short sword that's the second most valuable object an agent possesses, and I wound up and kicked him in the crotch hard enough to ensure whatever bastards he had running around wouldn't walk right for a solid week. A blow like that would have put a normal man out of action, hell, a blow like that would have outright killed most men, but Crowley and I were both well beyond that.

Still, it was enough to stun him for whatever fraction of a moment we were both operating in, and while it lasted I knocked the weapon from his hand. I had a selection of daggers about my person and I was damn sure Crowley had the same, but neither of us went for them. We went for each other, our hate so pure as to allow no intermediary.

I'm not sure what it would have looked like to someone peeking in through the window – flashes of color, vague kinetic bursts, each individual movement taking place far too quickly to make out. We were both spending our future at a tremendous pace, years, decades, there was no way of knowing. Whichever one of us survived this would come out an old man.

There was no art to our combat, just two people wailing on each other and waiting to see who dropped. He hit me in the chest with a punch that would have fractured stone, but it barely knocked the wind out of me. I returned it, three quick shots to his face, but on the third I broke a knuckle, could feel it crack against the bent cartilage of Crowley's nose.

I could feel myself losing the buff, my motions getting laggard, the honey-sweet spot that had kept me superhuman impossible to maintain. Crowley hadn't been under as long, or maybe he wanted it more than I did. Regardless, he was quick to take advantage of my weakness, wrapping both hands around my throat and squeezing with admirable intensity.

I fought back as best I could, short, savage blows against his face. My broken hand screamed at me every time I connected, begged me to stop, but I ignored it and kept throwing. Crowley's face was a haunch of raw meat, an open wound above a fat neck. But he didn't slacken his grip, indeed he strengthened it against the pain. I reared back and threw everything into one final blow, and it collapsed the socket of his eye, breaking the cavity, off-white ooze running down his face.

But still he wouldn't let go. At bottom, I think I was not the hater that Crowley was.

The gem fell from my hand, hit the floor and rolled into a corner. Crowley dropped down into normal time, smiling through a broken jaw filled with broken teeth, his one good eye jubilant.

Things went dark, the scope of my sight closing inward. The last time this had happened Adolphus had been there to save me. I'd let him die and I'd failed to avenge him, and I deserved what was coming.

The pain started to go away. The pain is always the last thing to go away, but I held onto it as long as I could.

Then the pressure on my throat eased, and the light came back. The boy was standing there, amidst the corpses. He had his hands positioned strangely, fingers interlaced as if to throw shadows against the wall. Crowley seemed not to recognize Wren, he was so caught up in the thrill of a fresh homicide. He started to say something, but never finished.

Wren reshuffled his hands. There was a very bright glow, like staring at the sun if the sun decided to come down and say hello. The pressure on my throat eased away. It was the only thing keeping me in place, and I collapsed onto the ground.

Crowley collapsed next to me. The skin and flesh on his torso were burned away, I could count each organ, watch his gray lungs heaving, his heart beat its last. His one good eye centered on me. I watched it flutter to a close.

It was less fulfilling than I had anticipated.

I lay there a while. I would have lain there a while longer, if I could have. I think I would have lain there till the end. Wren wouldn't let me though, that little bastard. Picked me up off the ground, steadied me against the wall. My legs collapsed beneath me. Wren helped me up again, and that time I managed to stay steady as he wrapped my arm around his shoulder and dragged me out of the abattoir and into the street.

45

We found ourselves in a bar just off the main quay called the Homeward Winds. It was a quiet little dump owned by an old comrade of mine, name of Lumiere. I used to slip in there on nights when the Earl was too busy for my tastes, when I wanted a little bit of quiet. The Winds had that in spades. Lumiere ran the bar as well as owning it, and he was a cold, unfriendly fellow, who seemed to have more of a taste for hitting people than he did speaking with them. He really had no business owning a bar, but it wasn't my place to tell him that.

Wren disappeared for a few minutes, ostensibly to the toilet, in actual fact to pull himself together. He'd well earned some time to himself. While he was gone I put enough breath into my body to allow it to forget some portion of its injuries. Then I had a quiet few words with Lumiere. He was nodding when the boy came back in.

I was up at the counter, but I walked him to a table in the corner. 'You hanging on?' I asked.

'I'm fine.' His face made a lie of his bravado. I signaled Lumiere for two draughts of ale. We waited silently until it came.

'To your father,' I said.

Wren drank it quickly. I didn't look into his eyes, but if I had I'd have noticed they were wet.

'Then Adolphus is . . .' Wren trailed off.

'Yeah.'

'And that man I . . .'

'Better you'd never learned what it felt like to put a fellow away,' I said. 'But since you had to – I'm glad it was him.'

Wren nodded, but he didn't seem to take much comfort in it. I watched him down his beer, trying to wash away the memory of the life he'd snuffed. A lot of them take to it, the young ones especially. I saw plenty of that in the war, quiet boys gone loud with their first taste of blood. Dangerous in anyone, doubly so for someone with the Art. But I could see from his eyes that Wren wouldn't go in that direction. He looked miserable, and lost.

I felt so damn proud of him, just then. He was maybe the only thing I ever got right in a long life of foolishness and barbarity.

We drank a while in silence.

'What are you thinking about?' he asked.

'My mother.'

'I thought she died when you were a kid.'

'Doesn't mean I can't think about her.'

'What do you remember?'

'Small things,' I said. 'There was a song she used to sing, to me and Henni. She was half-Islander, they've all got a touch of minstrel in them.'

'You never told me that.'

'Father was an Asher, I think. Unredeemed of course.'

'They must have cared for each other.'

'I suppose.'

'What did she look like?'

'I can't remember,' I said, which wasn't true.

We finished off our drinks, and I signaled Lumiere to bring us two more.

'What happens now?' Wren asked.

'The plan hasn't changed,' I said. 'You and Adeline are off to Kinterre at dawn. I'll be following you when I can.'

'It's a little late in the day to be squaring me out of accounts.'

'It's a little late in the day, period.'

'I'm part of this now, like it or not. I killed a man tonight.'

'Let's quit while you still feel bad about it.'

'You don't feel bad about it.'

'I am what I am. I'd like to see you be more.'

Lumiere had a mirror behind the bar, though it took me a while to realize who it was reflecting. My hair had been dun with streaks of gray in it two hours earlier. Now it was white as bone. How many years had that stunt with the Eye cost me? Ten? Twenty? I pawed at the fresh wrinkles on my face, lines like a gnarled oak. I hadn't ever been a vain man – I'd never had anything to be vain about – but still, it was a hell of a thing, sitting there and seeing what I'd sacrificed.

I was grateful for the boy's interruption. 'What's your plan, then?'

'Crowley wasn't the only one I owe something to.'

'You're going after the Old Man?'

I nodded.

'Then I'm with you. Adolphus was my father; he deserves that much.'

'You think he'd want you dead?'

'What he wants don't much matter anymore, does it?'

'Of course it does,' I said. 'It matters now more than ever.'

Wren looked into his beer a while. 'I got a right to make my own mind up on this one.'

'You do. You're a man, and I'm proud as hell to think I've had a hand in you becoming one. I'm not telling you to go – I'm asking you.'

He stared off into space for a while, thinking it over, bitter and confused and young, mostly just young. 'I won't leave you here to face it alone,' he said finally. 'I can't.'

'You're sure?'

Wren nodded firmly.

'All right.' I waved to Lumiere. He reached beneath the bar, filled two shot glasses and brought them over to us on a tray.

I took the one nearest me, handed Wren the other. We touched them against each other, then drank them in turn. Mine was strong whiskey, and it burned happily on its way down.

Wren set his own back on the table, frowning and licking his lips. After a moment he swirled his finger into the dregs, coming up with an unpleasant black slick. It took him another second to put it all together.

'Mother's Helper,' I said. 'A few grains of that will knock out a bull.'

He stood up from his seat, then promptly collapsed backwards. Lumiere was waiting to catch him, eased him slowly down to the floor. An unpleasant fellow, Lumiere, but reliable.

'Be easy, be easy,' I said, climbing out of my chair and kneeling down beside Wren. 'You fight you're only gonna give yourself a headache.' Actually, either way he was going to wake up in eight hours with the most awful fucking pain in his skull that you could imagine, but there was no reason to let him know that in advance. 'You look out for Adeline – she's already figured about Adolphus, but it'll take her a day or two to admit it. There's coin waiting for you in the Free Cities, enough to get a solid start at least. They say the practitioners there operate in the open, unregulated – you find the best one you can and you convince him to take you on. You want to do something for Adolphus, for me, that's what you'll do. Make every fucking drop you got in you count.'

He was too far gone to speak, but his eyes were furious, little dots of rage gradually swirling into unconsciousness.

'You'll forgive me at some point. At least you'll be alive to try.'

I waited another moment, then gave him a solid poke in the shoulder. He didn't react. Lumiere was standing over us silently, waiting for the nod. I gave it to him, along with the name of the boat he was to drop the boy's body off on.

'Pour me another shot before you leave,' I said. 'Straight up this time.'

46

Lord Charles Monck was a handsome, dignified man a few years older than I was. His hair was slate gray, but he had a broad chest and a youthful face. He looked like the sort of person you'd want in charge of the Empire – which, for most of the population, was far more important than actually being capable of running it.

Egmont, by contrast, looked very much the worst I'd seen him. He'd forgotten to comb his hair, or he'd simply undone his good work at some point during the day. His face was pale as curdled milk, and he was staring at me in a fashion that a man of weaker ego might find wounding. I assumed it had something to do with the letter I'd sent that morning, the letter that had in fact prompted the meeting that was about to begin.

It had read:

Egmont,

I know everything. At midnight, so will Black House. Should this possibility fail to meet with your approval, I'll be at your chapter house this evening at seven. Be there, and ensure your boss is as well.

After making sure of Wren's exit, I'd found a room at a nearby inn, slept for about twelve hours. I'd woken up feeling worse, feeling so old and tired I could barely keep my head up. It was small comfort to know that I wouldn't need to do so much longer. I'd spent the rest of the morning and the following afternoon chain smoking and trying to maintain that state of inebriation wherein tomorrow seems very distant, but unslurred speech is still a possibility. Around sunset I realized I'd overshot the mark, but I managed to right myself with the aid of a few vials of breath. I copped two more of these off a Tarasaighn on the way over to the Steps' headquarters. A member of my own stable, curiously. He was selling me what I'd sold him, at about a sixty-percent markup.

We were in a room in the chapter house that I'd never seen. They'd searched me before I'd come in, a thorough but not undignified pat-down. The Steps were big on gravitas.

'I was sorry to hear about your bar,' Monck opened smoothly.

'Don't be. I was the one who burned it.'

'And why would you do something like that?'

'I felt overburdened by the weight of my own possessions. Wanted to make a clear break.'

'How profound.'

'Thank you.'

'Normally, I don't interfere with Egmont's activities. He has my . . . utmost respect.'

'Clean hands are a valuable commodity.'

'But he says that you insisted my presence was necessary for this meeting to take place.'

'I didn't want to have to go over everything twice.'

'Well,' he said. 'I'm here.'

I rolled a cigarette overslow, playing out each motion with unnatural deliberateness. 'It actually wasn't a bad plan,' I said finally.

'Excuse me?' Monck answered.

'But you got carried away. Lack of subtlety, that's the first mark of an amateur.'

'I'm afraid I don't follow.'

'I can run through it, if that would make you feel better. But then again, we don't have a lot of time – it might be best to skip to the end.'

'Humor me.'

I lit my cigarette. 'You've been playing the long game against the Old Man. Slipping your people into Black House, doing what you can to wrong-foot him. At some point you made contact with the Nestrians. Your politics align vaguely, I suppose, and the enemy of my enemy and all that. They sent over a ringer, one of their top people, an old hand with deep roots in Rigus.'

'Go on.'

'It's been a few years, but I'm sure Albertine still had plenty to tell you about Black House, about the weaknesses in the organization. She might even have pointed you at an . . . acquaintance of hers, the Old Man's former protege.'

'She thought you might be of some value to us.'

'She's a sharp one – how much of it was hers?'

'Some of it.'

Most of it, if I had to make a guess. 'You needed a convenient excuse to make contact with me. You'd learned about Coronet from Albertine – it was her great coup, after all. And you've got enough ears south of the Old City to let you know about our sudden rash of murders, and about this new drug that had made its way onto the market. How am I doing so far?'

'Well enough.'

'It took me a while to figure out why, if you were all so concerned about project Coronet, you made a half-wit like Hume your point-man. But the answer was staring me in the face – you didn't care about Coronet, not really. Even if the red fever was some master plan on the part of the Old Man, it wouldn't go into effect quickly enough to upset your plans.'

'Coronet has never been our primary concern,' Monck confirmed.

'But while I was running around chasing leads, I stumbled upon all sorts of exciting secrets – secrets you knew I'd be passing on to the Old Man. Harribuld was your test case. Was he a complete patsy, or was he really working for you?'

Egmont fielded this one. 'We're always keeping our ears out for useful information. Harribuld didn't have much to offer, but we paid him a few ochres a month.'

'And all he had to do to earn it was get murdered,' I smirked. 'Anyway. You marched him past me the first time I visited, waited for me to tell the Old Man about it, waited for the Old Man to kill him. When that happened, you figured the game was on. You knew Black House was desperate to plug their leak, find out which of their people were secretly yours. And, lo and behold, last time I was in Egmont's office, I came across information pointing to five honest agents, trussed up as traitors. If the Old Man had bought that, you'd have continued feeding me false information, watched as Black House started amputating its own limbs. Did I miss anything?'

Egmont and Monck looked at each other for a moment. 'Not really,' Monck answered, turning back to me.

'A little over-clever, but not altogether a bad plan. The product of an impressively crooked mind, if I dare say so.'

'Thanks,' Egmont said, though he didn't altogether seem to mean it.

'Except the Old Man is more so – and he never bought any of it, not for a moment. You aren't playing him, he's playing you. He figured your scam out from the beginning, as soon as he discovered Albertine was whispering in your ear.'

'We didn't know he knew.'

'You should always assume the opposition knows more than

you think they do. If the Old Man is the opposition, assume he knows everything that you know, and a little bit more besides.'

'He went along with it well enough,' Egmont jabbed.

'You mean because he killed Harribuld?' I shook my head in bewilderment, only half-feigned. 'By the Scarred One, how you gonna play the game, you can't even read the score? Harribauld hasn't been of any use for a decade. Making him disappear didn't weaken Black House one fragment. All it did was get you over-confident, left me free to pursue my real purpose.'

'Which was?'

'What you don't seem to have realized is that your secret weapon can be turned against you. Albertine is a foreign spy. If anyone could prove you've had contact with her, you'd all be swinging from a gibbet before the week's out.'

'But no one can,' Egmont hissed. 'The Old Man's suspicions aren't hard evidence.'

'No,' I agreed. 'But her location would be.'

Egmont's composure shed like dead skin. 'What does that mean?'

I turned my attention towards him. 'You should have been more careful when you went to see her.'

'Bullshit.' It was the first time I'd ever heard Egmont swear. More evidence, if it was needed, that he was losing it. 'You don't know anything.'

I rattled off her address, enjoyed the effect hearing it had on the Director. His face went red, an unattractive contrast with his outfit.

'I'm hearing a lot of talk about secrets,' Egmont said, coming on heavy to make up for his moment of weakness. 'It occurs to me that if you weren't around anymore, this would cease to be a concern of ours.'

'If you were thinking of offing me, you should have done it before I was in a room with you and your boss.'

'I've got four very large men stationed outside this room.'

'If they were inside, that might even worry me.'

'We searched you before you came in.'

I dropped the blade in my sleeve out into my hand, made a little flourish. 'Not well enough.'

Egmont recoiled about three inches. Not so far, but then again we had a desk between us.

Monck didn't move, though – didn't so much as blink. 'There's no need for threats between friends,' he said finally, nodding towards Egmont but keeping his eyes on me.

'Friends, exactly.' The knife went back into its sheath. 'And as your friend, let me give you a piece of advice. This game you're playing with Black House – you aren't going to win it.'

'No?'

'No. The Old Man's slowed some, but your crew is only half-professional at best. Egmont bungled his play with Albertine. If the Old Man knew what I know, he could move on you this very moment, crush you beneath his boot heel, all under the full color of law.'

'And why doesn't he?'

'I'd assumed that much was obvious. It's because I'm not on the Old Man's side.'

'You're on ours?'

'I'm very much not on his.'

Monck took an ashtray out of his desk, then passed it over. 'You seem to be working yourself up to a suggestion.'

I rubbed out what little was left of my smoke. 'I assume you have a plan in case they move against you. An uprising within the city, a strike on Black House and whatever ministers you think will back it. Probably an attempt to, shall we say, safeguard the King? Perhaps even spirit him away to a location in which a careful watch can be kept on his well-being?'

'We have contingencies for every eventuality.'

'Good. Activate it tonight.'

Egmont bristled. 'Madness – our strength grows daily. We've got the votes in parliament, and thanks to your recent activities, Black House is short its top heavy.'

'I admit – the board seems weighted in your favor. But you're missing the critical point.'

'Which is?'

'You aren't as smart as the Old Man – you aren't nearly. And you don't have his resources, and it's always easier to hold on to something than it is to take it outright. You think your success is the result of your own abilities – I think it's a fluke, that he'll find a way to even it out if you give him the time.'

'That's an . . . interesting assessment,' Monck said, in a way that almost made me think he didn't really believe it.

'Thank you.'

'However, I'm afraid I'm going to have to agree with the Director. To move on Black House at this stage would be . . . premature.'

'But I haven't dropped my trump yet.'

Monck shot me a smile somewhere between mocking and placating. 'By all means, continue.'

'I can give him to you. Wrapped up in a pretty little bow. Without the Old Man to lead the resistance, you might even have a shot at pulling it off. Assuming you don't dally your way to the gallows.'

'What do you mean, you can give him to us?'

'I mean that I can arrange to have the Old Man arrive at a time and place of my choosing, and I can arrange to have him unguarded when he does.'

Suddenly the room got very serious. Monck and Egmont spent a while staring at each other as if trying to transmit information through their eyeballs.

'Also, I can ensure his second-in-command becomes yours.'

Egmont bristled.

'Or your third, if you're really so attached to the Director. Or, hell, you can put an ax in the back of his head, if you're that thick with blood lust. I wouldn't recommend it, though. Co-opting Guiscard might save you from outright war with the remainder of Black House.' But I didn't actually think that. Guiscard wasn't really the Old Man's number two, not in the sense that he could order anyone else in the shop around. The Old Man was not one to share the reins.

385

'And why would you do this for us?' Monck asked. 'Is it simply hate?'

'Don't underestimate hate – it's kept me going for half my lifetime. But no, that's not the only reason. You're going to do something for me, Lord Monck.'

'And what is that exactly?'

'Albertine,' I said. 'You're going to give me Albertine.'

Egmont didn't say anything, but then Egmont was no longer really a factor, hadn't been since midway through the conversation. Monck seemed to think so too, which is why before saying anything to me he turned towards his Director of Security and said, 'If you would give us a moment.'

No one likes being sent to the kiddies' table, though I think Egmont minded less than he might have. When the door had closed Monck looked at me for a while. I could feel the weight of the man's pupils on me. They would have held down a sheet of paper.

'You know,' he began finally. 'I've been hoping we'd meet for a while now.'

'It's a bit late in the day for flattery.'

'Not flattery. Albertine filled us in on the backstory. That you'd risen from street urchin to become the Old Man's number two. That if things had gone a different way, I'd be playing this chess game against you, instead of him.'

'You're playing it against me right now – or hadn't you noticed?'

'All that work, and you end up right back where you started.' He shook his head slowly, as if in sympathy. 'And all because of a woman. You must hate her very much.'

'I hate a lot of people,' I said. 'It gets hard to keep track. As it happens, there's something I'd like to ask you as well.'

He made a friendly sort of gesture with his hand. 'By all means.'

'Are you a fanatic, or a hypocrite?'

'Those are my only two options?'

'A hypocrite, then.'

'What makes you say that?'

386

'A fanatic would have gotten angry.'

His smile reminded me of the Old Man's. It had no meaning, it was just something to do with his face. 'I believe in the fundamental tenets upheld by the Sons of Śakra.'

'Not like Hume believes them, though.'

'It isn't required of Brother Hume that he gaze upon the larger picture. Brother Hume is lucky that way, I am not. But don't think my convictions false – the country requires a moral regeneration.'

'That's the task you've set yourself? The moral regeneration of the Empire? You'll have an easier time grasping the scepter.'

'Gaining power is only the first step.'

'Power isn't something you sit on, it's something you chase after. And it moves fast – if you want to hold onto it, you'd better not burden yourself with anything as heavy as decency.'

'I would think that a man with your background would appreciate what's required of someone, if they hope to make a change.'

'What is it with you would-be tyrants – it's not enough to rule the world, you want to be coddled for your megalomania?' I shook my head. 'I reserve my pity for the people that get caught beneath your tread.'

'No grand enterprise ever succeeded without sacrifice.'

'Not yours, though. Never yours.'

'Someone needs to be in charge.'

'Seeking the position ought to disqualify you from holding it.' I found myself wanting a hit of breath very badly, but didn't think it would go down well with Lord Monck, however tarnished his ethics had become. 'You don't need to sell me on anything – I don't care why you want what you want, don't even care what you'll do once you get it. You're a tool to me, like I am to you.'

'And what will you use me for?'

'To make sure the Old Man suffers, before he dies.'

'And Albertine? What do you want with her?'

'I'd like to take her to tea. I'd like to string her up by her thumbs and let the hounds loose on her. I'd like to hear her thoughts on a tapestry I've recently acquired. What does it matter to you, Lord Monck? I'm giving you the world in exchange for one member of it. A fair price, I think we can both agree.'

'Albertine has . . . done us good service. The Sons are unused to betraying our allies.'

'No grand enterprise ever succeeded without sacrifice.'

He didn't flinch, but he blinked in a flinch-like fashion.

'I'm not interested in debating morality. You've heard my proposal – we both know you'll accept it. There's moves to be made. Feigning righteousness is a waste of everyone's time.'

He folded his fingers together, gazed up at the ceiling, gave every impression of being deep in thought. 'Where should I send her?'

'Low Town,' I told him. 'Low Town is where it ends.'

47

The first thing I'd done after coming into the house was to shut all the lanterns save the one nearest the entrance. The second thing I'd done was take a seat in the darkness, light a cigarette and get to waiting. There was no point in being antsy, not this late in the game.

And yet, as I watched the door swing open I felt a moment of terror so exquisite that I had to stop myself from screaming. I'd been seeing her face in my head for ten years. In sweet repose, in mocking laughter, in reconciliation and crushed beneath my boot heel. The genuine article was something of a shock.

'Hello, Albertine.'

I wasn't sure if she recognized my voice, but she at least recognized it wasn't Monck's.

I flicked open the shutter on the lantern next to me. 'Don't try and run,' I said. 'I can't guarantee the men outside will be gentle in subduing you.'

I was obviously not who she was expecting. But she was a professional, and the first thing a professional learns is that they will, at some point, die in the service of their country. She took a long, deep breath, and closed her eyes. They were dry when she opened them.

'Hello, Sunshine. It's been a while.'

Something wrenched up inside my stomach. I hoped it didn't show on my face.

'Take a seat,' I said, gesturing at the other end of the table.

She tucked in the folds of her dress and set herself gracefully onto the chair. I stared at her for a long while, noting the lines across her face like a broken pane of glass, and the streaks of gray in her once golden hair.

'You've gotten old,' I said, but not unkindly.

'So have you.'

'But I was always ugly, so it's no great loss.'

'You aren't so ugly.'

I let that lie go unanswered.

'Does Monck know about this?' she asked. 'Or is he not a factor anymore?'

'Let's just say you no longer have a protector.'

She took that with something approaching equanimity. 'How did you find out about me?'

'I had someone watching Egmont.'

'Fucking child. I told him there was nothing to Coronet, and still you managed to frighten him enough to blow my cover.'

'I can be very convincing.'

Albertine reached across and pulled my cigarette out from between my fingers. 'I believe that convention allows the condemned a last smoke?'

I told myself I didn't feel anything when her skin had brushed up against mine, though I couldn't quite make myself believe it. I rolled another.

'You have it all figured out then?' she asked.

'Most of it. When I got a chance to look at the whole thing, it was easy enough to put together. Our past history aside, I'm

390

actually quite good at this. Though I admit, the fundamental crux is still a bit mystifying.'

'How so?'

'Why involve me at all? I understand, after ten years you don't have so many pieces left on the board, but still – best-case scenario, you put another shiv into Black House, skew the Old Man's vision. Seems like small reward, given the risk of setting me loose.'

'Perhaps I just wanted to see you again.'

My laugh was long, and bitter, and meant to cover how much I wished that was true.

'You're worth more than you like to pretend – the Old Man is a hard person to get to, he doesn't have much in the way of soft spots.'

'Soft spot? The Old Man hates me like a rabid dog does a frightened cat.'

'In our business, emotion of any kind is a weakness. Hate obscures the vision near as much as love.'

'Not quite so much,' I said.

She winced. I supposed it was a cheap shot, though I can't say she didn't deserve it.

Our conversation was interrupted by three loud knocks at the front door. I got up from my seat, one eye caught on Albertine, making sure she didn't try anything foolish.

Gusicard was outside, more nervous than I'd have liked. 'He's on his way.'

'Everything as planned?'

Guiscard nodded.

I closed the door and went back to the table. 'We don't have lots of time. There are a few things I'd like to ask you, before we get to what comes next.'

She raised her hands palms up, then brought them back together again. 'It seems I'm a captive audience.'

'Was any of what you told me about yourself true? Or did you just gin it up as cover? The brothers lost during the war, your little sister a student back in Nestria?'

'Some,' she said. 'I suppose not much.'

'And that house on the coast that you said your family owned. The one we were going to visit one day, that backed out onto the beach. Anything to that?'

She shook her head.

'Too bad,' I said. 'That sounded nice.'

I watched her smoke my cigarette, like I'd watched her smoke a thousand before.

'You had me picked out that first night I suppose, as an up-and-comer in Black House it would be wise to get your hooks into.'

'Yes.'

'Was I the only one? Or were you building a stable?'

'No one else. You were a big fish – it wasn't worth the risk, adding on a side project.'

'But then of course, you would say that.'

She shrugged, but wouldn't meet my eyes. 'Believe what you want.'

I wanted to believe her, though that was reason enough not to.

'Is there anything else?' she asked.

I'd had other things I'd thought of asking, but sitting there, looking at her, I decided I didn't really want to know the answers to them. 'That's it,' I said.

She took a long, slow drag, blew slow circles of white past red lips. 'Then perhaps you'd allow me a question of my own.'

'You can ask – I can't promise I'll answer it.'

But having received permission, she seemed slow to take it. She watched me for a moment, eyes like yesterday, or tomorrow. The flesh around them had withered, but that pair of blues were as bright and perfect as they'd ever been. 'What happened to you, that last night?'

'What do you mean?'

'You know what I mean.'

'You mean, why are you still alive?'

She nodded.

'Maybe I botched my play. Maybe I sent a squad of hitters around the front, just while you were walking out the back.'

'I don't believe that. You were not one to make that sort of mistake.'

'No? I botched everything with you, Albertine.'

She turned away.

I didn't say anything, content to watch her in profile, to think about what she'd been to me, and who I'd been when I'd known her.

'What I did . . .' she began finally. 'It was my job.'

'Of course.'

'You've done worse, in your time.'

'Much worse,' I agreed.

'That doesn't mean it was all a lie.'

'It doesn't matter,' I said. 'It really doesn't matter anymore.'

We smoked along in silence. I watched the ash build up along my cigarette with something much like regret. When the ember was down near the filter, I dropped it onto the floor, rose from my chair and opened the back door.

The night blew in on a chill wind. 'Well,' I said.

Albertine spent a long moment staring uncertainly at freedom. 'I don't understand.'

'Certainly you've got some bolthole secured for yourself? False papers, a stash of ochres?'

'Of course, but . . .' she faltered suddenly, lips fluttering.

'Now would be the time to use them.'

Whether it was real to her was a moot point. It had been real to me. Maybe the only real thing I'd ever had, the only thing that was ever all mine, that I didn't have to share with this sick fucking world I walked on. And if you can't keep faith with that then you're nothing, not a damn thing, not in my book.

I didn't say any of that. I knew why I'd done what I'd done. She could spend the rest of her life wondering. It was a magnificent sort of vengeance, the best I'd ever gotten.

Finally she got up from the table and crossed over to the doorway, stopping near enough that I got heady from her scent. Then she reached an arm around my neck and brought my face down to hers. It had been a long time since I'd been kissed by anyone like that. I did my best to return it.

When it was over, she touched my face with the back of her hand, smooth skin against scarred flesh. 'Farewell, Sunshine.'

I watched her walk off until she had disappeared completely into the darkness, watched a while longer to make sure. Then I lit another cigarette, and breathed in deep.

48

I went back to my chair, sat quietly, anticipating the inevitable.

I didn't have long to wait. The door opened abruptly, two agents filed in one after the other. They took a quick look around, saw I was alone, then went back outside and waited for the Old Man to make his entrance.

He was smiling. Not the smile he usually wore, the plastered-on thing he kept in place to fool bystanders, but a true smile, honest and cruel. 'My boy, my boy,' he said. 'You've certainly come through for us, haven't you?'

'I do what I can.'

He took a seat at the table across from me. He seemed very happy. 'Extraordinary, how life works.'

'Ain't it, though?'

'To think that all these years I've been cursing your name, furious at your failure to live up to your potential. And now . . .'

He let himself go silent. 'You've made good,' he said. 'You've made good in a grand fashion.'

'Your opinion means the world to me.'

He must have been aware that this was not the case, because after I said it he whittled his face back into its customary smirk. 'In any case. Where is she?'

'Albertine?'

'Of course.'

'Oh,' I said. I'd pre-rolled a cigarette for this exact moment, and I lit it with deliberate slowness. 'I let her go.'

'This is hardly the time for humor.'

'I'm quite serious. I only needed to hold her long enough to draw you out of hiding. And here you are.'

From outside there were the sudden sounds of a scuffle, steel on steel, screams cutting through the night. Then there was silence. Then there was a knock on the door.

'It's open,' I said.

Hume peeked his head in. There was blood on his collar, and a wide smile above it. 'Everything all right in here?'

'Just fine, Brother Hume, thank you for your concern. Can you give us a few minutes?'

'Of course. Just let us know when you're ready.' He shut the door behind him.

For the first time in his life – at least the first time I'd ever seen – the Old Man was utterly speechless. He opened his mouth. Then he closed it. Then he opened it again.

I smoked the remainder of my cigarette in the silence. It was the best damn cigarette I ever smoked.

'You,' he said finally, a condemnation and question.

'Me,' I admitted.

'But . . . security, the rest of my detail.'

'Guiscard realized which way the scales were tilting. I may have . . . slipped a finger onto the balance.'

'That foolish fucking blueblood. The Sons won't let him last the night.'

'I don't think so – Monck doesn't seem the type to let a good tool go to waste. Not really your concern either way, though.'

'And the woman? You would let her free, after what she did to you? After her betrayal?'

'It would seem so.'

'I don't understand,' he said, his final words on the subject.

'No,' I agreed. 'You don't.'

Some time went by while the Old Man pondered his predicament. Then his blue eyes recovered their customary twinkle. 'I must say, you've done a bang-up job with the whole thing, truly marvelous. Unfortunately, there is one bit you've mislaid.'

'Enlighten me.'

'You may have hoodwinked the half-wits that abound in your little corner of hell, convinced them of what a terrifying character you are. But the facade of impermeability is just that – your weak points are manifestly obvious to anyone who would care to look, and very nearly as easy to hammer at.'

'I just sound soft as tissue paper.'

'You imagined you would make this final play on me, accept the consequences with your family safely escaped.' He inflated his smile. 'Oh yes, I know all about that. I'm afraid your friend Yancey was quite forthcoming. I had intended to countermand the order to have them tortured and killed once on board their ship, but . . . it seems I won't have the opportunity.'

'Adeline and the boy, you mean?'

He bobbled a grin up and down.

'They went out on a Tarasaighn junk this morning.' I shook my head. 'Forget it. You slipped – dance long enough, it happens to everybody.'

The grin dropped off his face. 'You fool.' His cheeks filled with blood, and his hands shook in front of him. 'You damned fool.'

'Now you're just being rude,' I said.

'Anything they've promised you,' he said. 'Anything they've offered, it's a lie.'

'They promised me Albertine,' I said. 'And I've seen her already. The truth is, they want the same thing that I do – you on the end of a spit.'

'You won't live to enjoy your betrayal,' he said. 'Monck will make sure of that. You know too much.'

'I don't imagine my time line would extend out much further had you ended up on top,' I said. 'Of course, the point's moot. What's coming is coming – there's nothing either of us can do now but swallow it.'

There was another silence, a longer one. Across the table from me a man accepted his coming demise. It occupied the fullness of his thoughts, and he forgot to keep up his facade of humanity. Absent conscious effort his face was as empty as a doll's.

'What I did,' he began finally, 'I did for the Empire.'

'A simple public servant? It's a little late in the day to pull that one.'

'Have I grown fat off my position? Do I live in a mansion, do I wear silk and gold? Do I eat goose pâté, served by nubile courtesans?'

'You've gorged yourself on power for two generations – it doesn't leave much room for any other vice.'

'Who else would wield it? Bess? She spent twelve hours a day in church and the other twelve sleeping. Albert? He'll be mad of the pox in two years, you can already smell the rot. I've had to spend a fortune to keep it quiet. The Empire needed a steady hand. Needs it still.'

'It's unseemly, this attempt at justification. Remember who you're talking to. I know where the bodies are buried – and I know how many of them there are.'

'Bodies? Of course I've made bodies. Men and women, mothers and fathers by the hundreds and thousands. How many more live because of me? How many more go about their business every day, how many lives are lived happily and comfortably because of the things I've done?'

'There are always a lucky few at the top of the pyramid.'

'You think the Sons will be any fairer? Any more just?'

'I suspect Lord Monck will prove to be every bit the bastard that you were.' I shrugged, considering. 'Nearly so, at least. Regardless, it's not something that matters much to me. Tonight isn't about justice – it's about revenge.'

'The war won't stop with killing me – it'll start.'

'War was coming, anyway. All I did was nudge the timetable forward a bit.'

'You'll burn it all then?'

'We deserve to burn,' I said. 'You're just going to go first.'

It was getting late. That initial burst of feeling I'd gotten at seeing the Old Man humbled was starting to fade. I felt very tired. And I didn't suppose that Brother Hume's patience would last forever. I picked myself up. 'Well, then. I imagine the rest of this can continue without my presence.'

'Give me something to do it with, for . . .' he trailed off.

'For what? For old times' sake?' I buttoned my coat. 'It's for old times' sake that I'm gonna let them carve you up.'

He seemed very small there, at the end. In the dim light his eyes seemed sockets, his mouth a void. I knocked twice on the front door to let Hume know it was time to take his turn, then disappeared out the back.

49

My steps were light as a child's, I had to force myself not to sprint. It was hard to get used to not being dead by now – the whole play had been a hundred to one, I didn't have any real idea of surviving it. But it was done, and by some strange oversight I was still here. My heart pumped, my lungs drew breath. I was giddy – there was no other word for it.

I boxed myself into composure. It was too early to celebrate, too early by a long shot. I needed to find my way out of Rigus with something approaching rapidity. There was nothing here for me, the Earl was ashes, my family gone. And if I stuck around much longer I wouldn't be sticking around much longer after that. I knew more than was healthy – and even if I didn't, this was a bad night to be in Rigus. Tomorrow there would be a lot of dead men who'd had less reason to be made corpses than me.

If the Steps decided to play sly they'd send a team of hitters to trail me out the back door. But battered and bruised this was still my neighborhood – I cut a path down the winding back streets and alleys till I was confident a team of bloodhounds wouldn't have been able to follow along after. Then I made for Offbend with everything I was worth, squeezing the last drops of strength from my body. I needed to go to ground, find a hole to collapse into for a few hours. Tomorrow morning I'd reach out to my contacts at the docks, I knew enough people to call in a favor with whatever ships were still at berth. Most of my coin was waiting in New Brymen, but I had a few ochres stashed away, hell I'd work for passage if I had to, I didn't know the first thing about seamanship but there would be time to learn, wouldn't there? There would be time for lots of things.

I could smell the city's descent, anarchy in the air, violence like wood smoke. My actions had tipped Monck's hand, we'd see how well he played it. Guiscard might be able to convince some of his colleagues to lay down arms, but he wouldn't be able to convince all of them. There were plenty of men who knew they'd be worse off with a change of the guard. More of them than would be willing to swing around to the Sons' way of looking at things, if I had to guess – though they'd be slow to move, especially with the Old Man no longer around to lead the resistance.

Not that any of that mattered to me – I'd meant what I'd told Monck. I didn't care who ran Rigus, not one damn bit. If the Firstborn kept with me a little while longer, I wouldn't even be around to see it.

From the Old City to the northern corner of Offbend was a thirty-minute walk. I did it in a flat twenty. My breath was heavy and every part of me ached, but the thought of refuge kept me going, a warm bed to lie down in, a few hours of peace. I had a room above a tea shop, shuttered for the night. The neighborhood was quiet, middle class and residential. That was why I'd picked it.

I got a whiff in the same second I opened the gate, the last vestiges of my instinct towards self-preservation. Enough to pull myself out of the way of the short-blade coming fast towards my chest, enough to avoid a killing stroke.

Enough to delay the inevitable. I stumbled outside, a thin line of agony along my ribcage. I didn't have a sword and even if I did, I didn't have the energy to use it. The two men that followed me out into the alley had both, though, along with a grim air of competence that I associated more with Black House than the Sons.

'I suppose this is something of a surprise,' Guiscard said.

I still had a knife in my boot and for a moment I thought about going for it, seeing if I couldn't juke one of the thugs into joining me in the hereafter. But in the end I didn't bother. I was too tired to make any sort of serious go of it. And what was the point, anyway? Another corpse, another mother weeping – the Firstborn knows I've made enough of both. Given that we were about to have an interview, I didn't see any point in scarring another notch on my record.

'Not really,' I said. 'You're a slow learner, but you had good teachers. Or very bad ones, depending on how you look at it.'

Guiscard's heavies were waiting for the sign to move on me. What Guiscard was waiting for, I wasn't exactly sure.

'I am sorry about this,' he said. 'But it's no good leaving you alive, not with everything you know. And I needed to do something to make Monck clear on my value.'

'Take a last lesson from me. There's nothing you can say to make a man forgive you for murdering him.'

'I suppose not.'

Guiscard gave the go ahead. The thug on the right went left and the thug on the left came right and then there was something warm leaking down into my boots that I was pretty sure wasn't piss. I didn't see the point in remaining standing. There was a brick wall behind me and I stumbled back into it, slid down into the mud.

One thing about being killed by professionals, they didn't bother making my last moments any more miserable. The two heavies stood aside and left Guiscard room to come and make his last goodbyes. He knelt down till he was about level with me, though he kept a good distance, still wary even at this late stage. 'I wish things had gone a different way.'

I didn't bother to answer – I had other things on my mind, here in what seemed my final moments. Guiscard was well on his way to becoming the new Old Man, and that wasn't a position that ended happily. He'd get his, somewhere down the line. It was hard to care. The anger was seeping out with my blood.

He left finally, him and his boys, and I was alone again, at last. The wound didn't hurt like I thought it would have. A dull ache, a growing sensation of cold. It started to rain. I watched little droplets of rain beat down into the mud and listened to my breathing.

Things had gone better than could have been expected. Somewhere south west, where the bay runs into the ocean, Wren and Adeline were in the bottom of a Tarasaighn smuggler. The boy furious as a wounded hog, Adeline calming him down as best she could. They had the money I'd made off the Sons, and what else I'd scuttled away over the years. It was enough to give them a start. Shame that their father wouldn't be joining them, but there wasn't nothing for that now.

As far as Adolphus went, I'd settled up as best as could be done. Crowley was gone, and the Old Man with him. Fifteen years waiting on that last one, and as the rain wets down my hair, the memory of his face as I'd walked out the door keeps me warm.

I hoped Albertine was all right. She'd managed to escape Rigus once, she could probably pull it off a second time. Whatever security apparatus was still extant had larger concerns than the emigration of one middle-aged Nestrian. Even now I'm not sure if there was any part of what she'd given me that wasn't a con. But it's an abstract concern, would be even if I wasn't dying. I'm feeling quite magnanimous, now that it's too late to display it.

The light starts to fade. I clench and unclench my fists, for no better reason than I still can. Then I can't anymore, and I know I don't have much longer.

Things are coming at me quickly, fragments of my past, stray images and bits of memory. Adolphus at the counter serving drinks. Adeline behind him, silent and smiling. Yancey as he had been, strong and wild, hands tapping, head swaying. Celia as a girl, sweet and sad and innocent, before she'd gone so wrong. The Blue Crane laughing, long fingers leaving a trail of sparks in their wake. Crispin and I, brothers in arms, foolish and decent and brave. Albertine, so beautiful it hurts to think of her, hurts more than the hole in my gut. Wren when he was just a boy, willful and foolish. Wren as he is now, a good man, maybe a great one, something decent I'd left behind.

And then they fall away as well, and there's nothing left but the rain. And then there's nothing left at all. It's not so hard, dying. Just stop struggling for a moment, and let the night take you.

Acknowledgements

Many thanks (for various things) go out to . . .

My agent Chris, my editor Oliver, all the good folk at Hodder. My mother and father, Michael, David, Marisa and Mike. My grandmother and my extended family all the way down the line. Alex, Pete, John and co., William, Dr. Robert, Michael Rubin Esquire, Rusty, Sam, Elliot. Lisa. People I loved but forgot to mention specifically. Apologies.

Alice, Lucas at the House of the Wind, everyone who lives in Boipeba, Eduardo for letting me pretend to be a cowboy. Zero Piraeus. Mauricio and Mariann, who I will get into a book one day, as per our agreement. Francislane. Katerina. Andrea. Alex from Paris, I hope you got your movie done. Many other people. It is getting late.

There was a Brazilian hippie I met once on a path in a jungle near a beach who gave me a half of his coconut, and I never felt that I properly thanked him. So, thanks.

Thanks to anyone who read through all three of these (or even just this one, really) and maybe enjoyed it a bit. Regards.